LOVE'S BETRAYAL

Samson shrugged off Delilah's restraining hand. "It's okay," he murmured without taking his eyes from the man who faced him. He let his gunbelt drop to the ground. Almost immediately, the two men who'd dismounted kicked Samson's gun aside and then grabbed him by the arms, roughly turning him around to secure his hands behind his back. Casey saw the badge on Samson's shirt and removed it, smirking as he threw the piece of metal to the ground.

Samson turned and looked at Delilah. The sadness in his charcoal-hued eyes was enough to make her heart bleed. "Thanks for…the time we had. It meant a lot. Take care of yourself, Delilah."

"Delilah?" Casey repeated, looking at her and moving forward before Delilah had a chance to respond. "Are you Delilah Sterne?"

"Yes," she murmured.

"Mr. Telford wanted me to th[illegible]k you personal like for sendin' that telegram." A[illegible] stillness came over Samson in that instant, like the heavy calm [illegible] a ferocious prairie storm. "It[illegible] taken a lon[illegible] to collar Towers, here," Casey [illegible] ever done it without your [illegible] Mr. Telford promised [illegible] envelope.

Delilah shook her head [illegible] it."

Casey's eyes widened. [illegible]

"Take it!" The voice was [illegible]

Other *Love Spell* books by Christine Michels:
BENEATH A CRIMSON MOON
IN DESTINY'S ARMS
IN FUGITIVE ARMS

BEYOND BETRAYAL

CHRISTINE MICHELS

LOVE SPELL BOOKS NEW YORK CITY

This one's for "Candy," the mischievous and precocious Yorkshire Terrier who inspired Poopsy. And in memory of "Nikki," the ever faithful Maltese terrier who was my constant companion for thirteen years.

Also for my critique partners: longtime friend Bernice Carstensen, whose willing ear and unfailing support is always there, and for my sister, Esther Byrt, for the same reasons. Thank you both.

LOVE SPELL®

June 1998

Published by

Dorchester Publishing Co., Inc.
276 Fifth Avenue
New York, NY 10001

ISBN 0-505-52264-0

Printed in the United States of America.

BEYOND BETRAYAL

Chapter One

Montana Territory, May 1887

Immune to the soothing clackety-clack rhythm of the train, Delilah Sinclair tightened her black-gloved fingers on her reticule as she fell prey once again to anxious thoughts. The paper on which her sister's letter had been written crinkled beneath her grasp. She'd read it so many times she had it all but memorized. Still, with disquiet in her mind and a chill in her heart, she removed it and read it again.

Dearest Delilah,

I hope this letter finds you well. It seems that it has been much more than a year since we last saw each other, though I know it has not. I think of you often, and miss you dreadfully.

I wish I could tell you that good news had prompted the writing of this letter, but I cannot.

Although the hellish winter is thankfully over, the recovery process continues. The brutal winter hit us hard here in Montana. We lost much of our stock. Some of the cows calved too early, and Tom broke his leg badly when he and some of the men were out trying to rescue the little beasts from the terrible cold and waist-deep snows.

Then, a couple of weeks ago, we lost to rustlers a number of the cattle that had survived the winter. These were cattle that we had planned to sell ourselves. Many of our neighbors have suffered similar losses. The sheriff is investigating, but thus far the rustling continues.

In addition, the annual mortgage payment is due on the ranch in June. Having already spoken with the banker on numerous occasions, I can tell you that he is not in the least sympathetic to our situation. There are simply too many others whom hardship has hit as severely. In fact, some of the larger ranchers, not having any hay stores at all, are even worse off. So I guess I shall be grateful for small blessings.

I despise the necessity for asking, dear sister, but I must, though I do so without Tom's knowledge. If you have any means of assisting us, your kindness would be greatly appreciated. You know that I will repay you as soon as I am able.

Your loving sister, always, Eve.

Delilah closed her eyes briefly as she considered the implications hidden between the lines of script. Eve had as much pride and independence as any Sinclair. She'd never ask for help unless there was dire need of it. And, although she'd alluded only to the need for financial help, Delilah couldn't shake the certainty that there was something her sister wasn't saying. Regardless, the problem that Delilah faced at the moment was that she wasn't much better off financially than Eve. Yet somehow, in some way, she had to find the means to aid her. She'd promised Daddy long ago that she'd always look out for her younger sister.

With single-minded intensity, Delilah stared at the passing landscape as though the answer to her problems lay out there somewhere. Perhaps in the lee of a hillock or boulder where, in the higher altitudes, dirty clumps of snow still battled the inevitable onslaught of spring. Perhaps beneath the warmth of the sunlight in the greening meadows, where the spring warmth had coaxed the tender young grass and crocuses to the surface. Or perhaps in some of the more distant mountain peaks, where the snows receded, crowning the peaks while leaving vast valleys green with the moisture of their runoff. Valleys free at last for the cattle that had survived the winter to graze upon.

But she saw no answers there. With a sigh, she returned her gaze to the nearer landscape, and stared sightlessly at the newly emerged tender silver-green leaves on the sagebrush lining the railroad. In the seat across from her, she heard the rustle of Mrs. Higgins's skirts as the lady shifted position. She was no doubt settling her three-year-old daughter's head more comfortably on her lap; the child had been asleep for some time.

Mrs. Higgins was young—certainly no older than Delilah's own twenty-two years—and, Delilah had noted, she seemed rather naive.

On the seat next to Delilah sat a man who'd gotten on at the last stop—continuing a journey he'd begun some time ago, according to his initial conversation with the man across the way. From his direction came the periodic crackle of paper as he sorted through a sheaf that he'd pulled from a worn leather satchel shortly after seating himself.

"Are you a bounty hunter, sir?" Mrs. Higgins's quiet voice attracted Delilah's attention, the question piquing her own interest, and, despite herself, she listened for the reply.

"Yes, ma'am." The man's drawl was definitely southern in origin, diluted by years in the West. "Joseph Pike's the name."

"Mrs. Higgins. *Clara* Higgins," Clara introduced herself. "This is my daughter, Sarah."

"Pleased to meet you, ma'am." Pike cleared his throat. "I'm looking for these here three men." More crackling paper. "Heard they'd been seen up this way."

Her attention captured, Delilah looked. Noting her regard, Pike tipped his hat and introduced himself again. "Mrs. Delilah Sterne," Delilah offered with a nod, the lie coming easily to her lips after years of use. She'd been only seventeen when she'd claimed it as her own.

"It's right terrible to see such a young woman dressed in black. You been widowed long, ma'am?"

"Not long enough to forget him," she replied in a suitably subdued voice, as her blue eyes misted. Her statement confirmed her widowhood even as it erected a barrier against unwanted male attention.

"My sympathies, ma'am." Pike returned his attention to the WANTED posters and angled them so that both she and Clara could see them. "These here are the men I'm lookin' for. You jest let me know if you've seen any of 'em. Murderers and thieves, the lot of them. Butch Morgan, here," he said, pointing to the first poster, "is a rustler and a bank robber." The rendering on the poster revealed an individual with a long narrow face, unshaven appearance, and cold eyes. Pike slid Morgan's poster behind and revealed the next man he hunted. "This here's George Clark. He's wanted for robbin' a bank and killin' the clerk in Pine Bluffs. Word is he's travelin' with Morgan now." George Clark was a clean-cut–looking man with a large walrus mustache. Had it not been for the scar on his left cheek, he would not have appeared dangerous in the least.

"My parents live in Wyoming," Mrs. Higgins offered. "Not far from Pine Bluffs."

"That's nice country, ma'am," Pike commented, and switched posters. "This here feller is wanted for murderin' a kid in Cedar Crossing." He met Clara Higgins's gaze. "That's in Wyomin' too, ma'am." She nodded, and he transferred his gaze to Delilah. "Samson Towers is his name."

Despite the crudeness of the sketched likeness, Samson Towers was not an unhandsome man. He had dark hair and a strong jaw. "He shot the kid in the back, they say," Pike continued. Delilah listened to him with polite disinterest until she caught sight of the size of the reward offered for bringing Towers in alive: *One thousand dollars!*

"Big mistake him shooting Boyd Telford," Pike was saying. "He was the only son of Paul Telford." He raised his left brow as though that name should mean something to her. When Delilah merely shook her head, he looked at Clara Higgins expectantly, but she seemed at a loss as well. "The rancher," he explained. "Owns blamed near half of Wyoming Territory."

"Oh," Delilah said weakly. On second thought, she probably had heard the name, but her mind was still on that thousand dollars. "And you say Mr. Towers has been seen in Montana?"

Pike nodded and glanced around, ostensibly to ensure that none of his competitors were near. "Up near Helena or Butte, I hear," he replied in a low voice. "But you don't need to worry ma'am," he said to Delilah. "I doubt he'd be stupid enough to be in town. He'll be hidin' out in the hills somewhere. And I aim to get him."

Delilah didn't bother telling Pike that her own destination was neither Helena nor Butte, but Red Rock, a small town situated between and west of the two towns. Tom and Eve's ranch lay just south and a bit west of Red Rock. Anxious to see her sister, Delilah would be continuing on from Butte as soon as the train pulled into station, if that was at all possible.

At that moment, a sharp yap from the direction of Delilah's open carpetbag drew three pairs of eyes, and she reached down automatically to comfort the small furball which had recently become the bane of her existence. The dog had been a gift from an elderly woman Delilah had befriended. She didn't know why she'd allowed Mrs. Sharp to convince her to accompany her on her health-seeking excursion to the Soda Springs in Idaho Territory. Having learned long ago that self-reliance was the best policy, Delilah wasn't ordinarily prone to sentimental friendships. Nevertheless, she had accompanied the lonely old woman who'd traveled half a continent seeking a cure for her pain-ridden body. Perhaps she'd agreed because Mrs. Sharp had in some way reminded her of the mother she'd lost long ago. But regardless of whatever uncharacteristic and indecipherable reason she may have had, her compliance with the woman's wishes had resulted in being at Mrs. Edwina Sharp's bedside in the Soda Springs Hotel when she had passed on.

On her deathbed, Edwina had bequeathed to Delilah the thing she loved most in the world: her dog, Poopsy. She'd insisted that Poopsy had taken a shine to Delilah, and that she could leave her with no one else.

Now Delilah was stuck with a burdensome pet whose name she refused to utter. And, for the longest time, the dog had disdained to answer to any other appellation. She and Poopsy had, however, finally arrived at a compromise. She called the dog *Poochie*, and Poopsy tolerated the mispronunciation enough to respond.

"Perhaps she's hungry," Clara suggested.

Delilah shook her head. "Actually, I think she has to go. I just hope she can hold it until the next stop."

"What is it?" Mr. Pike asked, eyeing Poopsy with a kind of curious disdain.

Delilah looked at him in startlement. "Why, she's a dog, Mr. Pike. Of the Yorkshire breed I am told."

Pike's brows arched doubtfully. "Don't look like no dog I've ever seen. Way too small to be any good. One kick from a cow, and it'd be done for."

"Indeed," Delilah acknowledged. Privately, she found herself more than half in agreement with Mr. Pike. She'd spent much of her life on a farm, where animals either earned their keep or ended up on the dinner table. "However, I don't believe this breed was meant for herding, Mr. Pike. The elderly woman who owned her formerly regarded her as a companion, and nothing more."

"Companion?" Mr. Pike repeated in amazement. Then, with a disbelieving shake of his head, he fell silent.

"I didn't think bounty hunters took trains," Clara Higgins commented out of nowhere a few minutes later, her thoughts obviously having returned to their previous topic of conversation. It was that sort of remark which had caused Delilah to label her naive, but perhaps it was simply that Clara had managed to retain a youthful innocence that had long ago been lost to Delilah. "I thought you had to be able to track, like you can on horseback."

Pike smiled with a touch of condescension and explained. "We change with the times, ma'am. No sense in ridin' for days when we can just load our horses into the stock car and take the train to the area where the wanted man was seen. It saves time." Then he grimaced and shifted meaningfully. "Though I have to say that a saddle is a mite more comfortable than these benches."

Acknowledging his last statement with only a distracted little smile, Clara Higgins nodded and said, "I can see that it *would* save time. How interesting."

"And is your home in Butte, ma'am?" Pike directed his question to Clara.

She shook her head. "Helena, actually. I've just been visiting my parents. I expect my husband, John, will be waiting for me at the station in Butte, though. He said he had business there, so he planned to meet me and we'd continue on together. He's a lawyer in Helena, you know."

Delilah listened to the conversation drone on without paying any particular attention. Her thoughts returned once again to Towers and the impressive bounty being offered for his capture. Although vaguely aware that Pike had begun casting repeated glances in her direction as he regaled Clara with tales of his daring and dangerous efforts to bring the West's most vicious criminals to justice, Delilah ignored his interest.

One thousand dollars!

She surreptitiously studied the poster that Pike had left laying across his knee. Samson Towers was described as a big man in both height and figure, being over six feet tall with a solid muscular build. He had a drooping mustache, his eyes were dark, probably either black or dark brown, and, according to the description, he had no distinguishing marks or scars.

One thousand dollars! That kind of money would save Eve and Tom's ranch, and give Delilah herself a good stake for the future. If only there was a way she could take advantage of it.

Her father had been a bounty hunter. In fact, Garrett Sinclair had been among the best of the breed. Nothing like Joseph Pike who, in Delilah's considered opinion, was much too loquacious to be good at his work. Although she had to admit that, thus far, she didn't think that Mr. Pike was one of the men that her father would have accused of giving the occupation a bad name. Her father had always claimed there were far too many bounty hunters of that ilk—men as brutal as those they hunted—and he had carefully shielded his family from contact with such persons.

But despite her secondary knowledge of the profession, Delilah just couldn't think of a way to track down a murderer, capture him, and return him to justice—on her own—in order to collect the reward. So, finally, she faced the fact that there was no sense dreaming about *if only*, and forcefully returned her thoughts to her original plan.

She'd simply have to pray that her luck changed. If she'd been less depressed, and if the railroad hadn't begun warning passengers against members of her profession, she might have attempted to change her fortunes en route. She'd found that men often had a more pragmatic view toward financial losses incurred over a friendly game of cards during an otherwise monotonous journey. But instinct had told her that now was not the time for gambling, and her instincts had rarely failed her. Part of that feeling no doubt stemmed from the fact that many of the passengers were men heading to work on the railroad that was being constructed north of Helena. Small ranchers and farmers seeking work after a disastrous winter would have decidedly empty pockets.

At that moment, the train began to labor as the grade changed. "Sounds like we're gettin' closer to Butte," Pike commented.

Delilah looked out the window to see if she could catch a glimpse of the town. They were traveling through a breath-stealing mountain pass. Enormous granite cliffs bordered bottomless chasms. Wispy clouds settled on stone ledges to watch the passage of the tiny humans who thought they could tame this vast, wild land. And sunlight gilded the snowy peaks with gold. But Butte City was not yet in sight.

In fact, it was a good while yet before the train blew its whistle to announce its arrival in the town. When it did, Delilah looked out the window to see mammoth clouds of smoke rising into the blue sky from the smelters in the surrounding hills. Delilah had been told that mining was the lifeblood of the prosperous town, but hadn't realized how that would translate into actuality until she saw the billowing clouds. She frowned slightly, not quite certain how she felt about the smoke. It seemed a bit like a blemish, tarnishing the beauty of the landscape. Yet the mines obviously benefited a great many people, for she'd heard estimates which placed the population of Butte City well into the thousands, perhaps more than ten thousand.

The train whistled again, shortly thereafter adding the discordance of squealing brakes to the general clamor. The noise woke Sarah Higgins with a start and she began to wail in fright.

"Hush, darling. Mama's here. It's all right," Clara comforted her child.

Delilah studied the station. It didn't look that different from stations all over the West, for they were all fairly new. This station, belonging to the Utah and Northern Railroad—the first to enter Montana—was painted white with green trim.

Fully a third of the town seemed to have turned out to witness the arrival of the 11:25, for the platform was crowded with people of every description. Delilah knew there would be no one to meet her, however, for when she'd telegraphed to advise Eve of her impending arrival, she'd asked only that Eve have one of the ranch hands meet her in Red Rock. The reply which had arrived two days later had said merely: *Wes Powell will meet you and escort you to the Devil's Fork ranch.* The terseness of the response made it seem unlikely to have come from Eve. It had probably been answered by a hand who'd been in town for supplies and had been given the telegram.

The train whistled again, drawing Delilah from her musings. It was time to prepare to disembark. Delilah closed the carpetbag at her feet and watched as Poopsy immediately poked her small head through the carefully sized hole Delilah had cut into the side of the bag. The dog's black eyes glistened with excitement and the air of expectation that she sensed around her.

Eager to be on her way, and being more impatient than cautious, Delilah rose with Mr. Pike and a score of other passengers who began collecting their belongings before the train had come to a full stop. When the locomotive finally did jerk to a halt with a vicious snap, there was a chorus of delicate voices gasping "Oh, my!" as feminine hips were bruised. These cries were echoed by a few more earthy profanities—and apologies for the profanities—from men who had lost their footing. Delilah, thankfully, emerged unscathed.

Since Mr. Pike graciously offered to aid Mrs. Higgins with her luggage, allowing her to carry her tired and fractious daughter until they could find her husband, Delilah's own offer of assistance was politely declined. So, carpetbag—and Poopsy—in hand, she began to work her way through the tumultuous crowd and out onto the platform.

Children ran and squealed in the open grassy area next to the station, adding to the cacophony of the hissing train and the shouting adults. Aware of Poopsy's dilemma, Delilah headed for the grassy area without delay. Upon removing the dog from the carpetbag, Delilah slipped a leash on her and then stood watching the crowd while the furball did her business. Although the babble continued unabated all around her, Delilah was scarcely aware of it as she contemplated the next leg of her journey.

She hoped she would be able to procure a stagecoach, though she'd been warned that, in wild Montana, there were none of the established Wells-Fargo routes to which she'd grown accustomed. Failing a stagecoach, she would attempt to hire someone to take her to Red Rock, or, as a last resort, she would buy a horse and strike out on her own, shipping her trunk separately.

The last option held little appeal. Not only did she have little relish for a solitary trek through the unfamiliar Montana Territory, but it would destroy her plan to arrive in Red Rock with a modicum of refinement—something she viewed as critical. If her half-baked plan to help Eve were to succeed, it was requisite that she be viewed as a perfect lady. Which she was, of course—with the exception of her fondness for a good game of chance. And her unseemly independence. And her proficiency in shooting firearms. Delilah had discovered early on that *ladies* were trusted. And trust prompted moneyed gentlemen to empty their pockets more readily.

A quarter of an hour later, having maneuvered her way through the thinning crowd, Delilah approached the stationmaster. He was a rotund man whose thinning grey hair formed a halo around a shiny bald pate. "Excuse me, sir." Delilah called his attention from the papers he was perusing. "Can you tell me if there is a stage going to Red Rock?"

He huffed slightly, puffing out his cheeks. "No, ma'am. Mr. Waters runs a stage to Virginia City, but the only transport for Red Rock other than horseback is Mr. Didsworth's freight wagon. He takes on passengers readily enough, though."

"And when is Mr. Didsworth leaving?"

The stationmaster frowned and looked thoughtful. "Let's see. He made his last run . . . must be three days ago at least. He should be going tomorrow. Let me check." He turned away and entered an office to his right. Delilah observed him through the open doorway as he removed a clipboard from a nail on the wall and began checking entries.

"Yes, ma'am," he said as he stepped back through the doorway. "Mr. Didsworth is making his next run tomorrow. Would you like to send a boy around to let Ronnie know you'll be wanting a ride?"

"Yes, please," Delilah said with a nod, and resigned herself to spending the night in Butte.

She made arrangements for herself and her trunk to be delivered by hansom cab to the accommodations the stationmaster recommended for a lone lady such as herself, and minutes later she and Poopsy were on their way to Caledonia House.

It was seven the next morning, on the dot, when Mr. Ronald Didsworth pulled his wagon and four-horse team to a halt at 148 Arizona Street. Delilah, who had been asked to be ready and waiting, stepped from the boarding house laden with her reticule, her parasol, Poopsy in her carpetbag, and a small bag containing a roast beef sandwich and an apple which had been provided by her hostess. Thanks to an accommodating male tenant, her trunk rested on the stoop.

"Good morning, sir," Delilah called as quietly as possible, not wanting to wake anyone in the neighborhood who might have had the good fortune to sleep past sunrise.

"Ma'am," Mr. Didsworth tipped a battered old felt hat of indeterminate color. He was a tall, thin, string bean of a man with friendly pale blue eyes, stringy dark blond hair, and rotting teeth. After carefully wrapping the reins around the wagon brake, he descended and approached. "That your trunk?"

Delilah nodded. "Yes."

Didsworth looked back toward the wagon. "Tyler, come on down out of that box and make yourself useful," he called loudly, completely unmindful of Delilah's previous attempt at consideration for the neighbors. "And make sure you got room in the back there to slide in the lady's trunk."

"Yessir, Pa." A towheaded boy of about thirteen years popped up in the wagon like a jack-in-the-box. After hastily sliding a couple of objects around, he vaulted over the side to approach Delilah and his father. Without any verbal communication, the boy grasped one handle while his father grasped the other, and they carried the small trunk to the wagon while Delilah followed.

"Thank you Mr. Didsworth." She looked toward the boy with a smile, "And . . . Tyler, wasn't it?"

"Yes'm."

The trunk secured, Didsworth turned toward her and tipped his hat again. "Yer welcome, ma'am." He stuck out a callused hand. "Ronnie Didsworth, ma'am. And you'd be Mrs. Sterne."

"I am," Delilah acknowledged as she gripped his hand lightly in her black-gloved fingers. "I'm pleased to make your acquaintance, sir."

Didsworth nodded and offered her a smile that showed far too many discolored and broken teeth. "Likewise, ma'am. And now we best be gettin' on. Daylight's a'wastin'."

A moment later, Didsworth helped her up onto the

buckboard seat, settled Poopsy comfortably at her feet, and himself at her side, before setting the team in motion. As they traveled the still-vacant streets, Delilah couldn't help feeling there was something missing. Of a sudden, she realized what it was. "There are almost no trees here!" she exclaimed. The busy streets must have prevented her from making the observation the previous day.

"No, ma'am," Ronnie agreed laconically. "Not many. They don't grow good on Butte hill."

Delilah stared around her. It seemed as though the entire enormous mound on which the town had been constructed had been denuded. Many of the homes and buildings they passed were quite beautiful, however, and some compensated for the lack of greenery with window boxes containing colorful blooms of every description. Still, one would think that someone should have planted some shade trees.

"How far is it to Red Rock, Mr. Didsworth?"

" 'Bout twenty miles, ma'am. Give or take. Takin' a bit of time for lunch and to rest the horses, we should be there round about two or three this afternoon."

Before long, they left Butte City, and Delilah could not help but marvel at the changeable countryside. Leaving the scarred hillsides of the mines behind, they traveled through a grassy meadow from which they startled a small herd of deer; then, along a crystal-clear mountain stream in which Delilah could actually see the trout. By late morning, they entered a mountain forest so dense that it blocked out the sunlight, affording the day an unnatural twilight. At times it seemed almost as though the trees sought to reclaim the narrow trail that Didsworth dignified with the term *road*.

The road was deeply rutted, strewn with holes, and littered with gnarled tree roots. Delilah felt certain that at any moment her teeth would rattle out of her mouth.

She'd actually bitten her tongue when the right wagon wheel had fallen into that last crater.

"Do you make this trip often, Mr. Didsworth?"

"Yep, two or three times a week depending on what needs haulin'. And o' course that means travelin' this road four or six times." He obviously knew precisely why she'd asked.

"Isn't there another route?"

He shook his head. "None that I know 'bout. Course most o' the people that come this way is on horseback, so I guess most of 'em don't mind the road so long as they can keep their horses from steppin' in a hole. Ain't no fancy carriages goin' to Red Rock. Even wagons are like to break down."

"I can see why."

The words were no sooner out of her mouth than one of the wheels rolled up over a huge tree root, only to drop like a rock into a large hole on the other side. The drop was accompanied by another more pronounced lurch and the distressing sound of snapping wood.

"Damnation!" Didsworth exploded. He looked over his shoulder. "You okay back there boy? Anythin' fall on you?"

"No, Pa. I'm right as rain."

"Ma'am?" Didsworth asked.

Delilah straightened her bonnet and took stock. "I do believe I am completely unharmed, Mr. Didsworth." She felt a certain surprise at that.

Just as quickly as it had surfaced, Didsworth's ire dissipated and, with a shake of his head, he sighed, and muttered, "Well, guess I might as well see how bad it is this time."

A moment later, Didsworth and his son stood considering the damage to the right front wheel. Removing his hat, Ronnie scratched his head, then used his fingers to rake the shaggy strands of his thinning blond hair back into place before plunking his hat back onto his head.

Tyler, observing the gravity of the expression on his father's face, carefully copied his every action, although the replacing of the hat was accomplished with a bit less finesse.

Didsworth puffed out his cheeks, stuck his hands in his pockets, and rocked back on his heels as he considered the situation.

Again his son observantly mimicked his father's gestures.

Delilah almost laughed. She would have if the situation hadn't been so serious. Instead, she waited solemnly for some indication concerning the significance of their misfortune.

None came. Didsworth pulled a worn tobacco pouch from his rear pocket and tucked a pinch inside his lip.

Unable to stand the suspense a second longer, Delilah finally gave the man a verbal prodding. "Well?"

Mr. Didsworth looked up. "Well what, ma'am?"

"Is it bad?"

He looked back at the wheel and considered. "It sure ain't good. Spokes are busted and the blamed wheel came plumb off."

"Can you repair it?"

Didsworth shook his head and spit a stream of brown tobacco juice into the underbrush. "No, ma'am. I got a spare wheel, but there ain't no way I'm gonna be able to get it on there."

"So what are we going to do?"

Didsworth considered for a moment. "Well, we'll unload the wagon a bit and then I guess we may's well have us some lunch."

"Lunch?!" What did lunch have to do with being stuck out in the middle of nowhere?

Ronnie nodded as though he didn't quite understand

her surprise. "Yes'm. I was about to stop for lunch anyways."

"But . . . what about the wheel? How are we going to replace it?"

"We'll need help for that, ma'am."

Delilah stifled a sigh. She'd already assumed that much! Good heavens! Couldn't the man answer a simple question? She looked skyward, seeking the virtue of patience.

"And how, pray tell, are we going to get that help?" Delilah enunciated her words clearly, pursuing the matter.

Didsworth shrugged. "After lunch, I'll unhitch one o' the horses an' send Tyler on into Red Rock. He can bring somebody back."

Why in blazes hadn't the man just told her that instead of making her drag it out of him?

"Is somethin' the matter?"

Delilah opened her eyes and forced a smile. "Matter? No, of course not, sir. Whatever could possibly be the matter?"

Didsworth frowned and pondered her. "You've got the tone of a woman what's got her bloomers in a knot about somethin'."

Delilah opened her mouth, a ready retort on her tongue, but never got the chance to voice it, for Tyler tugged insistently at his father's shirtsleeve. "Pa, I think she's a bit like Ma."

"What are you talkin' about boy?"

Tyler grimaced and tried to lower his voice in an attempt to prevent Delilah from hearing. It didn't work. "I think she's mad 'cause you made her ask so many questions to get to the answer, jus' like ma gets mad atcha."

Didsworth considered his son's words. Then with a sigh of disgust he muttered, "Wimmen!" Ignoring Delilah now, he grasped his son's shoulder. "Son, you climb on up in the wagon and start shoving some of the heavier stuff to me so's we can be ready for gettin' that wheel on."

Tyler complied, and in short order the two had much of the wagon's contents piled neatly at the side of the road. Having had her offer of assistance declined, Delilah walked up and down the road with Poopsy on her leash.

Didsworth removed his hat, wiped the sweat from his brow with his shirtsleeve, and uttered a heartfelt "Whew!" before turning to Tyler. "You done good, boy. I think we can leave the rest. It ain't heavy. Now how 'bout you jump on up in that wagon an' open the basket your ma gave us." He looked around. "Don't look like there's no place to sit 'round here." That observation voiced, Didsworth wordlessly offered his assistance to Delilah to aid her back onto the canted seat of the buckboard before walking around and resuming his own seat.

"What we got in there for lunch, son?" he asked, looking back at Tyler.

"Two ham sandwiches, two egg sandwiches, some pickles, some o' that chicken we had for supper las' night, and a big jar of lemonade."

Didsworth looked over at Delilah. "Care for anythin'?"

"Some lemonade will be fine, thank you. I have a sandwich."

Didsworth gave her a sidelong look. "Still miffed, are ya?" he asked. Without giving her an opportunity to respond, he turned to direct Tyler in the pouring of the lemonade.

In actuality, Delilah had begun to forget her irritation. Now, taking the glass of lemonade from his hand, she nodded tersely. "Thank you."

She had just finished the roast beef sandwich, half of which she'd given to Poopsy, when the sound of hoofbeats broke the stillness. "Someone's coming," she said.

"Yes'm, it sounds that way." Didsworth peered along the trail behind them, waiting for the horse and rider to come into view. When they did, he flashed a wide smile that showed most of his discolored and decayed teeth. "Well, if that don't beat all. It's Sheriff Chambers, Tyler. Don't your ma always say that the good Lord will provide?"

"She surely does, Pa."

Delilah caught a glimpse of a huge black horse carrying a man dressed in a blue shirt, buckskin vest, and buff-colored Stetson hat before Tyler stood to observe the man's approach, blocking her vision. It was only a moment, however, before the stranger came back into view as he reined his horse to a halt next to the wagon.

"Ronnie." He greeted Mr. Didsworth with an abrupt nod before his gaze skimmed the listing wagon and its occupants. His hard, dark-eyed gaze stopped when it encountered Delilah, clinging without so much as a flicker of expression. "Looks like you could use a hand, Ronnie," he said, even as his powerful stare seemed to bare Delilah's soul for his impassive perusal.

"Yessir, Sheriff. I surely could."

"Let's have a look." The sheriff's steely gaze shifted and Delilah began to breathe again. As he dismounted and moved around the wagon with Didsworth in his wake, Delilah couldn't take her eyes from him.

There had been not the slightest glimmer of appreciation for her physical attributes in his eyes when he'd looked at her. Despite her determined avoidance of any kind of association with men, she'd grown accustomed to seeing that appreciation. Yet there had been . . . *something* there, for why else would he have stared? If not appreciation, what was it? She didn't think she'd ever encountered a man who hadn't found her attractive. Even more unsettling to Delilah, however, was the realization that, for the first time in her life, she herself found a man disturbingly compelling.

Why?

The sheriff was attractive in a very rugged manner, she supposed, though she'd seen many men in her travels whom she would consider more handsome. This man wore an aura of danger like a cloak. He was too rough-cut and too menacing to be handsome. His mahogany-brown hair had not seen a pair of scissors in too long. His complexion bordered on swarthiness, and the shadow of what would have been a full beard, had he allowed it to grow, lay darkly beneath the skin of his strong jaw. And his eyes. . . . They were chilling eyes. The kind of eyes that could stop a person in their tracks. Somewhere between blue and black, his eyes were the color of old steel, a deep charcoal grey.

"Ma'am, may I help you down from there so that we can try to get this wagon on its way?" The sheriff's deep baritone voice attracted her attention, and Delilah stared at his full-lipped mouth. Unable to move. Trying to remember what it was she'd heard him say a half second earlier. "Ma'am?"

She blinked and found her voice. "Yes?"

"May I help you down?"

"Oh. Yes, certainly. I should take my dog for another walk anyway." Rising, she held out her hand, expecting him to simply support her while she descended. Instead, she found herself grasped about the waist in a pair of very large hands, and lifted bodily from the seat. Instinctively, her hands sought his shoulders for equilibrium. The muscles there flexed, warm fluid steel beneath her palms. The heat of his hands penetrated the fabric of the clothing at her waist. The scent of him, a combination of horse, leather, soap, and perspiration reached her, disturbingly enticing. And then, her feet touched the ground.

Forced to look up in order to thank him, for her own five-foot-six-inch height reached only to his chin, Delilah found herself looking directly into dark eyes that seemed veiled in shadow. "Thank you, sir," she managed to murmur.

"My pleasure, ma'am," he responded. Yet no smile touched his lips as he turned back to Didsworth and the crippled wagon.

In that instant, Delilah's instincts told her this man was dangerous. There was a part of her that wanted to try to lift the shadows in his eyes. A part of her that wanted to see him smile—for her. A part of her that wanted to make him . . . *want* her.

Insanity! Pure lunacy! If there was one thing Delilah Sinclair did not need and would *never* need, it was a man.

Chapter Two

Despite the logic of her thoughts, however, Delilah found her eyes drifting to Sheriff Chambers again and again as she put Poopsy on her leash and walked the small dog up and down the narrow road. She still didn't know his full name, she realized, for he and Didsworth had forgotten the courtesy of an introduction in the face of the more pressing problem of the wagon wheel. But what was it about him that she found so . . . compelling? He wore denim trousers and boots that added a good inch or more to his already impressive height. The seams of his blue shirt seemed strained to the point of bursting whenever he bent his arm. His longish mahogany hair curled at the nape of his neck. In point of fact though, she could see nothing unusual about him save his size, and even that was not entirely unique—she'd seen a pair of lumberjacks once who had been the sheriff's match in proportion. And yet there was something . . . almost familiar about him.

Ridiculous! She'd certainly remember if she'd ever met the man.

Walking back toward the wagon now, she paused to observe the repair process. "I'll lift the wagon," the sheriff was saying, "and you and the boy can slide that wheel onto the hub." He looked toward Tyler, where the boy knelt with a pail next to the axle. "You got that hub greased up and ready, son?"

"Yes, sir." Picking up the pail, Tyler moved out of the way as the sheriff began unfastening the buttons on his shirt cuffs.

Delilah allowed her attention to wander to the dense forest surrounding them while the sheriff rolled up his shirtsleeves. The landscape was quite beautiful. Full of the scent of rich soil and cedar. Green with moss and ferns and heavy tree boughs. The sound of trickling water came from somewhere near. More distantly came the muted roar of a waterfall.

"Holy cow! I ain't never seen muscles like that!" Tyler's exclamation as he observed Sheriff Chambers drew Delilah's attention back to the men and the work on the wagon.

Her eyes widened and she almost echoed the boy's sentiment. Rather than simply rolling up his sleeves as she'd expected, the sheriff had removed his shirt and vest and draped them over the side of the wagon. For an instant, she gaped at the massive bronzed chest and muscular arms thus revealed. And then, remembering herself, she averted her gaze.

It did little good, for the picture was seared into her mind.

She'd seen men without their shirts before. Her father on numerous occasions as he washed up for supper, and other men a couple of times. But never had she seen a man like the sheriff. It was obvious that he went shirtless often, for the v-shaped line of demarcation at his throat was very faint, and his entire upper body was quite brown from the sun.

She'd encountered few men who had bared themselves so readily. In fact, she'd been told that some men wore long underwear year round, even going so far as to bathe in it. Personally, she'd always doubted the veracity of that assertion, but there was no getting around the fact that she was unaccustomed to the sight of half-naked men. And she'd *never* seen a man with quite as impressive a form as the sheriff's.

"Holy . . . !"

"Quit yer gapin', boy!" Ronnie Didsworth's admonition interrupted Tyler's second exclamation. "Get yerself over here an' help me get this wheel on."

Despite herself, Delilah looked back. Her jaw dropped.

Squatting at the side of the wagon, the sheriff put his back against it while he braced it with his hands. Then, he slowly straightened his legs, lifting the heavy wagon single-handedly while Ronnie and Tyler quickly slid the new wheel into place.

"Impossible!" Delilah whispered to herself, denying the sight.

Only it wasn't, because in the next instant the wheel was in place and Sheriff Chambers was donning his shirt and vest. "That should get you to Red Rock and home again."

Ronnie extended his hand. "Can't thank you enough, Sheriff. If there's somethin' I can do for you, you jes' let me know."

"I'll do that."

At that moment, there was a slight tug, and Poopsy's leash slid out of Delilah's hand. She whirled in time to see the small dog dashing for the forest. "Poochie! Come back here this instant." But the little miscreant simply ran faster.

Blast! If she'd only been paying more attention to what she was doing instead of gaping at the sheriff's naked chest, she wouldn't be in this situation. Delilah picked up her skirts and raced after the small dog, knowing that she had to catch the little beggar before it got too far.

"Ma'am, come back!"

Samson Towers, alias Sheriff Matthew Chambers, looked over his shoulder at Didsworth's shout in time to see Ronnie's lady passenger tearing off into the dense forest. "Damnation!" he muttered. Didn't the woman know better than to go dashing into a strange forest like that? He had a sudden and disturbing mental picture of that pretty lady sprawled at the bottom of one of the hidden canyons that laced their way through the dense forest, and knew he had to go after her.

Leaving the buttoning of his shirt for later, he loped toward the edge of the forest. "Ma'am!" he bellowed, and then looking back at Ronnie demanded, "What's her name?"

"Mrs. Sterne." Didsworth looked worried.

Samson plunged into the forest. "Mrs. Sterne, stop!"

The lady's dark widow's garb tended to blend into the shadow, making it difficult for him to see her clearly. He heard her shout "Poochie?" again and pinpointed her position as she paused to search for some sign of the dog in the intense gloom of the forest. It would be nearly impossible to see the small creature in the dense undergrowth.

"Ma'am!" he called as he followed the widow more deeply into the gloom.

Either ignoring him, or not hearing him, Mrs. Sterne hollered, "Here, Poochie!" once more before taking off at a run. This time, however, she only made it about three steps before she tripped, probably over an exposed root, and went flying in a jumble of white petticoats and black skirts, headlong into a copse of dense brush. Samson fleetingly wished that he'd been close enough to get a better view of the shapely white calf that was briefly exposed before the widow was on her feet again.

Blast! Would he never catch up with her? Switchback Ravine was close. Too damn close, he feared.

"Mrs. Sterne, stop!"

Delilah heard the sheriff's voice quite clearly, but whatever he had to say to her would just have to wait. If she didn't keep after Poopsy, she'd lose her. They wouldn't have time to wait around for the small dog to find her way back to the road and the wagon.

She was just about to plunge into a thick copse of undergrowth when she felt her arm gripped in a vise-like hold that jerked her back against a rock-solid form. "No, please . . ." she protested breathlessly, and then froze as she found herself confronting a massive expanse of bare bronzed chest. Jerking her fingers away from the disturbing contact, gasping slightly, Delilah slowly raised her eyes past the sheriff's shadowed jaw and bold blade of a nose to his eyes. Hard, dark eyes. Impassive, unreadable eyes. "I have to catch my dog," she explained weakly.

Without a word, the sheriff released his grasp on one of her arms to reach out a hand and part the brush. Then, with a nod in that direction, he said one word, "Look."

Slowly, Delilah turned her head. Her eyes widened. On the other side of the wall of underbrush, the ground disappeared. A narrow, but very deep chasm slashed its way through the forest, its rock walls moist with the water that trickled its way down to the streambed far below. Trees, perched precariously on the edge of the canyon, had a conspicuous lean, and seemed about to lose their balance at any moment. High overhead an eagle screamed.

"Oh, my!" Delilah said weakly. Had the sheriff not halted her when he had, she would have plunged to almost certain death. Dizziness assailed her at that thought, and she swayed. Then, without warning, the world tilted as the sheriff swept her up into his arms as though she weighed no more than a child.

She was about to protest that she could walk, but he only took a couple of steps before setting her down on the trunk of a huge cedar felled by the passage of time. "Stay here," he directed.

"But, Poochie . . ." Delilah found her tongue only to have her words quelled by a single glance from those intense charcoal-colored eyes.

"I'll look for her."

Delilah didn't begin to breathe normally until the sheriff's very large form had faded into the dense shadows. She told herself that her breathlessness had been entirely due to exertion, but she suspected she was lying to herself. The man had a very potent and rather overpowering presence, intriguing and disturbing at the same time.

A few moments later, the sheriff materialized out of the shadows carrying a small furball in the crook of his arm. At some point, he had apparently taken the time to fasten his shirt, for that disturbing expanse of wide male chest was now concealed. As he neared Delilah, he said simply, "Her leash got caught on a branch." Extending a hand to Delilah, he aided her to her feet.

Delilah looked up at him, expecting him to hand Poopsy to her, but he simply stared at her, his dispassionate gaze clinging to her features and doing strange things to her heart. Then, suddenly, he reached toward her face. Instinctively, Delilah flinched away from the gesture, her subconscious mind protecting her from potential violence at the hands of a stranger.

He frowned slightly. "It's okay," he murmured. "You have some dirt on your cheek."

Feeling foolish, Delilah stood immobile as his warm, callused fingers brushed at the spot and then plucked a small leafy twig from her hair before dropping to her elbow to turn her wordlessly in the direction of the road.

As they walked through the cool, shadowy forest, Delilah couldn't help casting sidelong glances at her companion. She didn't understand how she could feel both safe and threatened at the same time when in his presence, but she did. And it had something to do with the fact that he still looked vaguely familiar.

Something told her that she would be wise to spend as little time as possible in his company. If he wasn't from Red Rock, that shouldn't present a problem. If he was . . . Well, maybe she should just find out. "Sheriff Chambers . . . ?"

He looked down at her. "Ma'am?"

"I don't believe we've been properly introduced, sir. My name is Mrs. Delilah Sterne."

The sheriff reached up with one hand to tip his Stetson slightly. "Pleased to meet you, ma'am. I'm Matt Chambers."

Did the man never smile? Most people automatically smiled when meeting or being introduced to someone, but not the sheriff. "And in what town are you the sheriff, Mr. Chambers?"

"Red Rock, ma'am. Ronnie tells me that's where you're headed."

"Yes." Well, shoot! Why couldn't the sheriff have been from Butte or someplace?

A moment later, they stepped out onto the narrow road and their brief conversation ended. Didsworth was walking back and forth next to his wagon, impatience evident in every line of his body as he slapped his battered hat against his thigh. Spying them, he came rushing forward. "I was startin' to think I'd have to go on without ya, ma'am. Daylight's a'wastin', an' I don't know nobody who'd try drivin' a wagon over these roads after dark."

Delilah nodded. "Well, I'm here, Mr. Didsworth, thanks to Sheriff Chambers." She turned to the dark, enigmatic man at her side. "Thank you, Sheriff."

"Don't mention it, ma'am."

A moment later, Sheriff Chambers mounted his huge black horse. "See you later, Ron . . . Ty." He tipped his hat in Delilah's direction. "Ma'am." Then, with a light touch of his heels to his horse's flanks and the sound of hoofbeats, he was gone.

"He called me Ty. Did ya hear that Pa?"

"I heard."

"I think I like that." The boy's eyes glowed with hero worship.

Didsworth reached over and gripped his son's shoulder. "Has kind of a manly ring to it, don't it?" Then he turned to Delilah. "We'd best be on the move, ma'am. Lost us a couple of hours as it is."

As Delilah took her seat on the wagon once more, she was struck by the realization that, if Sheriff Matt Chambers was the sheriff of Red Rock, then he was doubtlessly also the sheriff investigating the rustling. And, Eve's letter implied, doing a pretty poor job of it, too. Much as Delilah would prefer to avoid the man in the future, she might have to talk to him about that.

It was late afternoon by the time Ronnie Didsworth finally guided his four-horse team and buckboard into Red Rock. "Well, now, lookee there," old Jeb Potter exclaimed in a low voice. "Didsworth done brung a purdy new filly to town."

His conversation with Potter thus interrupted, Samson straightened from his leaning position against the wall of Lowden's Mercantile and flexed a kink out of his broad shoulders. Potter was right about one thing: The woman with Ronnie was pretty. Downright beautiful, some might say. He'd noticed that this morning.

Widow's weeds or not, any man with eyes in his head could see she couldn't have been a widow for long. She had hair as black and shiny as new coal, skin as white and rich as the fresh cream Samson had poured into his coffee that morning, and eyes as blue as . . . well, hell, he couldn't think of anything quite as blue as her eyes.

"Seein' that purdy lady affect yer ears, Matt?" Jeb Potter demanded in a querulous tone.

Samson looked down at the old man with a cold-eyed gaze that had cowed more than one recalcitrant drover bent on raising hell.

"An' don't bother turnin' that look on me. I ain't yet seen the day that I'd be afeard of a young pup like you."

Samson's gaze didn't deviate. "What was it you said, Jeb?"

"I asked ya if ya knowed her."

"Nope. Never saw her before today." He looked back at the woman. Didsworth was helping her down from the buckboard in front of Mrs. Swartz's Bakery.

"Thought you didn't have no use for wimmin." Potter remarked.

Samson gave an almost imperceptible shrug. In actuality, he liked women quite a bit, but since he neither wanted nor could afford an entanglement with one who might have expectations for the future, he tended to avoid them. Except, of course, Lil. Lil was a widow in Butte City for whom the widowed state had been a boon. She liked variety in men and didn't like them to hang around too long. Sam's periodic friendship with her had been more of a convenience for both of them than anything else. Still, it had been a long time since he'd seen her.

"I like women well enough," he said finally, almost musingly, as he observed Mrs. Sterne. "There's just certain kinds I prefer to avoid."

"An' what kinds would those be?"

Samson narrowed his eyes as he watched the pretty young widow step up onto the boardwalk and pause to study the town. "The marrying kind that the good churchgoing ladies keep trying to foist off on me, and whores. Whores can be downright deadly." He was only half joking.

Potter shook his head. "Where in tarnation did you get an idea like that? Some of the best women I've knowed were whores. 'Sides, if you leave them out, there ain't nothin' left."

"There's widows," Samson murmured, wondering what in the hell he was saying. The last thing he needed was an entanglement with a woman. *Any* woman. With a past that shadowed him like a stalking wolf, he couldn't afford to let anybody get too close to him. But, damn, it had been a long time.

Potter followed his gaze. The lady was looking into the window of the Red Rock Savings and Loan. "I guess," he conceded. "But there ain't a whole lot of widders."

"I only need one." One that wouldn't need permanence. Marriage was not in the cards for a man like him. The trouble was, he hadn't quite stopped dreaming about having kids of his own someday. He'd always liked kids. And, unfortunately, you couldn't have the one without the other. At least not to his way of thinking. Nope. A nice cozy relationship with a beautiful widow would be about as perfect as he could get.

Potter frowned. "I still want to know where you got the idea that whores is deadly. Here all the time I've knowed you, I thought you didn't like wimmen. I swear, you an' Mayor Jack are the only fellas in town that ain't visited Cora's girls."

"I have an uncle who almost bled to death after catching the clap from a whore in Wyoming."

Potter snorted. "Now that's a stretcher if I ever heard one. Ain't nobody can bleed to death from catchin' the clap."

Samson looked down at him. "They can if they give it to their wives."

Potter stared at him as though he'd lost his mind. "You wanna run that horse by me agin?"

"When my aunt found out that Uncle Harry had been visiting whores when he went to town for supplies and then comin' home to her like nothin' had happened, she was so blamed mad she blasted him with the bear rifle when he came in off the range. He blame near bled to death before she could patch him up."

Potter looked up at him incredulously. "Why in blazes she shoot 'im in the first place if she was gonna try to patch 'im up?"

Sam shrugged and lifted his eyes to seek out the widow Sterne. She was making her way down the street past Doc Hale's office. "Damned if I know. Aunt Mazie always did love Uncle Harry something fierce. I guess she figured she didn't want to lose him after all. I was only about thirteen or fourteen at the time, but I've been real leery of catching the clap and giving it to another woman ever since." Not to mention the fact that he was just naturally fastidious. He didn't like the idea of being with a whore any more than he'd like the idea of putting on a pair of underwear or socks that had been worn by half a dozen men before him.

Potter frowned. "I can see how that could color a boy's view of whores a tetch. But it jest ain't healthy for a fella to go without a woman."

Samson was not about to tell old Jeb about his occasional visits with Lil—it was none of his business. So he said nothing.

"I think in your place I mightn't be so set agin marryin'."

Samson snorted. "No thanks." He had more than one reason for avoiding that exalted state.

There was a moment of silence. When Samson looked down at Potter, he saw the old miner looking up at him with a strange, knowing glint in his eye. "What?" Samson demanded.

"I know the sound of a man who's had his tail feathers singed when I hear one."

"Singed, hell!" Samson bit off a piece of the red-and-white-striped hard candy that he carried in his shirt pocket and replaced the remainder to be savored later.

"Well now, sonny, I know you ain't gonna believe this, but all wimmin ain't like the one that done you in. My Anna would'a walked to hell and back for me. Never saw a woman work so hard to keep her man happy. I never thought 'bout visitin' a whore when Anna was alive." He wiped his faded blue eyes with a handkerchief that may have once been white or beige, but was now of indeterminate color, and stuffed it back into his pocket. "Damnation, I miss that woman. Don't know why the good Lord hasn't took me to join her yet. Hain't got nothin' left to do on this earth that I can think of."

But Samson wasn't listening anymore. His thoughts were on the one woman he'd ever loved. Melissa Corrigan had been sweet, young, and innocent. Hell, they'd both been young, but they'd loved each other passionately nonetheless. He'd been a different person then, had even worn his own name. Somehow, unfailing optimist that he'd been, he had found the courage to ask Pete Corrigan for his daughter's hand in marriage, and the man had agreed . . . at first. Then, the wealthy railroad owner, seeking more power and prestige, had begun to demand things of his future son-in-law. Things that were not only morally wrong, but on the wrong side of the law. Things like sabotaging his competitor's lines or creating a scandal concerning his rival's family. When Samson had refused, Corrigan had revoked his permission for him to wed Melissa. Then, after having Samson thrown bodily off of his property by a number of his men, Corrigan had hastily arranged a marriage for Melissa to a man more amenable to performing the kinds of favors he needed. A man double Melissa's age who had needed a wife because he'd lost his own and still had a young son to raise. Samson had never learned his name, but he was a man who wouldn't have known the meaning of the word *tenderness* if it had reached out and touched him. Or so Mrs. Corrigan had said when Samson had asked about him. Mrs. Corrigan hadn't wanted to see her daughter married to the man but, having never before stood up to her husband, she didn't know how to begin.

Even now, six years later, the pain of what had followed had the power to bring a lump to Samson's throat. Poor sweet Melissa had not known what to do. She'd never in her life defied her father, and couldn't find the strength to do it then. Instead, terrified that her father would have the man she loved killed, she'd implored Samson to forget her and find another love. She'd made him promise not to interfere, saying it would only make matters worse. And so, he had stayed away and Melissa had done as her father demanded, marrying according to his choice. The day after the wedding, she'd tried to kill herself by jumping into the river. Only her mother's intervention had saved her.

It was that news, and images of what must have preceded her rash act, that had made Samson disregard his promise to her. He'd gone to the Corrigan property, still crowded with wedding guests, and landed a few very satisfying punches on both Pete Corrigan and the groom the man had chosen for his daughter. Samson couldn't even remember the man's face, and had never learned his name. Nevertheless, it had been satisfying to make that man feel a small measure of pain for his callous treatment of his new bride. Of course, Sam had sustained a few bruises himself when Corrigan's bodyguards pulled him away and threw him off the property. A day later, warned that Corrigan wanted him dead, and knowing that Melissa was forever lost to him, Samson had fled the area. He'd eventually become a hired gun—on the side of right—and lived a decent life until . . . until the day he'd made the mistake of stopping in Cedar Crossing, Wyoming.

He sometimes still wondered about Melissa, but he knew he could never again fall in love with such an innocent. Had she only had the strength to stand up to her father, or to leave behind the comforts of her affluent home and run away with him, they would have married despite Corrigan's ambition. But Melissa had done neither. Samson's young heart had eventually healed, though it still ached for what might have been, and he'd long ago decided that he never wanted to suffer that kind of pain again.

He would not, could not, love again.

And so, he avoided innocent women. Women who could worm their way into his heart with their need for protection. Women who admired his strength and appearance. And women who, not knowing the score, might grow to depend on him. He'd grown too old and too cynical to accept their admiration, and too interested in staying alive to be dependable.

Once more his gaze, of its own accord, sought the shapely form belonging to the young widow, Mrs.

Sterne. Her pace had increased as she came toward him on the opposite side of the street.

A safe, discreet relationship with an independent widowed lady who knew the score would suit him the best. There'd be no emotional commitment to make leaving hard when it became necessary. No parental interference. No clinging dependency. And, best of all, no more celibacy. Hell, it'd be blamed near perfect. He studied the object of his consideration intently.

Mrs. Sterne's small, rapid-fire steps echoed on the boardwalk. Her gown, dusty with travel from the tip of its high-necked collar to its hem, was in the process of picking up an extra layer of red-brown dust from the street. Still, despite her travel-worn state, his initial assessment stood. This lady was beautiful. Too damned beautiful. Getting near her could be about as smart as trying to stare down a grizzly. Maybe he should reconsider.

Yet he found himself fascinated by her obvious gentility. A man didn't get the opportunity to see very many ladies of her quality out here.

Carrying a black parasol to protect her delicate complexion from the brutal sunlight, she walked with her backbone as straight as a poker and her head held high. A small bonnet sat securely fastened atop her thickly coiled hair, but its purpose was obviously ornamental. Samson watched as she lifted her skirts, ever so slightly with the fingers of the same hand in which she carried her carpetbag, in order to skirt a small pile of horse manure as she crossed the street. He didn't even catch a glimpse of ankle. In fact, every move she made was as schooled and as graceful as though she was out for a Sunday stroll in a city park. The only thing that was even remotely unladylike about her was the carpetbag in which she carried that silly-looking dog of hers. It made the bag look as though it had sprouted an animal head. Carpetbag aside, however, this lady was all class.

"Breeding will always tell," his mama had often said.

For the first time in a very long time, Samson knew he was looking at the evidence of breeding. He tipped the brim of his hat as she drew abreast. "Afternoon, ma'am," he murmured.

Her big brilliant blue eyes lit on him for an instant as she acknowledged his greeting with the barest dip of her haughty little chin. "Sheriff Chambers," she said, and then she moved on. Her brisk steps carried her directly into the Lucky Strike Saloon.

Whoa! Back up them thar horses! The *saloon*?! Sam inhaled in perplexity, forgetting entirely about the hard candy he'd been sucking, and ended up inhaling the blasted thing. As a paroxysm of coughing gripped him, he continued to stare at the spot where the lady had disappeared into the Lucky Strike. Finally, old man Potter stood up and gave him a good whack between the shoulder blades, displacing both the candy and Sheriff Chambers's uncharacteristic fascination with one of the female persuasion.

Able to breathe again, Sam turned to speak to Potter. "Well, I better be getting back . . ." He trailed off as he realized the old man was grinning from ear to ear in toothless mirth. Potter resumed his chair and slapped his thighs in jocular rhythm. "You better stay away from that filly, sonny. She don't jest affect yer hearin', but yer breathin' too. And that's downright dangerous."

"Shut up, Jeb," Samson muttered, giving the old man a warning look.

"Sure thing, Sheriff. Just makin' an observation is all." Jeb's eyes glinted with unrepentant laughter.

He frowned. There were some definite advantages to keeping people afraid of you. There weren't many people in town who would have dared to enjoy a laugh at his expense. Perhaps that was exactly why Samson tended to seek out Jeb when he was in the mood for some honest conversation.

Ignoring Jeb's impertinence, Samson decided that on the way back to his office, he'd just stop in at the Lucky Strike to wet his whistle and have a peek to see exactly what that lady might be up to. Maybe she was one of those hellfire and brimstone preacher's widows come to Red Rock to reform the whores. If so, she had one heck of a job ahead of her, and it could prove downright interesting to watch. Besides, when Miss Cora threw her out of the saloon, she might just need someone to see her to the hotel.

By the time Sam entered the saloon, the bartender, Mitch Crebs, was pouring the widow a glass of what looked like peach cordial. With her carpetbag on the floor at her side and her back as ramrod-straight as a schoolmarm's, the widow stood at the bar slowly perusing the establishment. Samson followed her gaze.

The evening business hadn't yet begun, and there were only four other customers in the saloon. Simon Earl, a local rancher, his foreman, Frank Cook, and Simon's son, Travis Earl, sat at a table in the center of the room sharing a bottle of red-eye and a game of stud poker as they argued about the fate of the beleaguered cattle industry. They studied Mrs. Sterne with a measure of surprise and no small amount of interest before returning to their argument. Old Bill Crumley, the town drunk, sat in the back corner nursing a tumbler of cheap booze while he swatted halfheartedly at a blue fly buzzing near his head. The widow's gaze halted briefly at the poker table, its green surface dusty with disuse, and then moved on to the old piano which, come nightfall, would be belting out all kinds of lively ditties in response to Phil Marcham's dexterous fingers.

"What can I getcha, Sheriff?" Mitch asked as he moved down the bar toward Samson.

"Give me a shot of whiskey would you, Mitch?" Samson hooked the heel of his right boot on the brass railing at the bar, and waited.

". . . Course the damned rustling don't help," Simon Earl suddenly said in a loud voice. "You ever gonna do anything 'bout that, Sheriff?" he asked, drawing Samson's attention from the widow. "Or are you figurin' on the Almighty doin' your job for ya?"

"Aw, Pa . . . come on, don't . . ." Travis began.

He was interrupted by a cuff to the side of the head from his father. "You talk when I tell you to, boy, an' not before."

Travis lowered his gaze to the cards in his hand. "Sure, Pa." He was a grown man, and if he allowed his father to treat him that way, there wasn't much Samson could do about it, though his guts churned with cold rage.

Simon switched his gaze back to Samson. "Well, Sheriff, you got anything to say for yourself."

Samson's gaze sharpened. *Give me a reason, Earl.* "Well now, Simon, I don't remember anything in my job description sayin' I had to report to you. If that changes, though, I'll be sure to let you know." With those words, he dismissed the pompous rancher and turned back to his drink. Silence reigned. And then, slowly, Frank Cook began a conversation that drew his employer's attention, and they returned to the poker game they'd been playing.

With the tense moment past, Samson looked back at Mrs. Sterne. The widow had to have had some purpose in coming in here other than a drink—unless she was one of those suffragettes—and he figured if he bided his time, he'd find out what it was.

He didn't have long to wait.

"Bartender?" Mrs. Sterne called out in a soft voice.

"Yes, ma'am," Mitch responded as he moved back down the bar toward her.

"Would you be the proprietor of this establishment?" For the first time, Samson noted a faint southern lilt in her voice.

Mitch shook his head. "No, ma'am. That would be Miss Cora."

The widow smiled, though Samson wasn't sure he understood why. "And would you be so kind as to tell me whether Miss Cora will be in attendance here this evening?"

Mitch hesitated. "Yes, ma'am," he responded a bit warily. "Can I ask you why you'd be lookin' for Miss Cora?"

The widow sipped her cordial before responding. "Oh, it's nothing untoward, I assure you. I simply have a business proposition for her."

"A business proposition?"

"Yes." The widow didn't elaborate, but Mitch continued to stare at her expectantly. Finally she commented, "I notice your gaming tables appear to be in a state of disuse. I've been told that there is no dealer in town. Is that correct?"

"Yes, ma'am. Most folks in town don't quite cotton to professional gamblers."

The widow's expression sobered slightly. "How sad. There's truly nothing amiss in an honest game of poker, though. Wouldn't you agree, sir?"

Samson set his glass down with a definite clunk on the scarred wooden bar. He had a bad feeling about this. A *real* bad feeling.

Mitch flashed a glance his way, then cleared his throat. "I wouldn't know about that, ma'am. The ones we had here didn't know the meanin' of the word *honest*. Troublemakers through and through, they were. Here to swindle the local hands out of their month's pay and the miners out of their gold and silver."

The lady didn't respond.

"Is that what you want to talk to Miss Cora about, ma'am? Gamblin'?"

The widow drew a deep breath and then flashed Mitch a smile so dazzling that Samson caught the reflected brilliance. "Yes, sir, it is."

Sam grit his teeth. Dammit! The *lady* was a gambler!

If there was one thing Samson could not abide, it was professional gamblers. They were a coldhearted lot who brought nothing but trouble in their wake. And that trouble got good men killed. Men like his father.

Samson had started cleaning the town up when he'd taken on the identity of Matt Chambers and the sheriff's position in Red Rock two years ago. It had taken more than a year to do it, and he didn't intend to let all his work go for naught because a little slip of a woman with big blue eyes had a penchant for vice. Not on your life.

He turned to face the widow. "I'm sorry, ma'am, but if you've come here to set up a gaming table, you've come to the wrong place. We don't allow professional gambling here."

The widow pinned him with her blue-eyed gaze and moved down the bar to join him, sliding her glass of cordial with her. Then, setting her carpetbag at her feet once more, she got right to the point. "I'm afraid I don't understand, Sheriff. Isn't it the prerogative of the proprietor to decide whether or not gaming will be permitted in his or her establishment? Or has a law been passed of which I am unaware?"

Samson fought back a scowl. She sounded like a blamed schoolteacher. "There's no law against gambling, ma'am, but there is one against cheating. And, since I *am* the law in Red Rock, I'll see that it isn't broken."

Mrs. Sterne's left brow arched. "So then, your *law* doesn't include honest gamblers?"

Samson hesitated. "I've yet to meet a professional gambler who stayed honest when ridin' a losin' streak, ma'am. That's why we don't allow gamblers in Red Rock."

The widow's lips tightened perceptibly and the blue of her eyes deepened. "You mean that *you* don't allow gamblers in Red Rock, don't you, Sheriff?"

Samson nodded sharply. "That's what I mean. I run a clean town. Cheats get run out real fast."

Delilah echoed his nod and then turned back to Mitch. "Please inform Miss Cora that I will be by later to discuss a business proposition with her."

Samson couldn't believe his ears. Few men would have defied him so openly. That this little lady would do so left him flummoxed.

Picking up her carpetbag once more, ignoring Sam's presence as though she'd totally dismissed him from her mind, Delilah Sterne made for the door. Sam watched her retreating figure.

After tossing back the last of his drink and allowing it to blaze a trail of fire through his innards, he thoughtfully replaced his glass on the counter and left the saloon. One thing was sure. He couldn't let anyone undermine his authority. Not even a lady like her.

As the bat-wing doors squeaked in a discordant rhythm behind him, Samson paused on the boardwalk and observed the widow's retreating figure. She was headed for the hotel, her small double-time steps carrying her just as swiftly as any man's longer stride.

Pretty she might be. But if Mrs. Sterne proceeded with her gaming plans, she'd darned well find herself cooling her heels in his jail the first time she cheated. He smiled slightly, intrigued by the picture that came to mind. Yessir, now *that* would be interesting.

He had little doubt that she would cheat, for all gamblers did. And he'd taught himself to recognize most of their tricks.

He'd be watching Mrs. Delilah Sterne like a hawk.

Chapter Three

If that big galoot of a sheriff thought he could tell her what to do, he had another think coming, Delilah fumed with outrage. He might be as big as an outhouse, but he didn't scare her. As her daddy used to say, "Big men only have farther to fall."

Poopsy whined and, without conscious volition, Delilah stepped off the boardwalk into an alley to let the little dog do her business.

Who in blazes did that sheriff think he was? Why wasn't he out chasing rustlers instead of harassing a lady looking to do an honest day's work?

And why did he continue to strike her as vaguely familiar? Delilah frowned as she proceeded on to the hotel. Maybe it was simply that aspect of him that made him seem larger than life. But she didn't give a hoot how big he was, or how incomprehensibly dynamic she found him; she wasn't going to let him interfere with her plans to make some money to help Eve. If she got some good games going, she could make as much as twenty or twenty-five dollars a night, even after subtracting the saloon's cut.

Still immersed in her thoughts, Delilah opened one of the white double doors and stepped into the Mountain View Hotel. As she'd requested, Mr. Didsworth had brought her trunk on ahead. It sat on the dark hardwood floor to one side of the mullion-paned doors. Delilah paused to survey her surroundings. There was no one in sight. The lobby smelled of beeswax and old cigars. In the rear, she could hear voices, slightly accented, but could not make out what they were saying. On her right, an arched doorway led into what appeared to be a dining room. The smell of fried steak and potatoes—a true Western meal—wafted forward to tease her nostrils and tempt her empty stomach.

Stepping up to the gleaming mahogany desk, Delilah rang the bell and waited. A moment later, a curtain parted and a middle-aged woman with steel-grey hair secured in a braided coronet, stepped out. With a wide welcoming smile and a pronounced accent, she asked, "Vat can I do for you, missus?"

"I'd like a room please," Delilah said. "My name is Mrs. Delilah Sterne. This is my trunk." She indicated the small humpbacked trunk that carried all her worldly goods.

"Uf course. Uf course. We'll gif you a corner room. Zey are ze nicest. I'm Frieda Schmidt. I'll haf my Erich carry your trunk up for you." As she spoke, she turned the register around on the desk, placed a fountain pen in Delilah's hand, and tapped the page with a finger to indicate where exactly Delilah was to sign. "Erich is a goot boy, and strong, too."

Delilah signed and handed the pen back. "Can you tell me if anyone from the Devil's Fork ranch has been inquiring after me?"

Frieda frowned thoughtfully. "No, I don't sink so. I vill ask my husband." She stepped through the curtained doorway at her back, calling, "Marc?" A man's bass rumble responded, and then Delilah heard the murmur of voices.

Frieda returned a moment later. "Zere has been no one asking about you, Mrs. Sterne. Perhaps you should check vit ze sheriff."

Delilah nodded. "Thank you. I may do that." But she doubted that she would. She was too angry with the man at the moment. Besides, she didn't think it very likely that Sheriff Matt Chambers would know any more than anyone else.

"You vill be vanting a bat'?" Frieda asked.

"A bath? Oh, yes. Please." The mere thought of being clean again was heavenly.

Frieda smiled again, revealing strong white wide-spaced teeth. "I'll haf Erich carry up some hot vater for you. Vill you be haffing supper with us?"

"Yes, as long as your dining room will still be open in . . . say, an hour."

"Uf course. Uf course. It is likely there vill still be others dining." She held up a finger. "You yust vait. I vill call Erich."

Delilah smiled. "Thank you."

A couple of minutes later, Delilah followed a burly young man with short white-blond hair up the shiny mahogany staircase. Erich, who'd shouldered her trunk with surprising ease, led her to a room at the rear of the upper hallway. When he opened the door, Delilah saw that the room was a corner one as promised. It had windows facing both south and west, and the lowering afternoon sunlight slanted its way across the hardwood floor. In the height of summer, such a room would have been too warm, but now, in early spring, Delilah felt certain she would appreciate the warmth it would afford. The small room was well-furnished with a bed, a dressing screen in one corner, a night table, a dresser complete with pitcher and washbasin, and a small round writing table in the corner nearest the window.

"Where would you like the trunk, ma'am?" Erich had very little of his mother's accent. Delilah decided that he'd probably been born here.

"At the foot of the bed will be fine."

Erich set the trunk in place and then opened a closet door to remove a large serviceable and undecorated galvanized tub. "The chamber pot is under the bed if you need it," he said. "I'll be back in a few minutes with the water for the bath."

"Thank you, Erich."

He nodded. "My pleasure, ma'am."

He was just about to exit the room when Delilah had a thought. "Your mother wouldn't have any kitchen scraps that I could get for my dog, would she?" Delilah really didn't feel like carrying the little rascal down to supper with her, but if she didn't feed her before going down for her own meal, she'd feel obligated to take Poopsy with her. After all, the dog was no doubt hungry as well.

Erich shrugged. "I don't know, ma'am, but I'll check."

"Thank you, Erich." Delilah poured some water from the pitcher into the basin and set it on the floor for Poopsy to drink.

An hour later, having bathed and changed into a clean, albeit slightly wrinkled taffeta skirt and black shirtwaist, Delilah made her way downstairs to the dining room. It was empty of all save four gentlemen patrons. An older gentleman with grey hair and an equally grey beard sat near the window reading a recent edition of the *Helena Herald*. The meal before him looked neglected. A younger man sat near the center of the room shoveling food into his mouth with single-minded attention, as though eating were simply a tiresome necessity that must be gotten through as quickly as possible. He was dressed in a suit and Delilah pegged him for a young doctor or lawyer. The other two men sat together at a table against the opposite wall. A man dressed in denims and a blue flannel shirt was sitting with . . .

Delilah stopped in her tracks. Sheriff Chambers! Somehow she hadn't anticipated meeting him here, although she knew that in a town the size of Red Rock she could run into him almost anywhere. He'd changed from the blue denim and buckskin leather vest he'd worn earlier into black trousers and a black shirt on which his badge was prominently displayed. He wore a gun holstered on his right side, and for the first time she noted that the holster was securely tied to his thigh with a rawhide thong.

"You always gotta be careful of a man with his gun tied down," her daddy had said on more than one occasion. "When he pulls his pistol, he means to use it."

The black clothing Matt Chambers wore did not make him appear any smaller. On the contrary, in fact, his black-clad form seemed even larger and somehow more sinister against the white walls and red-checkered tablecloth. And yet, in some way, his hard features and intense unreadable eyes were even more compelling.

Tearing her gaze away from the sheriff with an effort of pure will, Delilah made her way toward a vacant table. She would simply ignore the man's presence and enjoy her meal. She had too much to do to spend any time thinking about the strangely charismatic lawman. She had to speak with Miss Cora tonight to put that portion of her plan into motion. Then, first thing in the morning, she wanted to be off to Eve and Tom's ranch . . . with or without her escort.

She couldn't help but worry about the fact that Wes Powell had not contacted her. Had something gone wrong at the ranch to keep him from leaving? Was Eve all right?

But Delilah would have no way of knowing the answers to her questions until Powell arrived, or until she got to the ranch.

Oh, darn! If her escort didn't arrive, she'd have no horse, and no means to get to the Devil's Fork. Unless . . . Just to be on the safe side, she'd make tentative arrangements for a mount. If her escort did show, she could always cancel.

At that moment, Mrs. Schmidt approached her table. "Dit your doggie like her supper?" she asked.

"Very much," Delilah responded with a smile. She was suddenly conscious of the sheriff's gaze on her, tangible, disturbing. "Thank you."

Frieda waved away her thanks. "It was notink," she insisted. "For supper ve haf roast beef vit' mashed potatoes and carrots, or t'ick, juicy T-bone steak vit' fried potatoes and sauerkraut. Also, I save you some apple cobbler for dessert."

"I'll have the roast beef, please. And the apple cobbler sounds heavenly."

"Goot. Goot."

"Mrs. Schmidt, would you be so kind as to tell me where I could find the livery stable? I may need a horse for a few days."

"Uf course. Uf course," Mrs. Schmidt replied. "But why go all ze way down zere when Mr. Metter, he is right here?" Before Delilah could respond, the woman turned to the table where Matt Chambers sat with his companion. "Mr. Metter?" Metter looked up. "Zis lady needs to talk vit' you about a horse. Yes?"

"Sure." Metter swung his gaze to Delilah. "Ma'am,"

he said, with a nod. "When do you need it and how long you aim on keepin' it?"

Studiously ignoring Matt Chambers's gaze, Delilah responded. "I'd like to leave at first light. And I'd only need it for about three or four days this time, but I may want to keep it longer." She paused. "Do you have anything?"

Metter frowned. "Depends. If you can handle a little spirit, I've got an Appaloosa gelding. Other than that, all I've got is an old mare who don't like to move too fast no more."

Of its own volition, it seemed, her gaze flicked ever so briefly to Sheriff Chambers and her heart leaped at the way he was looking at her. *Cold fire* was the only way to describe it. Did he find her attractive? She still didn't know. But there was definitely *some* emotion for her in that enigmatic gaze.

"The gelding will be fine, Mr. Metter," she managed to respond. "Where may I find the livery in the morning?"

Metter told her and she hastily looked away, unwilling to risk another meeting of glances with Matt Chambers.

"I hope you're not planning on travelin' far from civilization alone, Mrs. Sterne," Sheriff Chambers suddenly interjected. "This is dangerous country."

She had no choice but to look back at him. Their gazes locked. Studiously ignoring the riotous sensation that suddenly had her stomach in turmoil, Delilah managed to find her voice. "I can take care of myself."

"Whatever you say, ma'am," he responded with a dismissive shrug. "You have friends in the area?"

"My sister and her husband."

"Ranchers?"

"Yes," she replied tersely. Why in the world did he think he had the right to pry into her personal affairs?

"Let's see. That wouldn't be the Flying L, Mrs. Harlin would be a bit too seasoned to be your sister. Nor the Rocking E, confirmed bachelor there. Must be either the Devil's Fork or the Lazy M."

Delilah's lips tightened. The man was implacable in the pursuit of answers which were none of his business. Losing her manners along with her patience, Delilah said, "The Devil's Fork, if you must know, Sheriff."

At that moment, Mrs. Schmidt returned with her meal, and Delilah had an excuse to ignore the too-powerful presence of the man at the other table.

"I'll be ridin' out Devil's Fork way tomorrow. I can ride with you if you like."

Delilah paused with her fork midway to her mouth. Then, she carefully lowered it to her plate. The last thing she needed was to spend more time in the company of Sheriff Chambers. However, his offer was not overly forward, and for a woman alone to refuse his accompaniment would only raise questions.

"The road is free, Sheriff. You may, of course, ride where and when you like. I should think you'd be more concerned with catching rustlers and returning stolen cattle to the people to whom they belong, however, so please don't concern yourself on my account."

"Wouldn't think of it, ma'am," he drawled. Delilah thought she noted a trace of Texas in his tone. Either transplanted many years ago, or the son of Texans, she concluded. "And don't you worry your pretty little head about how I do my job." The statement was calculated to enflame her ire, and it served its purpose.

Bristling at his condescension, Delilah resisted the impulse to lambaste him—just the response he was seeking no doubt—and returned to her supper. Moments later, Sheriff Chambers and Mr. Metter rose to leave. Both men tipped their hats, and, as they walked by, Chambers said, "I'll see you in the morning, ma'am."

The devilish impulsiveness she'd inherited from her dear Irish mother came to the fore and Delilah responded, "Or, if you're planning to be at Miss Cora's this evening, perhaps you'll see me again tonight."

Whyever had she reminded him of that, she asked herself the moment the words left her mouth.

Chambers turned back to look at her, his stone-cold charcoal eyes pinning her in her chair. Then, slowly, he smiled. The expression transformed his hard features, and for the first time Delilah realized that the man was quite handsome. Yet the smile did nothing to negate the aura of danger that clung to him. In fact, it aggravated that quality for, like the snarl of a wolf, its only purpose was to show teeth. "Maybe," he acknowledged slowly in a tone barely above a whisper. Somehow the single word sounded vaguely threatening. And then he was gone.

Delilah shivered. The man didn't smile when he was supposed to, and then smiled when he was challenged. It could take a long time to figure out a man like that. More time than she had . . . or wanted.

A few moments later, Delilah reentered her room with the intention of putting Poopsy on her leash and taking her with her to the Lucky Strike. As usual, after having left the dog alone, Delilah was greeted by a chorus of complaints that sounded very much as though Poopsy was trying to talk. "Rr . . . ow, rah, rah, rr . . . ow." Delilah knew when she was being given what-for. She had come to the conclusion that Poopsy simply did not know that she was a dog. After all, Edwina Sharp had gone so far as to dress her canine companion in specially fashioned clothing and style her long silky hair. Quite simply, Poopsy thought she was entitled to go anywhere that Delilah went.

Being of an entirely different opinion, not to mention

a different temperament than Edwina, Delilah simply could not cater to the animal the way Edwina Sharp had. Since she had been saddled with the little rascal, she had decided that the only way to save her own sanity was to make Poopsy understand that she was a *dog*.

Now, stopping just inside the door of her room, Delilah placed her hands on her hips and stood looking down at Poopsy. "How many times have I told you that I will not tolerate that kind of behavior, Poochie? If you want to come with me, I suggest that you start behaving yourself immediately."

"Rraw, rrow, ruff." The little dog bobbed her head as though straining to form words.

"Poochie," Delilah said in a warning tone. "I *will* leave you here. Now do you want to come or not?"

As though sensing that her new mistress was at the end of her patience, Poopsy abruptly sat down, lifted her head, and curled her upper lip, baring her teeth. Delilah winced inwardly—to her the expression looked like a snarl—but she ignored her inner response because she knew that this was Poopsy's version of an agreeable smile. Why Edwina had ever bothered to teach a dog to smile, was beyond her, but she had. It was only one of Poopsy's bizarre little behaviors.

"That's much better. Now where's your leash?"

Poopsy cocked her head for an instant and then obediently pranced over to the carpetbag that, when laid on its side, doubled as her bed, and extracted her leash. Gripping the strip of leather in her teeth, she dragged it over to where Delilah waited.

"Good girl," Delilah praised. Bending, she fastened the leash around Poopsy's neck. "And I want you to continue to be a good girl tonight. Is that understood?" Poopsy didn't respond. "I mean it, Poochie," Delilah reiterated. "You should know by now that people in saloons will not meet Edwina's high standards. There is to be no biting or peeing on people's feet. All right?"

Poopsy smiled agreeably, and Delilah wondered what she'd missed in outlining her list of undesirable behaviors. The little dog appeared entirely too cocky.

Along with the warm yellow glow of lantern light, the lively and somehow bawdy sound of "The Yellow Rose of Texas" being played on a tinny-sounding piano spilled from the doors of the Lucky Strike into the dark and otherwise silent streets. Studiously ignoring the painful knot in her stomach, Delilah took a deep breath and stepped into the hazy blue atmosphere of the saloon as though she belonged there.

She'd never grown accustomed to being around so many men.

Still, gambling was much better than doing laundry until her hands bled, or taking in mending and working by the light of a lamp until her eyes teared from the strain. Her mama, Morgana Sinclair, had always said that everyone had a God-given talent and it was their duty to discover where that talent lay in order to make the best of life for themselves. Well, Delilah had discovered hers and was following her mother's advice. It was simply an example of nature's perversity that the gentle graces Morgana had taught her daughter aided her so well in a profession that she would have abhorred had she lived.

Viewing Delilah's aptitude for the gambling game as sinful, Morgana Sinclair had always compressed her lips with disapproval whenever her husband had bowed to Delilah's pleas and sat down to play poker with his daughters. Garrett Sinclair had done his best to convince Morgana that, when playing for nothing more than matchsticks, poker was merely good wholesome family entertainment. He had even managed to convince Morgana to play the game herself on occasion. But no matter how much she might have enjoyed the game, she would never have admitted it, for she could not quite forget the strictures with which she'd been raised.

"Sorry, Mama," Delilah whispered now as she looked around, studying the crowded tables. Most were occupied by miners, she thought, although a few cowhands seemed to have come to town. They were a loud, unruly bunch, and at a couple of tables the mood was distinctly ugly as the men argued.

The knot in her stomach tightened a notch, but she knew from experience that once she started playing, the tension would ease and she'd be in her element. So, taking a deep breath, she ignored it. Besides, she told herself, on the whole she'd run into very few men over the years who didn't treat a lady like a lady. It was simply a twist of fate that one of those she'd met had had the power to ruin her life.

She walked slowly through the room and approached the bar. As her presence was noted by more and more men, the noise in the room slowly decreased. She could feel their eyes on her, but she ignored the sensation. If she dwelled on it, she'd run out screaming and never again find the courage to face another man with hot greedy eyes.

And Delilah Sinclair refused to hide.

"Good evening, sir," she said to the bartender, her tone clear and full of confidence. "Is Miss Cora in?"

"Yes, ma'am. She is."

"Would you tell her that Mrs. Sterne is here to see her, please?"

"Sure thing." The middle-aged bartender considered her gravely. "You want something to drink while I go get her?"

Delilah smiled absently, her thoughts already moving on. "I'll have another peach cordial if you don't mind."

"Comin' right up."

In the past three years, ever since she'd seen Eve safely married off at the tender age of seventeen, Delilah had supported herself with her facility for gambling. As one of the West's few women gamblers, and certainly one of the youngest, she'd actually done quite well for herself. She'd definitely earned more than she had when she and Eve had taken in mending and laundry to keep the wolves from their door after their father had been shot, leaving them orphaned at the ages of seventeen and fifteen respectively. And gambling had been a lot less painful.

The problem was that luck came in streaks, as any gambler could affirm, and Delilah's luck hadn't been the greatest in the last few months.

"Mrs. Sterne, I presume," a woman's voice said. It was a low-pitched voice, but musical and clear.

Delilah turned to see a tall, statuesque redhead considering her with an astute brown-eyed gaze. "That's correct," Delilah said. "And you would be Miss Cora?"

The woman nodded. "Mitch tells me that you want to speak with me about working here."

"I do."

Miss Cora considered her quite openly for a moment, her eyes traveling over Delilah's lithe form from head to toe, lingering for a moment on the strange little dog sitting patiently next to Delilah's small feet. Then, just as the piano player concluded a lively ditty with a flourish and the barroom fell unnaturally silent, she said, "Come with me. We'll talk in my office."

Cora's office was small, barely large enough to hold the walnut desk and three chairs it contained, but its white walls were spotlessly clean, as were the bright yellow gingham curtains that hung over the single window. An oil lamp hung from a hook on the wall next to the door.

"You're not the usual sort of woman who comes in here," Cora said, giving Delilah another assessing glance. "Still, I'm afraid I have to tell you that I just don't have the room for any more girls at the moment."

"Oh, no! You've misunderstood!" Delilah was flabbergasted. Hadn't the bartender mentioned gambling? "I'm not here to apply for . . . *that* kind of work."

Cora frowned in perplexity. "Then I'm afraid I don't understand. Why are you here?"

"I was wondering if you'd be willing to discuss a business proposition concerning your card table. It appears to be quite vacant at the moment."

Cora's brows arched in surprise. "You're a dealer?"

Delilah nodded. "Poker primarily. I'm not as accomplished at faro, but I've played it."

Cora leaned back in her chair and surveyed Delilah with wide, astonished eyes. "Well, I'll be!" A second later, she regained her aplomb. "Still, I have to tell you, Mrs. Sterne . . ."

"Delilah . . . please. Call me Delilah."

"Very well . . . Delilah. I have to warn you that, even should we come to an agreement, gamblers do not fare well here in Red Rock."

Delilah compressed her lips and nodded. "So I've heard. However, I'm willing to take that risk."

"If Sheriff Chambers so much as gets a glimmer that you're cheating, he'll throw you in jail and run you out of town the next day."

Delilah stiffened her spine. "I may be a gambler, Miss Cora, but I do *not* cheat. I was raised in a good God-fearing family where dishonesty was not tolerated." She smiled then. "I am, however, uncannily fortunate at times, which has led people to accuse me of cheating."

Cora considered her with astute brown eyes. "I see." She drummed her fingertips on the desk thoughtfully.

"I'd be willing to offer you the standard twenty-five percent of the house take."

"Fifty percent," Delilah countered.

"Fifty percent!" Cora echoed. "You've got to be joking! The highest I could go would be thirty percent."

"Forty. After all, your table is sitting there earning you nothing at the moment."

"Thirty-five," said Cora, with a steely look in her eyes.

"Forty," Delilah reiterated.

Cora considered. "I thought you said you didn't cheat."

"I don't. I am enterprising. There is a difference."

"Forty percent of the house take is unprecedented."

"So don't tell anyone. I need the money, and you stand to make money on an otherwise empty table."

"Oh, very well. Forty percent. *Provided* that you're any good."

Delilah smiled. "You won't be disappointed."

"That remains to be seen, doesn't it?" Cora said. Slowly, however, she returned Delilah's smile and rose from her position behind the desk. Leaning forward onto her fists, she said, "I'll let you start tonight, to see how you do. Then, tomorrow night, you can start right after supper."

"I can give you a demonstration tonight, but I actually won't be able to start for three or four days, if that's not a problem. I'm going out of town in the morning. I just wanted to get this sorted out before I left."

She shrugged. "I can't see that it will be much of a problem. As you so kindly pointed out, the table is empty anyway.

"You have friends in the area, do you?" Cora asked.

Delilah shook her head. "A sister, actually. At the Devil's Fork ranch. I want to spend some time with her."

"Eve Cameron?"

Delilah nodded. "Yes, she married Tom a couple of years ago. Do you know her?"

"I know of her." Cora rocked back on her heels. "Well, I'll be! How long's it been since you've seen her?"

Delilah hesitated. Was there something in Cora's voice that shouldn't be there? "About a year, I guess. Why? Is something wrong?"

Cora paused. "There's been some trouble out that way recently. Rustling mostly. I haven't heard anything about the Devil's Fork, though, so it may not have affected them much."

She walked the few steps to the door and said, "Well, Delilah, let's see what you can do, shall we?"

"Certainly." The knot in Delilah's stomach tightened another notch. She ignored it.

Cora began to open the door and then stopped. After giving Delilah's attire a thorough examination, she asked, "Did you want to borrow a room to change in?"

"Change?" Delilah echoed. "Is there something wrong with what I have on?"

"You look like a preacher's wife. It's going to be kind of hard to dazzle the men with your charms when they can't see them."

Delilah compressed her lips. "I do not intend to use my charms, such as they are, to dazzle anyone. As I said, I play an honest game of poker."

Cora considered her with astute eyes that saw far too much, Delilah felt certain. Then, she held up her hands briefly, as though in surrender. "Fine. I just thought I'd mention it. Most women like to make the most of what they have." She opened the door and wordlessly indicated that Delilah should precede her.

Minutes later, Delilah took her place at the newly dusted gaming table, settled Poopsy firmly at her feet, and began shuffling cards. Laying the deck down, she spread the cards into a perfect fan shape before lifting the edge of one card with a fingernail and flipping the entire deck over and then back again. Scooping the cards up in a practiced sweep, she shuffled. The room was unnaturally silent as drovers and miners alike watched her. Then, she lifted her gaze and smiled.

It was the practiced smile she'd learned to use. A smile that rivaled the sunlight for brilliance and made every man who received it feel as though it shone just for him. It was her professional smile, and the only artifice she used to dazzle.

It was enough.

"Come on up, gentlemen," she called in a soft but carrying voice that conveyed culture and decorum. She sounded like a society lady inviting the men into her private drawing room to have their brandies. "Come on up and put your money down." She launched into the spiel she'd learned to use to attract her customers. "Lady Luck is smiling on the Lucky Strike tonight, gentlemen. It could be your night to strike it rich."

A few of the men began to stir. "I ain't never seen no lady dealer afore," one voice grumped.

"I have. Hell, once I played with Poker Alice herself."

"Poker Alice weren't no lady."

Delilah returned her attention to the cards in her hands, performing all sorts of dexterous movements designed to show her skill and attract attention. "Step up, gentlemen," she flashed her smile again, making every man there feel as though Lady Luck herself had smiled just for him. "Step up and put your money down. Everybody wins when Lady Luck is in town."

A couple of cowboys near the rear of the saloon rose and took their places at the table. Delilah looked to the one on her left. He was probably about thirty, but he looked older. His skin looked like old leather, brown and lined by the elements he faced. His eyes were grey-blue and his cheeks were covered with stubble.

"Good evening, sir."

"You can call me Tex, ma'am."

"Tex it is. And what's your game, Mr. Tex?"

"Five card draw, ma'am. An' it ain't *mister*. Just Tex."

Delilah looked to his companion. "Draw poker sound all right to you, sir?"

The cowboy tipped a battered Stetson and slid some money onto the table. "Yes, ma'am. Stud poker is my usual game, but draw is fine an' dandy too. An' I ain't never been *sir* to nobody. The name's Lance."

Delilah increased the brilliance of her smile as she counted out chips and began to deal. "I'm pleased to meet you Mr. Lance. I'm Mrs. Sterne."

Tex won the first hand. On the next hand, the cowhands were joined by a couple of old miners, and one man Delilah couldn't categorize. He was well dressed, but didn't have the look of a lawyer or doctor. The mayor perhaps?

As the evening progressed, the knot in her stomach eased. It looked like the few days she'd spent away from the game had turned her luck around. She'd lost only the one hand.

And then, she felt a powerful presence, and looked up to see Sheriff Chambers's gaze boring into her from his leaning position against the bar. Their eyes met and, for an instant, Delilah froze in mid deal. Then, without a flicker of expression, the sheriff mockingly lifted his shot glass as though in toast to her, and downed the whiskey he held.

The gesture doubled as a warning and a dare, and they both knew it. He was daring her to cheat—which she wouldn't do anyway, of course—but she hadn't realized how difficult it would be to play beneath Matt Chambers's watchful gaze. She made an error, throwing away a card she should have kept, and lost the hand.

Blast it all! She couldn't afford stupid mistakes like that. Not now.

Determination tightened her jaw. Somehow, she was either going to have to learn to ignore the sheriff's potent gaze, or she was going to have to get rid of the man.

At the moment, the latter option had some definite appeal.

Maybe she could stage a robbery and send him off chasing bad guys for the few weeks that she'd be here. Foolish thought. If she couldn't play an honest card game beneath his too-observant gaze, how in blazes would she plan and execute a robbery?

No, there had to be another way, an easier way, of keeping the good sheriff out of her hair. She just had to find it.

Chapter Four

The mountain morning dawned crisp and clear as Delilah made her way down the boardwalk toward the livery. It felt good to have an excuse to don split skirts and her black lady-sized Stetson again. Her father's Winchester, buried so long at the bottom of her trunk, felt familiar and reassuring in her hand. She had decided to risk the tarnish on her "helpless lady" image that carrying the Winchester might create, for the small derringer she carried in her reticule would be all but useless in the wild. Thanks to the absence of her escort from the Devil's Fork, she had little choice but to venture out on her own.

Lifting her head slightly, she took a deep breath of the fresh morning air and smiled. She was looking forward to escaping civilization for a time. It had been so long since she'd ridden a horse and traveled to places that a wagon would never go. So long since she'd camped and fished in the wild. So long since . . . her father had died.

The smile faded as memories stirred of a past that could never be recaptured. Years ago, Garrett Sinclair had taken his wife and daughters camping in the wilderness often. After they had established a base camp, he'd hunt venison while Morgana, Delilah, and Eve fished. Delilah remembered cleaning fish, smoking and preserving them until the barrels were full enough to supplement their larder for another winter. It had been hard work, and yet it had been a time full of laughter and promise.

Those carefree days had ended with her mother's death when she was just fifteen, and Eve thirteen.

It had taken over a year for Garrett Sinclair to begin to live again after losing Morgana. And even when he had, and had begun to take his daughters on wilderness treks again, their times together were never quite as joyful as they once had been. In the days after her mother's death, her father had focused more on instruction than on enjoyment. Although always a stern taskmaster, he'd also been kind, invariably offering praise or encouragement when it was due. He'd seemed determined that his daughters learn how to take care of themselves. Looking back, it seemed to Delilah almost as though he'd known he wouldn't be around to protect them much longer.

Lord, how she still missed him.

The swipe of a moist doggy tongue across her nose suddenly tugged her from her melancholy thoughts. She was carrying Poopsy in a saddlebag over her shoulder at the moment, and the little dog, no doubt sensing the abrupt despondent direction of her mistress's mood, had decided that she had to do something about it quickly. Now, she curled her upper lip and offered Delilah one of her most engaging smiles.

With a small hitching laugh, Delilah returned the smile and reached up to scratch gently behind Poopsy's left ear. "You're right, Poochie. Today is no time for thinking of things best left in the past." Poopsy, her mission accomplished, turned her head to gaze around from this new vantage point with glistening black eyes, her small pink tongue lolling from her mouth as she panted with excitement.

Delilah was just about to cross the street toward the livery when the stable's wide double doors opened and a buckboard wagon pulled by a familiar team of bay horses rolled into view. "Mornin', ma'am," Ronnie Didsworth shouted without heed for those who still lay abed on this fine morning. Then he pulled the wagon to a halt while somebody behind the conveyance—Mr. Metter perhaps?—loaded something onto it.

Delilah waved, but waited until she'd closed the distance between herself and the wagon before returning his greeting. "Good morning, Mr. Didsworth," she said just as Didsworth climbed down to move around the wagon and do some rearranging of its contents. Then she smiled at his son who, for the return trip, was seated on the wooden plank seat. "Good morning Master Tyler Didsworth."

The boy's eyes widened with pleasure at her very proper greeting. "G'mornin' ma'am," he returned as he reached one hand up to tip a hat that was not in place. His straw-colored hair, still uncombed after his night's sleep, stuck up in odd directions. Faced with the presence of a lady, he hastily raked it with his fingers before reaching behind himself in a blind search for the misplaced hat which, once found, was immediately plunked on his head. That accomplished, he looked back at Delilah. "Whatcha doin' up so early?" he asked, with the honest curiosity of youth.

Her smile widened. "I'm going to visit my sister. I haven't seen her in a long time, and I'm very excited."

"Oh." He looked vaguely disappointed by her response. "I got sisters, but I see 'em all the time." He shrugged. "Sometimes I wish I didn't." He glanced back at his father. "Pa has a sister, too, but we ain't seen her in a long time."

"That's unfortunate."

The boy shrugged. "It don't make no never mind to me. Truth be told, she's kinda uppity, if'n you know what I mean."

"Yes, I believe I do."

At that moment, Didsworth shook hands with Metter in farewell and climbed up onto the buckboard seat once more. "Well, I guess we'll be off. Ma'am, you just have Mrs. Francis down at the telegraph get hold of me whenever you'll be wantin' a lift back to Butte City. You hear?"

"I do, sir. Thank you." With a nod of acknowledgment, Didsworth clucked to the horses, and the wagon began to roll. "Have a safe trip," Delilah called out in their wake.

Both Didsworths raised their hands in farewell. As the morning once again regained its quiet, Delilah found herself scanning the area, seeking the tall muscular form belonging to Sheriff Chambers. He was nowhere in sight.

Dismissing as mere loneliness the faint surge of disappointment she felt, Delilah turned toward the stablemaster, who'd moved forward to stand at her side. "Is the Appaloosa ready, Mr. Metter?"

He nodded. "Yes, ma'am. His name's Jackpot." With a grin, he added, "I guess you'll be appreciatin' that more 'n most." It was obvious that either Sheriff Chambers or the local grapevine had made him aware of Delilah's occupation.

She smiled without comment. "May I see him?"

The livery owner led her into the warm, musty-smelling stable, indicating a stall about halfway down on the left. "Here he is."

Jackpot's head hung over the gate, studying them with a bright-eyed curious gaze. A good sign. "Can you bring him out please, so that I can get a good look at him?" Another of the many things she'd learned from her daddy was the value of a reliable horse.

"Sure thing." Metter removed a halter from a nearby hook and slipped it over the gelding's head with ease. A moment later, he opened the stall and led the animal out into the open.

Delilah studied Jackpot. He had good lines, strong hindquarters, and a nicely arched neck. There was no sign of lameness when he walked. She ran her hands over him. The muscles were smooth and in good shape. There were no saddle sores or scars to denote poor treatment. Bending, she lifted his hooves and noted that the shoes were in good shape, the hooves themselves well trimmed. There were no imbedded stones which would bring the horse up lame as he began to move.

"You know horses, do you?" asked Metter.

"Yes . . . yes, I do," Delilah acknowledged absently, without offering the explanation she knew he wanted. Satisfied, she gave the animal a pat on the rump. "He's a good-looking animal. What's the price?"

Metter named a sum. "That's for horse, saddle, and tack, since you don't got yer own."

Delilah considered. It seemed reasonable. "And how much will you refund when I'm finished with him?" she asked. She had never liked surprises. They haggled a moment more and then, content with the deal, Delilah saddled Jackpot. While Metter moved about his business, she settled her bedroll, canteen, and the saddlebags containing Poopsy and a change of clothing into place.

She was just leading the horse outside in preparation for mounting when Metter shouted, "Mrs. Sterne?"

She turned. "Yes?"

He came forward in a fast walk. "I blame near forgot to tell you that the sheriff said he'd catch up with you on the road. He had to ride out 'fore dawn this mornin'." Metter frowned. "There was more trouble last night. Some of Joshua Kane's men surprised them rustlers, and Jamie Cox got hisself shot right outa his saddle. He was a damn good hand too, if you'll pardon me for swearin', ma'am."

"Of course, Mr. Metter. Is he . . . deceased then?"

Metter nodded. "Deader 'n a doornail." He shook his head sadly. "What a waste." Then, taking a deep breath, he returned to the message at hand. "Anyways, ma'am, the sheriff asked me to tell ya to just stay on the road and be careful until he can join ya. Okay?"

Delilah nodded and mounted. "I'm always careful, Mr. Metter. However, I do thank you for the message."

"Yer welcome, ma'am."

Metter stared after the straight-backed young widow as she rode out of town. Somehow he didn't doubt her words. Not one bit. If he was a betting man, he'd bet there was more to Mrs. Sterne than met the eye. Way more. He sent a prayer of thanks winging heavenward that he had a good, solid woman waiting for him at home who was exactly what she seemed to be. Then, with a shake of his head, he dismissed the young widow from his mind and returned to his barn. There were stalls to muck out and halters to mend.

* * *

Samson studied the area in which he'd lost the trail. Nothing. Not the scuff of a shod hoof on stone. Not a broken twig. Not a single print. He'd lost them.

How could three men on horseback simply disappear? It didn't make sense.

Samson scanned the surrounding rocky bluffs for the umpteenth time. What was he missing?

But he saw nothing.

With a frown, he conceded defeat for the moment. Checking the position of the morning sun, he decided it was time to be on his way. He wanted to be back in Red Rock by the end of the day, and he had a goodly distance to go yet to get to the Lazy M. The Lazy M, like a number of other ranches in the vicinity, had been losing cattle to rustlers. And Carter McTaggert had demanded to see Sheriff Chambers about the latest theft. With the herds so seriously depleted after the winter just past, no one could afford the loss. Not even McTaggert, who up until this spring had been one of the area's most affluent and tyrannical ranchers. Of course, he still tended to be tyrannical. It was just the affluent part that had changed a mite.

But there was another reason Samson was anxious to be moving too. And that reason came in the form of a pretty young black-haired widow who was traveling his way.

Damn! The woman infuriated and enticed him at the same time.

With a cluck of his tongue, Samson set his horse, Goliath, into motion and did his best to ignore the sense of exhilaration invoked by the thought of once again meeting Mrs. Delilah Sterne. But, as his memory plagued him with a vision of how she'd looked the previous evening in the Lucky Strike, he discovered that ignoring his anticipation at seeing her again was not an easy thing to do.

He'd been surprised to see her still in her high-necked, concealing widow's garb. And yet, as the evening progressed, it became quite evident that she'd not needed the artifice he'd expected. Delilah Sterne, quite simply, had made the saloon her parlor. She'd had a calming influence on the men gathered there, and no one present would have ever suggested that Mrs. Sterne was anything other than a lady.

She was simply a lady who also happened to be a gambler.

And that was where the problem lay. He could not abide gamblers. Yet he couldn't deny the fact that he found Delilah Sterne damnably attractive. How could he reconcile the one with the other?

At that moment, Goliath went skittish on him, pulling at the reins and chomping at the bit as he side-stepped on the rocky mountain trail. Fighting to control the draft-size horse, Samson's attention returned to the present with a snap as he scanned the area, searching for the reason behind the big animal's distress.

The screaming roar of a mountain lion pierced his consciousness at the same instant that a streak of tawny fur launched itself toward him from a ledge above. There was no time to spur Goliath into motion. No time to draw his gun. No time for anything more than twisting as he kicked his feet free of the stirrups so that he could roll with the force of the big cat's attack.

And then he hit the ground with a couple of hundred pounds of raging, screaming wildcat upon him. Samson was desperate. Even as big as he was, a seething, savage cougar bent on his demise offered a significant danger.

Ignoring the painful but less life-threatening damage the beast's claws inflicted as they raked his chest and arms, Samson wrapped his fingers around its neck and concentrated on keeping its deadly fangs away from his throat.

Something was wrong here. Mountain lions rarely attacked people, and almost never one on horseback. But the instant Sam saw the blood-flecked foam edging the snarling creature's mouth, he knew the reason for its assault.

Rabies.

His heart almost stopped.

He felt the cat's warm breath on his face as he stared into wild, hate-filled golden-green eyes. Tightening his grasp, he felt the corded muscle in the neck beneath his fingers, the heaviness of the animal's body upon him, and the heat of its fur against his bare forearms. And he saw the exact moment that the lion realized the tables had been turned. Yet still it fought on, the unreasoning madness induced by the rabies eradicating any instinct for self-preservation and survival.

Had the animal been healthy, Samson would have hesitated to kill it. Most cougars would have run as soon as he'd begun to fight back. They preferred to kill swiftly, taking their prey by surprise. But this animal had made the choice for him. It would not run.

Altering the grip of his fingers slightly, he twisted the big cat's neck. Then, with a final jerk, he snapped its vertebrae. As the coiled tension faded from the beast's body, Samson thrust its carcass aside and sat up.

He immediately jerked his shredded shirt from his body and began a diligent search for any hint of a bite that had broken the skin. He had seen a man die from rabies once, and he'd sworn that he'd put a gun to his head and pull the trigger before he'd let himself die like that.

No bites. Nothing. And he didn't think any of the animal's disease-tainted slobber had fallen onto the scratches inflicted by its claws. He was winded and scratched up pretty good, and the left thigh of his denims had been shredded, but otherwise he was all right.

Closing his eyes briefly, he exhaled in relief. Then he scanned the rocky slopes for his horse. Goliath was nowhere to be seen. The horse had been well trained, however, and Samson knew he wouldn't have gone far. Putting his fingers to his lips, he released a series of piercing whistles, then leaned back to catch his breath while he waited.

Moments later, his sweat-flecked mount came clopping up the trail. If a horse could look sheepish, Goliath did. Still, he stopped a healthy distance away from the corpse of the lion. Samson rose, wincing as the scratches began to bother him, and discovered a few new aches and pains as well. Somehow, he seemed to have hurt his thigh. Probably when he'd been propelled out of the saddle. Limping over to his hat, which had been knocked off in the struggle, he slapped the dust from it and put it back on. Then he turned to Goliath.

The horse's head hung nearly to his knees. Goliath always seemed so ashamed of himself in the aftermath of an incident when horse instinct took over that Sam thought the animal must be part human. "It's okay, boy," he soothed as he stroked Goliath's sweaty neck. "It's okay."

Reassured, Goliath lifted his head and tugged affectionately with his lips at the shirt Samson held in his hands. There wasn't much left of the garment. The fabric had been cut to ribbons by the cougar's sharp claws.

Opening his saddlebag, Samson removed the blue chambray shirt that he always carried as a spare, and considered. He needed to do something to stop the bleeding before putting on his clean shirt, or he'd simply have two ruined shirts. He'd bind the wounds with his torn shirt and hope that would suffice.

* * *

Delilah had been on the trail, more generously termed a road, for a couple of hours, and there was one thing she could now say with certainty. Montana Territory contained some of the most beautiful country she'd ever seen. *Majestic* was the only word she could find to describe it. From its enormous blue sky to its distant snowy mountain peaks, it was an endless vista of natural beauty. She saw deep green forests, valleys bright with new grass and spring flowers, and colorful rocky crags striated with multihued stone. She saw bighorn sheep, bald eagles, and a herd of deer. A gaggle of Canada geese, a pair of bluebirds, and a porcupine. At every turn, as each new vista became visible, she gasped anew at some glorious sight.

She was observing a trickle of glacial mountain water that seemed to ooze from a rock face next to the road when suddenly she heard the sound of a horse approaching. Glancing over her shoulder, she immediately recognized the sheriff's form for, even at a distance, he looked gigantic. After waging a brief internal struggle, Delilah pulled up and politely waited for him to join her, though she found herself averting her eyes as he drew closer. Knowing the effect that his strange steely-eyed gaze had on her, the last thing she wanted to do was meet his eyes.

"Good morning, Sheriff," she said, barely sparing him a glance as he drew abreast of her.

"Ma'am." He greeted her with a nod.

Did his voice seem somehow tight? "Did you catch the rustlers?"

"No, ma'am. Lost the trail."

Delilah set Jackpot into motion and the sheriff followed suit with his huge black horse. Yes, there was some new aspect to his voice, but she was uncertain what it was. "That's unfortunate." Grief perhaps? "Did you know Mr. Cox well?"

"Just in passing, ma'am."

"Is something wrong, Sheriff Chambers?"

Silence. Then, "Nothing you should concern yourself about, ma'am."

Delilah's lips tightened. A condescending male response if she'd ever heard one. "I assure you, Sheriff, that I am quite capable of understanding the intricacies of law enforcement. My father was a bounty hunter."

No response. Delilah risked a glance in his direction. Did he seem paler than he had earlier?

"I'm afraid you've lost me, Mrs. Sterne," he said as he met her gaze. "Were we talking law enforcement?"

Delilah quickly looked away. "I believe so, Sheriff. Unless whatever is bothering you has nothing to do with your profession."

"Actually it doesn't, ma'am."

"Then, pray tell, what does it have to do with?"

Silence.

Delilah looked over at him to see that he was eyeing her with consideration. This time his dark eyes caught hers and held them. Her heart fluttered, robbing her of the ability to breathe properly. Desperately, she sought the thread of their conversation. "Well?" she prodded.

"Well what, ma'am?"

"Are you going to tell me what is bothering you, or not?" She frowned. He definitely looked a bit pale beneath his tan. "You don't look well, sir. Are you ill?"

He eyed her for a moment and then appeared to come to a decision. "In a manner of speaking, ma'am." He mopped his brow. "I got jumped by a rabid cougar back there."

"Jumped by a . . ." Delilah broke off as the words sank in. "Good heavens! Were you bitten?"

He shook his head. "Scratched up pretty good, but not bitten."

A horrifying possibility occurred to her and she hastily scanned the area. "Is it still alive?"

"No, ma'am."

"Thank goodness!" Her most immediate fear eased, Delilah turned her attention once more to the man at her side, who was quite obviously in considerable pain. More concerned than she ought to have been, but refusing to examine that emotion, Delilah sought a suitable place to stop, and spotted a downed tree. "Pull up over there. I want to take a look at those scratches."

She urged Jackpot in the indicated direction, then dismounted and secured him to a nearby tree limb. Turning, she expected to see Sheriff Chambers behind her, but he wasn't there. Rather, he was still sitting astride his mount in the middle of the narrow road they'd been following, watching her expressionlessly. "Are you coming, Sheriff?"

"I've already bandaged the scratches."

Delilah placed her hands on her hips. "Really? You cleansed them, disinfected them, and bound them with clean cloth?"

A pause. "I can't rightly say I disinfected them. I didn't think about it."

"Just as I thought. Do you have any whiskey in those saddlebags of yours?"

"I might have a bit."

"Good. Then I suggest you allow me to look after those scratches before they fester."

"You think it's that important?"

Delilah nodded. "Unquestionably, Sheriff. My mother saw two brothers die during the war from infections that she was positive could have been prevented. She made certain her daughters understood the importance of cleansing any wound."

He looked away, staring off toward a distant mountain peak. Delilah waited. Then, with a small shake of his head, the sheriff nudged his horse toward her and dismounted slowly, his face tensing with the pain of his injuries. After dropping his reins to ground-tether his mount, he removed the whiskey bottle from his saddlebag and turned to face her. "Over there?" he asked, indicating the fallen tree.

She nodded. Now that he was before her, so big and imposing and male, she wondered if she could, in fact, do what needed to be done. She hadn't willingly touched a man in anything other than a social situation since . . . since the day Jacob Sterne had entered her life. She'd certainly never touched bare skin.

Samson sat on the log, watching her, and waited. She was different than she'd been in town. More relaxed somehow? No, that wasn't it. More certain? Confident, perhaps? Maybe. Not that he'd noticed a lack of either quality before, but now the traits seemed somehow more obvious. As though Mrs. Delilah Sterne had returned to something she knew well. *That* was it. She seemed very at home suddenly. He suspected she knew very well how to fire the Winchester that rested in her saddle scabbard.

Interesting. A lady. A gambler. And an obviously accomplished horsewoman who knew rifles.

Who was Delilah Sterne?

"Take off your shirt, Sheriff," she directed in a brisk tone as she removed from her saddlebag an old petticoat that she no doubt intended to use as a clean bandage.

Her dog whined from the other saddlebag, and Delilah set her on the ground. "No running off this time, Poochie," she ordered distractedly as she continued to look in the saddlebag for something. "I don't intend to chase after you again." Poochie bared her teeth and then ambled a short distance off.

In the process of removing his shirt, Samson shook his head. "You talk to that dog as though it can understand you."

Delilah turned to face him. "I believe she can understand much more than people give her credit for. She's really quite intelligent."

"If you say so, ma'am." Leaving the blood-soaked torn shirt that he'd secured around his midsection in place, he draped his good shirt over the log and resumed his seat upon the log. "I've seen some pretty smart cattle dogs in my day." He left a *but* hanging unspoken.

"But you've never seen one that could understand more than a couple of words. Correct?"

"Yes, ma'am."

Mrs. Sterne nodded. "I hadn't either until I met Poochie." Her tone was final, and dismissed the topic. Samson got the message. He could either believe or disbelieve, it was of no concern to her. "Can you remove that as well?" she asked, gesturing toward the ragged shirt tied at his waist.

He nodded and watched as she retrieved her canteen, took a deep breath as though to gird herself, and then moved smoothly toward him through the bed of ferns that carpeted the roadside.

She gasped as the claw marks became visible, and Samson had to admit they looked a mite worse than he remembered. Four gaping bloody parallel lacerations marked his left side from his breast to the waistband of his denim trousers. Another deeper trio of gashes angled from right to left, starting just below his rib cage and ending at his navel. Even his forearms had gouges, though these were less deep, having been inflicted by the creature's front claws as it had tried to break his stranglehold. Every scratch continued to ooze blood, despite his previous doctoring attempt.

He noted that Mrs. Sterne paled visibly. "You're not going to faint, are you?" Damnation! If there was one thing he did not need at the moment, it was an unconscious woman on his hands.

"Of course not!" she assured him, though her complexion remained ashen. "But . . . goodness gracious! Those are more than scratches. They require stitching."

"I was figuring on seeing Doc Hale when I got back to town tonight."

"You could lose a considerable amount of blood by then," she pointed out.

He shrugged. "I've lost blood before, and I've got things to do. They'll wait."

With a grimace that suggested a certain amount of exasperation with male bravado, Delilah said, "It's your life."

"Yes, ma'am." He studied her. She seemed to be frozen in place. "Did you want to bandage these scratches or not, ma'am?"

She started slightly. "Yes, of course." Kneeling in the foliage at his side, she ripped some strips from her petticoat, which she then wet with water from the canteen. That done, she began to sponge the blood from his wounds. Her hands felt cool against his skin.

Samson stayed silent as she worked, watching her. She seemed to be avoiding looking at him, but he didn't mind. It was the first time he'd had the opportunity to study her this closely. She was a damned attractive woman, that was for certain. He imagined her with her midnight hair unbound and spread across his pillow, staring up at him with those deep pansy-blue eyes. He imagined her soft white body beneath him as she held him in her arms, her pouty red lips parting to accept his kiss. He imagined making love to her.

"Does that hurt?"

Her words jerked him back from the realm of imagination with cruel finality. "What?" he managed to ask, fairly barking the word.

Delilah looked slightly taken aback. "I asked if I was hurting you. You seem more tense all of a sudden."

"No, ma'am. I'm fine," Samson choked out. But he wasn't fine. Hell! He was about to bust the buttons of his trousers.

She eyed him doubtfully for a second and then nodded, asking, "Can you pass me the whiskey please?"

Samson handed her the bottle. It was only a quarter full, but he figured it would be enough.

She didn't seem to agree. "Is that it?" she asked.

"Yes, ma'am. That's all I've got."

She studied the contents briefly. "Well, I guess we'll just have to make do." She met his eyes for the first time since beginning to work on him. "This is going to hurt some."

He nodded and said nothing. He was fully aware of how much it hurt to have good whiskey poured into an open cut.

"Lift your arm," she directed. She indicated his left arm which, held snugly against his side, was blocking accessibility to the outermost cut. Obliging, he did as directed.

An instant later, liquid fire seared the parallel slashes created by the cougar's claws. He grit his teeth. As the strained muscles in his shoulder complained at having to hold his arm in the air after their already excessive use today, he rested his hand on Delilah's shoulder and focused his attention on his tormentor. On the subtle strength of the bones beneath his fingers. On the silken texture of the lock of hair that brushed his knuckles. On the delicate bone structure of her features.

The color had come back to her face now. In fact, she

looked decidedly flushed. Samson frowned and contemplated her. What was the matter?

Her bottom lip trembled slightly, and she caught it between her teeth to still it. A sheen of perspiration dampened her forehead. Even her breathing had altered, having become more rapid and shallow. It was almost as though she was nervous.

A thought occurred to him. Was she perhaps as attracted to him as he was to her? The idea pleased him immensely.

She poured more whiskey on the diagonal scratches and pressed a square of white cloth against his ribs to catch the excess.

"Your hands are trembling," he observed.

She jumped slightly, as though his words had startled her. Then, meeting his gaze she said, "Don't worry, Sheriff. It has nothing to do with you. I won't faint on you." Hastily looking away, she returned to the task at hand, but not before he saw what was in her eyes. It wasn't attraction; it was fear. He was momentarily disconcerted, but more than that, he was curious.

"What are you afraid of?" he asked.

She shrugged. "Nothing!" But she said the word too quickly. Seeming to realize that, she shrugged slightly and added, "Just ghosts."

She didn't look at him, yet he needed to see her eyes. Slowly, he reached out a hand and gripped her chin, bringing her gaze up. "Someone in your past?"

She nodded slightly and pulled from his grasp, looking away.

"Why now?" he asked. "What made you think of it?"

She looked down at her lap, staring intently at the torn cloths resting there as though the answer lay there. He began to think she wouldn't answer. Then, finally, she whispered, "I don't like . . . men . . . touching me."

"Pardon me?" he asked, certain he had to have misheard.

She shook her head. "Nothing. Forget it. I shouldn't have said anything." She passed him the end of a long strip of white cloth. "Here, hold that in place while I dress the scratches."

He did as she directed, but he couldn't get her words out of his mind. "Your husband?"

"No! My husband was a gentle, loving man whose equal I shall never find." She looked aside briefly, as though searching for words in the foliage to her left. Then she murmured, "Please, just forget I said anything."

Samson considered her. He wanted to know what had happened to her, because he wanted to know Delilah Sterne, to understand her. But he couldn't force her to tell him. "All right, ma'am." He looked down at the bandage she had secured in place by tying the two ends together. It was clean and tight enough to slow the bleeding, if not stop it all together. "Thank you."

"You're welcome." She took a deep breath and smiled a dazzling, albeit forced, smile. "And now, Sheriff Matthew Chambers, I suggest you try not to tangle with any more lions for a while."

"Yes, ma'am. If I could just convince those danged rustlers to give themselves up, maybe I could stop roamin' cougar territory."

She frowned. "Do you have any idea who is responsible?"

"I'm not real sure, ma'am." Retrieving his shirt, he put it on while Delilah collected her canteen and the now empty whiskey bottle. "I heard a while back that a fellow wanted for rustlin' in Wyoming was in the area, but I haven't seen him."

She passed him the bottle. "A bounty hunter on the train to Butte had WANTED posters on some men he said were in this area. One of them was a rustler."

"Do you recall his name?"

"Let's see, Samson Towers is the name that comes to mind most readily, but he wasn't the rustler. Let me think about it."

Something tightened in Samson's chest at her words. "Sure," he said, but he could hardly force the word past the constriction in his throat.

Ah, hell! After two years, it was starting again. Thankfully, the likeness on the poster was not very good. He'd destroyed enough of those that had crossed his desk to know that. Still, anyone who knew him well would eventually make the connection if one of the posters came into their hands.

Chapter Five

They'd been riding in silence for a while when Sheriff Chambers abruptly pulled up his horse and waited for Delilah to come abreast. His horse balked a bit as Jackpot drew near, but he quieted him, murmuring, "Whoa, Goliath," as he reached forward to pat the animal's neck. Delilah was just about to comment on the suitability of the name he had chosen for the huge horse when he looked at her, pinning her beneath his hard, too-discerning gaze. "You don't happen to remember that bounty hunter's name, do you?" he asked.

"Yes, I . . . uh . . ." But the power of the sheriff's scrutiny wrought havoc with her memory. Blinking, she diverted her attention toward the road ahead and managed to find her voice. "He introduced himself as Mr. Pike. Joseph Pike, if I'm not mistaken."

At that moment Goliath sidestepped again, irritated by Jackpot's proximity. Sheriff Chambers took him firmly in hand, and then, by tacit agreement, they began walking the horses. "Have you remembered yet who the other posters that he carried were of?"

She nodded. "The one fellow was named Butch Morgan, and the other . . ." she frowned, "Clark, I believe. I can't recall his first name."

"That would be George Clark," he said with a nod. "I heard about a month back that he and Morgan were in the area. But, since they were never seen around, I'd assumed they'd moved on. Though it seems like a heck of a coincidence that all this rustlin' is going on right when Morgan is rumored to be in the area." He frowned and mused aloud, "I wonder if Pike is going on old information or new?"

"I wouldn't know."

He turned his head to look at her for a moment, and his steel-hued gaze had a rather distant, thoughtful expression. Then, finally, he murmured, "No, you wouldn't."

They settled into silence, and much of the remainder of their journey passed quietly and uneventfully. Matt seemed deep in thought, and spoke little, which was fine with Delilah. She found conversation with him too disturbing.

Whoa! *Matt?* When had she begun to think of him so familiarly? Sheriff Chambers was fine. Even Matt Chambers was acceptable. But just Matt? Uh-uh. She'd have to watch that.

She'd begun to think that perhaps they'd make it through the entire journey without initiating a disagreement concerning their most fundamental difference: the fact that she was a gambler and that he hated them. Then, out of the blue, he spoke. "Do you mind if I ask you a personal question?"

Delilah felt tension invade the muscles of her back. "You can ask, but I won't guarantee you an answer."

He nodded. "Fair enough." He rode without comment for a bit, his eyes on the wall of forest ahead. Finally, he turned to look at her and said, "Why do you gamble? There must be any number of other occupations open to a lady such as yourself."

Delilah stared at him. Memories of how difficult life had been after her father's death came crashing in on her, and a rush of anger and bitterness suffused her, stiffening her spine and enabling her, for the first time, to meet his eyes without losing her equanimity. "Oh, yes, Sheriff," she said caustically. "There are any number of occupations available for a lady like myself. I could have become a whore. Though of course I wouldn't have been a lady for very long in that occupation, would I?" Without giving him the opportunity to respond, she continued. "Or, I could have continued to work my fingers to the bone doing mending and laundry until my hands crippled and my eyesight went from working long hours by lantern light. Or, hallelujah!" She mimicked the tone of someone having just made a wonderful discovery. "Perhaps I could have married into unpaid servitude, becoming old before my time. I mean, there are any number of men out there looking for a woman to keep their house, do their laundry, and warm their beds. Aren't there?" Lord knows she'd received enough proposals from lecherous old men to last her a lifetime.

A moment of stunned silence greeted her outburst. "You dislike hard work?" he asked.

Realizing that perhaps her passionate response had been inconsistent with the casual nature of the question, Delilah struggled to reign in her temper. "On the contrary, Sheriff. I've never been afraid of hard work if it is necessary for my own survival or the well-being of those I love." She paused, remembering her mother and father. "I know from observing my parents that love can make a lifestyle that is at times quite meager palatable.

But, until I find that kind of love for myself . . ." She trailed off, suddenly remembering her persona, and the lie she lived. In a choked voice, she continued, "Until I find that kind of love *again*," she emphasized the word meaningfully, "I fail to see what is so wrong with the way I make my living." She wondered if, in her anger, she'd betrayed too much of the truth concerning her circumstances.

Sheriff Chambers looked at her then, his steel-cold eyes looking deep into her soul as though to seek out the mysteries hidden in the shadows there. "I see," was his only response. Delilah was left with the distinct impression that Matt Chambers, being much more perceptive than most of the men she encountered, was beginning to question her story. "Tell me about your husband, Mrs. Sterne. What exactly happened to him?"

She'd answered that particular question often enough to be able to reply without stumbling. "Kenneth was killed by a cheater's bullet while gambling on the *Kentucky Dream*.

"That's a riverboat?"

"Yes. On the Missouri River."

"So your husband was a gambler too?"

Delilah nodded. "By continuing in my husband's profession, someday I shall meet up with the man who killed him and seek justice."

Sheriff Chambers studied her a moment. "Umhmm," he said. Was there still a note of disbelief in his voice? Then, to Delilah's relief, he nodded and said, "My condolences," before kicking Goliath to a faster pace. Delilah nibbled the inner flesh of her bottom lip nervously, thoughtfully. He was beginning to doubt her story, she was almost certain of it, but she didn't know what to do about it.

It was past midday when he finally reined in again. Then, pointing down into the vast green valley that lay before them, he simply said, "That's the Devil's Fork ranch." Nodding toward the east, he added, "The next valley over belongs to the Lazy M."

Delilah studied him, wondering what he was thinking, and then turned to look at the valley below. It took her breath away. Bordered by cedars, pines, and rocky bluffs, the valley was emerald green with rich moist grass. A narrow river ran through the southern portion, and not far from that lay the ranch buildings. It was beautiful. No wonder Eve had ignored her husband's pride and risked incurring his wrath by asking for help. Losing a place like this would be unthinkable.

"I'll ride on down with you," Chambers said. "While I'm here, I might as well check to see if they've had any more trouble."

Delilah snapped a look at him. Was he talking about the rustling, or something else? "What kind of trouble?"

In the process of studying the valley below rather intently, he shrugged and, without looking at her, said, "The rustling. Isn't that what you so kindly informed me that I should be most concerned with?" His sarcasm was not lost on her, but before she could think of a suitable response, he added, "It's been a while since I've heard anything from them." He then effectively ended the conversation by nudging his horse onto the narrow trail that led down toward the Devil's Fork. Delilah was left with little choice but to follow.

Upon nearing the ranch, a commotion from the direction of the corrals left no doubt in Delilah's mind that something of significance was taking place. Cattle bawled. Men shouted. Dogs barked. And a woman's voice rang out with a definite note of authority. The stench of burning hair hung in the still mountain air as they drew closer.

"Looks like branding time," Sheriff Chambers commented as they reined the horses in. He indicated the figure of a woman in the center of the corral. "That'll be Mrs. Cameron. Don't know how you're going to get her attention, though. She looks a mite busy, and I wouldn't recommend going into the corral."

Delilah stared in amazement. That was Eve?

The woman in the corral flipped a calf on its side with an ease Delilah would not have thought possible, hog-tied it, and then averted her face while holding it for the brander's iron. A moment later, the task completed, she released the calf and straightened.

Using a sibling's perception, Delilah studied her sister.

Eve wore what appeared to be a split skirt fashioned from leather. The garment was a little shorter than Delilah would have thought appropriate, for it fell only to mid calf, but Eve wore high work boots which preserved her modesty to some degree. A tan shirt, buckskin vest, well-worn leather gloves, and a green bandanna completed her ensemble . . . with one single exception. Eve wore a sidearm. A six-gun in a holster rested on her hip as comfortably as though she'd been born with it. Yet Delilah knew she had not.

Eve had always been the gentle one. The child who had been most like their Southern belle mother despite inheriting their father's tawny hair and cat-green eyes. She'd always hated guns. Heavens! She'd been so incapable of cruelty of any kind that she'd been unable to so much as watch a chicken being butchered for supper. Yet here she was branding calves!

This was not the sister Delilah remembered. In the year since they'd last visited, Eve had matured from a girl into a woman. A very determined woman, if appearances were not deceiving. And yet she was scarcely twenty years old. What had happened to induce such a rapid change in her baby sister?

Whatever it was, their mother would have been

proud of the result. She'd always wanted her daughters to be stronger than she had been, claiming that, had it not been for Garrett Sinclair's daring last-minute rescue, she would undoubtedly not have survived the Civil War. Delilah tended to think that her mother had simply been unable to recognize her own strengths, which lay in character rather than in physical constitution.

"I wonder where Wes Powell is?" Sheriff Chambers mused aloud, interrupting Delilah's musing. When she looked at him questioningly, he added by way of explanation, "The foreman."

"Powell is the man who was supposed to meet me in Red Rock," Delilah commented. "He didn't show up."

The sheriff stared off toward the corral and said nothing. Delilah was beginning to know him, though, and she believed he appeared thoughtful. In the next instant he said, "Looks like Eagle Shadow has finally decided to acknowledge our presence."

Delilah followed his gaze and saw a dark-skinned man, his long black hair secured in two braids which hung over his shoulders, raise an arm in greeting. "An Indian?" she asked, though she was reasonably certain the man had to be of native ancestry.

Sheriff Chambers nodded. "Jim Eagle Shadow." He looked over at her. "You don't have a problem with Indians, do you, Mrs. Sterne?"

She frowned slightly. "If you're asking if I have reason to hate them, the answer is no, Sheriff. The Indians I've encountered have always remained rather distant. Neither threatening, nor particularly cordial. Although I must say that, having heard the same tales as everyone else, I am naturally wary."

"Best advice I can give is to ignore the stories you've heard as much as possible, and make up your own mind about Jim when you meet him."

Delilah nodded without meeting his gaze. "I fully intend to, Sheriff."

At that moment, a cattle dog who'd just discerned their presence commenced a raucous barking and raced toward them. His proprietary attitude immediately set Poopsy off. Never one to back down from a disagreement with another canine, no matter the difference in size, she began to yap ferociously while squirming to escape the saddlebag. She was certain, no doubt, that she could set this disrespectful hound straight if only she could get at him. However, the only obvious result of her indignation was that she unnerved Jackpot and completely confused the cattle dog, which stopped short to eye, with a rather startled expression, the big horse from which the high-pitched barking erupted.

Delilah grinned, and then, hearing her name shouted, looked toward the corral to see Eve standing at Jim Eagle Shadow's side. Her sister waved and began to run in her direction. If the Indian had been the one to apprise Eve of her arrival, thus hastening their reunion, Delilah decided she liked him already.

Dismounting, scarcely taking her eyes from her sister, Delilah secured Jackpot to the rail of the corral fence and began to move along it, closing the distance between them. It seemed like an eternity until Eve slipped through the railing to throw her arms around her. Delilah, in turn, wrapped her arms around Eve's slender form, closed her eyes, and simply held on. Lord, she'd missed her.

Though Eve was only a little more than two years younger than herself, after their father's death, Delilah had raised her sister. Or perhaps they'd raised each other. Regardless, they'd grown extraordinarily close. Now, heedless of the tears rolling unchecked down her cheeks, she pulled back. "Let me look at you."

Eve obediently stepped back. With the sparkle of joyous tears in her own eyes and a trembling smile on her lips, she stood waiting for Delilah's impression. Delilah saw the newly developed strength of character in the set of her sister's jaw. She saw the confidence in her stance. She saw the light of determination in her eyes and knew, without a doubt, that Eve had come into her own.

Delilah smiled tremulously. "Oh, Evie, you've grown up."

Eve smiled. "It's about time, wouldn't you say?"

Delilah spread her arms and swept her sister into another embrace. "I've missed you."

"Not half as much as I've missed you. Why didn't you telegraph that you were coming? I would have met you in town."

"I did," Delilah assured her. "I received a reply saying that Wes Powell would meet me and provide an escort, but he didn't show. So I decided to set out."

Eve pivoted slightly, sliding her arm around Delilah's waist to stand at her side. Her expression sobered considerably. "Wes Powell quit a few days ago," she explained. "He never said anything about receiving or answering a telegram." She shrugged. "I'm glad you were able to ride with the sheriff."

Delilah opened her mouth to point out that she'd ridden over a lot of wild country without the benefit of the sheriff's protection, or anybody else's for that matter. But before she could get the words out, Eve read her expression and raised a conciliatory hand to halt her. "I know. I know," she said. "I have little doubt that you could have found this place based on the descriptions in my letters, but it's dangerous country just the same." She scowled. "Blast that Wes Powell. He makes me so angry. But I guess I should have expected that from him."

Delilah studied her sister's solemn expression. "What's wrong, Eve?"

Eve forced a smile. "Nothing I'm going to burden you with before you've even had a chance to refresh yourself." She looked toward the sheriff, and Delilah followed her gaze.

Sheriff Chambers had dismounted and was now talking to Jim Eagle Shadow and another hand. The dark blond hair that spilled over this cowhand's ears from beneath the brim of his hat made him easily recognizable as a white man, though he was well tanned.

"Come on," Eve said as she began moving toward the men. They stopped to one side of the group. As soon as the men paused in conversation and looked toward them, she spoke. "Mr. Eagle Shadow . . . Mr. Wright . . . I'd like to introduce you to my sister, Mrs. Delilah Sterne. She'll be staying with us for a while. Delilah, this is Mr. Jim Eagle Shadow."

Eagle Shadow tipped his black felt hat to her just as any white man would have, though his copper-skinned face remained solemn as he said, "Ma'am."

"Mr. Eagle Shadow," Delilah nodded in acknowledgment as she studied the man curiously.

"And this is Mr. Steve Wright," Eve continued, gesturing to the man with the long dark-blond hair.

Wright offered Delilah his hand, a gesture that not all men made when introduced to women, and spoke in a deep bass voice that seemed at odds with his stature. "Always pleased to meet a lady, Mrs. Sterne."

Delilah accepted his callused hand, met his kind brown-eyed gaze, and smiled. "A pleasure, Mr. Wright."

Eve turned toward Matt. "Sheriff Chambers," she said, extending her right hand to him, "I can't thank you enough for escorting my sister to me."

Delilah felt Matt's gaze touch on her before returning to Eve, but did her best to ignore her awareness of him.

Studiously avoiding eye contact, she focused instead on the exchange taking place between him and Eve. Matt accepted her sister's hand, his much larger one virtually swallowing Eve's. "Don't mention it, ma'am," he said.

And then, with a glance toward the man with whom he'd been speaking earlier, he took the conversation in another direction. "Steve tells me Powell quit." Eve nodded, but didn't have the opportunity to respond before Matt continued. "With Tom still laid up, it's going to be pretty tough going for you, isn't it?"

"I'm a lot stronger than I look, Sheriff. I'll be fine. But thank you for your concern."

Chambers studied her for a moment with the same dark steely gaze that so easily disrupted Delilah's equilibrium. Eve seemed remarkably unaffected, and Delilah's respect for her sister's newfound inner strength rose another notch. With a sharp nod, Matt finally accepted her assertion and said, "Jim tells me you haven't had any more problems with rustlers recently?"

Eve shook her head. "The additional twenty head we lost last week was the last straw. All totaled, we've lost more than half the herd we had left. I ordered the few head we still have herded into the corrals every night for safety. I can't afford to lose any more."

I can't? Delilah studied her sister, wondering at the solitary nature of her statement.

"Have you made any progress in finding out who's behind it?" Eve asked.

"Some, ma'am. But I'm sorry to say, not enough. This isn't just a few drovers out to make themselves some easy money." Matt stared thoughtfully down the valley. "I wanted to speak with Powell," he said a moment later. "Don't suppose you could tell me where I might find him?"

"Jim?" Eve looked toward the Indian.

"Last I heard he was workin' at the Lazy M," Eagle

Shadow said. His words positively dripped ice. Then, without another word, he turned and vaulted over the corral railing, apparently deciding to return to his work. After favoring the sheriff with a brief wave, Steve Wright followed in his wake.

Chambers looked at Eve. "What's goin' on here, Mrs. Cameron?"

"Well, Sheriff, it's pretty simple really. There are a lot of things that Powell doesn't like, and he seemed to find most of those things on my ranch."

"And what might those be?"

Eve shrugged. "Indians. Chinese people. And women who can give orders when necessary."

Sheriff Chambers nodded. "I see."

"Oh, my," Eve suddenly said. "In the excitement, I've forgotten my manners. Would you like a glass of lemonade, Sheriff? Fong usually keeps a couple of jars cooling in the well."

"That sounds real good, ma'am, but McTaggert lost some head the other night, so I still have some business to do over at the Lazy M. I want to get back to Red Rock by tonight. I appreciate the offer just the same."

"In that case, you'll probably be riding by here right about supper time," Eve deduced. "Why don't you at least let me offer you the hospitality of our supper table?"

The sheriff flicked a glance Delilah's way before responding. "I'd like that, ma'am," he said with a nod. "If I happen to be goin' by about that time, I'd sure like to take you up on it."

"Good." Eve smiled. "Then we'll be expecting you."

Delilah frowned inwardly. She sincerely wished Eve had not invited the sheriff to supper. She'd hoped to be free of his disturbing presence for a time. Still, she could always pray he wouldn't show.

Chambers doffed his hat to Eve, then turned his potent gaze on Delilah. "It was a pleasure riding with you, ma'am," he said, tipping his hat respectfully.

"Sheriff." Delilah favored him with a dignified nod. "I do hope you catch those rustlers. And thank you for your escort."

"My pleasure, ma'am," he said as he turned to Goliath.

He winced slightly as he mounted, and concern made her speak without thinking, calling, "Sheriff . . ." just as he was about to turn his horse. He halted, and she felt his gaze on her from beneath the shadowed brim of his hat as he waited for her to continue. Suddenly, however, she didn't know what to say. She couldn't very well demand to see his ribs again now. "Take care of those ribs," she concluded weakly.

He acknowledged her statement with a sharp nod, before reining Goliath around and urging him into a gallop.

"What happened to his ribs?" Eve asked, drawing Delilah's eyes from the rapidly dwindling figure.

"He was attacked by a mountain lion early this morning." Seeing the expression of horror dawning in Eve's eyes, and interpreting it, Delilah hastened to reassure her. "It happened before we met. I was in no danger."

"Well, thank goodness for that," she breathed.

Eve looked toward Jackpot. "I'll just have Mr. Wright take care of your horse, and then I'll take you on up to the house." Suiting action to words, she turned and shouted her request.

"Sure thing, ma'am," Wright replied.

That taken care of, Eve threaded her arm through Delilah's and began moving toward the house. Delilah took only two steps before she was brought up short by a sharp yap. "Oh, heavens! I forgot Poochie."

"Poochie?" Eve echoed as they turned. Poopsy was dividing her attention between the mistress who'd almost forgotten her, and the cattle dog which, having now discovered the origin of the earlier barking, sat gazing up at her. "When did you get a dog?"

"It's a long story," Delilah replied as they walked back to Jackpot. "I'll tell you later." Liberating Poopsy, she retrieved her saddlebags, settled them over her shoulder, and pulled the Winchester from its scabbard. "There, that should do it."

Minutes later, she and Eve were ensconced at a large, scarred, wooden table sharing glasses of cool lemonade while the Chinese gentleman that Eve had introduced as Fong bustled around Eve's kitchen preparing what looked to be a huge meal in a large wood-burning stove. Fong was quite small for a man, scarcely five feet tall—if that—with ageless skin, sharp-sighted, almond-shaped black eyes, and short, gunmetal grey hair. Clothed entirely in black, he sported a wispy goatee on his chin, sandals on otherwise bare feet, and a singing voice that sounded like nothing so much as rusty hinges. Still, he didn't seem to notice his melodic deficiency, for he sang, hummed, or talked to himself almost continuously as he worked.

Poopsy, having drunk her fill of water and been fed some scraps by Fong, lay on the floor beneath the table, sound asleep.

Delilah looked around. Since her previous visit with Eve had taken place in Jackson, Wyoming, where Delilah had been living briefly, this was the first time she'd seen Eve's home. She decided she rather liked the rustic charm of the log house.

In the center of the table, a canning jar performed the function of a vase, brightening the small house with a profusion of spring wildflowers. A large hewn-stone fireplace occupied the wall opposite the kitchen stove so that in winter the home could be heated from both sides of the room. A rocking chair, sewing basket, and pile of mending rested on a rag rug before the fireplace. Above the fireplace an old Springfield rifle, no doubt brought home from the Civil War by one of Tom's relatives, rested on the mantel.

To the right of the fireplace was the front door, leading to the forward veranda that stretched the entire width of the house. A back door, located next to the stove, exited onto a large enclosed porch which doubled as a pantry and a place to wash up before meals. The porch was even equipped with the convenience of an indoor pump to bring water directly from the well.

Access to the bedrooms was gained through either of two doors in the wall at Delilah's back. Though she'd seen neither chamber as yet, she decided that, all in all, it was a very nice home.

"So," Eve said, smiling across the table at her. "Oh, Delilah, I'm so glad you're here." But Delilah noted that the smile trembled on her lips and didn't quite reach her eyes. In fact, she looked on the verge of tears.

And instead of offering her solace, Delilah had to tell her that she didn't yet have the funds to help her. The thought made her want to weep herself, but instead she returned Eve's smile and said nothing. She dared not speak freely, for she didn't know how much Fong knew, nor how much Tom might overhear. "Where is Tom?" she asked by way of making conversation. "I haven't hugged the man who stole my sister's heart yet."

A shadow briefly darkened Eve's brilliant green eyes. "He's resting," she replied. "But I'm sure he'll do his best to be up for supper." After a brief pause, she said, "Let's go out on the front porch where we can enjoy the sunshine and not disturb him with our chatter."

For a long time they simply sat side by side on a wooden bench enjoying the sights and sounds of the ranch in the bright afternoon. Then Delilah found the courage to speak. "Your letter caught me at a bad time,

Eve. I've had a run of bad luck, and my stake is sadly depleted. I've convinced Miss Cora to let me operate a gaming table at the Lucky Strike, and I believe I can have the money for you when you need it, but it means I can't stay here with you as long as I'd like."

Eve nodded. "Sure. That's fine," she murmured softly. Then, afraid her words might have been misinterpreted, she hastily amended, "I mean I'm disappointed, of course, but I might be able to get away to come into town occasionally."

Delilah scrutinized her. "That's not it, is it?"

Eve took a deep breath and stared out at the corrals. "What do you mean?"

"The money's not what's bothering you, is it?"

For a time, Eve made no response, then she shook her head. "No. It isn't."

Delilah placed her hand on her sister's shoulder. "What is it, Evie? Talk to me."

Eve took another long shaky breath before responding. "I think Tom may be dying, Delilah."

Delilah's eyes widened in shock, and she set her almost empty lemonade glass down on the weathered floorboards of the front porch with exaggerated care. "Why? What happened?"

"His leg was broken very badly. The thigh bone pierced the skin. Doc Hale set it, but it never healed properly." She paused, swallowing audibly. "After about three weeks, the doctor told Tom that the leg needed to be amputated before the infection that was keeping it from healing began to spread, but Tom absolutely refused. He said he'd kill any man who took his leg, and despise me forever if I allowed it done. He said he'd rather be dead than live as half a man."

"Oh, my Lord!"

"Between Fong and I, we've kept the leg clean and disinfected with whiskey, just like mother always said.

I keep hoping the doctor was wrong. But I'm beginning to think that all I've managed to do is to prolong the inevitable. The leg looks . . . horrible, and Tom is getting weaker by the day now."

For the first time since they'd moved outside, Eve turned to look at her. "I didn't know what to do, Delilah, so I stood by Tom. Either way, I lose my husband, but I couldn't bear his hatred. Did I do the right thing?"

Unable to answer that question, Delilah swept her sister into her arms. Stroking Eve's tawny tresses, she murmured, "I don't know, sweetheart. Only you and Tom can know what's right for the two of you."

"But I don't know. That's the problem," Eve said over her shoulder. Delilah sensed the tension in her, the rigid control that locked in her pain. Eve lifted her head to look at her. "Perhaps if I'd argued with him just one more day I might have finally changed his mind. Or, if I'd gone against him, he might eventually have forgiven me. Now . . . now it's too late to change course. All I can do is hope and pray."

Delilah clutched her close again and closed her eyes. God help her, she didn't know what to say. Swallowing, she found words and prayed they were the right ones. "Then perhaps you should concentrate on cherishing the time you have left," she murmured hesitantly. "Build a memory strong enough to last you a lifetime, and . . . let him go."

Eve sniffled, caught her breath in an attempt to control the emotion, and then, as though Delilah's words had shattered the dam that held back the floodgates of her misery, she began to sob. Delilah ached with her, for her, yet she could do nothing but hold her and offer her the solace of her love.

Moments later, Eve pulled out of Delilah's embrace and dried her eyes on the bandanna she'd worn about her neck. "I'm sorry," she murmured. "I didn't mean to do that."

"Nonsense! You needed to do that. You can't keep it all bottled up."

Eve swallowed and sniffed. "You know what bothers me the most?"

Delilah shook her head.

"That we didn't have any children. We wanted one so badly, but it just never seemed to happen. We thought we had lots of time, so we didn't really worry about it. But now that time is gone, and I don't even have Tom's child to hold." Another silent sob gripped her, and her shoulders quaked. "Why couldn't the Lord leave me with at least that much of the man I love?" she whispered.

Feeling incapable of easing her sister's pain, Delilah shook her head in misery. "I don't know, sweetheart. I don't know."

They fell silent for a while, each staring out at the bright spring day but seeing only shadows. Delilah was worried about her. After a time, she asked, "How will you manage if Tom goes, Eve? Will you move to town?" But she knew as soon as she voiced the question what the answer would be. The Eve she'd known a year ago might have moved to town, but not this newly determined young woman at her side.

Eve shook her head. "This is my home. My ranch. I love it here, and I'm not going anywhere if I can help it." She looked at Delilah. "I've been learning as much as I can, from Tom and the hands that have stayed on. I've had to take Tom's place as much as possible from the start. The hands who refused to work for a woman have already quit." She took a deep breath. "I'll manage."

Delilah believed her. For even in thought, in conversation, Eve was preparing herself to stand alone. *I can't afford,* she'd said earlier. *My ranch,* she'd called her home.

Eve spent the remainder of the afternoon proudly showing Delilah around the Devil's Fork. Following Fong's assurance that it would be all right, Delilah had left a sleeping Poopsy safely ensconced beneath the table. While riding through an area Eve called the south quarter, they stopped to allow the horses to refresh themselves at the river. Stepping beneath the shady boughs of a weeping willow, Delilah sighed and took a deep breath of mountain air heavy with the scent of spring wildflowers and evergreens. As Eve joined her, she smiled. "I can certainly see why you love it here."

"You're welcome to come back and stay, you know." Her eyes were alight with an inner glow of pride and hope. "Between the two of us, we could not only save this ranch, we could make it prosper."

Delilah considered. The offer was tempting; it really was. Sadly, however, she shook her head. "No, Sis. This place is yours. It's in your blood, a part of you. Beautiful as it is, it would never mean quite the same thing to me, and I'd always feel like a visitor." She looked at her younger sister and smiled to soften her words. "If you ever need me, you have only to ask. You know that. But I can't stay."

Eve nodded, appearing suddenly more serious. "I thought you'd say that, but I had to ask just the same."

"Something's worrying you. What is it? Are you afraid the remaining hands will quit if Tom . . . ?" She trailed off, but the words didn't need to be said to be understood.

Eve frowned in reflection. "I don't think so. Most of the hands I have left are a ragtag bunch that nobody else would hire. Mr. Wright is a drunkard whom we constantly have to keep away from whiskey or his usefulness decreases proportionately. Mr. Stone is a good hand, but, like a good many Westerners, he has a past he doesn't want to share. He said he wouldn't work for anybody who didn't know how to mind their own business." She shrugged. "He might leave, I suppose, given the right offer."

She squinted into the sunlight, looking back toward the ranch. "Eagle Shadow and Mr. Fong are both good and reliable. But if somebody did hire them for their abilities, they would be treated with less respect. They might trade respect for more money, but I don't think so. And lastly, there's old Rattlesnake. He's so old he doesn't even remember his age." She shook her head. "He's slower than molasses running uphill in January, but he manages to tend the hogs and chickens adequately. Best of all, he doesn't demand much in the way of wages."

Delilah's brows arched. "Rattlesnake?" she repeated incredulously.

Eve nodded. "He calls himself Rattlesnake Joe." Then, grinning, she stuck her thumbs in her pockets, puffed out her chest and shoulders in obvious imitation of a strutting male, and said in a deep voice, "It's on account of bein' bit so many times he cain't hardly feel it no more."

They laughed. And, once started, it was difficult to stop. They laughed until they couldn't stand any more. Until tears rolled down their faces. Until their sides ached. Not because anything was that funny, but because they needed the release of mirth. Then, slowly, they sobered.

"Oh, my, it's been a long time since I laughed," Eve murmured as she watched the horses graze along the riverbank. Delilah pretended to do the same but, in reality, she was observing Eve.

"You never did answer my question, Eve," she pointed out.

Eve looked over at her. "What question?"

"Is something worrying you? Something besides Tom?"

Eve turned to stare thoughtfully at the swiftly flowing river. "Nothing definite," she said with a shrug. "Just a feeling."

"What kind of feeling?"

"Well, this is prime ranch land." She frowned as though trying to put her worries into words. "There are a lot of men in the area who don't have very open minds when it comes to a woman running a ranch. I learned that with Wes Powell." She turned to meet Delilah's gaze. "I guess I'm afraid that men like Powell might take it into their heads to try to drive me out."

Delilah's spine stiffened. She despised men who thought that the brute strength of a man made him superior, granted him entitlement to more than a woman. "Maybe it's a good thing Powell didn't meet me in Red Rock," she said.

Eve looked at her curiously. "Why's that?"

"I probably would have shot him with my derringer and landed in Sheriff Chambers's jail."

"I would have busted you out," Eve promised confidently. She pulled her Colt revolver out and sighted down its barrel. "I can shoot the neck off a whiskey bottle at forty paces."

"Have you ever shot anything that bled?" Delilah couldn't help asking wryly. She knew from the days when their father had taken them target shooting that Eve had steadfastly refused to kill anything. Even to eat.

Eve looked a bit sheepish. "Not yet," she admitted. "But I'm working on it. I almost shot a fox that was after one of my hens the other day."

"What made you start carrying a gun?"

"Tom did," Eve replied. "He said I had to know how to protect myself."

Delilah nodded. "I agree."

They sat in companionable silence for a few more moments and then Eve checked the position of the late-afternoon sun. "We'd better be getting back," she said, rising to her feet. "I like to help Fong with supper preparations whenever I can. I know how much work it is cooking for so many male appetites. And," there was a teasing glint in her eye as she looked at Delilah, "we want to make a good impression on your sheriff. Don't we?"

In the process of standing up, Delilah froze in mid rise. "He is *not* my sheriff!" she snapped. "Besides, he may not even show up."

Undisturbed by her sister's anger, Eve simply arched a brow. "Oh I wouldn't worry about that, dear sister. I think I can pretty much guarantee that he'll be here. No man who looks at a woman the way he looked at you can keep himself away for long."

"You're imagining things!" Delilah protested. "That man's eyes are gunmetal cold."

"Am I?" Eve mounted her horse and sat waiting for Delilah. "Gunmetal can get as hot as sin at times, you know?"

Chapter Six

A short time later, they arrived back at the house. After washing up on the back porch, they moved inside to help with the supper preparations. Since the Devil's Fork was a small ranch, and its owners completely without pretention, Delilah had already surmised that the hands would eat in the house with the family. Therefore, per Eve's instructions, after lighting two kerosene table lamps to dispel the gathering gloom of twilight, Delilah set the large table with nine places.

Eve, meanwhile, carved the huge ham that Fong had set out on a platter. Fong, Delilah discovered, ruled the kitchen with an iron hand, watching their every move with a critical eye. Once, he even corrected Eve in her carving technique. "No, no, missy. You do like this," he said, firmly taking the knife from her to demonstrate. As Eve, carefully following Fong's instructions, reverted to the task at hand, the diminutive Chinese gentleman next turned his eyes to the table settings. A careful scrutiny apparently revealed nothing untoward however, for he made a strange grunting noise in his throat, which Delilah translated as satisfaction, and turned back to the pots still on the stove.

Finished with the carving, Eve wiped her hands and surveyed the kitchen for another task needing attention. Seeing nothing, she turned to Delilah and said, "I'll just go change Tom's dressing and help him get ready. You won't mind helping Fong if he needs anything, will you?"

"Of course not," Delilah assured her. With worried eyes, she watched her sister disappear into the bedroom. She hoped that Eve wasn't pushing herself too hard.

"Missy . . . ?"

"Yes?" Delilah turned at Fong's call.

"You go out. Ling suppa gong. Call men. Yes?"

"Oh, yes. Certainly." She'd seen the triangular-shaped gong hanging from the porch rafter earlier. "Come on, Poochie," she said to the small dog, who had been following her around the table for the past few minutes seeking attention.

A sharp yap and an eagerly wagging hind end signaled the little canine's approval.

A cold sharp wind whipped Delilah's skirts about her legs, and tugged strands of hair from her chignon as she stepped outside. The afternoon sunlight had been smothered by a preternatural twilight. The sky overhead, so clear and blue earlier, was fast filling with ominous black thunderclouds.

They were in for a storm.

As Poopsy sniffed around the porch, Delilah rang the bell for a good long minute, cringing a bit at the assault on her own ears. Then, seeing an acknowledging wave from the direction of the barn, she called Poopsy and turned to go inside. It was as she was turning that she caught sight of a dark form descending a hillside to the west. Though the distance was much too great for her to discern the identity of the rider, instinct told her that she knew who it was.

Blast! Eve was right. Sheriff Chambers was coming to supper.

Opening the door, she let Poopsy scamper ahead of her and then entered the house in time to see Eve helping Tom to the table. She closed the door quietly behind herself in an effort not to disturb them and leaned against it as she observed them. Tom was supporting himself as well as possible on a pair of crutches, but it was obvious that he'd lost a considerable amount of weight and was very weak. His complexion was pasty white, perspiration beaded his brow and upper lip, and huge dark shadows marred the flesh beneath his eyes. He should not even have been out of bed. As Tom lowered himself slowly, painfully to a chair at the table, Delilah glanced at Eve to see an answering pain etched on her face.

Eve and Tom may have fallen in love at a young age—Eve had been just seventeen and Tom only twenty—but there was no question in Delilah's mind that they loved each other. Her heart ached for them. For her sister, who stood to lose the man she loved. And for the young man who, plagued by the insecurities and pride of the young, preferred losing his life to becoming less than a whole man. But if Tom passed, at least they had known love. Love, the kind of love shared by a husband and wife, was something Delilah had long ago resigned herself to living without.

"Delilah!" Tom exclaimed, having just noticed her presence. "Eve told me you were here. It's nice of you to visit." Tom's voice, labored and weak, nevertheless communicated a genuine gladness to see her. "Come on in and set yourself down, why don't you?" He continued to smile as Delilah moved forward to greet him.

Smiling, Delilah hugged her brother-in-law and tried not to notice how thin his broad shoulders felt. "It's nice to see you again, too, Tom." Straightening, uncertain whether to acknowledge his illness or not, she decided it would be foolish to try to pretend she couldn't see it. "I'm very sorry to hear about . . ."

"I know, I know," Tom interrupted her, weakly waving away her sympathy. "Let's talk about more pleasant things." He hitched himself a bit awkwardly into a more comfortable position on his chair, and Delilah noted that his injured leg was swollen to nearly double its normal size. "You know," he continued, "having you here will be like a breath of fresh air for Eve. She talks about you all the time, and rereads your letters until the blame things are near to fallin' apart."

Delilah smiled wistfully. "I do the same," she admitted.

At that moment, the door opened, and two men that Delilah had not yet met swept in on the tail of a brisk, chilly wind to hang their hats on pegs next to the door. "Storm comin'," the older of the two announced without preamble.

Moving to stand at Delilah's side, Eve introduced the grizzled old man as Rattlesnake Joe. The younger man at his side, who looked to be no more than mid to late twenties, she presented as Mr. Stone.

Mr. Stone looked at Eve with dark blue eyes that suddenly made him seem older than Delilah's initial estimate. "I told you before, Mrs. Cameron, the name's just Stone. Puttin' a mister in front of it makes about as much sense as spittin' into the wind."

"Would that be your first or last name, sir?" Delilah asked.

Stone swung his gaze to her. Looking into his eyes, Delilah would have wagered her last dollar that he'd already seen enough of life to last a lifetime. "Take your pick, ma'am," he replied coolly.

"I see. Well, I'm pleased to make your acquaintance, M . . . uh, Stone."

For an instant, Delilah thought she might have seen a glint of humor in Stone's eyes, and then it was gone. "Likewise, ma'am."

In a gust of wind that carried the scent of moisture, the door opened again to admit Mr. Wright, Jim Eagle Shadow, and, to Delilah's dismay, Matt Chambers. As they each hung their hats next to the door, Delilah hastily turned to find something to do to occupy her attention. As though reading her mind, Fong placed a knife in her hand and indicated a fresh loaf of bread that required slicing.

The noise level rose in direct proportion to the velocity of the wind wailing around the house, and to each additional person in the room. Now, Sheriff Chambers struck up a conversation with Tom concerning the rustling he was investigating; Mr. Wright and Rattlesnake Joe commenced to arguing about the merits of raising sheep versus cattle; and Fong launched into an impossible to understand diatribe while simultaneously swatting Eagle Shadow's hand with a wooden spoon for dipping into one of his pots before it was on the table. The kitchen became positively clamorous. Only Stone remained silent, standing to one side observing everything silently and, perhaps, with a touch of superiority.

"Delilah, you can sit there, next to Mr. Fong," Eve directed a moment later, pointing at a chair. "Everyone else pretty much has their favorite spot."

As the hands took their seats at the table, Delilah noted to her chagrin that the only vacant spot at the table for Sheriff Chambers, who was still in conversation with Tom and had not yet seated himself, was next to her. She tried to catch Eve's eyes to let her know just how unhappy she was with the situation, but Eve was industriously involved in passing fresh bread and bowls of steaming vegetables. A moment later, Matt took his seat.

"Hello, Mrs. Sterne," he said. He sounded weary, a bit pained perhaps. Still, she could not allow herself to be seduced by sympathy.

Delilah nodded, scarcely sparing him a glance, and carefully adjusted her skirts so that they stayed on her chair. "Sheriff," she murmured with a cool nod.

Plates were served and coffee was poured. Conversation quickly settled into a discussion of how many calves were left to brand, which cows were late dropping their young, and how many steers they had available to sell. Tom, in his seat opposite Delilah, was obviously laboring, though he tried to hide it by staying involved in the conversation. Eve aided him as much as possible without being intrusive, but Tom ate little.

Having nothing consequential to contribute to the conversation, and determined to avoid discourse with Matt Chambers despite her complete inability to forget for one second that he sat at her side, Delilah turned to the man on her right. "So, Mr. Fong," she said. "How did Eve happen to find such a wonderful cook?"

"Cook?" the man questioned. "She find diffelent cook?" His tone seemed a touch surprised.

"I meant you, sir," Delilah hastened to explain. "You're a wonderful cook."

"Oh. Is good." He nodded, accepting the compliment as his due without ever answering her question.

"So, how did she find you?" Delilah asked again.

"I find her. Lose camp cook job. Come here. Tell missy I cook. She say can't pay velly much. I say is okay. I stay." His story finished, the man shrugged and returned to his meal.

"Well, I'm glad you did." Delilah looked at her sister,

sitting next to Tom, letting the conversation flow around her as she pushed food around on her plate, eating little. Her attention seemed to be centered more on getting food into her husband than on her own sustenance. At least the cooking was one responsibility that would not burden Eve in the days to come.

At that moment, a blinding flash suddenly eclipsed the feeble light of the lamps, as lightning leapt across the sky. The cabin shook with the powerful resonance of the deafening clap of thunder that almost immediately ensued. Yelping with fear, Poopsy ensconced herself beneath Delilah's skirts and refused to move. Delilah felt the small dog's shudders against her legs, and reached down to pat her reassuringly as she stared at the windows. As though the bellies of the clouds themselves had been ruptured, a torrent so heavy that it made conversation all but impossible deluged the small log house. Rain poured down the windows in sheets so thick it was impossible to see. Nervously, Delilah returned to her meal. She had never liked storms. Involuntarily, she gave a small shriek of surprise herself as another brighter flash and louder crack reverberated through the house.

"My heavens!" Eve exclaimed. "We don't often get storms like this."

"Are you all right?" Matt asked, looking down at Delilah.

She made the mistake of meeting his gaze. Intense, unreadable, steel-hued, magnetic eyes. Her heart leapt into her throat to perform a staccato dance. As though he could see the pulse pounding there, his gaze dropped for a moment to her throat, liberating her as it did. "I . . . yes," she murmured hoarsely, finding her voice. She hastily lowered her eyes to focus on his mouth. "Of course," she added more strongly. "I was just startled."

He nodded, but said nothing. Delilah noted that he had a full lower lip and slightly thinner top lip. For the first time in recent memory, she found herself wondering what it would feel like to be kissed by a man. *This* man. Would he kiss her someday? Did he find her attractive enough to even try? He'd never given any indication that he did. But . . .

What was the matter with her? She neither wanted nor needed him to find her attractive! Wrenching her gaze away, Delilah focused her attention on the food on her plate.

"Well, one thing about this here kinda storm," old Rattlesnake commented, "is that they tend to wear theirselves out real quick, ma'am."

"I certainly hope you're right," Eve replied. "If it lasts too long, the house could end up floating down the river."

Tom smiled wearily. "I don't think you need to worry about that, my dear. Listen. See, it's already letting up."

And it was, though Delilah was more aware of Matt's elbow inadvertently touching her arm as he cut his meat than she was of anything else. Disregarding the urge to rub at the nagging spot, she took another bite of her supper and focused on the storm that had become the newest conversational topic.

Contrary to Rattlesnake's prediction, moments later it seemed obvious that the storm had settled in for a time. A good heavy soaking rain continued to pour down, while in the distance lightning flashed, as the more turbulent vanguard of the gale moved on.

An hour later, having finished coffee and a wonderful bread pudding with sauce that Fong had concocted for dessert, the rain had still not let up. The first to grow impatient was Stone. He pushed back his chair, scraping the legs noisily on the smooth plank floorboards, and said, "Well, I think I'll see if I can make it to the bunkhouse without drownin'. Thank you for supper, ma'am," he nodded at Eve.

"You're welcome, Stone," she responded.

Then he looked to Mr. Fong. "Fong," he said with a nod.

Fong favored him with an imperious wave of his hand and nodded. "Yeah, yeah. You go. Sleep good."

Moments later, the other hands began to straggle out into the pitch-black night. The first to follow was Mr. Eagle Shadow. The last was Rattlesnake, who looked out the door at the pouring rain with a decidedly disconsolate expression on his face. He looked at Eve. "If I don't make it in for breakfast in the mornin', will ya be so kind as to have someone check on me? At my age, I could catch my death in that."

"Of course, Rattlesnake," Eve assured him as she rose to begin clearing the table.

Rattlesnake stared at her a moment, then, shaking his head in apparent disgust over the density of the youthful mind, clapped his hat on his head and stepped out onto the porch muttering something about *no respect*.

Noting that Fong had set a tub of water on the stove to heat for washing dishes, Delilah rose to help clear the table, thankful to have an excuse to escape Sheriff Chambers's overpowering presence.

"Well, I guess I should be going, too," Chambers commented. His chair scraped against the floorboards as he moved back from the table.

"You can't ride all the way back to Red Rock in this downpour," Tom protested, "or you *will* catch your death. Especially when you're already feeling less than yourself from tanglin' with that cougar you were telling me about. If you don't mind sleepin' on the floor, you're welcome to spread your bedroll in front of the fireplace for the night."

"Sleeping on a warm, dry floor has never bothered me," the sheriff replied. "But I don't know." Moving to the window, he stared off into the distance. In a movement that seemed entirely unconscious, he began rubbing at his bound ribs. Delilah noted that a few spots of blood now marred the shirt that had earlier been clean. And she'd bandaged his ribs tightly with numerous layers of the fabric from her petticoat. It could only mean one thing: The worst of the gouges were still bleeding. Matt, obviously aware of that, was weighing the severity of the weather against his need for a few stitches to close the most serious of the wounds. But, with his body already weakened from loss of blood, would even this amazingly strong man be able to ride through hours of chilling rain without becoming ill? Delilah's instincts told her it would be a poor bet—and her instincts were usually right.

With a sinking feeling deep in her stomach, she made an offer she knew she'd regret. "Sheriff . . ." He turned to look at her. "If Eve will furnish a needle and some thread, I should be able to stitch the deepest scratches for you."

He stared at her for a moment without comment. Delilah sensed Eve's regard as well, though she didn't turn to meet her eyes. She knew from whence Eve's concern arose, yet Delilah had already tended this man's ribs once. With the additional security of being surrounded by people, she was certain she could do it again.

"Well, of course I will," Eve said finally, drawing Matt's gaze. "It's not like there's a shortage of thread." She looked at Delilah. "You can just help yourself to what you need from my sewing basket." She indicated the basket next to the stack of mending sitting before the fireplace.

Delilah nodded. "Thanks."

Matt spoke to Delilah. "You've stitched people up before?"

She nodded, but before she could say anything, Eve interjected. "Oh, my, yes. Delilah is quite accomplished in medicine. I cut my palm once—the knife blade slipped when I was carving a roast—and Delilah stitched it up almost as good as new." She lifted her left hand to display a narrow two-inch scar.

Matt's gaze hadn't left Delilah during the entire narration of Eve's brief story, except for a fleeting glance at the scar. Standing beneath that potent regard, Delilah was already beginning to regret her offer. "All right," he said finally in a low voice. Then, abruptly turning to look back at Tom, he added, "If you're sure it's not an inconvenience?"

Tom nodded. "I'm sure. Fong will be setting up a small cot on the porch for himself, and Delilah will be in the spare room, so that nice warm spot in front of the fireplace might as well get used. You go on out and collect your bedroll. For my part, I'm gonna head back to bed."

Eve immediately turned to help her husband. "Goodnight everyone," she said.

"Goodnight, Eve," Delilah responded as she focused on the dishes. "Sleep well."

" 'Night, Tom . . . ma'am," Matt said.

Fong said nothing.

Delilah waited for the sound of Matt closing the door as he left to retrieve his bedroll before she risked turning around. Blast! Was she never going to be rid of the man's presence? Now it seemed that even the weather conspired against her. She finished drying the last of the dishes as Fong threw the dishwater out the back door.

"Missy . . . ?" Delilah looked at Fong as he reentered

the house. "You need wata? You get now. Fong go sleep."

"Oh, yes. Certainly." She was glad to have a task to occupy her thoughts. Taking the basin Fong offered, Delilah entered the back porch to pump some water. She found that the pump needed to be primed quite extensively, with a large dipper of water kept for the purpose, before it began to work. Once her basin was filled, she moved back into the kitchen to place the water on the stove to warm. "You don't happen to have any extra whiskey, do you Fong?"

Fong nodded. "Missy Eve use lots. Fong make." He pulled a bottle from behind the sideboard and held it up. The liquid within looked like no whiskey Delilah had ever seen. It had a greenish tinge. Seeing her hesitation, Fong reassured her. "Fong whiskey betta for hu't." Then, shaking his head and briskly moving an admonishing finger from side to side he added, "No dlink."

"Pardon me?" Delilah asked, not understanding.

Fong mimed, tipping the bottle to his lips. "Not fo' drink."

Hesitantly taking the bottle from him, Delilah removed the cork and smelled the liquid within. Unprepared for the power of the fumes, she jerked her head back, blinking burning eyes. "Whew! That smells . . . strong!" She carefully raised it again to take a more cautious whiff.

Fong grunted. "Yes. Wo'k velly velly good for hu't."

Well, it would have to do, Delilah decided, though she would have preferred the good old whiskey she knew. "Thank you."

Fong nodded. "You need bandage too?"

"Yes. I was just going to ask if you had anything."

"Fong have." Going to a chest in the corner, he removed a stack of clean white rags and placed them on the table. "Need many for mista Tom." Then, without waiting for a reply from Delilah, he added. "Fong cook breakfast now. Then sleep."

"Breakfast!" Delilah repeated incredulously.

He nodded. "Need cook long time."

Delilah observed as he scooped raw wheat kernels into a double-layered cheesecloth bag, rinsed it in a pan of cold water, and then placed it in a large pot of clean water on the wood stove. After adding another log to the coals, he said, "Fong sleep now," and suiting action to words, he moved onto the back porch.

"Goodnight," Delilah called after him as he pulled the privacy curtain which—made of a yellow fabric with large white flowers on it—looked as though it had been fashioned from one of Eve's discarded dresses. She received a deep grunt in response.

She then arranged the bandages on the table, separating the thicker ones used for padding from the strips used for tying the dressing in place. After placing Fong's whiskey on the table next to the bandages, she retrieved a needle and thread from Eve's sewing basket. Pouring a small amount of Fong's whiskey into a saucer, she soaked the needle in it. Then, surveying the supplies, she wiped her sweaty palms against her hips. Now, if only Matt would get back in here, she could get this over with.

But Matt seemed to be taking his time. Watching Delilah pace back and forth, Poopsy whined. "Do you have to go, girl?" Delilah asked.

As though to answer her question, Poopsy went to the door.

After taking one of the lanterns off of the table to light her way, Delilah opened the door for the dog and stepped out onto the veranda with her. Poopsy, however, took one look at the cold rain pouring down from the eaves, and stopped in her tracks to look back at Delilah with beseeching eyes.

"There's nothing I can do about the rain, Poochie," Delilah said. "Now, if you have to go, hurry up. You'll dry once you're back in the house."

"R . . . row, raw, grr . . . row." Poopsy bobbed her head, sounding for all the world as though she was arguing the point.

Delilah shook her head. "You heard me. Now either go, or you can hold it until morning."

With her ears flattened against her head in annoyance, Poopsy sidled up to the edge of the porch, jumped off into the mediocre shelter of a lilac bush, squatted as briefly as possible, and leaped back beneath the shelter of the porch roof. Then, after shaking the water from her coat, she gave a series of exaggerated shudders and walked disconsolately back to the door.

"That is the dadburndest thing I've ever seen." The male voice coming out of the shadows to her right made Delilah jump.

With her fingers hovering near her throat, she searched the shadows until she recognized Matt's form. "Oh," she said. "You frightened me."

"Sorry. I thought you'd heard me step onto the porch."

"No, I didn't." Delilah stood staring at his shadowy form, not knowing what to say next.

Matt solved the problem for her. Nodding toward Poopsy, he said, "I think that blamed dog might actually develop a fit of the vapors if you don't soon let her in."

Delilah looked down. Sure enough, Poopsy was putting on quite a show. Anyone who didn't know that she'd been subjected to less than two minutes of rain would have believed the poor creature was about to die of a pulmonary illness from the way she sneezed and shuddered and coughed. "All right, Poochie," she said, opening the door. "You can go curl up in front of the stove."

Matt indicated with a hand that Delilah should precede him into the house. "Ma'am?"

Swallowing her renewed trepidation, Delilah stepped through the doorway. "I was beginning to give up on you."

"I had to bed Goliath down for the night," Matt explained as he removed his dripping wet hat and hung it from one of the hooks next to the door. Then, turning toward the fireplace, he spread his bedroll out before it to absorb some of the heat. It consisted of a waterproof tarpaulin outfitted with rings and snaps so the sleeper could pull the top flap over his head in wet or stormy weather. Folded neatly inside the tarp were a woolen blanket and a quilt. It was the kind of bedroll used by a person who knew what it was like to sleep on the land. Very similar to the one her daddy had always used, Delilah noted a bit wistfully.

"How are your ribs?" she asked quietly, mindful of those already abed in the small log house.

He gave her a long steady look, then said, "They've been better."

Summoning an impersonal attitude, Delilah nodded. "Well then, let's get them looked after, shall we? Take off your shirt and have a seat." She indicated the chair nearest the stack of linens she'd prepared.

Wordlessly, Matt did as he'd been bidden. For an instant, Delilah could only stare at the massive shoulders and biceps thus revealed. Then, with unthinking candor, she blurted the question that had plagued her since she'd first seen him lift a wagon single-handedly. "How in blazes did you get so big?"

Abruptly conscious of the personal nature of her query, her face flamed with embarrassment. "I'm sorry," she said quickly, averting her gaze though she felt his regard. "Please forgive my forthrightness."

"Nothing to forgive."

His deep quiet tone drew her gaze back to his face . . . to the dark eyes of such a deep grey that they seemed almost black. To the dark brown of his mahogany hair, tinged with flame now in the light from the fireplace. To the swarthiness of his complexion, with its whisker-shadowed jawline. There was something about this intense and powerful man that Delilah found much too compelling.

Suddenly he spoke again, tugging her gratefully from the dangerous direction of her musings. "Actually, size is a family trait. My father was a big man too, as are my uncles. We have contests to see who's the strongest whenever the clan gets together." He looked up at Delilah, and she thought he almost smiled. "I won last time for the first time," he said. "It wasn't easy. Took a lot of practice."

Delilah began to remove the binding she'd put on his ribs earlier in the day. Blood had soaked through in a number of places. "And how does one practice for a contest of strength?" she asked, purposely focusing on the conversation rather than on the man.

"By lifting tree trunks, dragging stone-beds and the like."

"I see." Delilah dropped the soiled bandages into a pile on the floor. "It sounds like an awful lot of work. Is there a prize for the winner of this contest?"

"It wouldn't be a contest without a prize."

"So what did you win?"

"Let's see. I got one of Aunt Mazie's prizewinning crab apple pies. A fancy embroidered shirt from Aunt Carlotta. A bowie knife from Uncle Dustin. And a real nice hand-carved leather belt from Pa." He sounded a bit wistful.

"You miss them?" she asked.

He nodded. "My father was killed shortly after that."

Delilah dipped a cloth in warm water and knelt at his side to begin cleaning some of the gouges marking his midriff. Then, pouring some of Fong's whiskey onto a clean dry cloth, she repeated the process. Samson sucked in air through his teeth as he felt the sting, but made no comment.

"How did it happen?" Delilah asked.

Silence.

She looked up into his face, saw a new tension settle in the lines around his mouth. Pain? Grief? "Forgive me. I shouldn't have asked," she said. "I didn't mean to stir up painful memories."

He nodded. Then, when Delilah had begun to think he would say nothing more, he said, "He was killed by a gambler in Green River." Delilah's hands froze in mid motion, but Matt didn't seem to notice. "He stepped in when a young, newly married farmer called the dealer on cheating and was about to be killed for his trouble. Of course, the young fool shouldn't have been gamblin' in the first place, and if the dealer hadn't cheated, Pa wouldn't have stepped in. But he was never able to abide cheats and swindlers."

"Was your father a lawman too?"

"Yes."

She didn't know what to say, so she said the only thing she could. "I'm sorry."

He made no reply. The only sounds in the room were the crackling of the logs in the stove and the more subtle hissing of the coals in the fireplace. Delilah felt judged in that silence. Judged and condemned without benefit of trial.

"Listen, Sheriff, I can understand how that experience could affect your view of gamblers, but, just as all lawmen are not created equal, gambling is a profession chosen by many different types of people. Some good, some bad. I neither cheat nor steal, Sheriff, and I would never kill anyone over a game of cards."

He looked at her, looking deep into her eyes as though to see her soul. Finally he asked, "Do you lie?"

Confused, Delilah looked at him. "Pardon me?"

"People usually say they don't lie, cheat, or steal. You left out the lyin' part. So . . . do you lie?" he reiterated.

Delilah shrugged. "I think we all lie when it suits us, don't you? I'd be very surprised indeed if I met a person who could swear they had never uttered a single prevarication."

Matt nodded, and silence fell for a few moments as Delilah worked. It was Matt who broke that silence first. "You might think you'll never cheat, but, given the right set of circumstances, you will. You're a gambler." He shrugged. "When you feel it's necessary to cheat, you'll simply gamble on not getting caught. But . . ." Extending a finger, he lifted her chin, forcing her to meet his gaze again. "But," he continued, "do it in my town, and you *will* be."

"Is that a threat, Sheriff?" To Delilah's chagrin, the words she'd meant to sound challenging, emerged huskily, almost breathlessly.

"Yes."

Delilah jerked her chin from his grasp. "I don't like threats, Sheriff Chambers."

He shrugged. "I don't think I've met anybody who does," he returned casually. The message was clear. "And don't you think it's about time you started calling me Matt?"

"Why?" she asked. "It smacks of familiarity. And I really don't want to know you any better, Sheriff."

For an endless moment, he looked at her, holding her gaze. Then he murmured, "Liar."

Managing finally to tear her gaze away, Delilah inadvertently poured an excessive amount of Fong's potent whiskey onto the deepest scratches. Nevertheless, she felt a certain amount of gratification to hear Matt suck in another breath through his teeth. Served him right!

But he was like a dog with a bone once on a particular topic of conversation, and he pursued it relentlessly. "I think you do want to know me better."

"And I think you're presuming a lot."

"Really? Well, regardless, I'm going to call you Delilah," he said. "Somehow Mrs. Sterne just doesn't suit you."

"And you think Delilah does?" She'd always disliked her name. Neither she nor Eve had been able to understand why they'd been named after the two women in the Bible most famous for their fallibility. But it seemed that their mother had simply liked the names and no connotation had been intended. "I would have thought you might find my name a bit off-putting, considering the less than honorable character associated with the biblical personage."

There was a brief pause, perhaps imbued with a significance that Delilah failed to grasp, and then he said, "I had thought of that actually."

She looked up at him. "And?"

He shrugged. "Well, you know the saying: Forewarned is forearmed."

"This is going to hurt," Delilah advised, just a fraction of a second before poking the small needle through the edge of one of the wounds. His stomach muscles contracted in reaction, but he said nothing. Curiously stimulated by their verbal sparring, Delilah returned to their previous conversation. "Does that mean that you think I'm capable of betraying you should the opportunity arise?"

He considered her for a moment with his hard, charcoal eyes. Finally he said, "Capable? Oh, yeah. But I would hope, not *willing*."

She glanced up at him. "You don't have a very high opinion of me, do you?"

"Actually, I have a higher opinion of you than of most people. You're beautiful, resourceful, independent, and ambitious." He frowned for a fraction of a second and added, "A mite misguided maybe. Still, that's not a combination often seen in a woman."

He does find me attractive! The words sang through Delilah's brain before she remembered that she didn't care a fig whether he found her beautiful or not. "Well, Sheriff, I'm hardly going to thank you for such a left-handed compliment. Nevertheless, I am gratified to learn that a man can appreciate my independence. Few do."

"Matt," he reminded her. "And sure, I admire independence in women. An ambitious and independent woman can go far. A bit of firm guidance from a supportive husband is all that's needed to—" Delilah's hand froze, and this time he seemed to sense it.

"To what, Sheriff?" she asked in a deceptively quiet voice.

He cleared his throat. "Could you maybe . . . uh, just finish that stitch?" he asked.

Delilah looked down and noticed that she'd halted in mid stitch, with the needle imbedded in his flesh. She finished the stitch and then realized that the other gash that needed stitching, being more centered on Matt's abdomen, was beyond her comfortable reach for stitching. She could try to accomplish the task anyway, by extending her arms and doing the best she could from the side, but she'd be unable to see it properly. The best position was to move between his sprawled knees and accomplish the task from that position. Such a situation, however, suggested a degree of intimacy that immobilized Delilah.

He sensed her hesitation. "Is something wrong?"

Delilah jumped as though she'd been scalded. "No, of course not," she said quickly. Too quickly? He stared at her strangely. "I . . . I'm just tired." The excuse was weak, but it was the best she could come up with. "Could I get you to turn to the side?" Perhaps if she worked from his other side, it would be less awkward.

"Sure thing." He swung his legs to the side as per her request.

If only the gouge was not so near . . . the center of his waistband. There was no help for it; she had to finish this and she wouldn't get it done from here.

Before she could change her mind, she extended her arms to begin working on the injury, and desperately sought the cord of their conversation. "Now then," she said, "do you want to continue with what you were saying?"

He considered. "Actually," he said, "I think that discussion might be best left for another time."

"Just when you'd managed to get my undivided attention."

"Well . . . maybe I'll reconsider," he murmured. His voice held a note that Delilah hadn't heard before. A husky, suggestive note, slightly tight. "I think I like the idea of having your undivided attention."

Oh, Lord! He sounded . . . provocative! Her hands trembled as an impossible combination of dread and excitement swept through her.

Chapter Seven

Samson looked down at the woman kneeling at his side and damn near choked. Though he could tell from her expression that the position she'd adopted was completely innocent on her part, and was simply necessary for providing the medical care he needed, he couldn't help finding her posture extremely erotic. Her hand was scant inches from a certain part of him. And that certain part was definitely taking notice, reminding him of just how long it had been since he'd been with a woman.

"Delilah . . ."

"Yes?" Her concentration remained on the stitch she was tying.

"Look at me," he whispered, reaching out to lift her chin again. It seemed he was always doing that, for she seemed curiously reluctant to meet his gaze. But this time, even though he raised her chin, she kept her eyes averted. "Look at me," he said again.

In an almost imperceptible motion, she shook her head.

"Why?" he asked, subtly stroking the soft skin beneath his fingers. He hoped she was getting used to contact with him. That she would stop fearing him.

"I think it's best if I finish your dressing and we say goodnight."

Samson studied her face for an endless moment, from her flawless creamy complexion to the exotic arch of her midnight-black brows. From her slightly uptilted eyes to her rosy pink lips. From the delicate shell of her ear to the corkscrew strand of hair that brushed the rosy slant of her cheekbone. "All right," he said finally, releasing her, though the words cost him. He didn't think he'd ever wanted anything quite so badly as he wanted to taste Delilah's oh-so-kissable mouth.

He sensed more than heard her sigh of relief. Damnation! How was she ever going to get over her fear of men if she didn't let one touch her? Preferably him.

He watched as she quickly completed the last few stitches, and then rose. She scooped up the soiled dressing that had once been her petticoat, throwing it into the stove fire, and then put away the needle. The more he observed her, evaluated her reactions, the more he realized that Delilah was a woman of contradictions. She'd been married, yet she was obviously quite discomfited by the sight of his naked torso—though she had disguised it well by talking incessantly. She feared the touch of a man, yet she claimed her husband had not abused her. According to what she'd said earlier in the day, she resented the servitude of being a wife in a loveless marriage, yet she claimed to have been so happily married that she could not stop mourning her husband.

"If you'll stand up now," Delilah said, "we can get a clean bandage on and we'll be finished."

"Sure thing, ma'am." He stood and moved a bit away from the chair.

Delilah pushed the whiskey out of her way as she collected a couple of padded dressings. Realizing for the first time that the whiskey had a strange greenish tinge to it, Samson frowned. "What exactly is that stuff?" he asked.

She looked to see what he was pointing at. "It's Fong's homemade whiskey. Apparently he makes it especially for disinfecting injuries."

Pressing a wadded dressing over the worst of the scratches, she directed him to hold it while she prepared a strip to tie it in place. As Samson looked down at her, at the vulnerable nape of her neck as she worked on him, he knew he could not . . . would not keep his word.

Finished securing the bandage, she tightened the last knot and said, "There, that should hold until you get a chance to have the doctor look at it."

"Thank you," he said quietly. He'd hoped that she'd look up to respond, but she only nodded and began to turn away. Instinctively, he reached out to halt her and then stared down in surprise at his own hand where it gripped her shoulder. "Delilah—"

"Yes?" The word came out in a whisper.

But he couldn't remember what it was he'd wanted to say, so he simply grasped her other shoulder and turned her toward him. Then, wordlessly, he once again lifted her chin, bringing her gaze up to meet his. The apprehension he saw shining from those beautiful blue eyes was like a kick in the gut. He wanted to hold her and protect her from her fear. But he couldn't protect her from himself, so he lowered his gaze to her pouty mouth. Her full lips trembled. The tip of her tongue darted out to moisten them, leaving them glistening, and he groaned deep in his throat, knowing he was lost. He'd simply have to prove to her that she had nothing to fear from him.

Lowering his head, he captured her lips with his. She stood frozen in his grasp, neither responding nor pulling away. Confused, he gently drew her into an embrace, reveling in the sensation of holding her soft woman's body next to his even as he sought the clues he needed to tell him how she felt. But there were none. Lingeringly, deliberately, he stroked her full lips with his tongue. He felt her tremble. Heard her breathing quicken.

Yes! But still she didn't open to him.

Slowly he drew back to look down into her face. Her eyes were closed, the midnight lashes fanning against her flushed cheeks. Her lips gleamed from his kiss. And yet her arms hung at her sides.

Baffled by the mixed signals he was receiving, but resolved not to give up on this yet, Samson let his hands slide down her arms to her hands, which he lifted and placed on his shoulders. She opened her eyes then to stare at him dazedly. "Open your lips for me, darlin'," he murmured.

"Wha . . ." but she didn't get any further because he captured her lips again, plunging his tongue into the moist warm hollow of her mouth. Damnation, she tasted good. Sweet. He'd always had a sweet tooth.

He caressed her tongue with his, expecting her to reciprocate, to show some kind of response, but again he was disappointed. She stood passive in his embrace, her breathing suggesting that she was as aroused as he, but she did not react overtly in any way. His frustration grew. What in blazes? Did she want this, or didn't she? Where was the experienced lover he'd expected to find?

Finally, his patience snapped, and he released her mouth. "Goldarnit, woman!" he exclaimed in a tone scarcely above a whisper, ever mindful of those who might be listening from behind closed doors. "Will you quit kissin' me like a blamed virgin?"

He regretted the words the instant Delilah opened her eyes, and he saw the hurt flare in those brilliant blue depths.

"Aw, heck. I'm sorry. . . ."

But it was too late. The hurt transformed to anger so swiftly that, had he blinked, he might not have seen it at all, and she pulled from his embrace, turning toward the table. "I apologize if my lack of expertise prevented you from enjoying the kiss, Sheriff," she said. Her words, although low, were clipped. "But I've never . . ." She broke off.

Samson studied the tense lines of her slender back. A vague suspicion began to come to life in his mind. "Never what?"

"I've never before met a man boorish enough to comment on it," she concluded. Samson was almost positive, though, that was not what she'd been about to say. "Perhaps your own tastes are more suited to the bordellos, Sheriff." She began bustling about, putting away the remaining bandages and whiskey.

Samson put his shirt back on, not bothering to button it. He was still trying to figure out what to say, how to negate the effect of his unruly tongue, when Delilah began to walk toward her bedroom door, saying, "Goodnight, Sheriff," over her shoulder without so much as glancing in his direction.

"Delilah . . ."

She halted, but did not turn.

"I didn't say that I didn't enjoy the kiss. I enjoyed it. Very much."

Without a word, she opened the bedroom door, stepped inside, and closed it again. Samson clenched his fists in frustration and muttered a very foul word under his breath. She'd probably never let him kiss her again.

Delilah leaned against the door, closed her burning eyes against the sting of tears, and pressed a shaking hand to her throat. She'd just experienced her first *real* kiss, and it had been a disaster. Not only had Matt made it crystal clear that he was sadly disappointed by her lack of expertise, but he'd then compounded her mortification by claiming that he'd enjoyed it anyway. But why hadn't he felt the same things she'd felt?

She'd been completely unprepared for such a carnal exchange. She hadn't even conceived that such kisses existed. It had been absolutely unlike the chaste meeting of lips she'd shared with the neighbor boy she'd thought to marry once long ago—in another life, it seemed. This kiss had been . . . exhilarating in a strange way. It had been warm, exciting, and very, very pleasant to be held in Matt's strong arms. To be cradled so gently against that big body. To finally experience the kiss that, despite all her fears, she'd been wondering about. It had been almost frighteningly foreign, and yet delicious at the same time. She'd never before experienced that strange melting sensation inside. Or the peculiar sense of light-headedness that should have been unpleasant, but was not in the least. And now that she had, she was more than simply afraid. She was terrified.

Terrified because she knew that, should he overcome his initial disappointment and someday kiss her again, she'd welcome his embrace. Terrified because, no matter how much she enjoyed his kiss, she knew she could never acquiesce to what he would expect to follow. Terrified because she was suddenly experiencing feelings she'd never expected to feel.

Oh, Lord! What was she to do? She could never allow

any man, even Matt, to touch her in that way.

She didn't understand how kissing could be so pleasant when . . . the rest was so hurtful and repugnant. If her mother had been alive, perhaps she could have brought herself to ask, to seek the answers she craved. But Morgana was long dead, and Delilah could not bring herself to ask her younger sister.

Delilah was the oldest. The one whom Eve had always turned to for answers. Perhaps it was silly, but Delilah felt that, should she ask Eve a question like this, she would in some way destroy the balance that existed between them.

Swallowing the lump in her throat, blinking back tears that she refused to shed, Delilah finally summoned the strength to step away from the door. In the light of the lamp that Eve must have left burning for her, she focused on the bedchamber. The furnishings consisted of a bed, a night table, and a dresser containing a pitcher and wash basin. On the night table rested a tattered copy of the *Ladies' Home Journal*, and a pair of books which on closer examination proved to be *Moby Dick* and *Uncle Tom's Cabin*. A white nightgown had been laid out on the bed for her. It would feel good to wash and get out of her dusty clothing.

She'd just begun to unbutton her shirtwaist when she was interrupted by a determined scratching at her door. Poopsy! Delilah cautiously opened the bedroom door only wide enough to allow the small dog to enter, but she couldn't help glancing into the other room. Matt had not yet sought his bed. He stood big, bold, and very dynamic at the end of the table. His gaze met and locked with hers, dark and mysterious, as though he'd been expecting her perusal. Her pulse leapt in her throat and Delilah hastily closed the door.

"Rr . . . raw, gr . . . ow, rrr," Poopsy demanded from the floor near her feet.

"Shush," Delilah admonished. "I'm sorry I forgot about you. But you have to be quiet or you'll wake somebody up."

The little dog gave her a censorious look and then searched around expectantly for its bed.

"We couldn't bring it, remember?" Delilah whispered. "Come here." Lifting Poopsy onto the foot of her own bed, she said, "You'll just have to sleep with me while we're here."

Poopsy bared her teeth, proclaiming her satisfaction with the arrangement, and settled down with a little snort to watch Delilah as she readied herself for bed.

As he lay before the fireplace in the other room, Samson's unruly mind conjured images to correspond to the muffled sounds emanating from Delilah's bedroom—images that were not in the least conducive to sleep. With an effort of pure will, he turned his thoughts to other things, contemplating the information he'd garnered at the Lazy M ranch, in the hope that sleep would follow.

Carter McTaggert had been his usual gruff self, demanding that Samson do something to earn his salary. McTaggert claimed that, including the twenty head he'd just lost, he'd been pilfered for almost a hundred head of cattle since the rustling had begun. Knowing McTaggert and his penchant for exaggeration, however, Samson estimated the actual number would be more in the range of fifty head. Still, it was a goodly number. And with the current beef shortage, someone out there was probably making a darn good dollar from the stolen beeves.

What Samson needed to know was where they were taking them prior to selling them. They had to be holing up somewhere immediately after each raid until the fuss died down enough for them to herd the cattle out of the territory. More than likely, they were using the waiting time to alter the brands on the cattle too. He was going to have to come back out here with his deputy, and a couple of other men if he could round some up, to start combing the hills.

He was also going to keep an eye on Wes Powell. To Samson's way of thinking, the man had not had an adequate explanation for why his distinctive piebald mare had been reported seen near the Bar K when Jamie Cox was killed. Powell merely claimed that it had to be a case of mistaken identity, because neither he nor his horse had left the Lazy M. A couple of other hands had backed him up on that, but Samson was suspicious. It would be pretty hard to mistake that mare. Especially since there just weren't that many in the area.

He frowned. A couple of the hands from the Rocking E might have piebalds, but he didn't think their peculiar coloring could have been mistaken for Wes Powell's mount. Still, maybe Samson would have to swing by and have a talk with Simon Earl on his way back to Red Rock. It might be interesting to see how many more head that rancher had lost to the rustlers recently.

Much as he hated to contemplate it, Samson was pretty much convinced that one of the ranchers had resorted to rustling to survive, and was simply rustling a few of his own cattle too in order to avert suspicion. All the ranchers were in dire straits. Callously, the guilty party's method of survival came at the expense of neighbors who could not afford the loss.

Samson closed his eyes, pondering the problem in that half-sleeping, half-waking state that he'd found often yielded answers that eluded the fully alert mind.

The problem was that his mental list of suspects was almost equal to the number of ranches in the immediate vicinity. He thought he could probably discount the Elk Creek ranch since it was owned by an absentee British landlord. Lord Fallon or something fancy like that. Samson had never met the man. Of course it was possible that the foreman, Rex Turner, had decided to conceal the ranch's losses from his employer in order to preserve his job, but Samson didn't think it likely. Rex was the kind of man you could trust at your back.

And Samson was pretty certain he could discount the Devil's Fork, since Tom was incapable of riding and Eve just didn't strike him as the type to stoop to rustling.

He wanted to reject the Flying L—he liked Mr. and Mrs. Harlin—but hadn't quite convinced himself yet. The Flying L had had some hay stores to tide them over the winter, and that had helped. They'd only lost about fifty percent of their herd to the starvation caused by the deep snows and long winter, versus the seventy-five-percent losses or higher that had been sustained by the larger ranches, which had relied entirely on pasture. The Harlins were good churchgoin' folks, but they were gettin' on in years. Certainly they were too old to start over. And that was what planted the seed of doubt in Samson's mind. There was no tellin' what a fellow might do in Harlin's situation.

His primary suspects, however, were the Rocking E—owned by Mr. Simon Earl, who'd always had a very high opinion of himself and his importance in the vast scheme of things—and McTaggert's Lazy M. A secondary suspect was the Bar K, owned by Joshua Kane, where Jamie Cox had been killed. Somehow, though, he couldn't see Kane killing one of his own men. Still, stranger things had happened. For all he knew, Cox could have been having an affair with Kane's beautiful and amorous young wife. Rumor was that more than one cowhand in the territory had had the pleasure. Kane could have used the rustling as an excuse to get rid of a rival. Maybe Samson would have to have another talk with Kane. . . .

Samson awoke with a start. It was still dark as pitch, but long years of experience told him that dawn was only an hour or so away. He instinctively reached beneath the edge of his bedroll, closing his fingers over the butt of his Colt for security before he realized that the noise that had awakened him was simply Fong stoking the fire in the stove. He relaxed, closing his eyes again, though he knew he would not sleep.

A few moments later, the door to one of the bedrooms creaked slightly as it opened, and he heard the quick light steps of a woman. Delilah? he wondered, though, stubbornly, he refused to heed the inner voice that prompted him to look. Then Eve spoke quietly, greeting Fong, and Samson knew that Delilah was still abed. Deciding that he wanted to be up and dressed before she rose, he rolled from his bedroll, tugged on his boots, and stood to recover his shirt from the back of the rocking chair where he'd draped it the previous night.

"Oh, Sheriff Chambers . . . you're awake," Eve remarked quietly upon seeing him. She walked silently toward him. "I wonder if you would be so kind as to go in and visit Tom for a while? He wants to speak with you, but I'm afraid he's not well enough to join us for breakfast this morning."

Samson studied Eve's face, searching for a clue as to what was in the offing, but saw nothing in her expression beyond fatigue and worry. "Sure thing, ma'am."

"Thank you," she said, offering him a weak smile. "Fong has the coffee ready, so I'll pour you and Tom each a cup and, if you don't mind, I'll let you deliver it when you go in?"

"I don't mind."

A moment later, Eve handed him two steaming cups laced with sugar and fresh cream and he turned toward the bedroom he'd seen Tom enter the previous evening.

Eve opened the door for him to enter and then closed it firmly behind him.

A lamp, its flame burning low, did little to dispel the gloom, but it provided enough light to see. In addition to the bed, the small bedroom contained a dresser with a scarred mirror, a wardrobe, a narrow washstand, and a chair which had been positioned next to the bed. Bright yellow curtains adorned the single window and the homemade quilt that covered the bed sported a flowered design of a corresponding yellow hue against a dark blue background. Tom, looking even more pale than he had the previous evening, was propped against a pile of pillows in bed.

He didn't even try to smile. "Have a seat, Sheriff," he said, gesturing weakly toward the chair.

Samson sat and placed Tom's coffee within easy reach on the edge of the washstand. He eyed the man on the bed gravely. "How are you feeling, Tom?"

Tom grimaced. "You've heard the rumors?"

Samson nodded, sipped his coffee, and said nothing. What could he say?

"Well, they're true. Unless the good Lord sees fit to deliver a miracle, it looks like I'm dying." Tom waved a hand weakly. "Oh, I still have the occasional good day, but they're getting farther apart. You know," he mused aloud, almost as though he was talking to himself, "death is a strange thing. It's a fact of life. We all recognize it and know that someday it will happen to us. And yet, I think there's a part of each and every one of us that believes we'll somehow escape it. Until one day you find yerself starin' down its throat."

The expression in Tom's fever-glazed eyes suddenly sharpened. "I heard that before you became sheriff, you were a hired gun. That right, Matt?"

Samson nodded. "On occasion, if I believed in the cause, I took employment as a hired gun."

"Never heard of a Chambers before, but that was probably because you were down South. Right?"

"Mostly," Samson conceded, not to mention the fact that he'd gone by another name then. "I was never a hired killer though," he added. "Folks tend to hear about those fellows a bit more often. There is a difference between a hired gun and a hired killer."

"I know. And it's a hired gun I'd be looking for." Tom coughed slightly and then spent a moment catching his breath.

"Why would you be looking for a gunhand?"

"For Eve."

"I don't follow."

"She won't leave this place, Matt—even after I'm gone. She says she belongs here. But there are a few people out there who don't agree with her. I've already had two crazy-low offers from thoughtful neighbors tryin' to buy me out. This valley has some of the best grazin' land in the territory, and they know it. But even if the price had been fair, I would have refused . . . for Eve's sake."

Tom fell silent and Samson read between the lines. "You think somebody will try to force her out."

Tom nodded. "I'm sure of it. Like I said, this valley is rich, and it borders on three other ranches. Two of those, the Rocking E and the Lazy M, could certainly use the pasture. The Rocking E wouldn't mind access to the river either. Earl's creeks tend to dry up in mid season. Then there's the Elk Creek. I haven't heard anything from Lord What's-'is-name, but he lost more head this past winter than any other rancher in the area. Near to ninety percent I heard. He could very well turn his eyes this way." Tom looked at Samson. "One way or another, I think it's a pretty safe bet to assume that at least one of those ranches will try to get this land. And I don't want my wife to be forced out."

"I'm not a hired gun anymore, Tom," Samson said. "I can keep an eye out for her, but I'm not sure what else I can do."

"I know. I know." Tom closed his eyes and swallowed, as though in pain. Then slowly he reached out a trembling hand to grasp the coffee cup on the washstand. Samson, knowing the strength of a man's pride, particularly in front of another man, didn't help him, but merely sipped his own coffee as Tom moistened his throat. Finally, Tom spoke again. "Do you know anyone, Matt?" he asked. "Someone you'd trust enough to safeguard your own wife if you had one?"

"That's a tall order, Tom."

"Yeah, it is. But do you?"

Samson leaned back in his chair, thoughtfully eyeing the ceiling as his mind turned back over the years and the men he'd encountered. "I can only think of one man who might be right for what you have in mind," he said. "Last I heard, he was in Dodge City, I think. But I don't even know if he's still alive."

"Who is he?"

"His name is Adam Colton. He's not a man you'd ever want to cross, but he's a good man where it counts."

"Adam Colton . . ." Tom repeated. He frowned as though trying to place the name. Then his expression cleared and Samson knew he'd either recognized the name and was satisfied with what his memory told him, or he'd decided to simply take Samson's word concerning Colton's character. "Can you contact him?"

"If he's still alive, I'll find him."

Tom's brow cleared, and for the first time since Samson had entered the room, he seemed to relax slightly. Then, reaching under the edge of the mattress, he removed a small package wrapped in brown paper. "Here," he said, passing it to Samson. "Give that to him.

It should be enough to pay him for about four months. Two if he's expensive."

"Won't Eve need this?"

Tom shrugged. "There's not enough there to make much of a difference as far as the ranch goes. Besides, the first thing she has to do is hold on to this place."

Samson nodded, and slid the package into his shirt pocket. Then he regarded the once vital young man lying in the bed. "I'll do my best to watch over her, Tom. You have my word on it."

Tom smiled weakly and extended a hand in thanks. As the two men shook hands, a wealth of meaning passed between them, unspoken but understood.

Two days later, Eve and Rattlesnake Joe escorted Delilah on her return to Red Rock. They planned to get some supplies for the ranch while they were there, thus Joe drove the wagon while Eve rode her favorite gelding, dubbed Sundance. Delilah might have stayed another day had things at the ranch been better, but she knew that Eve continually neglected chores on the ranch in order to visit with her. Besides, she didn't feel she had the right to rob Eve and Tom of any of the private time they had remaining. And if she was to help them, it was time to begin her work at the Lucky Strike.

Delilah and Eve had talked over the situation concerning the bank during her visit, and it had been decided the Delilah would simply deposit what funds she could directly into Eve's account at the bank. With luck, it would be enough to make the mortgage payment when it came due. If not, Eve would be forced to sell some of her cattle to take up the shortfall in order to meet the payment, which would leave the ranch unable to generate the operating capital it needed for the next year. Still, such a move, if it became necessary, would at least buy Eve and the Devil's Fork some time. Time enough for Delilah to try to increase the funds available to help her.

Tom, Delilah had learned, was not aware of the dire straits the ranch was in. Determined that he not waste his precious strength on worry, Eve had concealed as much of the reality from him as possible during his illness, shouldering the burden alone as she had begun to shoulder so much. Delilah worried about her. It would take a very strong person, man or woman, to weather what now faced her sister. Still, she had come from strong stock. They both had. They already had come through a lot, and survived.

"We're almost there," Eve said, her words drawing Delilah from her thoughts. "There's O'Hara's Lumber Mill." The lumber mill was on the outskirts of Red Rock, separated from the town by a swift, cold mountain stream dubbed Silver Creek. Past the lumber mill and across the bridge, on opposing sides of the road, were the whitewashed schoolhouse and church, easily visible in the distance against the verdant backdrop of rich meadow grass. "Civilization," Eve said. "Somehow it doesn't hold the same appeal it once did. Still, Red Rock is better than some of the places we lived—it's a nice quiet town, for the most part—especially since Sheriff Chambers took over."

"Yes," Delilah agreed. Except that in Red Rock she would once again have to face Sheriff Matthew Chambers. Her heart gave a little thud at the thought.

She'd managed to say a regally cool farewell to the handsome sheriff when he'd left the ranch, and she was certain nobody suspected the intimate moment that had passed between them. But in the days that followed his departure, Matt was never far from her thoughts. She'd see a thundercloud on the horizon and be reminded of the deep grey hue of his eyes. She'd see one of the ranch hands washing up and be reminded of

Matt's muscular chest. She'd see Stone's serious mien and be reminded of Matt's solemnity.

The horses' hooves clopped noisily over the planks of the bridge, and Delilah returned to the present. Children were playing boisterously in the schoolyard to her right, with the exception of a couple of girls sharing the seat of a swing suspended from a huge tree limb. Above them, a boy shimmied along the branch, obviously planning to take them unawares with some prank. Delilah smiled wistfully. The carefree days of youth numbered entirely too few.

Looking away before she got absolutely maudlin, Delilah stared ahead at the bustling little town and absorbed the ambience. The sound of lounging drovers arguing as they leaned on the hitching posts in front of Wilson's Saddlery. The sight of two ladies, children in tow, rushing into Lowden's Mercantile to get their shopping done. The smell of fresh baked bread and rolls emanating from Mrs. Swartz's Bakery.

"That's Mr. Cobb, the banker," Eve said abruptly, lifting her chin in the direction of a man emerging from the Red Rock Savings and Loan. A man sporting grey muttonchops closed the door of the bank and made his way down the boardwalk with a swift but small-stepped gait that seemed a bit effeminate. He wore black trousers and a matching suit jacket worn over a light grey vest and striped shirt. A gold watch chain dangled from the pocket of his vest. His ensemble was completed by a black bowler hat and a walking stick.

"How long has he been in the West?" Delilah asked.

Eve considered. "About two years now, I believe. His wife and children are still in Boston. She followed him here shortly after he took over operation of the bank but, rumor is, she refused to live in a town that was so lacking in refinement. So she went back East and nobody here has seen her since."

Rattlesnake Joe pulled the wagon to a halt in front of the mercantile. Eve and Delilah reined their mounts to a standstill and looked at each other. Neither was ready yet to say good-bye.

"Well," Eve said, "I guess I'll see you in a couple of weeks."

Delilah nodded disconsolately, and then inspiration struck. "Why don't I come into the store with you for a few minutes? I'm sure I could use a couple of things myself."

Eve's face brightened at the idea. "Would you? It'll be like old times." In the days after their father's death, they had done all their shopping together, sharing the decisions about what to purchase with their hard-earned money.

She smiled. "Certainly." Dismounting, she tied Jackpot to the hitching rail and removed Poopsy from her saddlebag perch, settling the small dog firmly in the crook of her arm and receiving a moist warm lick to her nose for her troubles. Eve waited for her on the boardwalk, and they entered the store.

Had she been blindfolded, Delilah would have known the instant she entered the mercantile. It smelled like general stores everywhere, of coffee and tea, tobacco and cigars, huge slabs of homemade cheeses and smoked hams. Pickle barrels and bushels of dried beans, peas, and corn crowded the aisles along with wooden slatted baskets of last season's potatoes, carrots, turnips, and onions. On the darkly varnished wooden counter next to three large jars of colorful penny candy sat a basket of eggs. A sign advertised them at fifteen cents a dozen.

Eve greeted Mr. Lowden and began going over her shopping list with him. ". . . Twenty pounds of flour, ten pounds of sugar, some matches . . ." Delilah allowed their voices to fade into the background as she examined a bolt of bright blue cotton fabric. Wistfully, she allowed the cool fabric to slide over her fingers. It would be so beautiful when fashioned into a gown. For an instant, she pictured the dress she could make with it, pictured herself attired in something other than black. She had always loved cheerful clothing.

Then, realizing what she was doing, Delilah jerked her hand away from the fabric and moved on. Wearing such clothing was impossible for her. She could not afford to give up her widow's garb. The thought of unwanted male attention terrified her.

Unwittingly, her thoughts turned to Matt. The impediment of her widowhood had done little to deter him. She didn't know what she was going to do about that.

"Mrs. Sterne!"

Delilah started at the unexpected male voice and turned. It took an instant before she recognized its owner. "Why hello, Mr. Pike. How are you?"

"I'm doin' all right, ma'am. Thank you kindly for askin'. I didn't expect to see you in Red Rock."

Despite the light of avid curiosity she perceived in the man's eyes, Delilah wasn't about to explain her presence to the bounty hunter. "Nor I you, Mr. Pike."

"Well, ma'am, I gotta go where the leads take me. When I showed the posters around, somebody said they thought they mighta seen that Towers fella in these parts. So, here I am."

Chapter Eight

As he rode back into town after another fruitless search of mountain canyons and valleys, Samson noticed a distinctive Appaloosa tied at the hitching rail before Lowden's Mercantile. Delilah was back! He felt a small thrill of anticipation—totally unlike him—but considering the way she'd invaded his thoughts lately, perhaps he should have expected it. Still, he couldn't allow her presence to distract him from his duties. This evening would be soon enough to let Delilah Sterne know that he hadn't forgotten her. After all, he had a firm duty to observe every move she made while gambling at the Lucky Strike.

In the meantime though, as soon as he stabled Goliath, he wanted to find old Jeb and have a chat. There was nobody quite as efficient as that old man at making observations. And since he spent darned near every waking hour lounging in front of either the mercantile or the barber shop, it stood to reason that he might have seen something that would help Samson.

It was almost an hour before Sam made it to Henry Newton's barber shop, where he found Jeb Potter sitting on a chair out front. He'd been sidetracked by a conversation with Mayor Ralston Jack, who'd wanted an update on the new dealer now employed at the Lucky Strike. Seems his wife had heard from Mrs. Swartz, who had heard from Mrs. Williamson, who had heard from God knew where, that Samson was actually going to allow another professional gambler to set up shop. The ladies were naturally concerned. Particularly when it was learned that the new dealer was, in fact, an attractive young woman.

"How's it goin', Sheriff?" Jeb asked as Samson approached.

"Not bad, Jeb. Not bad." He took up a leaning position against the wall, next to Potter's chair. "Anything exciting been happening in town?"

"Can't say as I'd call it excitin'. Intrestin' maybe."

"What's interesting?"

Jeb shrugged his skinny shoulders and smacked his toothless mouth. "New guy in town," he said without preamble.

"He heeled?"

"Yep. Has that look about him. Seems like he's fixin' to stay, 'cause he checked into the hotel."

Samson bit off a piece of hard candy and studied the street. "Lawman?"

"Mebbe," Jeb acknowledged. "More 'n likely a bounty hunter." Jeb spat a stream of brown tobacco juice into a tin can at his side, and Samson received the distinct impression that Jeb would have just as soon had his target be the bounty hunter's boot. Jeb had lost one of his two sons to a bounty hunter in a case of mistaken identity, and never had gotten over it. The old man considered bounty hunting to be nothing more than legalized murder. "Calls hisself Pike," Jeb added with distaste.

Samson nodded. He was afraid of that. Still, there was nothing he could do about it except continue to do his job and pray for the best. "You hear anything more about this rustlin'?"

"Heard old Simon Earl lost hisself another twenty head. And the Bar K fifteen head or so."

"Yeah. I heard that too." Samson squinted at a man coming out of the hotel. He wore dusty denims, a buckskin vest, a battered felt hat, and a pair of boots that looked like he'd probably been wearing them ever since bears grew teeth. The man paused to give the street a thorough examination, pulled a cigar from his pocket, lit it with a wooden match that he struck with his thumbnail, and then started walking toward the saloon. He had the gait of a man who'd spent a lifetime in the saddle. He also wore a set of matching pistols in holsters that had been secured to his thighs with rawhide thongs.

He had to be the bounty hunter.

As if in verification of his unspoken conclusion, Potter said, "Here comes that Pike feller now." He indicated the man across the street with a motion of his grey-whiskered chin.

Samson nodded. "He been askin' questions yet?"

"Not that I kin tell."

Samson shrugged. "Well, I guess we'll know soon enough why he's here."

"Yup." The door of the barber shop squeaked and the banker emerged, his hair and greying muttonchops once again neatly trimmed.

"Afternoon, gentlemen," he said, touching his walking cane to the brim of his hat as he went by.

"Hiram," Jeb said with a dip of his chin.

Samson shook his head inwardly. Potter knew that

Cobb hated to be addressed by his given name. But it was Jeb's way of reminding the pretentious banker that he regarded him as an equal—whether Cobb reciprocated the opinion or not.

"Cobb." Samson too nodded in acknowledgment of the banker's greeting.

As Hiram Cobb moved on, a companionable silence fell. That was another thing Samson had always liked about old Jeb. He didn't feel the need to fill every silence with useless chatter. They watched the people scurrying along the boardwalk, each intent on their own tasks. Mrs. Vanbergen, the laundress, was rushing along the opposite side of the street with an armful of white linens; her portly figure as she steamed along reminded Samson of a train's engine. Amy Sweet, dressed in men's clothing and smoking a cigarette, pulled her buckboard to a halt in front of the store; her youth and whatever natural beauty she might have possessed were camouflaged by her determination to be accepted as any man's equal. Doc Hale slammed the door of his office and, black bag in hand, hurried off down the street. The sight of him reminded Samson that the doc had told him to have the stitches Delilah had given him removed within the week. After demanding to know who had stitched his ribs, Doc had proclaimed Delilah's handiwork more than satisfactory and told Samson his ribs would heal just fine.

"That little lady you were so took with is back," Jeb commented out of nowhere.

"Oh. What little lady might that be?" he asked mildly, though he knew damn well who Potter meant.

Jeb snorted, not even dignifying Samson's question with a reply.

Samson decided it was time to get to the subject at hand. "Jeb, you know these hills better than most. That so?"

Potter nodded. "Seen most every piece o' them. Been here nigh on twenty years, Matt."

"So, if you were rustlin' cattle, where would you hide them? Especially if you were concerned about gettin' them out to market again fast?"

Jeb frowned. "There's lots o' good hidin' places. You'd be figurin' on them drivin' them out at night?"

Samson nodded in confirmation. "Yep. Any ideas?"

"Gimme a minute," Jeb demanded cantankerously. Then he started thinking out loud. "Le'see, you'd want somethin' that not just anybody could stumble across. Where d'you figure they'd have in mind ta take 'em?"

Samson shook his head. "Could be either Helena or Butte. They'd be wantin' someplace with a train though is my guess. Get the cattle out faster, less chance of questions."

"They'd be wantin' to use whatever range country between here and there they can. That'd narrow it down some." He frowned and stared intently at the dusty boards beneath his feet as he chewed thoughtfully on the wad of tobacco in his cheek. "Brokenback Canyon mebbe. It'd prob'ly be the best place ta hide 'em 'fore herdin' 'em out."

Samson shook his head. "I thought of that, but there isn't any way into Brokenback except above the falls, and there's no way around them. There sure isn't any way they're gonna drive a herd of cattle over them."

Jeb spat again before arguing. " 'Course there's a way into the canyon below the falls. It ain't easy ta find, an' a lot of folks don't know 'bout it no more. The ones that do can get downright panicky usin' it, 'cause it's real deep. It's fair wide, but once you get through a short tunnel, the walls is real high and sloped inward. Makes some fellers feel like the walls is closin' in. But if they didn't try to drive more 'n ten or fifteen head through at a time, it could be done."

Samson's gut told him this was it. Had to be. "How do I find it?"

After Jeb had explained, Samson wasn't surprised he'd missed it. The narrow access canyon began as what looked like a cave entrance concealed by a natural rock formation. In actuality, according to Potter, it was a natural tunnel. From his description, it was located very near where Samson had lost the trail the day that Jamie Cox had been murdered, which probably explained how the men had been able to disappear.

Tomorrow, Samson would go out for another look. Right now, he'd have a word with his deputy, Carl Wilkes, and see if anything of importance had happened while he was away. Then he was going to clean up and be ready to head over to the Lucky Strike this evening.

A couple of afternoons later, on the first truly hot summer-like day that they'd had, Samson left two recruits to watch over the cattle they'd found secreted in Brokenback Canyon and gained the complicity of Mrs. Schmidt in his pursuit of Delilah. The hotel proprietress, upon his request, created a picnic basket beyond compare, laden with fried chicken, lemonade, potato salad, and apple pie. Thus armed, Samson managed to convince Delilah to ride out with him. Actually he was a bit surprised by how easy it had been to convince her. Although he wasn't sure how he was going to go about it, Samson had decided to try the direct approach with her—especially since any attempt he had made at seduction only seemed to intensify her reserve.

As they pulled up in a beautiful meadow carpeted with bright yellow and purple wildflowers, she seemed a bit quiet and thoughtful. Samson loosened the traces on the buggy to allow the horses to graze, and then asked Delilah where she thought they should spread the blanket.

"It doesn't matter," she said. "Wherever you think is best."

Samson found himself disappointed by her lack of enthusiasm for the outing, but determined to make the best of it. So, as they settled down for lunch, he kept the conversation going, regaling her with tales of some of the town's more interesting moments. Like the time an inebriated Ray Fielding broke his brother, Tommy, out of jail only to find that he hadn't secured the horses to the rail and they'd wandered off toward home. With no way to run, Ray had joined his brother in jail until their father came to get them. Or the time a black bear had wandered down out of the hills to raid Mrs. Schmidt's garbage and had ended up getting tangled up in the clothesline. Some folks said that blamed bear was still wearin' Frieda's bloomers.

Poopsy interrupted them to coax tidbits of fried chicken from both Samson and Delilah before wandering off to explore the meadow again. Samson spared a moment to hope that the dog didn't scare up a skunk before concentrating once more on Delilah. He didn't seem to be making much headway with his humor either. Although she smiled politely, Delilah was obviously preoccupied with something else.

"What are you thinking?" he asked.

She shrugged. "I haven't been on a picnic for . . ." She cast her gaze into the distance. ". . . a very long time."

Since her husband had been alive, no doubt. Samson found himself despising this ghost of a man who still claimed her affections. "You loved him a lot, did you?"

She looked at him then, an expression of startlement in her brilliant blue eyes. "Who?"

He frowned inwardly. "Your husband. Isn't that who you were thinking of?"

"Oh, yes. Of course." She lowered her gaze to her lap and plucked at a loose thread on the black fabric of her skirt. "Yes, I loved him very much. I shall never marry again, for I could never love another man as much as I loved Kenneth. It would be unkind to marry and offer less than my whole heart."

Samson darn near choked on his lemonade. What she was telling him was that she'd sworn off men for the rest of her life! "That kind of life could get pretty lonely, don't you think?"

She shrugged. "I was never unfaithful to Kenneth, Sheriff. He was the dearest man imaginable. I don't see how I can be unfaithful to his memory. I feel that he is still with me, in spirit, watching over me."

Samson frowned. She was getting a bit over-emotional, wasn't she? Once again a vague uneasiness assailed him, but he could never put his finger on exactly what it was about the stories of her past that bothered him.

As though she sensed his subtle withdrawal, Delilah changed the subject . . . sort of. "Actually, Sheriff Chambers . . ."

"Won't you call me Matt?"

She searched his face for a moment as though seeking something, and then shook her head. "I'm sorry, I can't. Anyway, as I was saying, the reason I agreed to accompany you on this picnic was to ask you to please turn your interests elsewhere. Knowing my feelings for my husband as you now do, you can understand why I simply can't have anything to do with you."

Like hell! Samson thought. Being made aware of the depths of loyalty and devotion of which she was capable only solidified his determination to break down the barriers Delilah had erected around herself. He didn't want her love—he'd learned long ago that love was a painful trap that he could live quite well without—but he wanted her friendship, her loyalty . . . and, most certainly, her body. "Do you honestly believe that I will give up on you that easily?" he asked. Observing her all the while, he slowly began replacing items in the picnic basket.

Delilah stared at him as desperation flooded through her. "I had hoped . . . perhaps."

"I'm not after your love, Delilah. You can keep your heart and your devotion to your husband's ghost intact."

He didn't want her love, and yet he had kissed her. Was he proposing a marriage of convenience then? Had she not made her position on such a union clear to him just the other day, when he'd questioned her reasons for gambling? Did he think her so lacking in morals as to agree to such a thing? Anger suffused her, infusing her cheeks with heat, but she held it in check as she sought to understand *exactly* what he was saying. "Then *what*, pray tell, do you want from me?"

"Your friendship and . . . companionship."

She frowned slightly, trying to determine his meaning. Just friends? Companions? But they had nothing in common. Not even conversation over a friendly game of poker. Unless he had changed his mind. "I see. And as my *friend*, you would, of course, accept my profession without reservation?"

"Actually, I had hoped that, as my lady friend, you would no longer find such a pastime necessary. At least not as long as we continued to enjoy each other's company."

Delilah's mouth dropped open. Her eyes widened. The heat in her cheeks intensified. "Good heavens! You're suggesting that I become your *mistress*!" she exclaimed. "Aren't you?"

His steely-hued eyes swept over her, as unreadable

as ever. "I guess I am," he replied in a low voice. "We're both mature adults."

Delilah leapt to her feet. "I have never been so insulted in my life! I insist that you return me to town immediately!"

"Now hold on a minute . . ."

"Immediately, sir! I refuse to listen to another second of your insulting insinuations and propositions. And in the future, I suggest that your energies would be much better spent on recovering stolen cattle."

"Aww . . ." and then the sheriff cursed in a disgruntled tone beneath his breath as he rose. Delilah suspected she had not been meant to hear the word, but, once again, he had miscalculated. With a gasp of outrage at such rudeness, Delilah stalked toward the buggy, where she scooped Poopsy into her arms. It was one thing to inadvertently hear that kind of language in a saloon where men liked to be free of the strictures imposed by good company. It was another thing entirely, however, to know that she was the object of it. Without waiting for Sheriff Chambers's assistance, Delilah climbed into the conveyance to sit stiffly waiting for him to drive her back to town.

The entire picnic had been a disaster. Not only had she apparently failed to convince him that he should turn his attentions elsewhere, but she had learned that his pursuit of her was not nearly as honorable as she had supposed.

In fact, the only thing that made the day itself worthwhile was that Eve stopped in at the hotel for a visit shortly after Delilah had returned from the picnic. She'd come to get some more medicine for Tom from Doctor Hale, and used the excuse to stop for a brief visit with Delilah.

"Well, thank goodness something good is happening today, or I should have seriously considered returning to bed to get through it more quickly," Delilah said as she hugged her sister. Eve was dressed in a more traditional green suit, with a split skirt that reached her ankles, and a pleated white shirtwaist. And Delilah realized just how beautiful her sister had grown up to be.

"What do you mean? What's happened?" Eve asked as she pulled out of Delilah's embrace to look into her face.

After they were seated at the small writing table that occupied the corner of Delilah's room, Delilah told her about the sheriff's very indecent proposal. Eve was as shocked as Delilah had been. "Well," she huffed. "I would never have expected something like that from him. He's always seemed like such a decent man."

"You can bet I won't be going on another picnic with him. But, enough about that. Let's talk about something else. Has there been any change in Tom's condition?"

Eve's eyes clouded. "He's more feverish now. And complaining of the pain more. It doesn't look good."

Delilah swallowed, hating to see her sister's emotional pain. "I'll keep praying," she murmured. "Perhaps . . ." But neither of them truly believed that Tom would recover, and she broke off.

"So tell me," Eve said with false brightness as she changed the subject, "have you met any other handsome available men recently?"

Delilah shook her head. "None with whom I care to spend time."

Eve frowned. "I worry about you, Sis. You can't go through your entire life alone. You need a companion."

"I have Poochie," Delilah indicated the little dog who lay watching them with alert black eyes.

"I meant a man."

Delilah shrugged. "A man is a lot more work, and I haven't yet met one who was worth the trouble."

Eve considered her and then smiled. "Well, that's true. It has to be the *right* one to make it worthwhile. Remember old Mrs. Bitters?"

Delilah laughed. "Now there was one woman whose name definitely suited her. Up until the day she threw Mr. Bitters out into the street in his underwear, that is. I never saw a woman undergo such a rapid personality transition in my life. She became positively jovial." The sisters passed their remaining time together in fond reminiscence of times past until the chime of the bedside clock intruded and Eve had to leave.

Almost a week later, Samson lay in the shadow of a huge boulder overlooking Brokenback Canyon. He had found a herd of about sixty head of cattle, just as he'd suspected he would, but so far no one had tried to move them. Only two men maintained a more or less constant presence in the canyon, and thus far—since he was forced to keep his distance—he hadn't been able to identify them. In a canyon as isolated as Brokenback, there wasn't really a need for anyone to constantly monitor the herd except to protect them from predators, because there was nowhere for the cattle to go. Since he needed to catch all of those involved, if possible, Samson had little choice but to keep surveillance on the canyon and wait for the rustlers to make their move.

Normally, he would have asked the local ranchers for help with the situation. However, since in this instance virtually all the ranchers were themselves suspects, he, his deputy, and two recruits from town were doing the work themselves.

He and Bill Tillis, one of the recruits he'd managed to deputize temporarily, usually took watch from about midnight to early morning, because that was the most likely time for the rustlers to try to move the herd out.

Samson's deputy, Carl Wilkes, and the other recruit watched the canyon from late afternoon until Samson showed up to spell them at night. Tonight, though, he and Tillis had come out earlier because Wilkes's young wife Kimberley had gone into labor. Knowing Carl, he would have done his job anyway had Samson asked it of him, but his mind wouldn't have been on what he was doing, and that kind of thing tended to get good men killed.

It was nearing ten o'clock on a night that would have had a bright moon overhead had it been less cloudy. With the storm clouds scudding across the sky, though, the night was as black as pitch. Wind soughed through the branches of the cedars clinging to life on the rocky slopes of the gorge. He could hear the cattle lowing calmly below him. But there were no noises out of the ordinary. No hoofbeats or human voices. Keeping his senses attuned to the slightest sound or change in the mood of the herd, Samson allowed his mind to wander.

For the life of him, he could not figure out Delilah Sterne. And he didn't know what his next move should be. The only thing he did know was that, despite his frustration with her, he wanted her more now than ever. She was just about everything he wanted in a woman. And, if she was a bit lacking in the kissing department, Samson figured that was her husband's fault for not teaching her better. Samson could remedy that soon enough if she'd give him the chance.

Getting the chance was what was going to be the problem. She was still as jumpy about being touched as a jackrabbit downwind of a coyote. Samson had come to the conclusion that, whatever had happened to her to make her fear a man's touch, it must have happened *after* her husband's death.

He recalled the way she'd jerked away from his touch on that first day when he'd tried to wipe the dirt from her face. And he remembered the fear in her eyes when she'd been treating him after the cougar attack. It had been very real. Too real. It wasn't hard to imagine what must have happened to her. Whoever the man was who had hurt her, Samson would have liked to have given him a good beating before choking his worthless life from his body. He despised such men. But, since he was unlikely to get that opportunity, he decided instead to concentrate on undoing the damage. If he could.

That incident in Delilah's past would determine his next move. He'd been gentle with Delilah, as he was gentle with all women—he was too big not to be, for he was afraid of hurting them—but he hadn't been . . . slow. If he'd surmised rightly about the incident in her past, Delilah needed consideration and understanding as well as gentleness. She needed time to learn the joy of physical loving all over again. And since *dearest Kenneth* wasn't around to help her, Samson figured he was the next best choice. If there was one thing he knew how to do well, it was make love to a woman. Now, if he could just wrap up this darned rustling business, maybe he could get her to talk to him about something other than the Camerons' stolen cattle.

At that moment, there was a stir in the herd below and Samson shoved his thoughts aside to concentrate on his duty. Two riders below held up lanterns as they moved around the periphery of the herd. If they were simply adding more stolen bovines to the herd, there might be just the two of them. If they were moving them out, there'd be more men. Somewhere.

He peered through the impenetrable blackness until his eyes hurt. Then suddenly two more lanterns flared to life. The white patches on the herd below glowed in the light: white faces, white legs, horns. The herd began to move restlessly.

A short distance away, a match flared briefly. Tillis's

signal that he was moving down. Samson drew a match from his pocket and returned the signal before quietly summoning Goliath from the dense shadows.

He needed to get close enough to see who was involved before he and Tillis could put their plan into action. It was going to be tricky.

He suspected the rustlers were moving the cattle out, knowing that on a night as dark as this, with a storm brewing, they were unlikely to be seen. That meant there'd probably be about six men. Possibly more, but he doubted it in a rustling operation like this one. More hands meant more mouths to talk, and this had been a real closemouthed affair.

Six men against two. Not good odds, but he'd faced worse.

He mounted, slipped his gloves off, and tucked them into his jacket pocket. Then, releasing the thong on his gun, he removed the Colt Peacemaker, ensured that it slid easily out of its holster, and began to make his way quietly down the slope to the canyon floor. He wasn't much worried about the men catching sight of him before he was ready for them. It was a black night, Samson wore unrelieved black, and rode a black horse who, despite his size, was part mountain goat. Still, just to be on the safe side, Samson tugged the brim of his hat down a mite and pulled a black bandanna up over the lower part of his face. If the moon should peek out from all the cloud cover, he didn't want his face showing up like a painted target.

As he drew nearer the canyon floor, he noted that the herd began to surge a bit inside the ring of circling men. Calves bawled for their mothers; steers bellowed; mothers lowed, calling for calves from which they'd been separated. The ground began to vibrate slightly with the concentrated movement of the animals. Ignoring it, Samson focused instead on the men. He could now discern two more drovers, neither carrying lanterns, in addition to the four with lanterns.

Who were they?

Knowing that the rustlers would be driving the herd out through the same large natural tunnel that had allowed them to enter, Samson positioned himself in the shadow of a huge boulder next to the path they would have to take. As Tillis silently arrived, Samson signaled for him to do the same on the other side of the trail. Tillis knew Samson's goal was to identify the men involved and take them alive, if at all possible. Now they had only to wait and watch for the right moment.

Samson shivered as the night wind slid down off the surrounding stone walls. It was still early enough in the season for the nights to be downright cold. A meteor flashed by overhead, leaving a powdery trail of glowing coals in its wake. Goliath shifted restlessly beneath him. Damn, he was tired. Tired and cold. He blew on his chilled fingers, but dared not put his gloves back on. He'd never been much good at handling a firearm with gloves on.

Then, finally, he heard the bawling cattle coming nearer and tensed, his fatigue forgotten. He stayed unmoving in the shadow of the boulder as a few head of cattle passed him. It was too dark to make out any brands, of course, but he'd already recognized Wes Powell in the light of the lantern he carried as he rode point. He was sitting a bay horse this time and rode on the other side of the trail. Samson would have to leave him to Tillis, for one of the other drovers, swaying a lantern high above the milling backs of the cattle, was only a few paces away now, riding swing. Samson studied him closely. The way the man sat a horse was familiar, but he was having trouble placing him.

Then he looked up and the lantern light fell directly onto his craggy features. Spade Johnson!

Samson frowned. Well, hell! He hadn't expected that. A Bar K hand rustling cattle with a Lazy M hand? The rivalry between ranches, good-natured though it usually was, was often pretty stiff, and it tended to extend right down to the hands that worked for each brand. Something curious was going on here. Real curious.

"Git on up there!" Spade yelled at a dawdling heifer as his cow pony nipped the steer on the flank to propel it forward. Samson looked beyond Spade, pinpointing the whereabouts of his comrades as Spade moved by Samson's concealing boulder toward the canyon entrance. The two men riding drag were not carrying lanterns. They were just shadowy forms in the night, barely discernible from the milling herd. He'd have no chance of identifying them until they'd been caught. The problem was that, because they were bringing up the rear, if he came out of concealment before they'd passed by, they could catch him and Tillis from behind. Not a good option.

He frowned as he watched the next swaying lantern approach. He and Tillis would have to make their move soon, or risk losing the men up front. He pulled his Colt from its holster in readiness and watched the second lantern-carrying drover draw nearer. This man he identified as One-Eyed Jim Irish. Jim rode for the Elk Creek brand.

Three identified men. Three different ranches. Samson was beginning to get a picture of this operation, and he didn't like it. It smacked of a level of organization he hadn't suspected. From his vantage point, it looked like whoever was behind the rustling had recruited hands from different targeted ranches. The hands, working from the inside, would know when the best time to hit would be. If he was right, he suspected he would not catch the ringleader tonight. A man smart enough to organize this and tough enough to keep these drovers from cheating him was unlikely to dirty himself by coming anywhere near the actual work.

God, he hoped he was wrong. Because if he wasn't, his best chance of getting anywhere near the fellow behind it all would be to coerce his identity from one of these men. And drovers were, by nature, a close-mouthed lot. Even the outlaw ones.

He waited until One-Eyed Jim was almost upon him, and then he gave the signal he and Tillis had agreed upon: three waves of a large square of white cloth. He only hoped there was enough moonlight, feeble though it was, for Tillis to see it. But he couldn't worry about that now . . . because One-Eyed Jim had seen something. And just as Samson had hoped, the man was guiding his horse a little nearer Sam's concealing boulder as he peered into the darkness, trying to decide just exactly what it was he'd seen.

Before he knew what had happened, the rustler felt the cold steel of Samson's gun barrel pressing against his neck just below his left ear. "No sudden moves," Samson warned coldly, his voice low. "Unless you want me to pull this trigger."

Jim raised his hands carefully away from his sides. "Evenin', Sheriff," he said cordially. "Any chance we can talk about this?"

"None," Samson replied. "Dismount," he ordered. As Jim began to move a bit too eagerly, he cautioned, "*Carefully!* Where I can see you. And put the lantern down over there." He indicated a flat-topped boulder a few feet off the trail that would nevertheless be readily visible to the man bringing up the rear on this side of the trail.

When Jim had complied, Samson waved him back into the shadow of the boulder with a single meaningful gesture of the Colt. "Turn around," he ordered.

The drover turned slowly as Samson dismounted. "Aw, Sheriff, come on . . ."

"Shut up!" Samson interrupted him, prodding him with his gun for emphasis. He didn't know how much time he had before that lantern would be investigated.

Jim obeyed, and Samson hastily tied the drover's hands behind his back, then ordered him to his knees and secured the end of the rope to his ankles for good measure. That done, he jerked One-Eyed Jim's bandanna from around his neck and stuffed it in his mouth. "Quiet, now!" he warned.

He saw the glint of the man's good eye in the darkness and knew it was filled with an intense anger. One-Eye had been bested. His pride had taken a blow. But Samson didn't have time to worry about that now.

"One-Eye?" a voice called out of the darkness.

"Yeah?" Samson returned, in a deep generic tone that would be identifiable as male but not much else, as he hastily remounted.

He heard the scrape of a horse's hoof on stone as the caller moved his horse off the trail in search of One-Eyed Jim. "What the hell are you doin' you stupid son of a . . . ?"

The click of a revolver being cocked next to his ear cut the man off in mid sentence. His gun hand jerked toward his pistol. "I wouldn't," Samson warned.

"Who the fuck are you?" the man growled.

Samson could have asked the same question. "Get down!" he ordered, not bothering to reply. *"Slowly!"*

He repeated the process he'd used with One-Eyed Jim. As soon as the unknown rustler was securely tied next to Jim, he hastily returned to his surveillance of the trail. The last of the cattle had gone by. It wouldn't be long before the first drovers, Wes Powell and Spade Johnson, came back to investigate the disappearance of their comrades. Samson was ready. He just hoped Tillis was too.

In the next instant, though, a gunshot cleaved the night, its echo ominous and cold within the canyon walls. Then another rang out.

Something had gone wrong.

Samson quickly reached over to douse the wick in the coal oil lantern: It wasn't going to work as bait a third time. His eyes straining ahead, he spurred Goliath from cover, staying low over the horse's neck. He knew where Bill Tillis had been before the fracas, and he headed toward that spot now. Bill's camouflage had consisted of the dense shadow afforded by a clump of ancient cedars. Samson ducked beneath one of the boughs as Goliath moved into the trees. "Bill," Sam called quietly, searching the darkness for the hint of a human presence.

"Over here." The voice sounded labored.

A moment later Samson found him. "You okay?"

"Took one in the leg."

"Bad?" Samson asked, dismounting to kneel at Tillis's side.

"Feels worse than it is, I think. Musta hit the bone. I'll live, but I ain't walkin' anywhere real soon."

Hastily Samson folded the white cloth he'd used to signal Tillis earlier into a thick bandage and tied it as well as possible around the wound. There wasn't time to do more. "How'd you make out before you got shot?" he asked.

"I got Dick Burnett and another fella tied up back there." He indicated a dense shadow back from the trail. "Just like we planned. But one o' them others came back 'fore I was ready."

"Do you know who it was?"

"Powell, I think, but I couldn't swear to it."

Samson considered. So Wes Powell and Spade Johnson were still out there, and now they knew something had gone wrong. "Any idea where he is now?"

"You see that funny-lookin' tree on the bluff over yonder?"

Samson peered into the open space beyond the cedars. Just as he was about to give up, the moon slid from behind the clouds and he finally perceived the misshapen shadow, a black void against an indigo sky. "Yeah," he acknowledged.

"Below that," Tillis said. "And about ten or fifteen feet to your left."

"Got it." Leaving Goliath in the shadows with Tillis, he pulled his gun and began moving. He'd have to make his way around behind the area and see if he could locate the men. Then he could decide how to take them.

He was crouching behind a small boulder, peering into the shadowy night for his quarry, when he heard a bullet whine past his ear. He dove for cover.

Chapter Nine

Cautiously bringing his head up, Samson studied the area.

"Well, now, if it ain't the good Sheriff Chambers," a voice drawled loudly out of the night.

Samson tried to pinpoint the man's position. "Evenin', Powell," he returned.

"I sure wish you hadn't took it into your head to come by, Sheriff."

Had he seen a head move in the shadow of that large sycamore across the way? "Why's that, Wes?"

"I really *hate* the idea of killin' a lawman. But orders is orders." Samson heard the sound of him spitting. "No witnesses."

"That why you killed Jamie Cox?"

No answer.

Samson heard the crunch of boots on stone as Powell, emboldened now, tried to work his way into a better position for a shot. Samson fired in the direction of that noise. The bullet ricocheted off a rock and whined into the distance. He heard a faint curse a bit more distant and further to his right than he'd expected.

Spade Johnson?

"Give yourself up, Powell, and I'll guarantee that you get a fair trial." Before the echo of his words had even faded, he was moving, working his way up an incline that would give him a better vantage point.

Again, Powell didn't answer.

Samson peered into the night. The moon slid out from behind a cloud, bathing the landscape in silver light. He used the opportunity to survey the entire area. There was movement in the shadows not far from where he'd last been. Powell, he figured.

But where was Spade?

And then he saw a flicker of grey. A hat?

At that moment, there was a flash from the grey shadow and a bullet hit the boulder in front of him, spraying stinging rock shards up onto his cheek. He returned fire and was rewarded with a howl and a curse. He'd hit his mark. He didn't know how bad, and he didn't know if Spade would still be capable of fighting, but he couldn't worry about that now. Powell would be closing in on his position.

With that in mind, Samson moved to his right, away from where he'd last seen Powell, and searched for another vantage point. The moonlight had already begun to fade, and the night was once again growing black, but before it disappeared he spied another likely location and ran in a crouched posture toward it.

"Hey, Sheriff," Powell called. "I don't take kindly to people killin' my friends."

Samson didn't bother to answer, but noted that Powell's voice had come from close by. Once again he searched the shadows for a hint of movement. For a moment, he saw nothing. And then Powell fired four shots in rapid succession, each striking a number of feet from the last, as he tried to flush Samson out. None of the shots had impacted close enough for Samson to worry about, though, and he had been able to ascertain the general area of Powell's location by observing the muzzle flashes as each shot was fired. He figured Powell was about twenty or twenty-five feet away and moving to Samson's right as he closed in.

Samson settled down, took careful aim, and waited for a flicker of movement. An instant later, he fired.

A scream of pain rent the night as his bullet hit home. Then the night was silent.

After waiting a couple of moments to ensure that there'd be no return fire, Samson began to cautiously make his way toward the spot where he believed Powell had fallen.

He found him curled up against a boulder. He'd been hit high in the gut, just below the ribs, and was in a lot of pain. Samson disarmed him, lodging the revolver in the waistband of his denims, before holstering his own weapon. "I think you might make it, Wes," he said then. "If it doesn't take too long to get you into town, that is. Course, how fast or how slow we get movin' is gonna depend on you."

"What d'ya mean?" Powell gasped.

"Talk to me," Samson said. "Tell me who gives the orders in this operation."

"I talk, an' I'm a dead man."

"Maybe," Samson acknowledged with a nod as he casually scanned the trees and stone ridges surrounding the small clearing. He wouldn't feel safe until he knew where Spade was. "You don't talk, though, and you're a dead man for sure. Which way d'you wanna play it?"

"You ain't gonna kill me," Powell concluded.

"Not unless you give me a reason," Samson agreed. "But I ain't gonna save you either."

The moon reemerged, and Samson saw Powell considering him. "You ain't the kind of man to walk away an' let another man die."

"You're wastin' time, Powell." At that moment, there was a noise behind Samson. He spun and dropped to one knee, pulling his gun as he went. Spade Johnson was still slapping for leather when Samson shouted, "Don't!" and fired a warning shot that passed close enough to the drover's gun hand to singe it.

Wide-eyed, Spade slowly raised his hands. He looked dazed, and seemed a bit unsteady on his feet.

At gunpoint, Samson directed him to sit down next to Powell. "You hit, too?" he asked.

Spade shook his head. "You gave my hair a new part, an' knocked me out colder 'n a cucumber for a couple o' minutes, but I ain't hit bad."

Powell was eyeing Samson speculatively. "Somethin' on your mind, Wes?" Samson asked.

"You're mighty fast with that gun, Sheriff," he observed in a voice that was tight with pain. "There ain't many men that can draw like that an' still hit what they're aimin' at. An' I know the names of all the ones that can. So how come I don't know you?"

'Cause I haven't used the name you'd know in over two years. "I don't pull my gun unless I need to, Powell. You know that," Samson said with a shrug. "You don't earn a reputation that way." He turned to Spade. "Powell here needs to see the doc real bad, Spade, and he isn't goin' to until one of you starts talkin'."

"Sure thing, Sheriff." Spade nodded agreeably. He opened his mouth, frowned, closed his mouth, rubbed his whiskered jaw, and stared up at Samson. "Um, what 'xactly is it ya wanted me ta talk 'bout, Sheriff?"

Samson stared at him, wondering if perhaps his bullet might have done a touch more damage than old

Spade was aware of. "I want to know who you're workin' for tonight."

"Oh." Spade nodded. "Well, that's easy. *Him*." Spade jabbed a thumb in Powell's direction.

"Yeah?" Samson's gaze flicked to Powell and then back to Spade. "And who hired *him*?"

Spade frowned. "I dunno." He turned to Powell. "Who hired you, Wes?"

Silence.

"I can wait all night, Powell," Samson reminded him. " 'Course, I don't think *you* can. You workin' for McTaggert?"

Powell jerked as though he'd been shot again. "McTaggert! Hell, no! That bastard doesn't have the guts for somethin' like this. Nor the brains, neither."

Scratch one suspect. "Then who?" Samson demanded. "Earl?" Simon Earl was the man he'd tagged as the second most likely suspect.

Powell pressed against the wound in his stomach. "Come on, Sheriff, I'm bleedin'."

"Yeah," Samson acknowledged. "But you ain't talkin'."

"Go to hell, Chambers!" Pain and anger underscored his words.

"Not yet," Samson said mildly as he pulled a stick of hard candy from his shirt pocket and bit off a chunk. He leaned back against a rock and waited.

"Okay." The word came to him faintly from across the clearing.

"You say something, Wes?"

"I said, okay. I'll tell ya. But then you gotta promise to get me to the doc."

"You've got my word on it," Samson assured him.

"Yeah, it's Earl we're workin' for."

Now they were getting somewhere. "Tell me how he's got this set up."

* * *

The saloon was packed to the brim, and chaotic. Scores of drovers who'd just received their month's pay had descended on the premises to drink, argue, cavort with Cora's girls, and gamble. A handful of old miners had come down from the hills together and were sharing whoppers and a bottle of red-eye at a back table. Phil Marcham hammered out a rendition of "Buffalo Gals" unlike anything Delilah had ever heard, while Miss Dawna Star sang slightly off-key and at the top of her lungs. Dawna, who was one of Cora's upstairs girls, had told Delilah that she believed she'd have obtained fame and stardom with her singing voice if only life had dealt her a different hand. Like many of the women in her profession, Dawna had admitted she did not particularly enjoy her work. It was merely a means to an end: survival.

It had been a week and a half since Delilah had returned to town, and she hadn't deposited anywhere near the amount of money she'd planned to have for Eve by this time. With only a couple of weeks left until the date the mortgage was due, she was starting to feel desperate. She couldn't let her sister down. The thought of Eve possibly losing not only her husband, but also the home she'd grown to love, was too much. How much could one person be expected to endure in a lifetime?

If only Sheriff Chambers would stop coming in to stare at her. Delilah was convinced that he was the reason for her protracted spell of bad luck. She had difficulty concentrating with him watching her. His dark grey eyes seemed to mirror the exact color of a prairie storm front, as though their very color heralded the havoc he could wreak in her life if she let him. She'd learned to read the subtle changes in his eyes, had learned to discern the appreciation for her that she'd not been able to see before. And now that she'd gained that ability, she almost wished she hadn't. For Matt Chambers did not respect the barrier of her widowhood.

Where other men had been content to admire her from afar in respect for the grief she carried for another man, Sheriff Chambers seemed to systematically search for chinks in her armor. His eyes promised a passion that terrified her. Pledged a compassion that tempted her. And promised a pleasure she could not believe in.

He would kiss her again, she knew. Despite the fact that, since that disastrous day of the picnic, he'd scarcely approached her to do more than solicitously walk with her along the boardwalk, or to aid her across the street. And somehow, he doggedly managed to steer their conversation into the realm of the personal, no matter how determinedly she attempted to focus it on business. *His* business.

But tonight he had not shown, and for the first time in ages, the cards were going Delilah's way. Perhaps Sheriff Chambers had finally accepted her assertion that she would not cheat and had decided to go about the business of administering the law elsewhere. "How many cards, Tex?" she asked one of her more regular customers.

"I'll take two, ma'am," he drawled as he discarded the two he didn't want.

Delilah finished dealing the hand. "Dealer takes one," she murmured, and checked her hand.

Hallelujah! She had a full house, kings over jacks. It didn't get much better than that. She placed her bet and won the hand for the fourth time that evening. And the night was still young.

The evening continued to go well, although Delilah caught herself glancing repeatedly at the spot at the bar where Matt usually stood. Was something wrong? she wondered. She'd grown so accustomed to his presence, aggravating though it was, that without him there she felt as though something was missing. Finally, just before midnight, when Delilah's head had begun to pound with a headache from the incessant noise, she glanced up and he was there.

His clothing was dusty and dirty. There were lines of fatigue around his mouth, and a full day's beard shadowed his cheeks. Although darkened by weariness, his storm-hued eyes rested on her with a hint of admiration and the promise of passion and danger. Oh, how that aura of danger made her feel alive, made her pulse quicken and her blood sing. And despite her dislike of the man himself, of his arrogance, and despite his distrust of her, Delilah had to concede that there was little she found as exhilarating as sparring with Sheriff Chambers.

Somehow tonight the aura of danger he exuded was amplified, drawing her and unsettling her at the same time. And yet in another way, he was more appealing than ever. For something within him screamed of *need*—for comfort, caring, a woman's touch—and a part of Delilah she'd never known existed responded to that elemental call.

But she couldn't allow herself to falter. She could not allow a man into her life. Most assuredly not one like Matt Chambers. What she needed was to escape the turmoil of these smoky premises, get some fresh air and a good night's sleep.

"Last hand, gentlemen," she warned. "I'm afraid I'm going to have to call it a night."

There was a brief rumble of discontent, but nothing serious, and their disgruntlement was quickly forgotten.

Delilah focused on the hand, refusing to so much as

glance at the sheriff in the hope that she'd be able to ignore his presence enough to win this last hand too. She needed it, desperately, if she was to obtain even a portion of the money she'd planned to have made by now.

To her immense relief, it worked. Delilah rose from the table, bid her customers a good night, and then looked around for Poopsy before remembering that she'd left the little dog in her hotel room tonight. Mrs. Schmidt had given Poopsy a huge beef bone to which delicious scraps of meat still clung, and the dog had decided that she'd much prefer the bone to the saloon. Delilah certainly couldn't blame her.

Delilah headed for Cora's office—she was usually tallying profits at this time of night—to bid her farewell. "Could I speak with you a moment before you go, Delilah?" Cora asked as Delilah poked her head in the door.

"Certainly." She stepped into the room, closing the door quietly behind her.

"Have a chair," Cora invited, and then waited until Delilah had seated herself before proceeding. "I've noticed that something seems to be bothering you, Delilah. Do you want to tell me about it?"

For an instant, Delilah toyed with the idea of unburdening herself, but in so doing she would betray Eve's confidence, and she couldn't do that. And, despite the fact that she and Cora were fast becoming friends, she didn't yet know her well enough to talk to her about Sheriff Chambers's determined pursuit. So she shook her head. "Thank you. But it's nothing I can't handle."

Cora considered her gravely with her astute brown-eyed gaze, and then smiled gently. "If that's the way you want it. However, I want to point out that the level of profit coming from my gaming table is not quite what you led me to expect."

Delilah shifted uncomfortably. "I haven't been having the best of luck lately," she conceded. "But tonight went well. I'm hoping that's an indication of a turn for the better."

Cora regarded her silently. Finally she said, "Me too. And I don't mean that just for my sake, Delilah. I'll have your cut ready for you in the morning, as usual."

"Tomorrow is Sunday," Delilah reminded her.

She smiled. "I know, but I'll be here regardless, so you can come by if you like."

Delilah nodded and rose. "Thank you, Cora. And don't worry, I'm fine. I'll see you tomorrow then, all right?"

"Sure. Get a good night's sleep, honey. You look like you need it."

A minute later, Delilah headed for the main door of the saloon. Since there was no option but to walk past the bar, she prepared herself to very composedly pass the sheriff. She'd nod in acknowledgment perhaps, but she had no intention of speaking to him. He, however, forced a change in her plans.

"Hold up a minute, Mrs. Sterne," he said. He'd resumed calling her Mrs. Sterne when in public. "I'll walk you back to the hotel, since I'm goin' that way anyway."

"Thank you, Sheriff, but there's really no need," Delilah protested. "Stay and finish your drink."

He tossed back the whiskey remaining in his glass in a single swallow and said, "I'm finished."

Furious, Delilah could only nod and resume her walk toward the door as if she couldn't have cared less whether Matt joined her or not. But of course he did, grasping her elbow solicitously in the process. The heat of his hand burned through the fabric of her gown, deriding her guise of indifference.

Once they'd gone a short distance from the saloon and the clamor began to fade, Delilah heard Matt take a deep breath. "Nice night," he commented.

She looked up at the sky overhead with its myriad diamond-like stars. It *was* a nice night, but she refused to be lulled into complacency. "It was." The tone of her voice left no doubt as to her meaning, but Matt ignored the bait.

Seeking to change the subject, Delilah asked, "Did you find the rustlers yet?"

"Sure did. I've got them locked up in my jail right now. All except the one that Doc Hale's got, that is."

"Thank heavens!" Delilah halted to face him. "Were any of the cattle recovered?"

"Some, but not near as many as were stolen. Seems like they probably shipped some already."

"Were any Devil's Fork cattle amongst them?"

He shrugged. "It was too dark and too late to try to sort out the brands. Wilkes will be goin' on out to do that tomorrow."

Delilah nodded, taking in the lines of fatigue around his eyes, and resumed walking. "Is that why you were late tonight?"

Silence, and then, "Why, Mrs. Sterne, you didn't miss me by any chance, did you?"

"Don't be ridiculous!"

They came to the edge of the boardwalk and Matt gripped her elbow more firmly, as though to support her when she stepped off to cross the street. Heavens! One might assume her completely incapable of navigating the vast distance between boardwalks without the assistance of a man! A tart statement to that affect hovered on the edge of her tongue, but she merely tugged her arm from his grasp and quickened her step in the hope that he'd get the message.

"Is something wrong, Delilah?" The humor underlying his tone suggested a combination of intimacy and banter.

"Wrong? What could be wrong, Sheriff? You know how very much I enjoy your company."

" 'Bout as much as that dog of yours enjoys rain?" he ventured.

Delilah had to bite her lip to keep from smiling. Blast the man! He did have a certain appeal. "Less," she said. "Much less."

"I aim to change that."

"Really?" she asked. "I didn't know you knew any magic."

"Magic?"

"Of course, Sheriff. If I remember my mother's Irish tales of enchantment correctly, there are only two ways to change my opinion of you. Either you become someone else, or you use sorcery on me. Both options require magic."

"I see." Samson considered the woman at his side. Even in the moonlight, she was beautiful. His eyes slowly tracked over her, touching upon her face, her very kissable lips, moving over the fat sausage curl that fell artfully from the crown of curls upon her head to rest upon her right shoulder, down to her breasts. Perfect breasts, neither too small nor too large. "Well, I think I might know some sorcery," he murmured.

They halted in front of the hotel, and Delilah looked up at him. There was a slight frown between her brows. "What kind of sorcery?" Samson was staggered by the innocence in her eyes.

How could a married woman be so innocent of the ways of men? Of the courting rituals and sexual innuendo? Of kissing?

"Why don't you let me accompany you to the church social on Wednesday night, and perhaps I'll tell you," he said.

Delilah stared up at him. "You never give up, do you?"

He shook his head. "Never was a quitter." Especially when it came to something he wanted as much as he wanted Delilah. "We're meant for each other."

"What you mean is that *you* think I'm meant to be your mistress, isn't it?"

Samson wasn't stepping into that mess again, so he stayed silent. It didn't seem to matter, though. Just the memory of that conversation seemed to make her mad as a wet hen all over again. Her lips thinned. Her eyes flashed. And, even in the moonlight, he could see the color in her cheeks deepen. She sure was pretty.

"No answer, Sheriff? Well, I guess it doesn't matter, since you made it perfectly clear the other day what you thought. So my answer is: no, thank you, Sheriff Chambers. I have no desire to be insulted again. Neither do I have any desire to listen to another of your lectures on the evils of my gambling life. I'm here to make the money my sister needs to keep her ranch out of the hands of the bank, and then I'm moving on."

Samson filed away that piece of information for future reference. It seemed that the ranch wasn't as financially sound as Tom had believed when he'd given Samson the money to hire Colton. But the money was already in an account at the bank in Colton's name, so there wasn't much he could do about it now. He returned his attention to the woman at his side and the goal he had in mind.

"Will you go with me if I give you my word I won't lecture you or insult you in any way?"

Delilah gave a rather indelicate snort. "I don't believe you."

"Blast it all, woman!" Samson said, losing his patience. He didn't know how to woo her, let alone win her. "I can't be that bad."

"On the contrary, Sheriff, I find you insufferable. You profess to admire independence in a woman, yet you say a lady should not gamble, while at the same time you have no such strictures against gentlemen. That's an unfair and rather old-fashioned double standard for this modern age, wouldn't you say?"

"Old-fashioned!" Samson couldn't believe his ears. Damnation! He wasn't yet thirty years old. How in blazes could he be old-fashioned? "You think I'm *old-fashioned*?"

Delilah nodded. "Most definitely. And a bit of a hypocrite as well, I believe. You see nothing wrong in telling me exactly what is required of me to be an acceptable lady, when you yourself fail entirely to act as a gentleman should. In fact, as I believe I once told you, your manners are more suited to the bordellos, sir."

Damn, the woman had a tart tongue! "Anything else?" he asked quietly, warningly. Delilah, however, did not know him well enough yet to take heed.

"Yes, sir, as a matter of fact there is. I not only have no desire to accompany you to the social, but I am completely indifferent to your presence in my life. Were I to choose a male companion to accompany me to the church social, I would choose a *gentleman*. So, *please* leave me alone."

"Indifferent!" Now *that* hurt. The blamed woman had about as much snap and sting in her tongue as a bullwhip! But if there was one thing she was not, it was indifferent to him. And he intended to prove it. Before she could protest, he pulled her into his arms. Whether from surprise or because this time she knew what to expect, her mouth was open; ready for his invasion. He took it without hesitation.

Remembering his determination to overcome her fear of men, Samson immediately gentled his embrace, simply holding her against him as his hands roamed the contours of her slender back, memorizing it even as he committed to memory the shape of her mouth. The way her lips clung to his. The way she tasted. Just holding her was heaven. But it wasn't enough. His sex began to strain demandingly against the confines of his denim trousers. But he maintained rigid control. Until . . . uh-oh.

Lost in sensation, knowing only that she wanted, needed more, Delilah raised her arms to his shoulders. His too-long hair brushed the back of her hands with a warm, subtle caress. Heated satin against night-chilled skin. It felt so good. Turning her fingers up, she ran them through the soft hair at the nape of his neck, learning its texture. He groaned deep in his throat, an animalistic needy rumble, and everything within her went still as she strove to interpret the sound.

Had it been a response to her simple touch?

What would happen if . . . Slowly, cautiously, she began to kiss him back, guiding her tongue forward to stroke his as he'd been stroking the insides of her mouth. She was rewarded by a reflexive tightening of his embrace and another deep male rumble, almost a growl.

For the first time in her life, Delilah examined the possibility that, in male-female relationships, women, too, had power: the power to give pleasure or withhold it. It was a concept she'd never imagined, and wasn't yet sure she believed.

He lifted his mouth from hers for a fraction of a second as he sprinkled kisses over her forehead and temples, and Delilah was vaguely aware that they were moving. In the next instant, she felt the firmness of the hotel wall against her back and realized that he had moved them more deeply into the shadows. Upon the heels of that observation came the realization that she was allowing herself to be kissed, very thoroughly, on a public street. No matter that it was after midnight and almost everybody was abed. *Someone* might see them. But before she could even form the words of a protest, his mouth was back on hers and the brief flash of reason fled.

At that moment in time, there was nothing Delilah wanted more than the masterful possession of his mouth on hers. Nothing she cared about more than the intoxicating sensation of feeling the fluid steel of his big muscular body beneath her hands. Nothing she needed more than that brief moment of feeling her heart beat in unison with another—just this once no longer alone. Her breasts swelled and tingled, aching with a peculiar heaviness she didn't understand. Instinctively, she moved closer to him, pressing her throbbing bosom more firmly against his hard chest, snuggling closer to the furnace-like heat of his big body. It felt so good to be held in his firm, but gentle embrace. So good. . . .

And then, she froze as she felt something else. Its hardness pressed insistently against the soft flesh of her abdomen. Fear poured in upon her and she wrenched her mouth from his. Oh, God! How could she have forgotten? "Let me go, please." Her words were little more than a whisper. He didn't respond. "Please!" she begged a little more desperately.

As though he sensed the source of her sudden fear, he tried to comfort her. "I won't hurt you, Delilah," he murmured as he rubbed her back with soothingly warm hands. "You have my word on that." She made no response. Could find no words to say. "You believe me, don't you?" he asked.

Hesitantly, because she thought it might make him release her more quickly, she nodded. But in truth, she didn't believe him. He might not plan to hurt her—not the way Jacob Sterne had—but he would hurt her. How could he help it? The size of . . . that part of him made it incomprehensible that it could be otherwise. How she wished that she could accept that fact as other women seemed to. Perhaps it was the warmth and gentleness they found in their husbands' arms that made the other part of lovemaking bearable. She didn't know. But she did know that she simply couldn't accept it. Everything within her rebelled at the mere thought of that horrible invasion of her body. All she could think of was escape.

"I have to go, Matt," she said as she slowly, unsteadily stepped out of his embrace. Oh, Lord, she had to get away. Away from this man. Away from this town. Away from . . . the horrible conflicting emotions that threatened to tear her apart. "Goodnight," she managed to whisper.

"Goodnight, Delilah." His smooth baritone was so gentle, so seductive, that tears stung her eyes as she forced herself to turn away. Her knees trembled, but somehow she found the strength to walk toward the hotel doors. She half expected him to say something to stay her, but he didn't, and a moment later she shut the hotel door behind her with a sense of relief . . . and despair.

Slowly, with renewed exhaustion weighing down her limbs, she climbed the stairs to her room.

The next morning, Samson was in the process of washing up before breakfast when there was a knock at his door. Turning, he frowned at it. After a nearly sleepless night, he'd slept a little later than usual. The result was that he'd missed the church service—which he usually attended. Still, it was early for callers.

Continuing to frown with a combination of curiosity and impatience, he shrugged into the shirt he'd discarded over the back of a chair the previous night before falling into bed and, while buttoning the garment, answered the door. Mrs. Williamson, one of the town's most prominent matrons, stood on the stoop with one of her marriageable daughters, Honoria, at her side and a bevy of four or five slightly less forthright examples of Red Rock's ladies arrayed at her back.

"Good morning, ladies," Samson said.

Mrs. Williamson tensed slightly upon catching sight of his partially exposed chest, but did not allow herself to be deterred from her course. Fixing her gaze firmly upon his face, she said, "Good day to you, Sheriff Chambers. We were wondering if we might have a word with you?"

Samson glanced at the sparsely furnished interior of the log cabin the town had provided for his use. Not only was it untidy at the moment, but there were only three ladder-back chairs to be had. "Now's really not a good time, Mrs. Williamson. I'm afraid I don't have enough chairs."

"It won't take long," she persisted. "And we're quite willing to stand."

Reluctantly, Samson stepped back. "Then by all means, come in," he said drily.

He observed their expressions as they stepped into his humble home, trying to see it through their eyes. It was quite obviously the home of a bachelor. Mrs. Williamson noted yesterday's unwashed dishes still stacked in the basin on the table and raised her nose a fraction of an inch. After briefly making eye contact with him, Honoria Williamson's cheeks flamed and her gaze dropped to the rough planking of the floorboards, where it seemed permanently fixed. Mrs. Osbourne's examination found the open door of his bedroom, where his unmade bed was in plain sight, and her cheeks took on a flush—doubtlessly caused by the direction of her own thoughts. The other ladies centered their attention on him unwaveringly.

He leaned against the wall and tucked his thumbs into the outside edges of his jeans pockets. "So ladies," he said with a nod as they stood in a semicircle around him. "What can I do for you?"

Mrs. Williamson seemed to be their self-appointed spokesperson. "Sir, it has come to our attention that you seem to be spending an unsuitable amount of time in, shall we say, pursuits inappropriate to one of your position in the community."

"You don't say," he managed to return mildly as he rubbed his chin thoughtfully. The rasp of his callused palm across his unshaven jaw was the only sound in the room. If there was one thing he didn't like, it was other people telling him what was acceptable for him. Abruptly he recalled Delilah's words of the night before, and felt a twinge of guilt. Okay, so he could admit that he understood Delilah's feelings on the subject a bit better now.

Meeting his gaze, Mrs. Williamson took a hasty step back, and Samson realized he must not have controlled the evidence of his irritation as completely as he had supposed. Nevertheless, it soon became obvious that Mrs. Williamson wasn't about to be deterred so easily. "I do say, sir."

"And what pursuits *exactly* are we talking about?"

Mrs. Williamson's thin lips narrowed even further. "Why, the pursuit of that little trollop . . ." Samson's gaze sharpened and Mrs. Williamson hastily amended herself. ". . . er, widow that has taken up residence at the saloon, of all places. She is a lady of questionable character, Sheriff."

"I believe she has taken up residence at the hotel, not the saloon, madam," Samson corrected her in a deceptively mild tone. "Now let me get this straight. You ladies feel that it is inappropriate for me, as a fine upstanding member of this community," unfortunately his sarcasm seemed to be lost on them, "to pursue a lady of Mrs. Sterne's . . . um, *questionable character*?" He raised a brow to confirm her wording, and when she nodded, he repeated, "Mrs. Sterne's questionable character. Is that about it?"

"Yes, Sheriff, it is," Mrs. Williamson responded, emboldened once again. "Why, she gambles, sir! And the Lord knows she associates with riffraff of every sort in that . . . that *saloon*." The way she said the final word left no doubt in his mind exactly what she thought of such places. "It's unseemly. We had expected you to run her out of town long before now. Instead you're . . ."

"I can't run her out of town for being a gambler, ma'am," he interrupted. "It's a legal profession."

"But Sheriff . . ." Mrs. Osbourne sputtered in defense of her friend.

Samson held up a hand to forestall her. "If Mrs. Sterne cheats, I can run her out. But so far, ladies, she has proven to be the first *honest* dealer this town has seen in some time."

"So we just have to put up with this . . . this *woman* luring decent menfolk into that saloon to lose their hard-earned money," Mrs. Gage spoke from the background, the apparent failure of their cause giving her the courage to speak up.

Samson made a mental note to check to see if Larry Gage was spending a bit too much time at the gaming table. "From what I can see, ma'am, she's not doing much in the way of luring." *Certainly not where I'm concerned.* "And there isn't a man in there that has a gun to his head. Least none that I noticed."

"But surely, sir, just because we have to allow her to work here does not mean that you have to . . . to consort with her." Mrs. Williamson returned to the essence of her purpose. She, after all, had five marriageable daughters, as she'd pointed out to Samson on a number of occasions.

Inwardly, Samson grimaced. He had hoped that he'd deflected that course of questioning by focusing on the gambling aspect of the conversation. But he had an advantage in having been raised by a very Christian mother. "Mrs. Williamson, if you saw a lost sheep, would you not consider it your Christian duty to return it to the flock?"

Perceiving the direction his question was about to take her, she frowned, but could apparently think of no way to answer the question without seeming uncharitable. "Of course, but . . ."

"Mrs. Sterne is a lady with a Christian upbringing, ma'am. When her husband died, leaving her penniless,"—he was embroidering, for he had no idea what financial state her husband had left her in—"she was forced to make her way with the only skill she had. Would you do less?"

She stared at him, not prepared to give up hope yet of snaring him for Honoria. And he knew she certainly wasn't prepared to accept Delilah. But he hadn't left her much maneuvering room. "So your intentions are honorable, Sheriff? And you intend to put a stop to her gambling?"

Samson nodded as inspiration struck. The question had given him an opening to escape unwanted attentions. "Completely honorable," he assured her.

Mrs. Osbourne sighed in obvious relief and nudged her neighbor. "There, Eliza, what did I tell you? No man would permit his wife to gamble."

Samson stared at her. *His wife?* Somehow the words sounded distressingly appealing when associated with his mental picture of Delilah. *His* wife?

Uh-oh.

Chapter Ten

Delilah had spent the night pacing her room, only dropping into bed, fully clothed, and falling into a fitful sleep as dawn began to lighten the eastern sky. Now, as sunlight poured into the room and over her face, she awoke and groggily blinked at the clock on the nightstand. Good heavens! It was nearly noon. She couldn't remember ever having slept that late in her life. With a groan, she rose to wash her face and to make an attempt at pulling herself together. It didn't help. Once again, Matt Chambers invaded her thoughts. Damn the man! Why wasn't he discouraged in the face of her widowhood, as other men were?

Tears stung her eyes. She was too tired to deal with this. Too tired to find the answers she needed.

All she knew was that she had to get away. Away from Matt and his overpowering, seductive presence. Away from his town. Away from her own confused emotions concerning him. Simply *away*. But she couldn't go, because Eve still needed her. And if she didn't soon start earning some decent money with her gambling, she wouldn't have a hope of helping Eve make the mortgage payment on the ranch. In fact, it was almost too late already. She'd have to win a considerable sum every night from now until the date the mortgage was due to help as she'd promised she would.

She just didn't know what to do.

Unconsciously, Delilah resumed her pacing.

If she'd only managed to make the money she'd planned by now, then perhaps she could have left Red Rock. Although she'd have felt guilty for not being near to give Eve the emotional support she needed to face Tom's illness, at least Delilah would have been secure in the knowledge that her sister would not lose her home. But Delilah hadn't made the money because she just couldn't seem to work with Matt Chambers watching her like a hawk.

"Drat the man!" she muttered. At every turn his name arose as the source of her troubles.

Having given up on diverting her mistress from her thoughts during the night, Poopsy now watched Delilah from her bed with a disconsolate expression. Delilah knew the little dog, sensing her distress, wanted reassurance, but she just didn't have any to give right now.

Pausing, Delilah looked in the mirror and gasped at the change in herself. Huge bluish shadows marred the flesh beneath her eyes. A frown line etched the normally smooth skin between her brows. And her typically pale complexion was downright pasty, not a trace of color remained. She didn't understand how a man, any man, could have this effect on her. She was a Sinclair, after all. She was made of sturdy stuff. But in the short time she'd known him, Matt Chambers had invaded her mind and her life.

Her stomach rumbled loudly, and she realized she

was hungry despite her inner turmoil. She welcomed the interruption. It was another direction in which to focus her thoughts, for all the worry and pacing was getting her precisely nowhere.

She'd put on some fresh clothing, take Poopsy out for a walk, and then go for breakfast. Or rather lunch.

Three-quarters of an hour later, carrying Poopsy in the crook of her arm, Delilah made her way into the dining room. It was rather more crowded than she'd expected. A good many families seemed to have decided to treat themselves to Sunday dinner at the hotel. As she stood in the entrance seeking a small table for herself, a few speculative glances were flung her way. Over the years, however, Delilah had grown accustomed to the way tongues invariably wagged about a young widow turned gambler, so she ignored them. She had never been a really gregarious person anyway, and traveling as much as she had precluded making lasting friendships.

"Mrs. Sterne—" A sudden loud call startled her, and she turned her head to the right to locate its source. At a table near the front of the restaurant, a man had risen to his feet to wave at her. To her surprise, she realized it was Mr. Pike. "I'd be right honored if you'd join me for lunch, ma'am." He indicated the empty chair across from him. "I'd hate to see such a pretty lady go hungry."

And, in truth, Delilah realized that there were no vacant tables. "Thank you, sir," she said with a smile as she moved to join him. "That's very kind of you."

He shook his head as he moved around the table to pull out a chair for her. "No, ma'am. Not kind at all. My reasons are purely selfish. I just wanted the chance to sit across the table from such a pretty lady."

Delilah smiled and settled Poopsy on the floor at her feet, where she could unobtrusively feed her tidbits. She noticed Pike's collection of WANTED posters lying on the table to his right. Nodding toward them, she asked, "Have you had any luck with your search?"

"Not yet, ma'am. I heard this morning that the sheriff brought in a couple of rustlers last night. Thought I'd mosey on over there after I eat and take a look. I figure it could be Morgan and maybe Clark too. If so, it might be that I'll have to set my sights somewheres else."

"No luck with that other one either?" she asked.

He shuffled his stack of posters, placing one on top and turning it toward Delilah. "Towers?" he asked, pointing to the picture. She nodded. "Naw," he said, shaking his head. "It's the dangdest thing. He seems to look a mite familiar to folks round here, but most swear up an' down they never seen him. Almost makes me wonder if he might have kin in these parts or somethin'. I ran into that down Arizona way once. Trailed a fella nigh on a month, 'cause folks kept sayin' they'd seen him. Then, when I finally caught up with him, turned out I'd been chasin' the cousin of the fella I wanted to find."

"I take it the cousin wasn't wanted?"

"No, ma'am. Wasn't worth a penny. And ta top it off, he hadn't seen the man I was after in more 'n two years." Pike shrugged. "But sometimes it goes like that. It's part o' the job."

At that moment, Mrs. Schmidt approached the table with a plate for Pike. "Missus Sterne, I didn't know you vere comink or I vould haf brought you a plate too." She set Pike's plate down with a smile and looked back at Delilah. "You vant dinner, no? It is roast turkey today."

Delilah's stomach rumbled at the mere mention of food. And *turkey*. She couldn't remember the last time she'd had turkey. "Oh, my, that sounds lovely. Yes, please."

Frieda smiled her friendly gap-toothed smile, and

winked. "I be right back." Delilah wondered where she got the energy to cook and serve so many people every day. Oh, she knew that Frieda's husband, Marc, did a lot of the cooking, and her son, Erich, helped with serving the guests and washing up. Still, it was a lot of work, even split between three people. But when Delilah had suggested once that they might hire help, Frieda had very decisively said, "No, missus. Zis is a family business."

Despite his rough appearance and roving lifestyle, Pike obviously knew his manners. He politely ignored his dinner and continued to regale her with tales about his work as a bounty hunter until Frieda Schmidt returned with a plate for Delilah. Then, conversation waned as they both delved into the delicious meal. In the silence, Delilah stared sightlessly at the poster still laying on the table and found her thoughts returning once again to the intrepid Sheriff Chambers.

The kiss they had shared last night had been . . . wonderful, and terribly frightening. Instinct told her that she was in more danger from Matt Chambers than she had been from any man since Sterne. Yet Matt was nothing like Sterne. And perhaps that was exactly where the danger lay: in the subtle seductiveness of his caring attitude and the erotic power of his kisses. A knot clenched in her stomach at the mere thought of what he wanted from her. And yet she found herself yearning for the gentle warmth of his embrace. Remembering the intoxicating pressure of his lips on hers. Visualizing his hard masculine features.

She blinked to dispel them, but they obstinately remained. Then, slowly, Delilah came to the realization that the features she's been seeing in her mind's eye were actually quite similar to those in the likeness on the poster of the wanted murderer, Samson Towers. *Very* similar. Almost identical, in fact.

Her heart skipped a beat, and her gaze sharpened. A coincidence, surely?

Once more, she superimposed the image of Matt Chambers over that of Samson Towers. If one removed the large walrus mustache from Samson Towers's image . . . it could be. The shape of the face was the same. The hairline was the same. Even the contour of the eyes was the same. Towers's nose looked a bit broader than Matt's, but that could have been an error on the part of the artist.

She read the description again:

> Samson Towers is a big man in both height and figure, being more than six feet tall with a muscular build. His size seldom goes unremarked. His eyes are dark, either black or dark brown. He has no distinguishing marks or scars.

With the exception of the eye color, which again could be just an error on the part of the observers, the description fit Matt Chambers.

Was it possible?

But with each passing second, Delilah grew more certain. How a wanted killer could have become the sheriff of Red Rock, she didn't know. But she'd have bet her last dollar that Samson Towers and Matt Chambers were one and the same man. The depiction in the poster was not that good, for the mustache altered his appearance considerably, concealing his upper lip entirely. Undoubtedly, nobody had yet put it together because they didn't expect to see it. After all, who would suspect a sheriff?

The question was, now that *she'd* put it together, what should she do about it?

She'd been raised to believe in justice. Any man guilty of murder, no matter how nice he might seem, had to stand trial for his crime. It was the way things were. But . . . an image of Matt being hanged invaded her thoughts, and she almost choked. No! If he was innocent—which, knowing him, she was almost certain he was—then a trial would simply clear his name and set him free. *That* was what needed to be done.

She paused in mid bite as she realized she just might have the means to expel Matt Chambers from her life, *and* help her sister. Could she do it?

She squirmed inwardly at the mere thought of turning him in. Had she been faced merely by her own desire to be quit of him, then she would not even have considered it. But . . . there was Eve to consider. With Matt out of the picture, perhaps Delilah's luck would turn.

But even if she did turn him in, how could she go about it?

If she told Pike, she had little doubt that he'd take advantage of the information. And Delilah would get Matt Chambers, or rather Samson Towers, out of her life. Which was what she wanted. She ignored the twinge in her chest and hastily propelled her thoughts onward. But even with Matt gone, she was no longer certain that she had the time to win the money she needed to help Eve and Tom. And she'd promised to help.

She lay her fork on her plate as she considered the WANTED poster once again. *One thousand dollars reward for the return of Samson Towers—alive—to the authorities in Cedar Crossing, Wyoming.* Surely she should be entitled to a portion of that if she supplied information that led to his capture. How else could she get the money to help Eve save the Devil's Fork?

"Is something wrong with yer dinner, ma'am?" Pike interrupted her thoughts.

"Hmm? Oh, no, it's delicious. I'm just . . . not as hungry as I'd thought."

"There's carrot pudding for dessert," he informed her. "Might want to save some room for that."

"Yes," Delilah responded distractedly. Picking up her fork, she began to pick at her meal once more.

She simply was not capable of returning Towers to Wyoming on her own. Pike *was*, but she was under no illusions as to the nature of his character. He was a bounty hunter. He would do the work, collect the reward, and keep it. The thought of offering her a portion of the reward would never occur to him. At any rate, doing things that way would take too long. She needed the money within two weeks.

Poopsy nudged her leg, and Delilah automatically leaned down to offer her a small piece of turkey.

For a moment, she was appalled at the direction her thoughts had taken. Not only was she considering the betrayal of a man for whom she had feelings—confused though they were—but she was contemplating doing Pike out of the reward for a man he'd obviously spent considerable time tracking. Perhaps she should just tell him and let him take Matt back.

Matt.

Lord, she'd begun to care for him despite her fear of getting too close to him. But if he was innocent of the charges, he would be freed. She had to believe that. And if he wasn't . . . if he wasn't innocent, then he was not the man she thought he was; he was not the man she had begun to care for.

And letting Pike take him back to Wyoming would do nothing to help Eve. There had to be a way to turn this into a positive thing all the way around. A way to help Eve and Tom save their ranch. A way for Matt to face justice and clear his name. And a way to free herself from Matt's attentions, allowing her to return to her safe, untouched existence.

And slowly, as she ate her delicious meal without really tasting a morsel, Delilah came up with a plan. It was risky. It might not work. But she had to try. Knowing that it was too late to accomplish her plan that day, she resigned herself to waiting for the morning, but refused to allow herself to falter in her decision.

It was the best way. The *only* way to accomplish all that had to be done.

Dawn the next day found Delilah at the livery stable putting Jackpot's bridle on and coaxing him from his stall. She'd left Poopsy in the care of Mrs. Schmidt for the day, and had managed to escape without telling the gregarious woman where she was going. Or why.

As she put the saddle on his back, Jackpot nudged her shoulder and Delilah produced an apple for him. It was a bit wrinkled and soft from having been stored in the hotel's root cellar over the winter, but the horse didn't seem to mind. He munched happily while Delilah cinched the girth and slid her Winchester into the scabbard.

She was just mounting when Mr. Metter's voice came from the shadows behind her. "You're up right early this mornin', ma'am."

She sighed inwardly, wishing she'd been just a few minutes faster, then turned to face him. "Good morning, Mr. Metter."

"Mornin', ma'am. Where you off to?"

"I just have a couple of errands to run in Butte City. I'll be back by nightfall."

He frowned. "If you don't mind me sayin' so, ma'am, that's a long way to ride for a couple of errands. Unless you turn around an' come back near as soon as you get there, you'll be hard-pressed to make it back 'fore dark."

Delilah mounted and looked down at him. "I'll be fine, Mr. Metter. Really." And she kicked Jackpot into motion, ducking beneath the stable door, before the well-intentioned stableman could delay her further. Within moments, she'd cleared the confines of Red Rock and was on the road to Butte. Not allowing herself to think about what she was doing—it was the *right* thing after all—she thought instead about Eve and Tom.

She remembered the laughing young man who'd swept her sister off her feet. At the time, she and Eve had been living just south of Salmon, Idaho, in the village of Bragg Creek. A small one-room cabin had been their home, and they were taking in laundry and mending to make enough money to survive. It had been just over a year since their father's death, and she and Eve had just been leaving the mercantile when Tom, who was talking over his shoulder to his uncle, had run into them—quite literally.

From the beginning, he'd had eyes only for Eve. Love at first sight. After apologizing profusely, he'd introduced himself with gallant flair before permitting them to pass and go on their way.

Then, later that night, he'd shown up on their doorstep—the Lord only knew how he'd managed to find them—asking if he might call on Miss Eve Sinclair before his heart broke for lack of sight of her. Despite Delilah's determination to protect her younger sister from men, she found herself quite taken with young Tom Cameron, and agreed to allow him to call while he was in the area visiting his relatives.

He'd stayed for a little more than a month, but during that time Delilah and Eve came to know him well. A laughing, carefree young man, he was also hard-working. After saving every cent he'd earned over the last four years, he had just purchased a piece of virgin property in Montana on which he planned to build the ranch he'd dreamed of all his life.

It turned out that, when he'd run into Eve and Delilah, he was in the area to buy reliable stock and gain a bit of advice from his Uncle Brady about the ranching business. Serendipitously, though, he'd also fallen in love during his stay, and when he left to return to Montana and his new ranch, he'd taken Eve with him as his wife.

Delilah shook her head. The possibility that he might die still didn't seem quite real to her. Life was so cruel at times. Closing her eyes briefly, she sent a prayer winging heavenward that the good Lord could find it in his heart to provide a miracle. Not just for Tom, but for Eve, who had already lost so much in her young life.

A short time later, Delilah took note of her surroundings and realized that she would reach Butte before much longer. Once there . . . but she refused to think about it. If she did, she wasn't sure she'd have the courage to go through with it, and she needed to. For Eve's sake as well as her own.

She returned to her memories. It was upon finding herself alone after Eve's marriage that Delilah had decided that preserving her reputation was not worth all the pain of dry, cracked, and bleeding hands, stabbed fingers, and strained eyes. What reason, after all, was there for preserving one's reputation but to attract a marriageable man? Since she had no such desire, and Eve was gone, Delilah saw no sense in maintaining the facade. So she'd turned her eyes toward the saloons, and never looked back. As a young, attractive widow, she'd been accepted surprisingly easily.

It hadn't been easy for her, though. The first time that she'd stepped into the shadowy and mysterious confines of a saloon and approached the gaming table, she'd been so nervous that she had almost retched all over the dealer. It hadn't helped that the dealer was an ex-lawman with a fast draw and a reputation to match. But, for herself, Delilah had found him to be a gentleman.

Remembering the person she'd been then, Delilah smiled and shook her head. Life was exceedingly strange at times. Looking back, she could clearly see the major turning points in her life. The moments that had propelled her in new directions, gradually forging her into the person she was today. Yet at the time those moments had been nothing more than trials to be lived through or decisions to be made.

If she had never walked into that first saloon, where would she be today, she wondered.

And then, there was no more time for thought as she came to Butte City. It was something of a culture shock, returning to the booming industrialized mining town after spending so much time in Red Rock. No less than ten or fifteen blocks in the downtown area consisted of three-and four-story brick buildings, some with fanciful trim and arched windows. Electrical lighting had come to Butte, and tall poles belonging to the Brush Electric Light and Power Company lined a number of the streets in the business district. Horse-drawn carriages of every description lined the streets and avenues as top-hatted gentlemen went about the business of making money. From all appearances, a good deal of money. Of course, it was rumored that there were more than 200 mines being worked in the area at the moment. Copper mines like the Anaconda and the Parrot, silver mines like the Bluebird and the Lexington, which was said to ship $60,000 in bullion every month. That was a lot of money. No wonder the city looked so prosperous.

Delilah's gambler's heart beat just a little faster, but

she ignored it. What she sought at the moment was not a saloon, but a telegraph office. For what she was about, she couldn't risk using the telegraph office in Red Rock.

She passed a number of banks, hotels, insurance companies, and laundries. Even a jewelry store which she would have loved to have browsed through, but dared not take the time. A beautiful blue gown displayed in the window of one ready-made clothing store slowed her as she gazed at it with envious eyes. She passed the post office, where a sign in the window reminded customers that postage was now two cents per ounce. And then, finally, a little further on, a telegraph office.

Dismounting, she secured Jackpot to a hitching rail with a convenient water trough beneath it and, as the horse drank, she went inside. The telegraph office was quite dark, being fashioned almost entirely of wood, probably mahogany, and it took a moment for Delilah's eyes to adjust to the gloom. The first thing she noticed was the young man behind the counter. He wore a white shirt, thin black necktie, and a small black cap. The second thing she noticed was a strong smell of peppermint. "Afternoon, ma'am," the young man greeted her.

Delilah smiled. "Good afternoon. I'd like to send a telegraph to the sheriff's office in Cedar Crossing, Wyoming."

"Sure thing, ma'am." He placed a piece of paper and a pencil on the desk for her. "You just write out what you want to say, and I'll get it out right away."

Delilah went still. She hadn't thought about what to say. Looking around a little desperately, she spied a small table and chair in the corner. "Is it all right if I do it over there?" she asked. "I . . . I'm not certain how to word it."

The young man nodded. "You just let me know when you're ready." He immediately returned to whatever task he'd been doing when she entered. Slowly, thoughtfully, Delilah walked over to the table, sheet of paper and pencil in hand.

After much deliberation, wasting more time than she could afford, she finally came up with:

> Have information regarding S. Towers. Stop. How much reward for details leading to capture? Stop. Will wait two hours for reply. Stop. Delilah Sterne.

She gave it to the young man, paid for its transmission, and then asked where she might go while she waited. The telegraph operator suggested a restaurant just down the street.

An hour later, having drank enough tea to set sail and having eaten her fill of pastries, Delilah returned to the telegraph office to see if she'd received a response yet. To her disappointment, she hadn't. With a sigh, she took up residence in the corner chair to wait out the second hour. If she didn't hear by then, she'd have no choice but to return to Red Rock without an answer. As it was, she might be late getting to work tonight, though she doubted Miss Cora would say anything.

She observed as people came and went. Sometimes people came in themselves to retrieve messages, but in a number of instances the clerk would send young boys racing off with messages to be delivered. A man, whom Delilah took to be a miner due to the grimy state of his clothing, came in to send a message. He paid, and left.

"Ma'am," the telegraph operator called twenty minutes later, just as Delilah was about to give up.

"Yes?"

"Your message is here."

Having convinced herself that, in all likelihood, she would not receive a response, Delilah only stared at him for an instant. Then, as his words sank in, she rose and quickly made her way to the desk. He handed her a piece of paper on which the communiqué had been transcribed.

It said simply:

> Five hundred dollars. Stop. Half now. Stop. Will send to your bank. Stop. Other half when Towers in custody. Stop. Waiting reply. Stop. Paul Telford.

Delilah swallowed. Good Lord, it was going to work. Her hands began to shake from a combination of fear for the irrevocable act she was about to commit, and relief for finally having the funds to help her sister. She was certain that the immediate $250 that she would receive for the information, on top of what she'd already deposited on their behalf, would be more than enough to meet Eve and Tom's mortgage payment. She sighed, not realizing how worried she'd been until the weight was lifted from her shoulders.

It was mid afternoon before Samson learned that Delilah had left town, unescorted, to go all the way to Butte. He'd spent part of the morning talking to Pike, the bounty hunter, about Morgan and Clark, who had been the two unknown men he'd captured the other night. And, of course, all the time he'd talked to Pike, he'd done his best to conceal his own features. Keeping his hat brim pulled low. Never looking right at the man as they talked. Until, finally, Pike had left.

Samson's first reaction, upon talking to Metter and learning about Delilah's trip, was fury. How could she do something so irresponsible? There were bears, wolves, and cougars in these mountains. Not to mention any number of two-legged predators that roamed the wilds. Then, as his anger slowly cooled, he thought to wonder at its source.

After all, he had no rights where Delilah was concerned. Though, truth be told, ever since he'd told Mrs. Williamson and the bevy of town matrons who'd come to call that his intentions toward Mrs. Sterne were honorable, he'd found himself more than a little intrigued by the thought of marriage to her. Still, it was not his place to worry about her. So why was he?

He wanted her friendship. He wanted her in his bed. Nothing more. And if it didn't work out, well, they could both move on to other things. Couldn't they? And even if she never agreed to an intimate relationship between them, he could simply go back to the life he'd led before she had come to Red Rock. Delilah would move on to another town, another gaming table, and, someday, another man who would teach her to love again.

Samson scowled at the thought. Dammit! He didn't want to go back to the life he'd led before she came. Contemplating life without her in it, in his thoughts, seemed suddenly exceedingly empty. And he certainly didn't want another man touching her, teaching her the joy of loving. That man was supposed to be him. He couldn't imagine it any other way without wanting to hit something.

But he wasn't supposed to care that much. His plan had been for a reserved, friendly relationship. Yet somehow, somewhere along the way, he'd begun to care about Delilah Sterne. Too much. And he didn't know what to do about it.

When dusk began to fall, and she hadn't returned to town, tension began to seep into his muscles. He couldn't concentrate on the papers on his desk. He snapped at Deputy Wilkes for no good reason, and had to apologize. And he couldn't seem to stop going to the window to look for her.

Finally he gave up. Cursing, he slammed out of the office. After checking with Metter to see if perhaps she'd returned and he'd missed seeing her—though he was pretty sure it hadn't happened—he mounted Goliath and headed toward Butte. The only thing that would ease his mind would be to find her, so he might as well meet her.

Blast the woman!

He wanted to give her a good talking to for her foolishness, but didn't even have the right to do that. Somehow, he was simply going to have to find a way to marry her. He sure as hell couldn't have the woman he loved traipsing all over the countryside driving him crazy with worry and not be able to do anything about it.

Whoa! Back up there. *The woman he loved?* What in blazes was he thinking? He didn't love her! Did he? The idea of loving another woman scared the bejesus out of him. All that pain and impulsiveness and need. . . . He never wanted to go through that again.

But he *was* going through that again.

"Aw, hell!" The shock of that discovery made him pull Goliath up. He considered galloping back to Red Rock as fast as the horse could carry him. Was there still time to get out of it? Could he leave Delilah to her own devices and never see her again?

He stared into the night. It was a clear night, thankfully one of the first warm ones. There was a moon overhead, but it was still dark—especially here in the forest. He could scarcely see the trail in front of him. He listened to the hoots of owls and the scurryings in the grass and the mournful wail of a distant wolf, and wondered if Delilah was hearing those things too. Was she frightened?

Well, hell, she deserved to be frightened.

Could he leave her to the night and its creatures and the fright she might be feeling?

No.

With a grimace of self-disgust, Samson set Goliath into motion once more. He'd ridden about two miles before he finally heard the sound of a horse approaching.

Delilah?

He moved Goliath off the road into the shadow of the trees to wait and watch. When the horse came into sight, he could see by the silhouette in the moonlight that the rider was indeed a woman. It had to be her.

And once again his anger returned. The blamed woman needed a good scare thrown into her, that's what. Maybe she'd think twice about taking off by herself the next time. With that thought in mind, Samson sat in the shadows observing her approach.

She looked small and vulnerable in the moonlight, her shoulders slumped with tiredness. He hardened his heart, refusing to allow himself to be swayed. This was for her own good.

As she drew nearer, he tugged Goliath's head up from the succulent grasses on which he was nibbling, and shortened the reins. Samson waited until she'd gone about ten paces past the spot where he was concealed, then he kicked Goliath into a gallop and raced after her. She was just beginning to turn to investigate the sounds behind her when he was upon her. Grasping her around the waist, he plucked her from her saddle and pulled her into his lap.

Chapter Eleven

As she felt the arm clamp about her waist, Delilah screamed. Mindless unreasoning terror gave her strength, and she fought like a wildcat. With feet and teeth and nails. She would not let it happen to her again. She wouldn't! She would fight with every last ounce of breath in her body.

"No!" she screamed, this time in rage, as her assailant pinned her hands together behind her back. She arched her body away from him, using her feet to kick at his leg, at his horse to spook it, at anything within reach.

"Goldarnit, woman! What are you trying to do? Emasculate me?"

The voice sounded vaguely familiar, but she was too frightened to identify it. Since her last kick seemed to have produced a result, she attempted to duplicate it.

"Oh, no, you don't," the voice growled in her ear. His grip on her shifted as he pulled her more firmly against him, limiting the effectiveness of her kicking.

"No! Don't! Please, don't," she cried out as tears of frustration and fear and rage boiled up inside her and began to pour down her cheeks.

"Delilah, stop it! It's Matt. I'm not going to hurt you."

She heard the words, but her fear rendered her incapable of understanding them, and she struggled on.

"Dadburnit, woman! Will you calm down and listen? I'm not going to hurt you. It's Matt."

She went still, not quite certain she could trust her ears. "Matt?" she echoed, hating the tremble in her voice but unable to prevent it.

"Yes, darlin'. It's Matt."

Slowly she turned in his lap to look up into his face. The moonlight had transformed his familiar visage into one comprised of shadows and angles, but it was definitely Sheriff Matt Chambers. Her relief quickly transformed into anger, however, as she realized that he had deliberately frightened the wits out of her for some reason only he knew. "You . . . you *bastard*!" she exclaimed, swearing for one of the few times in her life. She swiped in embarrassment at the tears still trickling down her cheeks.

There was a moment of tense silence. Then he spoke. "I know you won't believe this, Delilah, but I'm sorry. *Really* sorry. I . . . forgot that . . . God, I'm a fool."

"Well, you won't get any argument on that score," Delilah said stiffly. "Now, put me down please." She wanted nothing more at the moment than to put some distance between them.

Obligingly, he carefully lowered her to the ground before dismounting himself. To her further dismay, Delilah noted that Jackpot was nowhere in sight. No doubt the poor horse had been as startled as she was, and had taken off at top speed for the security of his stable.

Buoyed by her anger and not much else, Delilah turned to face the cause of her current distress. "I'd appreciate an explanation for your outrageous behavior, Sheriff. *If* you would be so kind." The sarcasm in her voice was impossible to mistake.

He considered her in silence for a moment, the darkness cloaking his expression. Then he said, "I wanted you to understand the dangers of going off alone."

Delilah's eyes widened and she turned her back to him before she did something unseemly like . . . like slapping him. Oh! The man was infuriating. "Do you honestly think I don't *know* the dangers, sir?" she asked in a tight voice. "From man and from beast?" Though on some occasions it was difficult to separate the one from the other.

"I guess maybe you do." His tone was tense.

"You're darned tootin' I do."

"Then why are you out here alone?"

She whirled to face him. "Because I value my independence. Unless I need a guide, I see no reason to sacrifice my liberty for the company of a man. Would you have me cowering in my room afraid to venture out without an escort?"

"Most women would consider waiting for an escort to be simple good sense."

"Well, I'm not one of them. In case you've forgotten, in my profession, I travel alone all the time. I go into places where few women go and associate with men whom decent women won't even allow to brush against their skirts." How could she make him understand without revealing too much of herself? Or perhaps it no longer mattered. "And every time I do, I feel sick to my stomach with fear. Frightened that I'll encounter another brute who will . . ." She broke off, unable to put her repulsion into words. But he remained silent, waiting, so she took a deep breath and continued. "I live with my fear until I get to know the people in the town. Until they have accepted me for who I am."

"You mean until they accept the boundaries you establish?"

Delilah turned away from him to gaze into the blackness of the forest lining the narrow road. How very perceptive of him. "Yes," she agreed. Though that was something *he* had refused to do, she might have added.

"So, why do you do it?" His quiet baritone came out of the darkness at her back.

Delilah tilted her chin up as though looking at the stars and closed her eyes. "You wouldn't understand."

"Try me."

She took a deep breath. "I do it because I am a Sinclair by birth, and a Sinclair always faces her fear. I do it because being with people, lots of people, keeps me from remembering too much. And I do it because gambling is the only work for which I have a certain amount of talent and which I truly enjoy. Why is that so hard for you to understand?"

"But . . . you're a woman, darnit!"

She whirled to face him. "And because I'm a woman, I must enjoy sewing seams in men's shirts or trousers day after day for a few coins that barely keep starvation at bay? Well I don't! The tedium drives me so crazy that I could scream with the frustration of it all."

"There are other professions, and not just menial ones. I heard tell there's a woman doctor somewhere in Colorado. You're good at doctoring. And there's a lady newspaper reporter in Idaho or Wyoming I think. You're good with words too. I bet you could do something like that. Heck, you could probably do anything you set your mind to."

Delilah stared at him, puzzled by the admiration she heard in his words. Matt Chambers admired her despite every attempt she had made to drive him away. He had faith in her intelligence, in her abilities, in *her*.

And she had just betrayed him. Guilt rose in her throat like bile, choking her into silence.

"You should do something less dangerous," Matt was saying. "I don't like wondering night after night if some drunken cowhand is gonna take it into his head to try to recoup his losses at gunpoint. And I don't like worrying about you when you go off half-cocked all by yourself."

Delilah could only continue to stare at him. Was that where all this was coming from? He had been worried about her. Would a cold-blooded murderer, the kind that would shoot a kid in the back, care that much about a woman like her?

So, he would be cleared of the charges against him. *But what if he wasn't?* Oh God! What had she done?

"Aw, hell! I don't know why I'm standin' here talkin' to you about this now. Come on. I'll get you home. We'll probably catch up to that blamed horse of yours a mile down the road." He turned and mounted Goliath, then extended a hand down to her.

She looked from his big capable hand to his hard night-shadowed features and shook her head in protest. "I'm not going to ride double with you."

"Well, I'm not walking. So unless you intend to walk, you have about one minute to make up your mind."

Delilah looked at the narrow band of road that faded into absolute blackness ahead. There wasn't much moonlight.

"Delilah—" he said, with a note of warning.

"Oh, very well," she responded less than graciously as she grasped his hand and felt herself hoisted with surprising ease onto the big horse's rump. It took her a moment to get her split skirt arranged so that it covered her legs properly. Once settled, she reverted to conversation. "You know, since it was you who got me into this predicament in the first place, I should think you would have offered to walk. It would have been the gentlemanly thing to do."

"I'm not a gentleman. Leastways, not tonight. I'm not in the mood."

Delilah didn't know how to respond to that, so she said nothing. Besides, she was busy trying to figure out how to hold on to him firmly without pressing her body against his in an unseemly fashion. She settled for knotting her fingers into the sides of his leather vest. This worked quite adequately until he quickened the horse's pace. Then, however, she found herself being jounced from side to side in a manner that could easily result in mishap. He seemed to realize this too, for he grasped her hands in his and pulled them about his waist, joining them securely together. This position, of course, had the disadvantage of bringing her front up solidly against his back, which was disconcerting to say the least. Still, there was little sense in protesting, so she supposed she must bear the discomfort as well as possible until they reached town. God willing, it would not be long.

They rode in silence for a time . . . until Delilah's stomach growled rather loudly. "What was that?" Matt asked.

Delilah flushed. "Don't concern yourself, Sheriff. It seems that my stomach is protesting the lack of a decent supper."

"What did you have to eat today?"

Delilah thought back. She'd left before breakfast had been served. "I had some pastries around lunchtime."

"That's it?"

"Don't worry yourself, Sheriff. I'll have something at the restaurant when I get to the hotel."

"I don't think so."

She regarded the back of his head quizzically. "Why do you say that?"

"The restaurant is closed. It's after eight."

"Oh." She hadn't realized it was that late. "Well," she said, after a moment's thought, "I'm certain I shall survive until morning. I'm not exactly undernourished."

No, she was nicely rounded in all the right places, Samson concurred silently. The sensation of her nicely rounded breasts pressed up against his back was one that would no doubt invade his dreams for nights to come. Still there was no need for her to go hungry when he had a larder full of food at his place.

"Or perhaps I can get something from Miss Cora's kitchen," Delilah continued, unaware of the direction of his thoughts.

"I told Cora that you might not be in tonight."

There was a second of stunned silence. "Whyever did you do that?"

"When you were so late getting back to town, I thought something might have happened to you. Since I remembered that you'd used the last of my saddlebag whiskey on those cougar scratches, I stopped at the saloon to get another bottle. And, well, it just kind of came out." He paused, waiting for an angry response, but there wasn't one. That made him even more uncomfortable, because he didn't know what in blazes she was thinking. "Are you upset?" he asked, wishing he could see her face.

"No. Actually, I'm a bit relieved. I'm quite tired and the idea of sitting in that smoky saloon until midnight did not appeal to me. However, I do not want you to think that gives you free rein to interfere in my life whenever the inclination takes you. Is that understood?"

There she went with her schoolteacher voice again. Samson grinned. "Yes, ma'am."

They were on the outskirts of Red Rock before they finally came upon Jackpot, who was grazing at the side of the road. Rather than dismounting and allowing Delilah to ride her own horse, Samson simply gathered Jackpot's reins, wrapped them around the pommel of his saddle, and kept going.

"I'd like to ride my own horse now," Delilah protested.

"No, ma'am," he said, knowing that should he allow her to ride her own horse she would refuse to accompany him to his home. "You can ride later."

"Why . . . but . . . this is . . ." Delilah sputtered. "Well, this is very high-handed of you, Sheriff."

"Yes, ma'am."

She didn't seem to know what to say when he agreed with her. Silence prevailed for a moment. Until she noticed he had turned off of the main street and was not heading toward the hotel. "Where are we going?"

"I thought I'd take you to my place and cook you an omelette." Thank goodness he'd taken an hour to clean the place up after the visit he'd received the other day.

"Oh, no! I don't think that's a good idea!"

"You don't like omelettes?" he asked, purposely mistaking her meaning.

"Of course I like omelettes. I just don't think . . ."

"Then don't *think*. For a change, just *do*."

A pause. "I'm not sure I can do that," she said quietly.

"Trust me, you can. All I'm going to do is feed you."

Fifteen minutes later, Delilah sat tensely at his table, looking around his spartan cabin as though she'd bolt for the exit at the slightest noise. Samson set about stoking the fire in the wood stove. "My coffee isn't the greatest, but it hasn't killed anybody yet either, so I figure it can't be all that bad. You want some?" he asked.

She looked at him with blue eyes as big as saucers in her pale face and nodded. "Yes, please. I feel a little chilled all of a sudden."

Samson nodded and took a couple of cups off of the

hooks set into the battered sideboard that had come with the house. He wished he knew how to start a conversation that would relax her. But he didn't. Truth was, he wasn't very relaxed himself at the moment.

He'd had an ulterior motive in bringing her here, one he hadn't admitted even to himself until a short time ago. He wanted to tell her about himself. No, he didn't *want* to, but he needed to. He needed to know how she'd react, how she'd feel about his past before he got himself ensnared any more deeply in this so far one-sided relationship. But now that he had her undivided attention, he felt awkward and didn't know how to begin.

Considering the problem, he set about making the omelette he'd promised her, slicing bits of onion and ham into the egg mixture. He supposed he could just ask her if she recalled the name Samson Towers—which of course she had, because she'd mentioned Pike showing her his poster—but somehow that seemed a little sudden. He was so deep in thought that when Delilah spoke, he didn't hear her words. "Pardon?" he asked, turning to face her.

"I asked if there was anything I could do?"

He nodded toward the sideboard. "You can set a couple of plates out, if you want. Other than that, I think I've got everything pretty much under control." He watched her as she moved about the cabin, finding the plates and utensils they would need and setting them on the table. It sure felt good having a woman around. Now, if only he could convince her that she belonged with him, they might have a future. He hadn't decided how long he wanted that future to be as of yet. But he did know he wanted one with her.

But when the omelettes and coffee were ready, he still hadn't decided how to go about talking to her. With the exception of the occasional comment about the weather or the Wilkeses' new baby, they ate in silence.

Finally, Samson could wait no longer. Once they were finished eating, he'd have no reason to keep her from returning to the hotel.

"Delilah—" She looked up and waited. "I wanted to talk to you about something."

A hint of wariness might have entered her eyes, but she nodded. "All right."

He plunged ahead before he could change his mind. "I . . . I'm not the person you think I am. My name is Samson Towers, not Matt Chambers."

Her eyes widened, though he couldn't quite read the expression they held. "I see." She looked down at her plate. "So why are you going under an assumed name?"

He shrugged. "It's a long story." Sipping at the dregs of his coffee, he rose to pour another cup for each of them as he sought the words to continue. "I told you that my father was a sheriff, didn't I?" She nodded and he went on. "Well, one of the things my father disliked about being a sheriff was that his hands were sometimes tied by the very law he was supposed to uphold. There were cases where what was morally right was not necessarily what was legally right. He told me never to let myself become the tool of rich and powerful men who knew how to make the law work for them. So, rather than following in my father's footsteps, I chose to become a hired gun. That way, I figured I could choose my fights and what side I wanted to be on." He shrugged. "I didn't make a heck of a lot of money, of course, 'cause the side I picked was usually poor as church mice, but at least, unlike my father, I could live without regrets." He fell silent, remembering. "For a while," he added in a murmur.

"What happened?" she asked softly, as though she didn't want to disturb his thoughts.

He shook his head. "Something I never figured on. See, I was good at my job. I watched the way the wind was blowin', picked my battles real careful, and hardly ever lost a fight. And because of that, I started to get a name as a fast gun." He shook his head again, still unable to believe it. "I just about keeled over from surprise the first time one o' those young guns lookin' for a reputation called me out.

"I managed to avoid killin' him. Heck, I beat him to the draw by a mile. He was still tryin' to get his gun out of its holster when I asked him if he wanted me to pull the trigger or not. Scared the daylights out of him. He ran off and I never saw him again." Samson looked at her. "I was more prepared after that and usually found a way to avoid the kids."

Delilah nodded, waiting for him to continue, but the next part was going to be the hardest to put into words. Rising, cup in hand, he walked to the window and stood looking out at the darkened streets of Red Rock. The town had become his home. He liked it here. It was quiet—leastways it was now that he'd cleaned it up. He liked the people—most of them anyway. And he didn't want to lose the life he had here. Was he doing the right thing in confiding in her? Yet this conversation had become irrevocable in its conclusion the moment that he'd admitted he was Samson Towers.

"I guess I should have figured that my luck wouldn't last forever and that I'd have to face down some kid eventually. But I didn't. And I was in a little town called Cedar Crossing in Wyoming when I came across a kid that wouldn't bow out. His name was Boyd Telford. 'Course I didn't know at the time that his last name was Telford, or that his daddy was Paul Telford, or that Telford owed the whole blamed town. The young fool was callin' himself Kid Boyd and aimin' to make a reputation for himself no matter what. The first time he came gunnin' for me, I made the mistake of embarrassing him in front of the townfolk by takin' his gun away and kickin' his butt into a water trough to cool him off. He came back the next day, just as I was about to leave town."

Samson stared at the blackness beyond the window, not seeing it or the town or anything but the scene in his mind. God, he hated remembering.

"What happened?" Delilah's voice prompted from the room at his back.

"He was about to shoot me in the back, but I heard the click of the hammer. I drew, turned, saw a man with a gun aimed at me, and fired. It was pure instinct. The same instinct that had kept me alive in my line of work.

"I didn't realize until he lay dead on the ground that it was the kid." Samson shook his head, swallowing the lump of regret that still lodged there. "Aw, heck, Delilah, he was just seventeen. A kid. But with a Colt six-shooter in his hand, he could kill like a man, and he was bound and determined to do just that." Samson shrugged. "I wasn't ready to die."

"So, if it was a fair fight, why have you changed your name?"

Samson shrugged. "It was in the minutes following the kid's death that I found out Kid Boyd was Paul Telford's *only* son. The kid had been spoiled since the day he was born. Paul Telford was one of the most influential men in the territory—had the biggest cattle spread for miles around—and, like I said, he owned that blamed dirtwater town. So, what it came down to was my word against his. A gunfighter against a respected businessman."

He turned to look at Delilah over his shoulder, but she was staring down at the table. "Who would you believe?"

She lifted her gaze to his and he was surprised by the depths of the sorrow he read there. She shook her head. "Weren't there any witnesses?"

"A few. But none that couldn't be bought." He shrugged. "I'd killed Telford's only son, and he wanted revenge. He was willin' to use the law to get it.

"You know what's really funny is that I've never even met the man. I wouldn't know him if he passed me in the street."

"So, how did you get to be Matt Chambers?" Delilah asked, her tone scarcely above a whisper.

"Telford had men tracking me all over Wyoming territory—it was getting harder and harder to avoid them—so I headed up into Montana. I was travelin' one day when I noticed something in the distance that looked like it could be a downed man. I found Matt Chambers. He'd been on his way to Red Rock to take the job as sheriff when he'd had a run-in with some horse thieves that had shot him, stolen his horse, and left him for dead. He was gut-shot, so there wasn't anything I could do for him except stay with him. And since he was dyin', and not likely to try to arrest me, I told him my story. It was him that suggested that I take his identity and come to Red Rock. Said that that way I'd be able to keep anybody from seein' the WANTED posters Telford was sending everywhere. I figured it was worth a shot, so I took the job. Even swore an oath of office on Chambers's Bible.

"After Chambers passed on, I buried him, shaved my mustache, took his spectacles and badge, and came on to Red Rock, where I took his identity." He stared thoughtfully at the streets for a time, remembering, then murmured, "I never could get the hang of wearin' those spectacles. They made me trip over my own feet."

"How long have you been here?" Delilah asked a moment later.

"Goin' on three years, I guess. Took the whole first year to clean the place up."

The silence stretched after that, and Samson waited.

What was she thinking? Did she hold him responsible for the kid's murder because he'd chosen to live by the gun? Did she understand?

"Samson—"

He closed his eyes. God, it was good to be addressed by his own name. It had been a long time. "Yeah?"

"Why have you told me this?"

He turned to face her. God, she was beautiful—even in the yellow lamplight. "Because I like you, Delilah. I like you a lot. And I wanted you to know who I am. Who I *really* am. You know what I mean?"

She considered him silently for a moment. "I think so," she whispered. Then, "Why haven't you tried to clear your name?"

He shook his head. "As long as Telford is alive, it isn't possible. He's too rich and too powerful, and there are too many people out there who can be bought."

Like me, Delilah thought, staring at the big obdurate male whom, only a few hours ago, she'd wanted so badly to get out of her life. To be blunt with herself, she had to admit that she'd been bought by the reward offered for this man. This man, who had one of the finest characters of any she'd ever known, with the exception of her father. The thought of the wheels she'd set in motion made her want to vomit, and she sought desperately for some thread of hope that what she'd done could work out for the best. "Surely not all the judges are corrupt?"

He shrugged. "Maybe not. But knowing Telford's reputation, I doubt that I'd live long enough to stand trial."

Oh, God! "So you just live another man's life, always afraid that your past will catch up with you? There has to be something you can do? Some way to clear you name?"

He didn't respond, and finally Delilah rose from the table to approach him. He must have heard her footsteps but, even as she stopped directly behind him, he didn't turn to face her. Finally, she placed her hand gently on his shoulder. The tense muscle beneath her hand leaped in response. "Matt—?"

He turned, and she reeled beneath the force of the pain in his eyes. "So tell me what you would have me do, Mrs. Sterne."

And as he spoke the name she'd appropriated for her own, Delilah realized with sudden startling clarity that they were not so very different, she and Samson Towers. She too had assumed an identity to protect herself. Only she had been protecting herself not from a rich man's vengeance or a hangman's noose, but from the ostracism of so-called polite society. Society had insisted on telling her what was acceptable for one *in her position*, so she had altered her position in the eyes of society, and in so doing had found the freedom to live.

"What would you have done?" Samson asked now, in the face of her silence.

Delilah gazed up into his handsome face, into the dark charcoal-grey eyes that, against her will, she'd learned to read, and shook her head. "I don't know." *Probably the same thing you did*, she admitted silently, as shame threatened to choke her. She stared into storm-dark eyes burning with pain and need, and felt something within her respond to that elemental call. "Oh, Matt, I'm so sorry."

He frowned slightly, as though not understanding. "Delilah, I . . ." But whatever he'd been about to say faded into oblivion as Delilah, heeding impulse, placed her hands on his broad shoulders and rose onto her toes to place her lips against his. She sensed his surprise as, for a brief moment, he failed to respond. Not knowing quite how to proceed, she was about to break away when, groaning deep in his throat, he swept her into his embrace and deepened the kiss.

His tongue invaded her mouth, stroking and coaxing, and Delilah's toes curled. He caressed the soft interior of her mouth, stoking a passion she was only just learning, and her pulse roared in her ears. His hands crept downward to grip the twin cheeks of her bottom, and Delilah's heart fluttered wildly in her chest. More confidently this time, she sent her own tongue forward to explore the mysterious recesses of his mouth, to do erotic battle, and was once again rewarded for her efforts by a very masculine growl.

He broke off the kiss then to feather soft little kisses along her hairline and over her temples. "Damnation, woman," he murmured in her ear. "Do you have any idea how much I want you?"

With her eyes still closed, the better to bask in the sensations he bestowed by tracing the whorls of her ear with his tongue, Delilah gasped and shook her head slightly.

"As much as I want my life back," he murmured.

Delilah moaned as a tangled combination of passion and guilt, impossible to separate, rose in her throat.

"Do you have any idea how much I need you?" he whispered.

"No," she murmured as she too sought his ear and lightly nipped the lobe before soothing it with her tongue.

"As much as my next breath," he murmured before slanting his mouth across hers in another consuming kiss.

Tears of self-reproach burned Delilah's eyes as the memory of what she'd done that afternoon intruded on the moment, and she responded to him almost desperately, seeking forgetfulness in the passion he spawned with his caresses. His hand closed over her breast, testing its weight, inflaming the nipple with his thumb through the fabric of her shirtwaist, until Delilah could do nothing but clutch him to her. For he was suddenly the only stability that existed in a dizzying world of pure sensation.

And then, without quite knowing how it happened, she felt his big warm hand on her bare skin as he brushed aside the lacy fabric of her camisole to caress the soft flesh of her breast. They groaned in unison. And then, abruptly, he slowed. "Delilah, darlin'—"

But she didn't want words right now. Words . . . and thinking . . . and guilt. She wanted only to feel, to forget, to . . . truly live as other women did. And so she covered his lips with hers once again.

But the distraction only worked a moment. "Delilah, are you sure? I promise I won't hurt you, but you have to be sure, honey, because . . . well, I don't think I'll be able to stop if we go much further."

As his words penetrated her consciousness, Delilah went still. He was talking about doing . . . that. Her stomach fluttered nervously as remembered terror struck fear into her heart. But this was Matt. The man who'd never been anything but gentle with her. The man she had betrayed with her unthinking actions. The man she had perhaps condemned to death. After what she had done . . . perhaps she owed him the momentary comfort of her body. Perhaps she even deserved a measure of hurt.

"Delilah?" he asked again.

She looked up at him and her heart tripped a beat at the emotion blazing in his eyes. He cared for her, of that she had no doubt. He would not hurt her unnecessarily. "I'm sure," she murmured.

Chapter Twelve

He crushed her to him then, brushing her face with little kisses. "You won't regret it," he murmured.

And he lifted her in his arms to carry her into his bedchamber, where he stood her next to the bed while he lit the bedside lamp. Delilah received an impression of a large, pine-framed bed draped by the colorful pattern of a homemade quilt. A mirrored dresser in the shadowy edge of the room. And a chest of drawers upon which rested a set of books bracketed between horsehead bookends. Then he turned her toward him, once again becoming all that existed in her immediate world.

His arms encircled her and his lips claimed hers, masterfully, fiery with passion. He demanded a response she was powerless to deny as his hands began to roam her body, investigating, exploring, testing. Her breath caught in her throat at each tantalizing caress. "Matt," she breathed.

"Call me Samson," he urged. "Just for tonight."

Eyes closed, she nodded, and whispered, "Samson."

As though her acquiescence to his simple request had given him immeasurable happiness, he clutched her more tightly for a moment before backing away slightly to finish undoing the buttons on her shirtwaist. Within very short order, he had removed her outer garments and petticoats, and he stepped back to study her as she stood before him in her thin camisole, bloomers, silk stockings, and shoes. Feeling more than a little shy, Delilah's hands fluttered in a self-conscious attempt to conceal what was not yet revealed. He gently gripped her wrists to still them. "Beautiful," he pronounced with a tense smile as his eyes glittered with a raw hunger that should have frightened her, but didn't.

This was Matt, or rather *Samson*. But whatever name he used, she knew he would not hurt her. Not the way . . . but she wouldn't think of that now. She wouldn't!

"Sit down for a moment, darlin'," he bid her as his hands guided her onto the edge of the bed. Then he knelt to undo the laces on her shoes, slipping first one shoe off and then the other, dropping both unceremoniously to the floor. Keeping her left foot cupped in his hand—it looked ridiculously small when cradled in his large hand—he raised it to his mouth. Delilah gasped as his warm mouth closed over her big toe, silk stocking and all, and sucked tenderly. An inferno of sensation raced up her leg to settle heavily in her loins. Her eyes widened, for she had never imagined feet to be capable of delivering such befuddling sensations. So involved was she in the new perceptions, that she was unaware that his hands had drifted up her leg to the edge of the silk stocking until she felt his warm fingers brush against the cooler skin of her bare thigh. His fingers blazed a trail of fire down her leg as he rolled the stocking down, garter and all, and slid it off her foot.

Then his gaze locked on hers, holding her captive, immobile as he once again raised her foot to his mouth and gently kissed each of her bare toes. Delilah gasped as his tongue emerged, hot and moist, to caress her little toe. She found herself racked by a trembling she couldn't explain. Gripped by a panting breathless excitement that frightened her as she felt it gnawing away at the edges of the rigid control she'd always maintained. And suddenly she was aware of the textures of his quilted bedspread beneath her thighs, of her camisole, and of the flesh of his hands in a way she'd never been conscious of before.

When Samson repeated the entire process with the silk stocking on her other leg, Delilah felt as though her heart must burst through her chest, its pounding was so violent. Her control snapped, and she gasped audibly.

He rose then to rain kisses over her face as his hands threaded themselves into her hair, releasing pins, uncoiling the heavy mass of her waist-length hair. Letting it cascade to her hips, he gently spread it over her shoulders as though memorizing its texture. Then, lifting one coal-black tress in his hand, examining the curl as it coiled around his finger, he lifted it to his nose and breathed deeply. Did the lavender scent she'd used in her bath water still cling to it?

And then, gripping her fingers in his hands, Samson raised her to her feet again. Delilah felt every ridge and fiber in the rag rug beneath her bare soles. And when he slipped the strap of her camisole off of her shoulder and lowered his head to sweep hot, sensuous kisses over her sensitized flesh, she felt the gentle coolness of the night air on her fevered skin. An erotic counterpoint to the subtle abrasiveness of his jaw against her skin. He lowered his head to kiss the breast he'd exposed, to capture the taut nipple in his mouth, and a jolt of lightning sliced through her, sharp and potent and hot.

Clinging to him, she gasped as a liquid heat she didn't understand sluiced through her to settle heavily in her loins. She clamped her thighs together in an attempt to stem the tide. Good heavens, what was happening to her? Was it supposed to happen?

But she had no more time to wonder, for he lifted his head, claiming her lips once more. The kiss was all-consuming, devastating to the senses, and her fingers curled helplessly in the fabric of his shirt. Part of her was aware of his hands moving over her, removing the last of her clothing, and that part of her cringed at her lack of modesty. But Delilah could do nothing to heed that internal voice, for her passion-drugged faculties had focused on a strange potent need that had risen within her. She didn't know what it was—had never before felt it—yet it thrummed through her body with a power that ravaged her senses.

And then, even the ground beneath her feet fell away as Samson lifted her in his arms and placed her gently on the bed.

His bed.

The fabric of the spread was cool against her back and, without the furnace-like heat of Samson's big body next to her, cold, hard reason began to intrude. Her fingers curled into the fabric of the quilt as an ancient fear tried to regain its foothold. Looking up into his face as he stood over her, she saw the heat of naked hunger blazing from his eyes, and felt that fear grow more desperate, clawing for purchase in her dazed mind. No! She reminded herself that she owed him at least this much. And she'd already declared that she was sure. She would not go back on her word.

And then the sight of Samson removing his shirt distracted her. Her breath caught in her throat as he bared his muscular bronzed chest to her view. His smooth flesh gleamed with a health and vitality that not even the still-healing scratches inflicted by the cougar could diminish. Her gaze roamed the wide expanse, absorbing the restrained power evinced by his massive pectoral muscles. Seeing the brawn evident in the corded muscle of his abdomen. Discerning the tempered strength in the rippling muscles of his bronzed arms. And her heart stuttered.

He was magnificent! Like the picture she'd seen of a Greek god once in one of her mother's treasured books.

Samson pulled the boots from his feet, dropping them unceremoniously wherever they might land, and then lifted his hands to the waistband of his denims. He hesitated then as his gaze searched her face. She had no idea what he saw there, but whatever it was apparently made him decide to leave his trousers on for a while longer.

Delilah was a bit uncomfortable with that—she didn't want to be naked while he remained partially clothed—it made her feel exposed . . . somehow, more vulnerable. But before she could put her nebulous feelings into words, he lay down at her side on the bed and leaned over to kiss her again.

This kiss was different. Although still a carnal assault she was powerless to resist, it was harder, making her aware of the restrained power, the controlled savagery of the man behind it. Yet, somehow, instead of frightening her, the kiss only made her feel more feminine. Fragile versus his strength. Delicate versus his solidity. Diminutive versus his massive size. And yet, cared for, protected.

His hands roamed freely over her body, exploring, tormenting. Delilah raised her hands to explore his body in turn—his shoulders, his chest, hesitantly at first, and then more boldly. It was smooth, hot, and hard. Fluid steel beneath heated flesh.

He broke off the kiss, trailing his lips down her throat and chest until his hot mouth closed over the tip of one passion-swollen breast. Delilah moaned softly with the exquisite agony of the sensation that rushed through her. Her entire body felt ablaze with heat. Fevered with need. Adrift in an inferno of sensation. She clung to him, her anchor in a sea of wondrous impressions, and pressed her mouth to the back of one hand—an effort to stifle another moan that was even now rising in her throat.

He pulled her onto her side then, facing him, and his arm slipped lower, sweeping over the indentation of her waist until his hand caressed the twin mounds of her derriere. Parting her legs gently with his knee, he pressed his denim-clad thigh against that secret part of her. The part that burned with a curious aching need. And she could no longer restrain the moan that clawed at her throat.

Her hands clutched at his shoulders, pulling at him, begging him for something she did not understand and could not voice. Groaning deep in his throat, he captured her lips in an intense, ravaging kiss as his large hand closed over one aching breast. So sensitized to his touch was she becoming, that that simple act caused a renewed onslaught of liquid heat to race through her, and instinctively Delilah flexed her hips against his thigh.

Sensation raced through her like a prairie fire. And she did it again, setting an intuitive cadence that coincided with the pulsing need engendered by his rhythmic caress of her aching nipple. Then, lifting his head, he shifted their positions once more, rolling Delilah to her back, removing his thigh from between her legs as he lay on his side next to her. Delilah groaned in instinctive protest as he withdrew the one source of assuagement she had found for the burning that centered there.

"Soon, darlin'," he promised in a whisper. But her hips flexed again, involuntarily, seeking . . . something.

He leaned back, then, to sweep her with his gaze. A savage glitter lit his eyes now, and she shivered beneath his regard. But it was not from fear. Rather it was an exhilaration as old as humankind that provoked the tremble. Her flesh tingled beneath his smoldering scrutiny. The nipples of her painfully swollen breasts contracted even more tightly. Her breath came in little panting gasps.

Continuing to watch her, he trailed his hand slowly down her body, stopping to dip one finger into the well of her navel. Delilah's hips arched again, instinctively, demandingly, and her face flamed with mortification as his lips curved in an infuriatingly self-satisfied smile. But in the next instant, she forgot her embarrassment as his mouth closed over the distended tip of her breast, scorchingly hot and tantalizing, tugging at the tiny crest as he raked the sensitive nub with his tongue. A mewling sound escaped her lips. Her body arched uncontrollably. And every vestige of strength left her limbs as her body became a mere compilation of superresponsive nerve endings for him to manipulate at will.

Before she'd even recovered from the paralyzing burst of heat that ricocheted through her system, she felt his hand at the junction of her thighs, parting the crisp curls nestled there. Fear nagged at the edges of her consciousness again, but she ignored it as she strained against his hand, seeking an end to the torment. A release that she'd never before felt the need of, but which she knew instinctively that he could give her.

But his touch was only more torment, as he stroked the soft inner flesh of her thighs, combed through the curls of her mound, and trailed his fingers delicately over the most heated part of her, stoking the hot coals of desire into an inferno that all but consumed her. "Samson!" she cried, involuntarily.

He lifted his head from her breast to look into her face with a dark, smoldering gaze. "Soon, darlin'," he promised again. "Don't be impatient. I want to make absolutely certain you're ready for me."

Ready? She didn't know what exactly was involved in reaching the satisfaction she craved, but she couldn't get more ready, could she?

Yet as he lowered his head to exact exquisite penance for her impatience from her other breast, and casually pressed one finger into the moist crevice between her thighs, Delilah learned otherwise. A sob caught in her throat at the desperate yearning that sent her hips surging upward in search of the release he withheld. "Matt, please!" she cried, as the last vestiges of modesty and virtue were swept aside. Forgotten was her agreement to call him Samson, for passion crowded everything from her mind but the tremendous need blazing through her.

In the next instant, he left her, and Delilah cried out at the loss. Then she realized that he had merely risen to strip himself of his denims. She had a fleeting glimpse of his sex as it sprang from a thick nest of curls at his groin, but it was too fleeting for her to even get an impression of size. And perhaps that was best, for she didn't truly want to know beforehand. Then he was back on the bed with her, nudging her knees apart as he knelt between her thighs.

Delilah, dazed by desire, could only stare at him in puzzlement. So there was no satisfying conclusion to all these sensations, then? There was only the intoxication of the feelings themselves before the painful part? Disappointment flared in her mind and she tensed slightly as the blunt head of his shaft pressed against her.

"Relax, Delilah. I won't hurt you," he murmured, as he leaned forward to suckle her breasts, each in turn, again.

She didn't believe him. But then, despite her disappointment, her hips surged upward in involuntary response to his actions, and Delilah found that the feelings he'd aroused had not diminished.

"That's it," he rumbled as he pressed his hips forward a tiny bit.

The head of his sex entered her and, involuntarily, she felt her body tense again. The anticipation of the pain to come was almost as bad as the pain itself. *Relax!* she told herself. *Get it over with.* But once again he halted in response to her tension, holding himself immobile. He kissed her, caressed her, fanned the flames of her desire until her hips lifted in instinctive invitation again and, once more, he pressed forward a bit.

"Damn . . . you're tight," he murmured through gritted teeth, on the heels of a groan, and she wondered at the strain she saw on his face, but knew not how to ask about it. "So hot," he gasped. "Oh, Delilah, I want to be inside you."

"Yes," she whispered, clutching him close. She knew what he wanted. "Yes." Not knowing what else to say, not able to think through the feelings he aroused in her, unconsciously she raised her hips again. And again he pressed forward a tiny bit.

It took him an awfully long time to enter her, inch by torturous inch, with a consideration and gentleness that she had not known was possible. By the time the deed was accomplished, perspiration beaded his brow in great droplets that he whisked from his eyes with an impatient hand. He groaned then.

"It . . . it doesn't hurt," Delilah voiced her surprised

realization. It was a strange sensation, this invasion of her body, but not unpleasant.

He lifted his head to meet her gaze. "It's not supposed to," he said tenderly as he stroked her soft cheek with his thumb. "At least not after the first time. Not if it's done right."

"Oh."

A frown flickered briefly between his brows, and Delilah realized hazily that, had she been the married woman she portrayed, she would undoubtedly have known that. Samson, no doubt, wondered at her ignorance. And then, as his sex pulsed within her, her hips flexed, and he groaned. Capturing her lips with his, he withdrew and slowly squeezed back inside.

The friction of his sex as he filled her, huge and hot and rock-hard, was exquisite agony, and she lifted her knees to grip him better with her body. He repeated the stratagem, withdrawing completely with each stroke. Quickening the pace with each stroke. Driving her closer to the edge of madness with each stroke. Until . . .

Delilah cried out as a wave of sensation impacted, carrying her away on its surging crest. And another. And another. He smothered her cry of release with his mouth. And then his hips began to pound against her, and he lifted his head, uttering a hoarse male cry. A moment later, he collapsed against her.

Panting with complete enervation, Delilah opened her eyes to gaze upon the man who had thrown her senses into chaos. She had never suspected . . . never imagined . . . would never have believed how consuming lovemaking could be. Their hearts hammered in union as she gazed into his storm-hued eyes with a sense of marvel and discovery. Words eluded her.

Samson rolled to one side, taking her with him, and Delilah settled her head in the hollow beneath his chin, listening to the comforting thud of his heart as she closed her eyes. In the grip of a lassitude unlike any she'd ever felt, she drifted off to sleep.

Being careful not to wake Delilah, Samson reached over to extinguish the lamp, and lay staring in the darkness. If it hadn't been for her obvious lack of virginity, he would have sworn that the woman in his arms had been a virgin when he took her. She was simply too naive, too lacking in expertise, and too innocent of the ways of men to have been married for any length of time. And yet it had been obvious that she'd received rough handling at some time in her life, so not all of what she had told him was untrue. Still . . . he couldn't help but wonder who Delilah Sterne really was.

Their lovemaking had been spectacular. In fact, he couldn't remember ever being so aroused. He had wanted nothing more than to drive himself into her slick sheath, to bury himself within her to the hilt. But Delilah had needed gentleness, she had needed to take it slow. And he wanted to give her everything she needed and more. He wanted to erase every other man she'd ever known—whether the recollection was pleasant or otherwise—from her memory until *he* filled every crevice of her mind. He'd wanted to teach her what lovemaking should be. And he thought that perhaps he'd succeeded in that last goal.

But somehow he was going to have to get her to tell him about herself. So much of what he'd thought he'd known about her now seemed in doubt that he wondered exactly how much of Delilah was a lie. Yet, for the moment, with her in his arms, he was content to simply hold her and dream. Dream of what life might have held for them had he not been a wanted man. Dream of taking Delilah as his wife. Dream of the children they might have had.

His eyes flew open. *Oh, damn!* He'd completely forgotten about the necessity of taking precautions. For all he knew, Delilah could now be pregnant with his child. The thought pleased him even as it terrified him. What kind of life could he offer a child? Children needed security, the one thing he would never have.

Then, deciding there was no sense in worrying about it at this point, he closed his eyes and rested his nose next to Delilah's lavender-scented hair. He would simply have to ensure that he took precautions in the future and pray that this once had not borne fruit.

Delilah opened her eyes to the greyness of predawn. She frowned dreamily at the strangeness of her surroundings. There was a delicious heat at her back, and an unaccustomed weight laying across her waist. Slowly, memory returned. Moving carefully, she looked over her shoulder to see Matt, or rather Samson, sleeping behind her, his big body curved around hers.

She studied his features in repose, noting how sleep softened his expression. He had an aquiline nose, thick dark lashes that Delilah envied, and full sensual lips. She remembered all the things those lips had done to her the previous night, and flushed even as she felt a faint stirring in her loins.

Who would have guessed the pleasure to be found in a man's arms? Certainly not she.

She wondered if there were more lovemaking techniques that Samson could teach her, or . . . And then reality came crashing in with a vengeance.

There would be no time for him to teach her anything. Because of her, Telford's men were even now on their way here to arrest Samson. Because of her, he would lose the respectable life he'd created for himself here in Red Rock. Because of her, he might hang for a crime he had not committed.

A sob caught in her throat at the thought of him dying.

Oh, no! She had to warn him. She had to tell him what she'd done.

But she was afraid. Afraid of his anger. Afraid of his hurt. And most of all, afraid of his hate.

Why? If you want him out of your life, why should you care what he thinks of you? a voice argued in her mind.

But she did, she realized with a suddenness that surprised her. She cared a lot. When that change had been wrought, she didn't know. Perhaps sometime during his revelation the previous evening. Perhaps some time during the past weeks, without her realizing it, as he'd relentlessly but gently pursued her. Or perhaps during his caring lovemaking last night. But suddenly the thought of a life without Samson in it was more frightening than it was desirable.

She no longer wanted Samson out of her life!

The realization stunned her. She again looked over her shoulder at the man sleeping at her back. Had she grown to care for him? In that instant, with stunning force, Delilah received a revelation: She not only had grown to care for this big, intractable male, she *loved* him.

How could she have fallen in love when everything within her had been afraid of intimacy? Although from the first kiss she'd shared with Matt she'd realized that not all aspects of a relationship with a man would be repugnant, she hadn't known until last night that the sexual aspect of lovemaking could be anything other than painful and disgusting. So how could she have fallen in love? It didn't make sense. One simply did not fall in love overnight.

Somehow, when she hadn't been expecting it, hadn't been looking, Samson Towers, alias Matt Chambers, had wormed his way into her heart. And now, thanks to her, they had no future.

A sob caught in her throat. What was she going to do? She couldn't bear the thought of Samson losing his life because of her. There had to be something she could do. Some way to undo what she'd done without making Samson hate her.

Return the money?

No, that wouldn't work, because it had been deposited directly into Eve and Tom's account, to which Delilah had no access. Besides, Telford already had the information he needed and, even if she tried to recant, he would no doubt insist that the details be checked out. He wanted Samson.

Oh, God, she had to get away. She had to think. The thought of facing Samson with the knowledge of what she had done standing between them was more than she could stand.

Moving carefully, a tiny bit at a time, she slid out from beneath Samson's arm and made her way to the edge of the bed. Pausing, she held her breath as he stirred slightly. When he resumed breathing evenly, she hastily sought out the articles of her clothing still scattered about on the floor, and dressed. Deciding that she'd put her shoes on in the main room, where walking in them stood less chance of disturbing him, she picked them up and slipped out of the bedroom.

The fire in the stove had gone out, and the early-morning chill of the house brought goose bumps to her arms, yet her internal anguish was such that she scarcely felt it. All she could think of was escaping before she had to face him again. Escaping while she thought of a plan to help him, to help them both. Escaping . . . the tremendous guilt that weighed her down, though she doubted that she would ever do that.

She tied her shoelaces with shaking hands and then

rose to tiptoe to the door. "Don't tell me you're leaving without saying good-bye," a deep male voice rumbled behind her.

Delilah jumped, squealed, and turned to face him. Wearing nothing but his denims, which he'd not yet buttoned, Samson was leaning against the doorjamb of the bedroom, looking more appealing than any man had the right to look. Delilah's heart flipped over. "I . . . yes . . . I have to go."

"Without saying good-bye?"

"I didn't want to wake you."

He smiled then, a devastatingly seductive smile that showed strong even white teeth. "I wouldn't have minded," he said as he strolled slowly toward her.

Delilah read the purpose in his eyes, and knew she had to escape before he wove his way even more firmly into her heart. She jerked the door open. "I have to get back. Poopsy has been alone for too long," she explained hastily, forgetting in her anxiety that she'd sworn never to utter the dog's name aloud.

"Poopsy?" he asked, frowning, advancing until he stood before her.

"My dog." She looked up at him, into eyes the color of old steel, and wanted nothing more than to throw herself into his arms, forgetting everything. But if he was to stand any chance, then she had to come up with a plan of some kind. And she couldn't do that with him distracting her.

"I thought her name was Poochie."

"It is. I mean, her name was actually Poopsy when she was given to me, but I call her Poochie."

His hand snaked out to grasp her wrist. "Don't go yet?" he asked. "Stay, and I'll make you breakfast."

"No!" His brows arched at the panic in her voice, and she swallowed. "No," she repeated more calmly. "I have to go."

"All right," he replied, frowning as he tried to understand her decision. "I'll let you go if you agree to accompany me to the church social tomorrow night."

Tomorrow? Of course, it was now Tuesday morning. She tugged at her wrist, but he wasn't releasing his grip without an answer. "I . . . oh, all right. I'll go with you to the social."

"That's about the most ungracious acceptance I've ever received," he drawled, "but I'll take it." And again he smiled. "I'll pick you up at six."

Delilah nodded and tugged her wrist from his grasp before racing toward the lean-to stable where he'd put both horses the previous night. "Good-bye," he called after her. Delilah glanced over her shoulder and raised a hand to wave, but didn't reply. After swiftly saddling Jackpot, she mounted and left at a canter.

Samson watched her ride away. "Now what in blazes has gotten into her?" he murmured to himself.

Chapter Thirteen

By midday, Delilah had come to the conclusion that all of her parents' lessons on strength of character had come to naught. Not only had she set a sequence of irreversible events into motion without sufficient consideration, but she was a coward to boot. Having come to the conclusion that there was no way out of the mess she'd created that would not hurt either Samson or herself, she'd decided to leave Samson a note and run away. Hopefully, the note would allow him to elude his pursuers, if not retain the life he'd made for himself. And by running away, Delilah would avoid facing him, avoid seeing the hurt and anger that she knew she would see in his eyes.

Of course it meant that, despite the feelings she now carried for Samson, she could no longer have him in her life. But perhaps that was as it should be. A sacrifice on her part to pay for her terrible deed.

She'd already decided that perhaps somehow she'd

be able to help him. She might be able to hire a lawyer that could clear his name. She vaguely recalled that the woman she'd met on the train, Clara Higgins, had said her husband was a lawyer. But whatever happened, Delilah knew she couldn't face Samson again.

She'd checked with the bank and had been assured that Eve and Tom now had enough money in their account to meet their mortgage payment. Delilah had kept her hotel bill paid up-to-date out of her earnings at the saloon, and she still had some wages coming. Enough surely to pay Mr. Didsworth for a return trip to Butte and to buy a train ticket out of Montana.

Eve!

The guilt bowing her shoulders was compounded when she thought of her sister and considered the fact that Eve might still need her emotional support. But this new, stronger Eve had not seemed to need her as badly as she would have only a year ago. That realization came with a sense of relief for, though she wouldn't have admitted it, at times Delilah had found the promise she'd made to their father to always look out for her younger sister a bit difficult. There had been occasions when, weighed down by responsibility, and fear for their future, she'd wished that she might trade places with Eve.

But that was long ago, and she and Eve had weathered those trials together. They were grown now. And without the financial worries that had plagued her, Delilah was certain Eve had the strength to face whatever came her way.

Delilah would leave a note with Mrs. Schmidt for Eve explaining briefly why she'd had to leave so suddenly. Though she would be angry with her for a while for what she had done, Eve would forgive her. Eventually. If there was one thing she could always be certain of in this world, it was her sister's love. Delilah just hoped she was able some day to forgive herself, for she was finding that self-loathing was a very difficult emotion with which to live.

Her decision made, Delilah sat down to consider how to word the two correspondences she must write. She'd begin with the one for Samson. Tears blurred her vision as she stared at the blank sheet of paper before her, but they were tears of regret and self-pity, and she refused to allow them to fall. Regret for the loss of a love she had found too late. Regret for the future that might have been and could now never be. And self-pity as she pictured herself becoming another Edwina Sharp, dying alone and unloved in some distant place with only strangers to bury her.

Poopsy whined in commiseration, and Delilah automatically leaned down to pat the little dog reassuringly on the head. Then she focused on the paper before her.

> Dearest Matt,
>
> What I have to tell you is extremely difficult, and I know you shall never forgive my betrayal, which is why I haven't the courage to face you. I won't bother begging for your forgiveness. I do beg of you to try to understand, however, that my actions were the result of impulsiveness and thoughtlessness rather than malice.

At that point, she halted and simply stared at the paper. The words necessary to say what needed to be said eluded her. And despite her determination, tears began to track silently down her cheeks. She had fallen in love only to lose him in almost the same instant that she'd realized she loved him. It wasn't fair.

At that moment, a knock at her door made Delilah jump guiltily. She hastily slid the letter she'd been writing beneath a stack of paper. After quickly wiping the tears from her face, she called, "Just a moment," before rising to peer into the mirror. She dabbed a cloth over the tear stains, pinched some color into her cheeks, and smoothed her skirts. Unfortunately, there was nothing she could do about her reddened eyes.

Moving to the door, she asked, "Who is it?" hoping against hope that it would not be Samson.

"It's Frieda Schmidt, Mrs. Sterne. I haf a message for you."

Delilah quickly unfastened the lock and opened the door. Frieda took one look at her and said, "Oh, my. You haf heard already?"

Delilah stared at her blankly. "Heard what?"

"Zat your sister came to town with poor Tom laid up in ze back of ze wagon. Zey are wit' Doc Hale now. Eve, she is asking for you."

"Oh, no!" Delilah stared at Frieda in horror. And then she mindlessly grabbed her reticule and headed for the door. "Will you watch Poochie for me again, Mrs. Schmidt?"

"Uf course, uf course. You go."

Delilah remembered nothing of her walk to the doctor's office, but suddenly she was standing before the door. Incongruously, she noted that the dark green paint on the door had begun to peel. Closing her eyes, she took a deep breath to marshal her inner resources, then firmly reached out to turn the handle. Stepping into the waiting room, she immediately noticed the smells associated with doctors' offices everywhere: a combination of herbal remedies, strange concoctions, and timeworn books. The waiting room was small. It held two armchairs against one wall, and another two exactly opposite. Across from the entry, a curtained alcove led off into the inner sanctum of the doctor's domain.

The waiting room was empty.

Delilah stepped in, jumping as a bell over the door

jangled, and then halted and stood wondering what to do. Straining her ears, she listened for the sound of voices, but the place was as silent as a tomb. Oh! She winced inwardly at her unfortunate choice of wording. Abruptly, a voice bellowed, "Who's there?"

Delilah jumped—her nerves must have been positively frayed, for it was not like her to be so easily startled. Then, finding her voice, she called back, "Mrs. Sterne."

"I'll be out in a minute," the voice shouted. "Have a seat."

Delilah heard the murmur of a woman's voice—Eve?—and then quick, light steps coming toward her. An instant later, the curtain moved aside, and Eve emerged. "Oh, Delilah," she said, throwing her arms around her sister. "Thank you for coming."

There was a desperation in Eve's embrace that worried Delilah, and she felt another stab of guilt—a common circumstance in the past few hours—for having considered leaving her to face this alone. "How is he?" she murmured.

"Unconscious. From all the laudanum, you know. Doc says it'd be a blessing if he goes in his sleep." Her voice hitched and she broke off, swallowing audibly.

"Oh, Lord! Evie, I'm so sorry."

Eve sobbed against Delilah's shoulder. "It's my fault, Del. If only I hadn't listened to him."

If there was one thing Eve did not need to suffer, it was guilt! Gasping her sister by the upper arms, Delilah pulled back from her until she could look into her face. "It is *not* your fault, Eve. The decision was Tom's, and he's the one who made it. He doesn't blame you, and he certainly wouldn't want you blaming yourself, now, would he?"

Eve simply stared at her with misery shining from her luminous green eyes.

"Would he?" Delilah asked again.

Slowly Eve shook her head. "No, I suppose not."

"All right then. Now what did the doctor say?"

"He said that it's probably just a matter of hours now."

Delilah studied her and put a cap on her own tear ducts. "And has everything been said between you and Tom that needed to be said?" she asked quietly.

"Oh, yes," Eve said, as renewed tears shone in her eyes and she turned away to pace the small waiting room. "More than enough, I think. I'm so angry with him, and I don't want to be angry with him because I love him and he's . . ." She bowed her head and her shoulders shook in silent misery.

Delilah placed an arm around her. "Why are you angry with him, Evie? What's happened?"

Eve hiccuped. "I'm angry with him for choosing to die when I need him so. And I'm angry with him because . . ." She broke off to stifle a sob. "He told me he wants me to marry again, Delilah." Her lip trembled. "But only for love, he said. Not to save the ranch. Not for companionship. Not for any reason but love." Then, turning to Delilah, she said, "He made me promise to let myself fall in love again. How can he think that's even possible when my heart feels like it's being shattered into a thousand pieces?"

"Hearts heal, honey. Tom knows that. He loves you and he wants you to be happy. Don't be angry with him for that. And as for marrying again, I don't think you need to worry about that now. Once some time has passed, you can think about the promise you made."

Eve nodded. "You're right. Right now, I just want to sit with Tom in case he wakes again. I don't want him to be alone when . . ."

She broke off as her face twisted with grief and Delilah enfolded her in her embrace once more, her own heart aching with the need to protect her sister from her pain. But that was an impossibility. "It's all right to cry, sweetheart. Let it out."

Delilah held her younger sister as her body convulsed with the force of her grief, and wondered how the Lord could be so cruel as to take everyone they loved from them. Their mother, then just two years later their father, and now . . . Tom. Someone of Eve's tender age should not have to suffer so much.

A moment later, Eve regained control. Pulling away, she dried her eyes and looked up at Delilah. "Will you stay with me?"

"You know I will."

Delilah followed Eve down a narrow hallway to a back room. The smell of sickness was horrid, but she did her best to pretend she hadn't noticed. An intense young man with dark hair and spectacles worked over Tom; he didn't even glance up as they entered. "I've cleaned the leg as well as possible," he said. Delilah gasped as she caught sight of the limb to which he referred. Tom's trouser leg had been sliced from hem to hip, exposing his leg for the doctor's care, but Delilah doubted there was much that could have been accomplished by anything short of a miracle. The limb was quite literally black with putrefaction. Ugly red streaks radiated upward over Tom's exposed chest from the decaying limb, offering mute evidence of the spreading infection. "If he does happen to wake," the doctor continued, "and is in pain, you can give him some more laudanum." Doctor Hale indicated a brown bottle sitting on a stand that also contained a number of strange-looking metal instruments. "It can't hurt him now. Other than that, just sponge him occasionally to keep him as comfortable as possible."

Eve nodded. "All right, thank you. Doctor, this is my sister, Mrs. Delilah Sterne."

He glanced up then and nodded. "I've seen your handiwork, Mrs. Sterne. Nice job of stitching you did on the sheriff. Don't suppose you'd be interested in a job as my assistant? It's demanding work, and doesn't pay much except in satisfaction, but you have some definite talent there."

Delilah's eyes widened in startlement. "Well, I, um . . ."

He waved away her stumbling response. "Never mind. Just let me know if you change your mind."

"I will, sir. Thank you."

"Delilah is going to stay with me for a while if it's all right with you, Doc," Eve interjected.

Doctor Hale nodded as he draped a sheet over Tom's inert body. "Sure. I only have one other patient," he gestured toward the wall on his right, which presumably shielded another room, "and he's the kind that's secured to his bed with a pair of handcuffs anyway. I doubt that her presence will bother him."

The doctor left them then, and Eve and Delilah pulled up chairs next to the table on which Tom lay. The change in his appearance since Delilah had seen him last was startling. His skin was pale, but flushed with the unnatural blush of fever. His lips had a bluish tinge. And he'd lost so much weight that he was mere skin and bones, with the exception of his grotesquely swollen leg.

The afternoon passed slowly, the only sounds in the room those of Tom's ragged, labored breathing and Eve's occasional sobbing as she rose to sponge Tom's wasted body. She wouldn't allow Delilah to help with Tom's care. "I won't have the opportunity to do things for him much longer," she murmured in explanation.

With all of her energies focused on Eve and Tom,

Delilah pushed aside her own problems for a time, though Samson's plight was never far from her mind. She had to help him!

Later.

Time passed. Her tears spent, Eve sat staring at Tom's sunken face with dry, tortured eyes. Feeling inadequate, Delilah placed a hand over her sister's; the comfort of her presence was all she had to offer. Eve turned her hand palm upward to grip Delilah's fingers with crushing force. After that, she simply held on, as though in Delilah's hand she'd found the anchor she needed to keep from falling into a pit of despair and self-blame.

Some time later, the bell over the door in the outer room jangled and Delilah heard muted voices. A moment later, Doctor Hale came in carrying two supper plates. "Mrs. Schmidt sent these over with young Erich." He set the dishes on a cabinet nestled against the wall and then moved to the examining table, where he lifted Tom's eyelids briefly to peer into his eyes. "How's he been doing? Has he roused at all?"

Having blanketed herself in numbness, Eve didn't stir to reply, so Delilah looked at him and shook her head. "He's the same," she murmured.

Hale shook his head sadly and checked his patient again, taking his pulse and checking his leg, though it was obvious even to Delilah that there wasn't anything he could do for him. Then the doctor met Delilah's eyes meaningfully and shook his head again. "If you need anything, just call," he said. "And try to get Mrs. Cameron to eat a bite or two."

Delilah nodded in silent agreement as the doctor left the room.

A while later, although she wasn't very hungry herself, she rose to retrieve the plates the doctor had left. Each plate had a small dish of custard nestled on one edge. In addition to the custard, Mrs. Schmidt had provided them with a hearty beef stew and homemade buns. Taking one of the plates over to where Eve sat staring blankly at her husband's face, Delilah gently nudged her. "Eve, honey, I want you to take this. You need to try to eat something."

In blind obedience, Eve accepted the plate, lowering it to her lap, without so much as looking at it.

"Will you try a bit?" Delilah asked.

Eve shook her head. "I'm not hungry," she murmured so quietly that, even standing right before her, Delilah had to bend forward to hear the words.

"I know, Evie. I'm not either. But we have to eat just a little bit. Please? For me?"

For the first time in hours, Eve looked at Delilah. Then, slowly, she nodded and picked up the fork on her plate. Piercing a small piece of carrot, she put it into her mouth. Satisfied that Eve would at least try to eat something, Delilah turned to retrieve the other plate for herself and then resumed her seat next to Eve.

Neither of them was able to eat more than a few bites, but at least it was something. Sometime later, she didn't know how long, Delilah replaced the plates with their now cold fare on the cabinet. She was tired, discouraged, and feeling particularly helpless, so she took a moment to lean against the cabinet, close her eyes, and simply breathe. A groan came from across the room, and she whirled at the sound. Tom was stirring, very slightly, and Eve had risen to lean over him.

"Tom, I'm here."

Tom opened fever-glazed eyes to look at her. "Evie, darlin'?"

"I'm here." Eve clasped his hands and squeezed. "I won't leave you."

A lump rose in Delilah's throat, choking her, and tears swam in her eyes, blurring the scene before her.

"Are you in pain?" Eve asked.

Tom nodded. "But it's worth it to be awake. I wanted to see your beautiful face just one more time," he murmured. "If there is one memory I want to take with me, it's that." He raised a trembling hand to trace the curve of Eve's cheek while she tilted her face into his touch. "Can you smile for me? Just one last time?"

A sob caught in Eve's throat, but she nodded and smiled for him. The smile wobbled, but it was apparently enough for Tom.

"Thank you, darlin'. You know how much I love you, don't you?"

Eve nodded and the sob finally escaped. "Oh, Tom, I don't want to lose you."

"I know darlin'," he murmured as he stroked her hair as though attempting to memorize its texture. "Now give me a hug so that I can smell your perfume."

Eve nodded and bent forward to kiss the side of his face. Tom's arms wrapped around her briefly, and he sighed. And then slowly, so slowly, his arms dropped back to his sides. "Tom?" Eve said.

But there was no reply, and Delilah had seen what Eve had not. On his final sigh of contentment in holding the woman he loved, Tom had left this life.

Eve pulled back to look down at him, but his eyes stared sightlessly at the ceiling. "Tom?" she cried more loudly.

Delilah went to her. "He's gone, sweetheart. Tom's at peace now."

"No," a wail of denial rose in Eve's throat. And then turning into Delilah's embrace she asked, "How will I live without him?"

Delilah didn't bother murmuring reassurances now. Nothing she could say would ease the pain Eve was feeling. Later she could remind Eve that although Tom had passed, his love for her wasn't gone. Later she would remind her that she would always hold Tom in her heart. Later she would remind her that as long as she remembered him, a part of Tom would always be alive and with her. For now though, she simply held her sister and let her weep.

"I don't know . . . how I'll manage without him," Eve sobbed brokenly.

But Delilah had recognized what Eve had not yet realized: the fact that Eve had been functioning quite well without Tom for some time now. She'd been doing everything that managing a ranch entailed. She would now lack her husband's counsel, but she had her own strength, determination, and intelligence. Eve would triumph. Delilah said only, "You'll manage. You have my word on it."

At that moment, the doctor entered the room. He looked at Delilah wordlessly, but the question was plain in his eyes.

Delilah nodded. "He's gone," she murmured.

"Did he wake?"

"Yes. He talked for a moment and then . . . he just sighed."

Doctor Hale nodded. "It happens like that sometimes." He glanced at Eve and then back at Delilah. "You're going to take care of her?" he asked.

"Of course."

"See that she gets some sleep. I'll get hold of Mr. Howard and Reverend Duncan to make arrangements for the funeral. It'll probably be best if we get that accomplished tomorrow."

Delilah stared at him numbly, glad that he was thinking about necessities, because her own mind suddenly felt as though it was slogging through a dense fog. "Mr. Howard?" she repeated in a deadened tone.

"The undertaker."

Delilah nodded. Of course. They would need an undertaker.

Some time later, once Tom's body had been taken by Mr. Howard, the undertaker, to be prepared for his funeral in the suit that Eve had had the foresight to bring along, Delilah took Eve back to the hotel with her and tried to get her to rest.

Samson sat astride Goliath, concealed in the shadow of a huge cedar where he'd been sitting for the past few hours observing Simon Earl's Rocking E Ranch. He needed to catch Simon Earl red-handed if he was going to jail the man for rustling. Otherwise, he had only Powell's word on Earl's involvement. And truth be told, Samson would not bet his life on Powell's honesty. Neither would a judge. 'Course the other hands had backed Powell's statement once they learned the cat was out of the bag, so to speak. Still, Samson had no proof that Earl was involved. He'd caught the others red-handed, but not Earl. And the idea that the powerful rancher might get away with saving his ranch at the expense of his more respectable neighbors grated like sandpaper on Samson's sense of decency.

So Samson had done something he would have preferred not to have done. He and Deputy Wilkes had made a deal with One-Eyed Jim. They would talk to the judge on One-Eye's behalf if old Jim helped them get Simon Earl. Jim had balked at first: He wanted to be set free—period. But when he realized that Samson wouldn't agree to that, he accepted the offer he'd been given. Or rather he had seemed to accept it. Samson wouldn't put it past him to try to escape if he got the chance. That was why Samson and Carl had provided an escort for One-Eyed Jim, bringing him out here. Then they'd hidden in the hills above the ranch to watch him ride in.

The plan was that One-Eyed Jim would go to Simon Earl and tell him that the rest of the gang had been caught with some of the cattle *outside* the canyon. He'd tell Earl that the remaining cattle—animals that Samson had ensured were still carrying brands belonging to Simon Earl's neighbors—needed to be moved that night before the sheriff came back and found the access to the canyon. If Earl was real smart, he'd do nothing, and Samson still wouldn't be able to link him to the operation with any tangible proof. But Samson figured that Simon Earl's greed would hang a lickin' on his intelligence. Samson and Carl Wilkes figured that Earl would make one of two moves. Either he'd try to herd the cattle out of the area immediately, concluding that he could avoid the deputies that would be combing the hills. Or, he'd herd them back to his place real quick and hide them amongst his own cattle. Samson's bet was on the second move, because he figured that's what he'd do in Earl's position, but he was prepared for either eventuality.

Once Simon Earl and whomever among his own hands he would trust were in the process of moving the cattle, either back here to the ranch or off to sell, Samson and Carl would arrest them. It wasn't a very elaborate plan, and even from Samson's point of view it was as full of holes as last year's socks, but it was the best he could come up with on such short notice.

And he needed to catch Earl quickly. If he didn't and, for whatever reason, Earl didn't set up another rustling operation, the rancher would get off scot-free.

With the exception of One-Eyed Jim, Earl's other partners were still languishing in Samson's jail under the guard of Bill Tillis who, although he was hobbling around on crutches, could still wield a gun well enough.

Jim had entered Earl's ranch house a few hours ago. There'd been a brief flurry of movement on the part of the ranch hands after Jim's arrival, then nothing. Samson itched to know what was going on down there. But as the waiting dragged on, his thoughts inevitably turned to Delilah and the social.

For the first time since coming to Red Rock and being pegged as the most eligible bachelor in town, Samson was looking forward to the monthly church social. He couldn't count the number of socials he'd attended where his primary thought the entire evening had been *escape*. Nor could he count the number of socials that he'd managed to avoid for the sake of duty. Duty being *anything* drastic enough to keep him out of the ladies' clutches for just one more month. Being the sheriff, he'd been informed upon his arrival in town that it was his responsibility to attend all town functions with the exception of those times when his duties as sheriff precluded attendance.

By Samson's definition, a sheriff's duties were pretty varied. Anything from rescuing kittens to catching bad guys. Young Sarah Jennings's kitten, Mischief, had offered him the excuse he needed for missing one social. It had taken him most of the evening to save that cat. Unfortunately, in a town the size of Red Rock, there weren't all that many timely rescues to be made, and Samson had had to attend more socials that he cared to remember. Heck, when he thought about it, he'd been embroiled in so many female machinations in the last two years that he figured the good Lord might let him skip purgatory when he died on account of time already served. Tomorrow night was the first time he'd be attending a social with a lady of *his* choosing on his arm.

And Delilah was *all* lady.

He frowned abruptly as he recalled Mrs. Williamson's reaction to Delilah Sterne's presence in town. He hoped he hadn't made a mistake in inviting Delilah. He would feel responsible for her discomfort if the town matrons were rude to her.

The more he thought about it, the more worried he became. Why hadn't he thought of that? "Damn!" he muttered to himself. Then, a stirring at the ranch house below distracted him.

Somebody went running from the main house to the bunkhouse. Then, a couple of minutes later, three men emerged. They saddled five horses and rode up to the main house, where they sat waiting out front with the two extra horses.

Something was definitely happening.

Samson looked over at Wilkes where he lay dozing in the shade of a tree with his battered hat pulled down over his face. Apparently the new addition to his household had not yet learned to sleep more than a couple of hours at a time, and Carl's rest was suffering as a result. He'd been napping for almost an hour now, though. That should help to refresh him. "Carl," Samson called softly.

When the man didn't so much as twitch a muscle, Samson pulled a cone off of a nearby tree and threw it at him. Carl jumped and shoved his hat back. "Come on, Wilkes," Samson said quietly. "Time to join the party."

Wilkes nodded, ran his hands over his face to clear the cobwebs, and rose to mount his sorrel mare, Bella, which he'd left ground-tethered a short distance off. He brought the mare to a halt next to Goliath. "What's goin' on, Matt?" he asked.

Samson shrugged. "I don't know, but they're gettin' ready to ride out, so we'd best follow them and find out what old Simon has in mind."

The moon had set, and it was nearly dawn the next morning before Samson and Wilkes trailed Simon Earl and his boys back onto Rocking E land with their small herd of stolen cattle. To Samson's surprise, rather than immediately herding the cattle in with his own, Earl had them driven into a small dead-end canyon that formed a natural corral some distance away from the ranch buildings. A minute later, when he saw the branding irons being brought out, Samson understood why: Earl was going to destroy all evidence that the cattle weren't his. Or at least he was going to try.

Figuring that the commotion would help conceal their approach, Samson and his deputy waited until the branding was underway before riding down. He expected trouble: Earl did not have much respect for the badge Samson wore or the law it represented. And once again the odds were five or six against two. But he figured that most of these men were good men who just happened to work for Earl. He hoped he was right. In case he wasn't, though, he'd sent word to each of the ranches involved, letting them know that he was bringing Simon Earl in for the rustling of their cattle.

By his calculation, if he failed somewhere along the way tonight and Earl won this little battle, the man would have about twenty-four hours before his neighbors took care of the problem. Samson didn't approve of vigilante justice, but it had worked in Montana Territory back in '63, when the miners had organized to get rid of Henry Plummer and his road agents. There were still times when it had its uses.

Samson and Wilkes rode almost within shouting distance of the rustlers before dismounting and secreting their mounts in the dense shadow of a large outcropping. They made their way forward on foot from there.

Cattle bawled. Men shouted. The fire crackled. Hair and flesh sizzled. Smoke hung in the chilled air of early morning. Samson waited for a lull in the action before drawing attention to their presence. "Simon Earl—" he shouted.

There was a moment of stunned silence. "Who's there?" a voice demanded.

"It's Sheriff Chambers."

He vaguely heard someone cuss and then Earl asked belligerently, "What d'ya want, Chambers?"

"Tell your men to throw down their arms, Simon. I'm here to take you in."

"What for?" His tone of voice hadn't changed.

"I think we both know what for," Samson replied.

He saw Earl make a gesture that looked like he was telling his men to make their way around behind him. "Maybe you'd better spell it out for me, Chambers. Just so's there's no misunderstandin' an' all." Earl was killing time.

Samson let him think it was working, but motioned for Wilkes to watch their backs. "Seems like the brands on those cattle aren't Rocking E's."

"How do you figure that?"

"I checked them out yesterday and watched you drive them out."

A man poked his head around a tree trunk a short distance away. Splinters lanced their way into his cheek when a bullet from Wilkes's Colt struck the edge of the trunk right in front of him. He yelped and hightailed it back to join the others. Earl took one look at him and said, "You're fired, Rydan."

Rydan brushed at the blood staining his cheek. "That's fine by me, Earl. I signed on as a cowhand, not a goddamn gunfighter. You want gunfighters, you'd better hire 'em straight off next time."

Samson decided to talk directly to the hands arrayed uncertainly at Simon Earl's back. "You men throw down your weapons; my business is with Earl, not you. Unless you figure he's gonna make it worth your while to make his business your business."

The men hesitated, looking at each other, looking at

Earl. "I figure Simon's neighbors are none too happy with him right about now," Samson continued, "so you might want to practice with those guns a bit if you're sidin' with Earl. You'll probably have to use them." The knowledge that Simon Earl's neighbors might be gunning for Earl and anyone who worked for him seemed to do the trick. Dean Bradford dropped his Winchester first and slowly, carefully unbuckled his gunbelt, dropping his sidearm to the ground. Then he raised his hands.

"You're fired too, Bradford," Earl growled.

"Yessir, I reckon so," Bradford replied. He didn't seem too concerned.

A second later, the man Earl had called Rydan followed suit, dropping his weapon to the ground with a thud. He'd already been fired, after all. Then a young man that Samson had never met dropped a pair of pearl-handled pistols to the ground. Samson stifled a sigh of relief. He'd had the young man sized up as another *Kid Something*. "Bradford, pick them all up and put them over by the tree to your right." The tree was far enough away that the guns would be out of Earl's reach, and the path Bradford would have to take to get to it would ensure that he didn't cross between Samson and Simon Earl.

"Yessir." Bradford bent to the appointed task, accomplishing it quickly and efficiently without any attempt at treachery.

"Now, you three can mount up and ride out," Samson directed the drovers.

"What about my guns, Sheriff?" the young man argued. "I saved a long time to buy those."

"They worth your life?" Samson asked.

"No, sir. But I want them back."

"If you drop in to the sheriff's office tomorrow, you can have your firearms back."

The three cowhands mounted and rode off without looking back. Cattle milled, lowing restlessly. Only Simon Earl and his son Travis remained. Simon was bold and belligerent. "You ain't takin' me in alive, Chambers. I'm not gonna lose everything on account of some goddamn cows."

"Pa!" Travis looked just plain scared.

"Shut up, boy! You just do what I tell ya and everythin'll be fine."

Samson didn't like the looks of things. Glancing at his deputy, he saw an echoing worry in his eyes. With a gesture, Samson suggested that Wilkes move around and try to get behind Simon Earl. Just in case.

Carl nodded and slipped off into the greying darkness.

"He's lying, Travis," Samson said. He wanted the young man out of the cross fire, but he wasn't holding out much hope of getting him to ride out. "Your Pa's not going to get out of this, and if you aren't careful, you'll go down with him. Wouldn't it make more sense for you to run your Pa's ranch for him rather than to go to jail with him, maybe die with him? Why let some stranger take over everything you've worked for all your life?"

"Pa?" Travis looked at his father.

"I told ya to shut up boy!" And then, without warning, Simon Earl pulled his side arm. Samson ducked behind a rock as a bullet whined over his head.

Damnation! He'd hoped that it wouldn't come down to another gunfight.

When next he cautiously peered over the boulder, he was flabbergasted to see Simon Earl using his own son as a shield. "Pa?" Travis was obviously stunned as well.

"They won't shoot you, boy. Will you, Chambers?"

Samson didn't bother answering the question. "I can't let you leave here, Simon. You know that. Besides, you've got no place to go. What do you think this is going to accomplish?"

Earl didn't answer except to fire at Samson again. The bullet ricocheted off of the boulder and whined off into nothingness. There was another shot. And another. He dared not lift his head above the boulder to see what Earl was doing, so he tried moving to the side a bit. Another shot and something stung his arm. Samson jerked back behind the security of the boulder and glanced at the wound.

Just a graze. Nothing serious.

He figured Simon had two shots left before he either had to reload or switch guns. Of course, Travis's pistol was real near to hand. Still, it would be a momentary reprieve.

Taking off his hat, Samson lifted it slowly above the boulder, attracting another round of fire. One shot. Two. That should do it.

"Hold it right there, Simon." It was Carl's voice.

Cautiously, Samson peered over the boulder to make certain everything was under control. Wilkes had his pistol pressed to the back of Earl's neck.

"Let the boy go and drop the gun." Wilkes ordered. "Now!" Slowly, as hate suffused his features, Simon Earl obeyed. Carl's gaze flicked briefly to Simon's son. "Travis, I want you to step away from your pa and drop your gunbelt. You understand me?"

Travis nodded, and carefully, without making any sudden moves, complied. The young man still looked stunned. He'd learned something about his pa in the last few minutes that no man should have to learn.

Chapter Fourteen

It was almost noon before Samson had everything tied up at the jail. Truth be told, his jail was getting a mite crowded, but Judge Niven was supposed to be back in town on Thursday, so it wouldn't be for much longer. Heck! Thursday was *tomorrow*. A man sure could lose track of the days when he didn't get any sleep. Samson had been out of town for more than twenty-four hours. All he wanted to do was go to bed and get a few hours of sleep before the social, but with his stomach gnawing at his backbone the way it was, he figured he'd better grab a little something to eat at the hotel first. He didn't trust himself to cook. With his eyes as blurry as they were, he wasn't sure he could boil water without burning it, let alone fry an egg. At least if he fell asleep over his plate at the hotel restaurant, Mrs. Schmidt would give him a nudge to get him moving on home.

"Hey, Sheriff," old Jeb greeted him as he passed the mercantile.

"Jeb," Samson nodded and halted. He was really too tired for a rundown of the local news, but he thought he'd better ask, just in case. "Anything been happening?"

Jeb nodded. "Yep. You want the funny stuff first or the sorrowful stuff?"

Samson sighed. He'd have to hear the sorrowful stuff eventually anyway, but he could sure use a laugh right now. "The funny stuff," he said.

Jeb narrowed his eyes, considering. "On secon' thought, ya might not think it's as funny as I do. I sure hope ya didn' have any laundry over at Mrs. Vanbergen's." Jeb chuckled and shook his head.

As a matter of fact, he did. "Why's that?" Samson asked.

"One o' them sachet kittens su'prised her real good when she went out ta hang stuff on the line."

"A skunk?"

"Tha's what I said, wasn' it?" Jeb demanded.

Samson ignored the question. Oh, boy! He hoped his good shirt hadn't been on the line when it happened. He'd wanted to wear it tonight. "Did the skunk spray her?"

Jeb grinned. "Got her real good. She done come runnin' over to the mercantile to get all the vinegar an' bakin' soda she could carry. 'Course, old man Lowden was yellin' at her ta get out of his store, tryin' to chase her out 'fore she stunk up the place. An' him no bigger than a bar o' soap on wash day next to her," he grinned. "Coulda told him it wouldn' work. Mrs. Vanbergen wouldn' budge till he promised to deliver all the vinegar and soda he had over ta her place." Jeb shook his head again. "It sure was somethin' ta see."

A tired smile tugged at Samson's lips. Yeah, he could imagine the scene. Though he wouldn't have wanted to be too close to it himself. "I guess I'll have to find another shirt to wear to the social tonight."

"Social's postponed to Saturday," Jeb informed him without an explanation.

Samson's brows arched. "Why?"

"On account o' the funeral taday. That's the sorrowful news I was talkin' about b'fore."

"Whose funeral?" he asked.

"Tom Cameron's." Jeb shrugged and looked down the street toward the undertaker's. "He passed on las' night. Howard said his leg was darn near rotted right off. Hell of a way to go." He shook his head sadly. "Funeral's over at the church at four o'clock."

"Aw, hell!"

"Yep," Jeb returned in full agreement. "That little lady of yours seems to be holdin' up purdy good. She's been keepin' Mrs. Cameron over to the hotel with her." He looked up at Samson. "You gonna go to the funeral, Matt?"

Samson nodded solemnly. "Yeah."

Jeb nodded. "I figured."

"I'll talk to you later, Jeb."

Samson wasn't very hungry anymore, but he had to eat, so he continued on down to the hotel. He wondered if he should bother Delilah and Mrs. Cameron to express his sympathies or just wait until the funeral to do it. Over a lunch of fresh trout which Frieda Schmidt proudly proclaimed had been caught by her son Erich from the creek, Samson decided to wait to speak with Delilah and her sister. If they were managing to rest, he didn't want to disturb them.

He noticed that Mrs. Schmidt seemed to be affected by the news of young Tom's passing too. Her smiles were not quite as wide, her eyes were sad, and her conversation a bit stilted. In addition, that blamed dog of Delilah's was following Frieda around looking so forlorn and lost that Samson began to believe Delilah's assertion that the dog understood far more than dogs usually did. Then again, Delilah had told him that she'd inherited the dog from some older lady who'd passed on, so maybe the little dog was simply wondering why she'd been handed over to yet another mistress.

His lunch over with, Samson decided to go home and try to catch a couple of hours of sleep before the funeral. He'd been really looking forward to spending time with Delilah tonight, but he was exhausted. . . .

After a brief funeral service, the congregation of Red Rock's only church gathered in the cemetery to bury one of its members. It was a bright sunny June day. "Or ever the silver cord be loosed, or the golden bowl be broken, or the pitcher be broken at the fountain, or the wheel broken at the cistern.

"Then shall the dust return to the earth as it was: and the spirit shall return unto God who gave it." The words began to run together, becoming little more than a jumble of sound to Delilah as she stared sightlessly at Reverend Duncan's black-suited figure as he read from his worn leather-bound Bible. Stifling a sob, she used a sodden handkerchief to blot a fresh bout of tears that rolled down her cheeks.

She hated death. It was one thing in life that you could not fight against and win. At best, you could delay it. Young and old alike were struck down indiscriminately. There was no sense of correlation between a life well lived or poorly lived and the depths of the pain and suffering associated with dying. The entire process seemed completely random.

She gave Eve's hand a small squeeze; reassurance that she was at her side, a gesture to keep her from sinking too deeply into herself. Delilah was concerned about her. Eve hadn't slept much the previous night, but neither had she cried. In fact, she hadn't cried since the moment of Tom's death. She seemed almost too calm. Yet whenever Delilah had asked her if she was all right, she'd responded with a softly uttered, "I'm fine," and offered a wan smile before sinking back into a kind of stupor. Even now she stood tall, straight, and pale; her eyes were dry. But Delilah could sense a brittleness, a delicacy behind the rigidity that worried her. Eve reminded her of a piece of delicate china, beautiful but so fragile that it could shatter into a million pieces if not handled with exquisite care.

The hands from the Devil's Fork had arrived in town for the funeral and now stood on either side of herself and Eve, silently supportive as they cast the occasional anxious glance Eve's way. Delilah didn't know who had sent word to them, but someone must have, for she'd been so involved with Eve that she'd forgotten. It had probably been Doc Hale. He had taken care of most of the details.

Delilah saw other faces in the crowd she knew: Frieda, Marc, and Erich Schmidt had come to pay their respects. Doc Hale stood near them, his hat in his hands and his head bowed. There were the Lowdens from the mercantile and the Metters from the livery. Miss Cora had come too, heedless of the ever-ready-to-criticize matrons of Red Rock. Since she had only known Eve in passing, Delilah felt certain that Miss Cora's presence was a gesture of support for herself, although Delilah had developed a thick skin long ago and was seldom bothered by wagging tongues. She noted that the town's respectable ladies kept their husbands firmly at their sides, and as far away from Delilah as possible. If she'd been feeling less depressed, she would have greeted the men whom she'd had occasion to meet in the Lucky Strike. However, of all the people in attendance, the presence that Delilah found the most disturbing by far was that of Samson Towers.

She couldn't help but look at him. He was so handsome. And she so wanted to feel his arms around her again. But every time she looked at him, she found his eyes on her, gentle, compassionate, and caring—and that made her guilt swell to near choking proportions. The letter she had planned to write him still lay unfinished on the table in her room. Yet she didn't have the courage to tell him in person. To see the expression in his eyes transform into hate. To see that gentleness become rage.

Oh, God, what had she done? Her heart constricted with pain and she stifled another sob, this one for Samson.

"Ashes to ashes," the reverend intoned. "Dust to dust." The hollow sound of a clump of dirt hitting the coffin drew Delilah's eyes and thoughts back to where they ought to be at a time like this. Reverend Duncan said another prayer and then the mourners began to slowly move away. She refused to watch, refused to watch Samson walk away from her. It would be too painful, symbolic though it might be.

The church ladies had organized a supper at the town hall on behalf of those mourners who'd come from greater distances, and this was where everyone would head now. Delilah dreaded attending with Eve, though she knew it was obligatory. The thought of making polite conversation and the possibility of running into Samson were both extremely frightening prospects in her current state of mind. Nevertheless, she looked at Eve. "Are you ready to go?" she queried softly.

Eve shook her head. "Just a few more minutes, please." She looked at the Devil's Fork hands who waited uncertainly for her. "You go on to the hall and have something to eat if you like. I'll be along shortly."

"Yes, ma'am," Wright and Stone murmured simultaneously.

As soon as they'd moved off, she turned her attention to the two men in denim overalls and chambray shirts who'd stood back from the mourners while they waited to complete their job of filling in the grave. "Before you . . . fill it in, could I have a few moments of privacy please?"

They nodded, uncomfortable as men always are when faced with a grieving woman. "Sure thing, ma'am," the older one murmured before backing off to a discreet distance. "You take yer time."

"Would you like me to stay, Mrs. Cameron?" Reverend Duncan asked.

Eve shook her head. "No. It's all right." And then, as though afraid she might have offended him, she offered him her hand. "But I do want to thank you, Reverend. It was a beautiful service."

Reverend Duncan accepted her hand and nodded, though a slight frown settled between his brows. He glanced questioningly at Delilah, but since she didn't understand the precise nature of his concern, she could offer him no assurances. "You're quite welcome, ma'am," he said to Eve. Worn Bible in hand, he began to walk away, trailing after the other mourners, and then abruptly he stopped and turned to face Eve once more. "You're sure you'll be all right, ma'am?"

Eve nodded. "I'll be fine," she said softly. "If I need anything, my sister will be with me."

Reverend Duncan looked at Delilah and she received the impression that he wasn't all that certain that she could offer Eve what she needed. Delilah's spine stiffened as she stared back at him, meeting his gaze boldly. Then, finally, his expression softened. He nodded and turned away.

Delilah gripped Eve's elbow to support her and

moved with her sister nearer to the graveside. For the longest time, Eve simply stared down at the pine coffin, her face as expressionless as though it had been carved from stone. And then, with an abruptness that startled Delilah, Eve's legs crumpled and she fell to her knees. The first sob convulsed her entire body. Delilah dropped to her side to cradle her against her shoulder as the pain Eve had been holding inside suddenly erupted, breaching the walls of her defenses to free a deluge of healing tears. Eve crumbled against her as great choking sobs gripped her body in a paroxysm of grief.

When the storm was over, Eve dried her eyes and said good-bye to her husband for the last time. "I won't cry for you again Tom," she murmured. "I have to run our ranch alone now, and there's no more time for grieving. I still don't understand the decision you made, though I know you said that you didn't regret it. I suppose, though, that I've finally accepted it. Perhaps it will stop hurting some day. Good-bye, darling. I'll visit you when I'm in town." Pulling a daisy from a batch of wildflowers that someone had left at the graveside, she dropped it down onto the coffin.

Rising then, she looked at Delilah, at the tears brimming in her eyes, and hugged her. "Don't cry for me, Delilah. I'm all right now. I don't want you to worry about me. All right?"

"I'll always worry about you, Evie. You're my sister and I love you." She sniffed. "But I think you've grown into a strong woman, and I won't worry about you nearly as much as I used to."

Eve released her, nodded, and almost smiled. "I guess I can accept that."

Eve, being the perceptive person that she was, had sensed by noon the next day that something was bothering Delilah other than Tom's demise. Upon returning to Delilah's room after lunch, she'd wanted to know what it was. Delilah stared at her and couldn't bring herself to tell her. To tell Eve about the situation she now found herself in, she would have to tell her why she'd acted as she had. And nothing about her reasoning had been admirable. Fear of the sheriff's determined pursuit of her had been only part of the reason—and perhaps it had been the most understandable. But Eve would not thank Delilah for saving her ranch at the possible expense of a man's life. Especially a man whom she liked and respected.

"It's nothing, Evie. I won't burden you with my problems at a time when you have so many of your own."

"You're sure?"

Delilah nodded. She would bear this horrible guilt alone, and pray that when she finally found the opportunity to finish the letter to Samson, he would still have time to evade Telford's men. It was Thursday now. She had sent the telegram on Monday. If they rode hard, or came part of the way by train, Telford's men could be almost here. The thought terrified her.

"Well, I have to get back to the ranch," Eve was saying. "I might as well go back with the hands. I think the ranch is the best place for me right now. I miss it."

Her words suddenly penetrated Delilah's numbed mind. "Already?" she asked. "But . . . would you like me to come with you until you're feeling more yourself?"

Eve shook her head. "I'm going to be working most of the time anyway. And Fong is there to run the household. I want you to worry about yourself for a change, Delilah. I want you to find someplace you can be happy, and with any luck *someone* with whom to share that happiness. I want you to try to forget the past, and Sterne, and everything that happened to us back then, and start to live again. Will you do that?"

Delilah stared at her. "I didn't know you . . ." She trailed off, uncertain as to how to finish. Never before had Eve adopted the role of the caretaker. Never had Eve given her advice or told her what her opinion was of Delilah's personal life. Never had Eve shown she understood quite so much as that simple statement revealed. It brought tears to Delilah's eyes.

"You didn't know I what?"

"Understood," Delilah breathed. "I didn't know how much you understood."

"I've always understood, Delilah. And I've always felt guilty for not fighting harder to help you."

Delilah was stricken to learn that her younger sister had been suffering on her behalf. "Oh, Evie. Why should you feel guilty? You tried to help. It wasn't your fault. He knocked you unconscious. There was nothing you could have done."

Eve shrugged, her eyes shimmering with tears. "I could have fetched some kind of a weapon before I tried to help. I could have done something besides simply jumping on his back and pounding his shoulders with my fists."

Delilah hugged her. "You were only fifteen, Eve. Fifteen! You have nothing to feel guilty for. Please don't blame yourself."

Avoiding Delilah's gaze, Eve released her and turned to look out the window. "I'll try not to, if you'll promise me you'll think about what I've said. It's time to put the past behind you and start to live again, Delilah. Please?"

"I promise I'll think about it," Delilah said.

"Good!" With a forced smile, Eve turned back to her. "And now, it's time for me to go. Write to me?"

"You know I will."

"You'll be leaving Red Rock right away?" Delilah nodded and Eve asked, "Where will you go?"

Delilah shrugged. She hadn't really thought about

anything except getting away. "Colorado perhaps. I hear the scenery there is almost as beautiful as it is here."

Minutes later, Eve mounted a tough old buckskin mare that Rattlesnake Joe had brought to town, and left Red Rock to return to the Devil's Fork ranch. *Her* ranch. Rattlesnake drove the buckboard wagon that Eve had driven into town carrying Tom, and the other hands trailed out behind them. They made a strange and solemn procession as they left Red Rock: a lady rancher, an old man, an Indian, a Chinaman, a drunk, and . . . the solitary man who called himself Stone, whoever he might be. And yet, as Delilah stood on the boardwalk outside the hotel and watched her sister ride away, for the first time in memory she was not worried about her, for something told her that Eve would be fine.

"I've been trying to get a chance to talk to you for days," a deep voice said from behind her, making her jump. "Will you join me for supper tonight? I hear Frieda's making cabbage rolls."

Samson! Delilah closed her eyes and swallowed. "I . . . uh . . ."

"Come on. It's just a meal, and you have to eat."

Yes, she did. And perhaps she could simply tell him about what she'd done. She didn't want to, but she had to admit that the letter was a coward's way out. And she'd never before considered herself a coward. "All right," she murmured, turning to face him. At the sight of his handsome face, her heart gave a peculiar lurch and the bottom fell out of her stomach.

He smiled, and her pulse began a double-time cadence. "Good," he said. "I'll pick you up at seven."

Delilah nodded. "All right."

He hesitated a moment as though there was something more he wanted to say, and then he shook his head. "Well, I guess I'd best be going. Judge Niven's in town and we have some business to take care of."

Delilah nodded again. "Later, then."

She watched him walk away, knowing that the next time he did so it would be for good, and her heart ached for what might have been. "Afternoon, Mrs. Sterne," a loud voice called from the street.

Startled, Delilah turned to heed the greeting and realized that it had been delivered by Mr. Didsworth, who was driving his freight wagon, loaded high with merchandise, through town. "Good afternoon, sir," Delilah returned. "Are you just arriving or just leaving?"

"Arriving, ma'am. I'll be headin' out agin in the mornin'."

Providence! Delilah decided. She'd go see Mrs. Francis at the telegraph office and see if she could book a seat on a train out of Butte late tomorrow. Then she'd book a seat on Mr. Didsworth's freight wagon, returning to Butte. He would be leaving bright and early in the morning, she knew, for that was his routine. Oh, and in the morning, she'd have to see Mr. Metter regarding Jackpot. The funds she would receive for selling the horse back to him would aid with travel expenses.

Thus it was that Delilah had a busy afternoon. Her final stop was the Lucky Strike. She couldn't very well leave town without saying farewell to the only woman, other than Frieda Schmidt, who had befriended her during her stay. Delilah waved to Mitch on her way past the bar and asked, "Is Miss Cora in her office?"

"Yes, ma'am."

A second later, Delilah knocked on the office door. "Come in," Cora said in her low-pitched musical voice. Then, as Delilah opened the door, a genuine smile. "Delilah! Come in. I've been thinking about you. How are you?"

"I'm fine," Delilah said, returning her smile, albeit a bit less widely.

"Please sit," Cora said, indicating one of the chairs before her desk. "Eve headed back to the Devil's Fork already, I hear."

"Yes. Actually that's why I'm here. I've come to say good-bye and to apologize for the fact that the gaming table was less prosperous for you than I had hoped it would be."

Cora waved her apology aside. "No need to apologize. An honest dealer can't make guarantees, and you *were* honest. Besides, I made more on that table than I would have if you hadn't come at all, now didn't I? But I'm really sorry to hear you're leaving. Are you certain I can't talk you into staying a while? Red Rock's not a bad place to live, you know."

Delilah shook her head. "No. I can't stay. I have to get away."

Cora considered her with a grave expression. "That sounds like man trouble. Anything I can help with?"

"No. But thank you."

Cora grimaced. "Darn that Matt Chambers! I knew the way he was chasing you he was just going to break your heart."

Delilah's gaze flew up to meet Cora's. "Oh, no. It's not Matt's fault. It's mine." After what she'd done, she couldn't bear to have anyone think badly of him.

"Yours," Cora repeated incredulously. "What did you do?" Her tone suggested complete disbelief. "Except try to avoid him, that is?"

"Yes, well . . . in trying to avoid him I did something . . . unforgivable. I betrayed . . ." but she couldn't bring herself to voice the extent of her perfidy, so she changed tack. "I betrayed his trust and the trust of everyone who befriended me." And then, to her horror, tears of self-pity welled in her eyes again. Oh, Lord! She didn't want to cry in front of Cora.

But it was too late.

Cora quickly rose and moved around the desk to sit beside Delilah. Placing an arm around her shoulders, she handed her a clean handkerchief and murmured, "You just let it out, love, and then we'll talk. There's always a way to fix things. We just have to find it."

But Delilah knew there was no way to fix this. No matter what she did, Samson would have to be told what she had done. And once he learned what kind of person she truly was, he would hate her. As he should. As she would were the shoe on the other foot.

"Heavens!" she hiccuped as she dried her tears. "I've done more crying in the last few days than in the last year."

"Sometimes it happens that way. That's why they say that bad things happen in threes." Cora leaned back to study her with compassionate eyes. "Now why don't you tell me what this is all about? Sometimes it helps to talk about it even if that's the only thing that can be done."

Delilah hesitated. She was afraid, if she told her, that Cora would hate her just as she now hated herself. Yet she desperately wanted advice. Finally, she sighed. "You'll undoubtedly hate me," she said. "But . . . will you promise me that you absolutely will not tell another soul?"

"Of course, if that's what you want," Cora replied.

Delilah nodded and twisted the handkerchief in her hand. Now that she'd agreed to talk, she didn't know where to begin. Finally she sighed, and simply started talking. "I've been afraid of being alone with men, or getting too close to them, for a number of years now. I won't go into the reasons why, but I'm sure you can guess. So when Matt didn't respect my widowhood as other men did, it terrified me."

Cora nodded understandingly without comment, and, after a bit, Delilah found it easier than she'd imagined to confide in this worldly woman who'd seen enough of life not to be shocked by anything she heard. Delilah told her about her desperation to help Eve save her ranch. She told her about meeting Pike on the train and then later in the hotel restaurant. And she told her about recognizing Matt's face in the WANTED poster of Samson Towers.

"I think you can guess what follows, can't you?" Delilah asked. There was an acerbity to her tone that she couldn't help.

Cora studied her face for an instant. Her expression hadn't altered. "Maybe you'd better tell me," was all she said.

And so, Delilah told her what she'd done. She told her about returning to Red Rock only to be met along the road by Matt. She told her what Matt had told her about how he'd come to be a wanted man. And she told her about the realization that had come too late that she loved him. "Now," she said, "there's only one thing left to be done. I have to tell him what I've done and move on, out of his life and away from here. The only chance I have to save him now lies in telling him the truth."

Cora nodded and sighed. "Oh, Delilah. I can certainly understand why you're upset. It's one heck of a tangle, that's for certain. I wish you'd talked to me about the Camerons' situation sooner. I could have lent you the money you needed to help her, and then you could have worked it off here at the tables and it wouldn't have mattered if you had a few slow nights. But . . . well, that's all hindsight now.

"As for the other, I think you're right. The only thing

you can do is to tell him. He has to at least have the opportunity to be prepared for that man . . . what's his name?" Cora rose and moved back around her desk to face Delilah.

"Paul Telford."

"Yes, he has to have the chance to prepare for Telford's arrival, if nothing else."

Delilah nodded, and dabbed the last of the moisture from her eyelashes. "Thank you for listening, Cora. I . . . I'm sorry."

Cora frowned. "I don't understand why you're telling me you're sorry. What are you sorry for?"

Delilah shrugged. "I don't know. For not being as good a person as I should be, I guess."

Cora laughed. "Delilah, love, there isn't any one of us that's as good as we should be." Then she sobered. "I won't say that what you've done isn't serious. It's a terrible thing that could hurt a good man." She shrugged. "But we all make mistakes, love, and some of them are pretty bad ones. I don't think there's anyone that can sit in judgment of you except yourself and Matt."

"You don't hate me, then?"

Cora shook her head. "Of course I don't hate you. I've done things that weren't exactly admirable either, you know. It's part of being human."

Samson couldn't stop looking at Delilah. Thank goodness the dining room was almost empty, so there weren't that many people present to witness just how much of a fool he could make of himself over her. But, damn, she was beautiful. Even as pale and tired as she was. Her lips didn't have their usual color and there were faint blue shadows beneath her eyes, but that only made her look more fragile. It made him want to hold her in his arms again, to protect her and take care of her. And that made him think of the direction his thoughts had taken in the last couple of days.

It had been more than two days since he'd held and kissed her. Heck, it had been that long since they'd been able to have a decent conversation. He had wanted to go to her and comfort her after Tom's funeral, to give her a shoulder to lean on. But she had seemed too busy being the strong shoulder for her sister, and he hadn't felt he had the right to barge in on their grief, no matter how good his intentions. But he wanted that right. He wanted it badly.

He hated the frustration of not knowing when he could hold her again. When he could kiss her and make love to her again. When they could simply talk again as they had that night. And he hated not having the right to care about where she went and with whom. And that was when the idea of marriage began to solidify in his mind.

Heck, she knew about his past and it hadn't really seemed to bother her much. Maybe, just maybe, she'd be willing to take the risk involved in marrying a man like him. Maybe she'd be willing to give them a chance.

He looked at her, and couldn't help wondering once again if, even now, she carried his child. The idea didn't terrify him as it had. In fact, now it gave him a kind of tight excited feeling in his chest. He wanted Delilah for his wife, and he wanted her to bear his children. He wanted them to build a wonderful life together as a family. He wanted . . . oh, God, he wanted her to say *yes* when he asked her. But he needed to get a conversation going first. He couldn't just blurt out a question like that.

He took another sip of his coffee and looked at Delilah over the edge of the mug. She hadn't said much since they'd come in. She seemed a bit shy or something and, for the most part, had been avoiding his gaze. Now she whispered something to the little dog she held on her lap while they awaited their meal, and then fiddled with the linen napkin on the table.

Samson cleared his throat. "I saw Eve head out this morning. How do you think she's doing?"

Delilah lifted her eyes to meet his gaze briefly, and then allowed them to slide away again. "I think she's doing much better than could have been expected. She'll be fine."

"That's good."

Delilah nodded. "Yes."

"We were able to return some of their cattle, you know."

"No, I didn't know." She looked at his mouth this time, not meeting his eyes. "That's wonderful news."

He nodded, and cleared his throat again. This wasn't working, and he didn't understand why. He didn't know if something was bothering Delilah, or if his own tension was to blame for the awkwardness he felt.

At that moment, the meal arrived, and he was able to concentrate on something else. Delilah set Poopsy on the floor at her feet, and they began to eat. The silence stretched, and the tension grew.

Finally Samson couldn't stand it anymore. "Delilah—"

"Matt—"

Having both tried to speak at the same time, they broke off and stared at each other. Samson smiled. "Ladies first."

"Oh, no," Delilah said. "You go first. Please?"

Samson cleared his throat for the umpteenth time. "I . . . well, there is something I wanted to talk with you about."

"Yes?"

He looked around the dining room to ensure that there was no one within earshot. "Well," he said in a low voice, "now that you know about me, I was wondering. . . . That is, my past didn't seem to upset you that much, and I thought that maybe . . . Aw, heck, this is harder than I thought it would be."

She frowned slightly, obviously trying to perceive his meaning from what he *hadn't* said as yet. "Go on."

Samson took a deep breath. "Delilah," he said.

"Yes?"

"I was wondering if you would consider . . . That is, will you marry me?" There! He'd said it.

It took him an instant to realize that, rather than appearing happy as he had hoped she might, she looked stricken. She dropped her fork to her plate as though her fingers had suddenly lost their strength. Her eyes grew moist. And her throat worked. Finally, she gasped out, "You want to marry *me*?"

He frowned. What was so goldarned surprising about that? "Yeah. I do." His tone was almost defensive.

"Oh, Matt!" Her lower lip trembled with emotion.

Obviously she wasn't happy about the idea. Samson swallowed his disappointment. "I know it's sudden," he managed to say. "But will you at least think about it?"

She stared at him with tears shimmering in her brilliant blue eyes, and nodded.

He exhaled in relief. Well, that was something at least. "Good," he said, smiling. "Now what did *you* want to talk about?"

But at his words, her face crumbled. With a sob, she scooped her dog up in one hand and rushed from the dining room.

Chapter Fifteen

The man she'd fallen in love with wanted to marry her! Oh, how she wished she might have the opportunity to say yes. Life could be so cruel at times.

Delilah spent the evening alternately raging at the fates, plunged neck-deep in self-castigation, and weeping for a love lost before it had been found. By the time her anguish had dulled to a numb ache and she was able to focus on the need to be doing something more constructive, it was nearly midnight, and too late to do anything.

She dried her eyes for what she promised herself would be the last time for a good long while, and then took a seat at the little writing table in the corner of the room. Pulling the letter to Samson from the bottom of the small stack of paper, she lit the lamp and reread what she'd written. Somehow, she had to find the words to complete it, since her resolve to tell him in person had certainly come to naught.

After staring at the paper for endless minutes, she realized that there was no easy way to say what she had to say. No way to soften the blow. And so, she simply put pen to paper and began to write.

I guess for me to have any hope of you understanding my actions, you will first have to gain an understanding of me, of who I am and the fears and hopes that have shaped the course of my life for so long. So I suppose I must tell you an abbreviated version of my life story.

My mother, Morgana Tate, was a Southern lady whose fortunes were changed drastically by the Civil War, as so many people's were. My father, Garrett Sinclair, was born in the West to a pioneering family who had relatives in West Virginia. He became a bounty hunter. I believe I told you his occupation at one time, though why I did, I don't recall. It's not usually something I tell people, given the dislike so many people harbor for bounty hunters. My father was the exception in that trade, however, for he was a good man, neither cruel nor violent, and he treated everyone fairly.

Eve and I had a happy life with our parents, although early on it was a bit unsettled, as we moved from town to town. I think Daddy had a hard time with the concept of having roots. We, Eve and I and Mama, used to collect *WANTED* posters when we saw them so that Daddy could look them over. I guess that's why, even today, I pay more attention to such things than other ladies do. But I'm getting ahead of myself. Eventually, although Daddy continued to seek men for bounty to supplement the family income, we did settle down on a small farm in Nebraska.

Mama passed away when I was fifteen. She'd

been getting progressively weaker for more than a year, and one day she just went to sleep and never woke again. A weak heart, the doctor said. Eve and I took over the running of the household, taking care of Daddy and, for the most part, running the farm as well. Daddy wasn't much use for a long time; Mama's death hit him pretty hard. He started getting drunk quite regularly, which was something he'd never done before. I guess it was then that I realized that it was possible to love someone too much. For that reason, I didn't argue when Daddy arranged my betrothal to Trent Lider, a neighboring farm boy. I liked Trent, but didn't love him and, after watching Daddy suffer, I considered that a blessing.

Delilah wrote long into the night. By the time she'd finished the letter, it was more than ten pages long. She rose and went to the bed, where she lay on her side and stared at the darkened rectangle of the window. She hoped that the letter would help Samson to understand her and perhaps, someday, to forgive her. But she was too exhausted to think about it any more. The act of putting all those memories, good and bad, on paper to be read by the eyes of another, even someone as kind and gentle as Samson, was a draining and traumatic experience in itself. Especially for someone who rarely spoke of the past. Someone who tried, with an almost single-minded determination, to always look forward. Yet sharing her past with him was the least she could do after . . . No, she was tired of thinking about that.

So tired. She'd just close her eyes for a minute and then take the letter down to the sheriff's office and slide it beneath the door before she left at dawn.

* * *

Delilah's eyes shot open to a room filled with early-morning sunlight. Ten o'clock! "Oh, my heavens!" For an instant she could only stare numbly at the clock as she realized that she'd missed her ride to Butte with Mr. Didsworth. "Blast!" She hadn't meant to fall asleep.

Well, there was no help for it. She'd simply have to ride Jackpot to Butte and sell him to a livery there. It was a good thing she'd decided to wait to return him to Mr. Metter until this morning.

She looked at the sealed envelope propped up against the lamp on the writing table. Slowly, hesitantly, she rose to retrieve it. It shrieked of cowardice. Faced with the light of a new day, she knew she had to tell Samson herself, or never again be able to face herself in a mirror.

It was Friday! There was no more time to delay.

Even as she performed her ablutions with indecorous haste, a sense of impending doom crowded into her mind and heart. As quickly as possible, Delilah changed out of her rumpled gown, tucked the letter she'd written into her reticule, and left the hotel at a near run. But when she opened the weathered wooden door of the sheriff's office a few moments later, Samson wasn't in. With her instincts telling her that she had to find him quickly, she stared at Deputy Wilkes in dismay. "Where is Sheriff Chambers?" she asked breathlessly, heedless of courtesy and decorum.

"Calm down, ma'am," Deputy Wilkes said. "He's just gone over to Doc Hale's office for a moment to . . ." He broke off as he realized that Delilah was already turning away. Then called after her, "Is it anything I can help with, ma'am?"

Delilah didn't waste time responding, but raced off down the street. She approached Doc Hale's just as Samson emerged and turned in the other direction. "Matt!" she called, halting him.

"Delilah—" He smiled in greeting. It was a slow, sexy smile that told her exactly how attractive he found her; and it hurt as though he'd taken a stabbing weapon to her heart, for she didn't deserve his smile.

"Matt, I need to talk to you."

Perceiving her urgency, his smile faded and he studied her face. "All right. I was just heading to an appointment with Mayor Jack. Why don't we meet for lunch?" He began crossing the street.

Racing along at his side, Delilah was shaking her head before he'd even finished speaking. "No! No, it can't wait! I've put it off too long already. There's no more time."

Samson frowned now. "No more time for what, Delilah?"

Delilah swallowed. How could she make him understand? In sudden inspiration, she reached into her reticule and extracted the letter she'd written. "Read this as soon as you get out of town," she said, handing it to him. "It's all explained in there."

"What is?" He stepped up onto the boardwalk in front of Lowden's Mercantile. "And where am I going? Delilah, you're not making any sense."

She shook her head in frustration. "Matt, you have to leave town. Now! Immediately. The letter will explain why, but please . . . just go."

He halted and stood looking down at her, a frown of confusion between his brows. "Where is it you want me to go, Delilah? To the Devil's Fork? Has something happened there?"

"No, it's nothing like that. It's—"

"Towers!" a deep male voice shouted from behind her.

Delilah winced and closed her eyes. "It's Telford," she finished quietly, somehow knowing without turning that she was too late. But she didn't think Samson heard her. With his attention focused beyond her, he absently folded her letter and tucked it into the pocket of his denims before moving around her.

With a sense of unreality gripping her, Delilah turned. She had to step sideways to see, for Samson had shifted protectively in front of her. Then, as her gaze fastened on the street, Delilah gasped. Like the manifestation of a nightmare, six men on horseback leading two riderless horses came down the center of the street. Six pairs of stone-cold gunfighter's eyes fastened on Samson. Samson's gun hand twitched. The man in the lead must have noticed too, for he yelled, "Don't even think about it, Towers. Less'n you want innocent people to get hurt."

The men halted their horses and the leader dismounted to face Samson. He had a pair of matching pistols in tied-down holsters and the most glacial eyes Delilah had ever seen. "I'm here ta take you in, Towers," he said. "Do I need to draw my gun, or are you gonna come peaceable like?"

Samson just stared at him for a moment as though considering his options. "Who are you?"

"The name's Casey," the man said in reply to Samson's question. "John Casey. I'm ramrod at the Cross T in Wyomin'. You heard of it?"

As though upon some kind of signal that Delilah had missed, two more of Telford's men dismounted and approached. Ignoring them, Samson nodded in response to Casey's question. "I've heard of it. So, where's Telford?"

Casey grinned, but not kindly. "Waiting for you. Now you wanna drop that gunbelt, or do we have ta do this the hard way?"

Samson's eyes assessed the street. Then, slowly, he nodded and his hands moved to the buckle of his gunbelt.

"Matt, no!" Delilah put a hand on his arm. Somehow she had to put a stop to this. But how? Peripherally, she noted old man Potter rise from his chair and take off down the street as fast as his skinny old legs could carry him, but she was too worried about the drama unfolding before her to heed his action. Distantly, she heard the questioning murmurs of a crowd of nervous but interested onlookers who were gathering on the boardwalk behind her.

Samson shrugged off her restraining hand. "It's okay," he murmured without taking his eyes from the man who faced him. He let his gunbelt drop to the ground. Almost immediately, the two men who'd dismounted kicked Samson's gun aside and grabbed him by the arms, roughly turning him around to secure his hands behind his back. Casey saw the badge on Samson's shirt and removed it. "You won't be needing this anymore," he said with a smirk as he threw the piece of metal to the ground. "Where's your horse?" he asked.

"At the livery."

Casey turned to a man who'd remained mounted. "Get his horse." With a nod, the man turned his horse and rode off down the street.

"Give me a moment with the lady, will you, Casey?" Samson asked when Casey turned back.

Casey considered him with a cold-eyed gaze, then smirked again. "Sure. Why not?"

Samson looked at her. The sadness in his charcoal-hued eyes was enough to make her heart bleed. Why, oh why, had she ever learned to read his eyes? "I guess I should have known better than to dream of a future," he said. Then, with a self-conscious glance over his shoulder at the men who remained close enough to hear every word, he added, "Thanks for . . . the time we had. It meant a lot. And if . . ." His gaze fell and he seemed to look at her abdomen for a moment. "No.

Never mind that. Just take care of yourself, Delilah. Will you do that?"

"Delilah?" Casey repeated, looking at her and moving forward before Delilah had a chance to respond. "Are you Delilah Sterne?"

She wanted nothing more than to deny her identity, but she saw by the confusion in Samson's eyes that it was already too late. "Yes," she murmured, not taking her eyes from Samson's.

"Well that do make matters a whole lot simpler. I was wonderin' how we were gonna find you. Mr. Telford wanted me to thank you personal-like for sendin' that telegram." A horrible stillness came over Samson in that instant, like the heavy stillness before a ferocious prairie storm. Denial and disbelief flared to life in his eyes, replaced only a moment later by a terrible bleakness that cleaved her heart in two. "It's taken a long time for us to collar Towers, here," Casey went on. "And we might not'a ever done it without your help. Here's the rest of the reward Mr. Telford promised ya." For the first time, Delilah took her eyes from Samson long enough to look at Casey. He was holding a thick brown envelope out to her.

Delilah shook her head. "I . . . I don't want it."

Casey's eyes widened. "Well now—"

"Take it!" the voice was Samson's, but there was a quality in his tone that Delilah had never heard before. She looked at him and saw the turbulent storm of myriad emotions raging in his eyes. The sorrowful acceptance of her betrayal. The accusation and hurt. The rage and hate. Disgust and loathing. "Take it!" he said again. "You'll need a stake for the next town . . . and the next poor sucker you find."

Oh, Lord, he thought she'd planned . . . everything.

"Take it," he growled in a tone that threatened violence if she didn't obey.

With tears of shame burning her eyes like acid, Delilah accepted the envelope. Then, refusing to allow herself the cowardice of avoiding Samson's eyes, she lifted her gaze to his once more.

"Good luck, Widow Sterne," he said. "Take care of yourself. But I guess that's what you're best at, isn't it?"

Delilah just looked at him, memorizing his features. She felt the loss of his gentleness and compassion and love like a physical blow, but it didn't matter. She deserved the pain. She deserved his hate. She deserved every unkind word he wanted to throw at her. "I know you won't believe this," she said, "but I'm sorry. More sorry than you'll ever know."

He nodded, but she could see he didn't believe her. "Just tell me one thing: Did you send that telegram before or after?"

Delilah didn't have to ask what he meant. Before or after he'd confided in her? Before or after they'd made love? Before or after the single night that had changed the course of their relationship?

"Before," she replied in a whisper. "I could not have done it after." Peripherally, she was aware of a man arriving with Samson's horse, Goliath, in tow.

Samson nodded, but was not given the opportunity to say anything, as Casey gripped his arm to turn him. "Okay, that's enough jawin'. We gotta get movin'."

They pushed Samson roughly toward his horse, and the sight of him being taken out of her life, the thought of what he had yet to face, hurt her more than if those rough hands had been upon her. "I'll hire a lawyer," she called after him. "I'll meet you in Cedar Crossing and see that you get a fair trial."

Samson turned back to her then, just for an instant. "You still don't understand, do you Delilah? There's not going to be any trial. I'll never see Cedar Cro—" He grunted then as Casey slammed a fist into his stomach.

"Stop it!" Delilah shouted instinctively, her voice ringing out with a power and volume that would never belong in a ladies' parlor. Six pairs of eyes fastened on her and, although none reflected the surprise they felt, the rapidity of the movement itself suggested some astonishment. "Mr. Casey—"

"Yes, ma'am?"

Delilah noted that the other men were forcing Samson to mount, but she needed all of her attention on Mr. Casey. "I intend to meet Mr. Towers in Cedar Crossing. If he does not arrive, I will hold you personally responsible, sir. Do I make myself clear?" Her tone was low, icy-smooth, and sugar-free for the first time in a very long time.

He smirked. "You gonna call me out, are you?"

"Hardly, sir. I don't intend to give you that much warning."

Casey's smirk slowly faded as he stared at her with a gaze that might have cowed someone with less to lose. Delilah returned it stare for stare. "You wouldn' be threatenin' to shoot me in the back now, would ya, ma'am?"

Delilah's eyes widened and the dulcet, slightly southern lilt returned to her voice as she said, "Mr. Casey! I am a lady who respects the law. As should you."

Casey stared at her a moment more as though trying to figure her out. Then, with a shake of his head, he dismissed her and mounted. Delilah sensed that he'd dismissed her warning. How could she ensure that Samson's prediction did not come true?

"Hey there! What's goin' on now?" a voice yelled as booted heels clomped along the boardwalk in hasty approach. It was Deputy Wilkes, with old man Potter trailing in his wake.

"This ain't none of your affair, Deputy. Just mind

your own business an' you might live to see another day," Casey warned.

Wilkes came to a halt and stepped off the boardwalk to grab Casey's horse's reins. "Well, now, as the law in Red Rock, I figure pretty much anything that goes on here is my business, so I think you got some explainin' to do."

Casey looked as though he'd like nothing better than to simply shoot Wilkes like he might an annoying critter, but after a moment's consideration he said, "That man," he stabbed a thumb over his shoulder in Samson's direction, "is Samson Towers. He's wanted in Wyoming."

"W'all, heck, I know that." Delilah saw Samson start slightly at that information. "Doesn't change the fact that he's a damn good sheriff an' a good man to boot. Way I figure it, that prob'ly means he's not guilty of what they say."

Casey's eyes narrowed. "I'm takin' him in."

Wilkes looked past Casey at Samson, but Delilah couldn't see his expression. Samson simply shook his head. At that, Wilkes shook his head as though in disagreement, then took a deep breath, spat in the dust, and released the reins of Casey's horse. Looking up at Samson once more, he said, "I hope to see you again, Matt."

Samson nodded. "It was good workin' with you, Carl."

As she watched Samson ride out of town surrounded by six cold, hard men, Delilah felt terror lodge in her belly. With shock numbing her thought processes, she turned blindly away and stumbled over Samson's gun. Bending to pick it up, she wrapped the belt around the holster and tucked the weapon beneath her arm. It was the only thing of Samson's that she had. Paralyzed by disbelief and a continuing sense of unreality, she lightly stroked the cold metal of the pistol grip. Then, lifting her gaze, she stared numbly at the people still clustered nearby. Old man Potter was looking at her as though she was some sort of insect. Deputy Wilkes's eyes were colder than she'd ever seen them. Mrs. Williamson was looking at her as though she'd like to have her burned at the stake. In fact, only Miss Cora standing in the doorway of the Lucky Strike looked at her with anything approaching compassion.

"Go after him, love," she said. "Make sure nothing happens to him."

Yes! She could follow. That's what she could do.

With a nod at Cora, Delilah absently tucked the envelope of money into her reticule and sped down the street toward the hotel. Her mind raced at breakneck speed as she planned what she'd need to take, what she'd need to store, and what she'd need to buy. She'd need her bedroll and her Winchester. She'd have to leave her trunk, but she was certain Mrs. Schmidt wouldn't have a problem holding on to it for a while. She needed to buy a pack horse, some food supplies, and a decent pistol, too. The derringer she carried in her reticule was useless except in close quarters, and she didn't want to rely entirely on the Winchester.

A scant twenty minutes later, having hastily packed, paid her bill, and made arrangements with Frieda for the storage of her trunk, Delilah emerged from the hotel. For the first time in a very long time, she had cast aside her widow's garb. Clad now in the trappings of the young woman her father had taught to camp in the wild, to hunt deer, and to track men, Delilah wore a denim split skirt which she'd fashioned herself for much-decreased fullness, a matching jacket, and her black felt hat. Instead of her black elbow-length lady's gloves, a pair of buckskin leather gloves were now tucked into the waistband of her skirt. Her bedroll, which also contained an oilskin coat to be worn in the event of inclement weather, and her saddlebags were draped over her shoulders, and she carried her Winchester in hand. Poopsy, pink tongue lolling, was once again happily ensconced in a saddlebag, looking forward to another adventure.

The first stop Delilah made was at the livery, where she swiftly negotiated with Mr. Metter for a packhorse. In actuality, the only beast he had available was an old mule he'd taken in on trade, and in her haste, Delilah's dickering had undoubtedly been less than proficient, for the mule would be slower than a horse. But in the end it wouldn't matter. She needed it. Minutes later, with the pack-mule in tow, she rode Jackpot hastily down the street to the mercantile.

She noted a number of pairs of eyes observing her, both judgmental and curious. Mutterings reached her ears, but only the occasional word was intelligible. ". . . knew she was bad news. . . . absolutely scandalous. . . . Why . . . poor Sheriff Chambers. . . . puts me in mind of them britches Amy Sweet wears . . ." But all the muttering and stares scarcely affected her, for her mind already ranged far ahead.

It took two trips for her to get all the supplies she thought she might need loaded onto the pack-mule. "Easy, Betsy," she murmured as the animal sidestepped trying to avoid the second load. Chafing at the extra time it took, but aware that she needed to remain as inconspicuous as possible, Delilah carefully wrapped in a blanket the coffeepot, tin plates, frying pan, and Dutch oven she'd purchased in an effort to lessen any noise they might make. It was ironic that all her purchases had been made with the money Casey had given her; the money that Samson had demanded she take. Had she not had the money, she would have been unable to outfit herself adequately for a long trip on horseback. It wouldn't have prevented her from following, of course, but it would have reduced her chances of success. Delilah took a small measure of comfort in that irony.

With her supplies satisfactorily packed, Delilah mounted Jackpot and rode out of Red Rock. Miss Cora met her gaze solemnly as she rode past the Lucky Strike, then in that last moment before Delilah was out of sight, she called, "Good luck!" Delilah nodded and turned her eyes forward, toward the future, toward the man she loved.

She was a bit more than an hour behind Telford's men, but they'd made no effort to conceal their tracks, and she followed their trail without effort. She traveled as quickly as she could with the old pack-mule in tow, still she feared she was falling farther behind, for the tracks she followed indicated the men were riding swiftly. That worried her, for it seemed to confirm Samson's assessment of the situation. Surely any man who planned on riding a horse over two hundred miles, and maybe nearer to three hundred, would not set off at a gallop. Come to think of it, Telford's men hadn't even stopped at the mercantile to refresh their supplies. Something was definitely strange. But she vowed that Samson would reach Cedar Crossing alive. If she got any indication that Telford's men intended otherwise, there would be hell to pay.

A few hours out of Red Rock, Delilah noted that Telford's men had begun to slow their pace. It was as though they'd wanted to leave the Red Rock area behind as quickly as possible and, now that they had, they could ease their pace. Whatever their reason, she was glad of it, for it allowed her to begin closing the distance between them. Since they would probably make camp at dusk, she hoped to close that gap even more by riding on after they'd camped, though she'd have to make certain not to lose their trail. She didn't want to risk losing even more time by having to backtrack in order to pick it up again.

Delilah estimated that it was probably around ten o'clock when she caught a glimpse of a campfire in the distance. Stopping, she assessed the area. Telford's crew had made camp in a small sheltered depression through which a narrow stream flowed. She wouldn't be able to get too close without giving herself away, so she headed upstream a bit to make her own camp. She hoped they weren't watching for anyone following them.

She wouldn't bother with a fire; she was too tired to cook anyway. Besides, after she'd settled Jackpot, Betsy, and Poopsy down for the night, she wanted to work her way closer to Telford's camp to check on Samson.

Over the next two days, Delilah settled into a routine. She'd follow their trail during the day, catch up to them at night if she'd fallen behind, and then camp a short distance away—but far enough not to be detected—before slipping closer to check on Samson.

Then, on the third day, Delilah was working her way down the slope of a mountain far in the wake of Telford's men when she saw another man on horseback join them. Halting, she strained to see. Who was this?

There seemed to be something almost deferential in the way the other men responded to him. Was this Telford himself? And, if so, why? What need would Paul Telford have to meet his men out here if they planned to take Samson to court?

Delilah swallowed apprehensively. She didn't like this. She didn't like this at all.

She liked it even less when she discovered that Telford's men suddenly seemed to have become more concerned with obscuring their backtrail. Orders from

Telford? She lost them for a time when they traveled down a streambed. She wasn't certain which way they'd gone until she found their exit point. And, cagily, they'd exited at a point where the stream was bordered by huge flat rocks in which there would be no tracks. Had she not seen fresh horse droppings, she might have missed it.

It was only late afternoon when she caught up with them. They seemed to have made camp early for some reason. And this time they were encamped in a small, very secluded dead-end canyon. She didn't like the sounds coming from that camp. Not one bit. They sounded almost . . . festive. The men shouted and laughed, but their laughter was edged with cruelty. Poopsy growled and Delilah hastily reached a hand back to soothe her. "It's all right girl," she murmured. But she wasn't certain it *was* all right. She wasn't certain at all. The question was, what could she do about it?

She couldn't go racing in there like an avenging angel. She'd probably just get herself hurt, or worse, and be no help to Samson at all. And there was no way she could enter the canyon without being seen. What she needed was a vantage point overlooking it.

She studied the terrain. The small canyon was bordered by rocky crags on both sides. Either side would provide numerous vantage points from which to see into the canyon. The hard part was going to be getting up there. The only thing even remotely resembling a trail was something that looked like a mountain goat track. She'd have to leave Jackpot and climb on foot.

With fear and desperation sinking their teeth more firmly into her with every passing moment, Delilah looked around for a place to conceal the animals. There! Not far from the entrance to the canyon, but far enough not to attract attention, was a natural rock overhang bordered by thick brush. She kicked Jackpot toward it.

After hastily tethering both Jackpot and Betsy near a copse of grass that would, hopefully, keep them occupied, she removed Poopsy from the saddlebag and put on her leash. She didn't know how long she'd be gone, and the little dog probably had to go. With her leash on, Poopsy looked at her expectantly, but Delilah knew she couldn't take her—she wouldn't be able to trust the dog to keep silent—so she quickly tied the leash to a sturdy bush. "I'll be back soon," she told her as she moved back to Jackpot's side. "Just be patient, and for heaven's sake be quiet. All right? No barking! Do you understand?" The little dog bared its teeth.

With the animals taken care of as well as possible, Delilah pulled the Winchester from its scabbard and, on impulse, pulled the oilskin overcoat from her pack, putting it on before heading for the trail. The Smith & Wesson revolver she'd purchased along with a battered secondhand holster felt heavy against her hip as she rapidly climbed the narrow path, but she wouldn't have wanted to be here without it. Loose gravel crunched beneath her feet and she slipped slightly, only managing to stop herself by grabbing the edge of a boulder. Then, halting for a second to catch her breath, she listened. The noise made by the men in the canyon had faded somewhat; deflected by the wall of rock no doubt, but no one appeared to have heard her. Delilah's sense of urgency remained undiminished, each passing second grating on her nerves like sandpaper.

It took only moments to reach the top—although how she would get down again was something Delilah refused to consider—and they were the longest moments that she had ever known. Taking a deep breath to settle her racing pulse, she scurried cautiously toward the opposite edge of the stone precipice, using a large boulder perched at the edge of the escarpment as a shield. Then, warily, apprehensively, she peered down into the canyon below.

She gasped. Oh, Lord! Samson had been stripped to the waist and his arms had been secured to the saddle horns of two large horses which stood facing away from each other. As he stood, arms outstretched helplessly to the side, Telford's men were beating him. Brutally. Even from this distance she could tell that he was badly bruised and covered with blood. With each blow that landed on his body, the startled horses tugged at the ropes that secured Samson's arms. Every muscle in his large body tensed and bulged as he fought the pull of those huge horses. And then the next blow landed.

Goaded by a rage unlike any she'd ever known, Delilah raised the Winchester and fired at one of the men about to strike Samson. Then she fired again. And again. Uncertain if she hit her targets or not. Knowing only that she had to stop the butchery below.

And then, abruptly, her father's teachings echoed in her mind. *Never fire a gun in anger, girls. Anger can get you killed. It keeps you from assessing a situation*. Delilah closed her eyes for a scant second, swallowing the horrible rage that threatened to consume her, and then forced herself to evaluate the circumstances. There were seven men. She couldn't tell if any of them had sustained an injury from her firing or not, but they all remained standing. Guns drawn, their attention was now focused on the cliff face above them rather than on the man they'd been brutalizing. At least she'd accomplished that much. She studied them more closely, clearly recognizing Casey. Each of the men below was armed with at least one handgun. A couple of the men, like Casey, carried two pistols, and four of them were now also armed with rifles.

Delilah swallowed. She was one person against seven men. Lord help her . . . and Samson.

Chapter Sixteen

"What the . . . ?" Three men began firing wildly in the direction from which they thought the shots had come. Most of the bullets missed her by a considerable distance, but a couple of rifle shots impacted uncomfortably close. Delilah moved a few feet and returned fire. A couple of her shots missed, but she managed to hit two men. One would never fire a gun with his right hand again. The other would walk with a limp for a very long time, for her shot appeared to have caught him just above the knee. Then there was a lull in the firing, as a score of eyes scrutinized the ridge.

"Who are you?" a man shouted. Delilah figured it was Telford. "What do you want?"

Delilah considered. She didn't want to have to speak, because as soon as the men below knew that they were dealing with a woman, their male egos would make them foolhardy. Yet she wanted them to leave—*without* Samson. So how was she going to accomplish that?

She looked in the direction of the late-afternoon sun, then down at the men below, and her eyes widened with inspiration. Now she knew why she'd brought the overcoat with her.

Keeping an eye on what was happening in the canyon, she moved away from the edge and along the top of the canyon to a point that would put her directly in front of the lowering sun when seen from the point of view of the men below. With the aid of the bulky overcoat and her felt hat, she hoped to make herself look like a man. And, if she managed to pitch her voice low enough when she spoke, perhaps the men's perception of her shape would allow her to fool them. She hoped.

When next Delilah looked into the canyon, Telford—at least she thought it was him—seemed to be directing a couple of men to search for her. She loaded and fired a couple of rounds at the men who were trying to slip away. The shots merely stirred up dust at their feet, but the threat halted them in their tracks. Then she took another hasty inventory of every man's position and what guns were at his disposal. She wasn't too worried about the pistols—as high as she was in this new position, their accuracy would be greatly diminished were any of the men to shoot up at her. But rifles were another matter. Then, cognizant of the possible threats, she moved out cautiously from behind the boulder she'd been using as concealment and, Winchester in hand, stood in front of the setting sun. Pitching her voice as low as possible, she shouted, "Drop your guns and move out!"

Her own words echoed back at her.

As soon as Casey saw her, he lifted the rifle in his hand to fire. But Delilah, prepared for the move, fired first. A moment later the gunman lay writhing on the ground. Delilah thought she'd hit him high on the shoulder, but it was difficult to know for certain.

"Move out," she shouted again. "Leave the big man." She didn't want to betray the fact that she knew Samson. Not unless she had to. The less Telford's men knew about her, the better.

"Like hell," Telford shouted. Then with a foul curse he asked, "Who the hell are you?" Without waiting for a response, he lifted his rifle. Delilah ducked behind the protection of her boulder just as his bullet struck the stone where she'd been standing. Delilah returned fire, but missed. After evading the passage of another bullet, she fired again. He shouted obscenely and she thought perhaps she'd hit him that time.

Cursing softly beneath her breath, she moved to the protection of a different boulder where she could look out onto the valley below. Blast! One of Telford's men was missing. Probably gone in search of her. Was there another goat path up from their side that he would be following? But she had no more time to wonder, for the men below had begun to untie Samson. Telford was giving orders, but she couldn't hear what they were.

Refusing to focus on Samson himself, for fear rage would hinder her thinking, Delilah studied the men supporting him. She wouldn't be able to get a shot at the man on Samson's far side, but the man on this side, if she was careful, she should be able to take out of commission without hitting Samson. Praying for accuracy, Delilah sighted down the barrel with painstaking care and fired, then quickly jerked back to the protection of her boulder—hopefully before they'd spotted her.

The echo of her rifle report was punctuated by a horrible scream from below as the bullet found its mark. The man on Samson's far side continued to hold him up, remaining shielded from her by Samson's big body, and she shook her head in frustration. Then she noted the man she'd shot in the knee limping toward Samson with a broken whiskey bottle in hand. Were they planning on finishing Samson off, leaving him to bleed to death while they made their escape? Not if she could do anything about it. Gritting her teeth, she fired at the man with the whiskey bottle. He fell, cursing loudly and clutching his thigh. "Will somebody get that son of a bitch?" he yelled.

In that instant, a scraping noise to her left made her aware of the fact that she was no longer alone on her rocky escarpment. Telford's missing man had undoubtedly joined her. Panting with the urgent need to get this over with and to help Samson, she looked around, desperately seeking inspiration. None came.

An instant later, a voice very nearby yelled down to Telford. "Hey boss, you ain't gonna believe this: It's a woman!"

Damn! So much for anonymity. But what worried her more was that, if he could see her, why couldn't she see him? And why hadn't he fired yet? Drawing her pistol, a better bet in close quarters, Delilah hastily moved to another boulder. One that, hopefully, offered more protection.

"Kill the bitch!" came the decisive reply. "She damn near shot my goddamn knee off."

So she had hit him. She hadn't been sure.

Telford's previous orders obviously had been for his gunman to find out who was firing at them, but those orders had now changed. An instant later, a bullet whined past her ear just as she caught a glimpse of a grey Stetson scarcely fifteen feet away. She returned fire, but heard her quarry scrambling to one side and knew she'd missed.

Damn! She didn't have time for this. She needed to keep watch over Samson until she could drive these men away.

She strained her ears, listening for the scrape of a

booted sole on gravel, or the rasp of clothing against stone. Nothing. Cautiously, breathing shallowly, with gun at the ready, she began to move in the direction she thought he'd gone. Suddenly there was a scrape to her right. Delilah whirled, saw a man coming around a boulder scarcely ten feet away, and fired instinctively. To her horror, the bullet struck him in the forehead, and she found herself staring into wide, disbelieving blue eyes as the man slowly crumpled to the ground. As though his gaze had somehow been locked upon her, his dead eyes continued to stare directly at her.

Oh, Lord! She'd killed a man. Closing her eyes, she clutched her stomach to still its sudden rebellion, and then turned quickly away.

"Did you get her, Canfield?" Telford demanded.

Regaining her position at the boulder, Delilah looked down into the canyon. "Your man is dead, Telford," she shouted, not bothering to try to disguise her voice. Firmly shunting aside the picture of the dead man's face, she decided to turn his death to her advantage—if she could. "You've got two minutes to mount up and get out of here, *without* Mr. Towers, or you'll be joining Mr. Canfield." She prayed they'd heed her threat, because she wasn't at all sure she could kill again. Listening to their movements, glancing down every couple of seconds, she reloaded her weapons and waited.

Two of the wounded men had dragged themselves over to their horses and appeared to be leaving. Telford was talking heatedly to the man supporting Samson. Then he drew his pistol and aimed it at Samson's head.

No! Without a second of hesitation, Delilah pointed the Winchester and fired.

"Son of a bitch!" The gun flew from Telford's grasp as he cradled his arm against his body.

Knowing now that they planned on killing Samson, Delilah was through with giving them time. She kept firing. Kept the pressure on. Until . . . finally . . . Telford and the rest of his men ran for their horses.

Samson stood, swaying almost drunkenly on his feet. "This isn't over yet, Towers," Telford yelled. "You're a dead man."

Then the men spurred their horses toward the canyon entrance. At the last moment, one of them turned, Winchester in hand, aiming at Samson. Again Delilah fired, and this time her target was too far away for her to check the shot. He flew out of his saddle while his horse continued on.

Dead? She didn't know. And with her concern for Samson crowding all other thoughts from her mind, at the moment she didn't care. As soon as his tormentors were out of sight, Samson sank slowly to his knees and then simply keeled over to lay on his side. Was he unconscious? She prayed not, for how would she get him out of this canyon if he was?

Delilah didn't know how long it took her to work her way down from the ridge. She found the trail that Telford's man Canfield had used, but at times she had to lower herself gingerly from one ledge to another. In other instances she was able to scurry down narrow paths, sending small rocks and gravel crashing down ahead of her. No matter how quickly the descent was accomplished, though, with worry and fear gnawing at her, it seemed like forever. Finally, she knelt at Samson's side.

Delilah sucked in a breath. His face was a bloody mess of torn and bruised flesh. His nose looked broken. Both his eyes were swollen almost shut. There was a jagged cut along his neck, right over the jugular vein, deep but not fatal. It looked as though they'd been taunting him with the possibility of a quick death. Her gaze roamed lower, taking in his bruised and battered torso. A broken or dislocated finger on his left hand. A jagged cut through his denims that had drawn blood on his thigh. For a moment, overwhelmed by the extent of the maltreatment he'd suffered, Delilah could only stare. It would be a miracle if he didn't have any broken ribs. And he would almost certainly have a couple of cracked ones. How would he ride? How could she even hope to get him on a horse?

And then, a groan from Samson spurred her to action. She had to stop the bleeding and then get him somewhere where she could tend him properly. Spying his discarded blue chambray shirt and black bandanna laying in a careless heap on the ground, she ran toward them. The shirt was already a tattered rag, so she certainly couldn't do it any more harm by ripping it into strips. Hastily, she tied one strip of cloth around his bleeding thigh, and another around the cut in his throat. Then, she examined his ribs. They needed to be supported enough for him to ride. If she tied a number of strips from the shirt together, surely that would do the trick. She was in the process of doing that when Samson groaned again. "Samson?"

A frown puckered his brows as he tried to focus on her through eyes that were mere slits in swollen tissue. Then he licked his parched and swollen lips. "Delilah?" he asked, in a voice rusty with pain.

"Yes. I'm here. I'm going to help you."

He tried to shake his head, and then winced. "Go away."

His words hurt, but she refused to accept them. "I'll go away when you're better, if that's what you want. But right now you need me. Can you sit up? I need to bind your ribs."

Slowly, laboriously, leaning heavily on his right arm, Samson pushed himself into a sitting position. Without looking at him, without meeting the expression glaring from his swollen eyes, Delilah accomplished her task, binding his ribs tightly and then knotting the strips of cloth together to prevent their loosening. "There," she said. "Now, I have to get you somewhere where I can take care of you. Do you know anyplace?"

Turning sideways, he tried to rise. She quickly moved to help him. Once again, he rebuffed her, so she stood back and let him make the attempt on his own. He didn't make it. Falling back with a curse, he stared up at her. The next time she extended her arm, he didn't refuse it, though she knew it galled him to accept her aid.

"Is there someplace we can go while you heal?" she asked again.

He nodded slowly, painfully. "Yeah. There's an old miner's cabin," he gasped, as though every word, every breath was agonizing, "about three miles west of here. Did you see . . . a rock that looked a bit like a hat sitting on top of a hill?"

Delilah thought back. "Yes. I think so."

He nodded slightly. "The cabin is right below that rock."

"I'll find it," Delilah promised. "Can you ride?"

"I'll damn well ride out of here," he muttered. "Goliath?"

Delilah nodded. "He's here. So are three other horses they left behind." She didn't bother pointing out that two of these were the horses to which they'd had Samson tied. The third was probably Canfield's horse. He wouldn't be needing it anymore. Since each horse was carrying a small amount of supplies or a bedroll, Delilah intended to take the beasts with them.

As though he'd heard his name, Goliath came clopping over; he was still saddled and bridled. The wild look in his eyes and the nervous rippling of his hide made it obvious that the big horse was spooked. He nudged Samson's arm gently and Samson grabbed his bridle, patting the big horse's neck reassuringly before working his way painfully back to the stirrup.

"Do you need help?" Delilah asked.

He shook his head. "I think I know how to get on a horse by myself," he returned coldly, deliberately misunderstanding her.

Nodding, but keeping a watchful eye on him, Delilah turned to the task of stringing the other horses together. All of them remained saddled and bridled, so Telford had doubtlessly planned to move on before making camp this evening. When she noted that Samson had managed, by pure force of will, to pull himself into the saddle, she mounted the smallest of the three horses and came up alongside Goliath.

"We have to stop just outside the canyon for a moment," she said to Samson. "I need to get Jackpot and my supplies."

Refusing to acknowledge her words in any way, Samson merely peered straight ahead through slitted eyes. His body was hunched and tilted in a way that made it obvious that he was in terrible pain, probably from the ribs on his left side. But since there was little she could do for him without her supplies, and since she wanted to get him to safety and shelter before his body stiffened up or he lost consciousness, Delilah moved out.

By the time they came into sight of the cabin, it was almost completely dark. Samson had been hanging on the edge of consciousness for some time, and a while back, Delilah had been forced to take Goliath's reins and lead him. Yet somehow, even injured as he was, Samson had managed to stay in the saddle. Now, spying the small dark cabin, Delilah chafed at the passage of time, wanting nothing more than to urge the horses forward at a quicker pace, but knowing that, for Samson's sake, she could not. Finally, though, they reached it, and Delilah leapt from Jackpot's back.

The cabin was constructed of logs. It had a sagging front porch with a protective roof. A coal oil lantern and a metal box of wooden matches hung next to the door. Delilah quickly lit the lantern and opened the door. A musty smell greeted her, but she ignored it. A hasty inspection revealed a single large bed, a wood stove, an old table, and three wooden chairs that had obviously seen better days. It would do just fine.

Leaving the lamp hanging on a nail stuck into one of the porch's roof supports, she returned to Samson's side. "Samson?" She had to call him twice more before he was roused. "We're here. Can you get into the cabin?"

After getting Samson into the house—where Poopsy took up residence beside him on the old bed, refusing to budge from his side—Delilah hastily unloaded all the supplies from the horses. Then she led the animals around to a lean-to attached to the side of the cabin, where she unsaddled them and got them settled in. Thank heavens the lean-to had some hay stores in it, because Delilah hadn't the time to waste seeking food for them. And there was enough rainwater in the bottom of an old trough to keep the beasts content for a time. Later, once Samson was cared for, she'd worry about filling it with fresh water for them.

With the horses cared for, Delilah took a pail from the cabin and sought out the well. It was the old windlass type—no pump—and she quickly lowered the old wooden bucket into the shadowy depths. "Please, God, don't let it be dry," she murmured. After endless seconds, she was gratified to hear a splash.

Back in the cabin, she was about to start the stove in preparation for heating the water when she discovered one other thing she needed: wood. The wood box next to the stove was almost empty. Blast! Why was nothing ever easy?

Since Samson had sunk into unconsciousness anyway, Delilah took the lantern and hastily looked around the cabin for a woodpile. But the darkness had become so absolute that it was difficult to see for any distance, even with the lantern. She was just about to conclude that the wood stores must have been used and not replenished by the cabin's last tenant, when she spied a small pile in the shadow of the lean-to.

"Thank you, Lord," Delilah murmured. Setting the lantern down, she scooped up as much wood as she could carry and hurried back into the cabin.

For the next week, Delilah cared for Samson almost continually, helping him take care of his most basic and intimate needs, while he drifted in and out of consciousness. She hovered constantly on the edge of exhaustion herself, refusing to allow herself to contemplate anything but the next task that needed doing. Driving herself to exhaustion so that she couldn't think, couldn't contemplate the magnitude of her error. Finally, by the end of the week, Samson began to rouse himself. Though after his first twenty-four hours of consciousness, she almost began to wish he had stayed unconscious throughout his entire convalescence. The man was rude, ungrateful, uncooperative, and resentful. And with nothing but time on his hands to think, his resentment grew.

"I guess I shoulda paid more attention to the biblical connotations of our names after all," he said suddenly.

Delilah looked up from where she sat before the stove, altering a man's shirt she'd found in one of the bedrolls to fit Samson's imposing size. The swelling on his face had gone down, though the flesh remained discolored. He stared at her now with steely-hued eyes that were as hard as flint. Delilah merely nodded, too tired to argue. "I suppose you should have," she agreed quietly. "Do you want some soup?"

He scowled. "I'm sick of soup. I want something with some substance. What are you trying to do? Starve me to death?"

Delilah ignored his question. "If you think you can keep it down, I can fry some bacon. And I found some tins of beans. I can open a couple of tins."

"I just got finished telling you I'm starving, woman. Of course I can keep it down."

Feeling unaccountably near tears, Delilah nodded and rose, turning to the task. She was just tired, she assured herself. That's why his anger hurt so. If she'd been feeling better, she would have told him what an ungrateful lout he was. Then she sighed. No, she wouldn't have, because she deserved his anger. She deserved every unkind word he flung her way. After all, he'd almost been killed because of her.

While the food was cooking, Delilah turned to the task of dressing his injuries and checking his ribs, as had become her habit. He stared at her resentfully the whole time, chilling her with the expression in his eyes. Swallowing nervously, Delilah did her best to ignore his anger—but it wasn't easy. She was alone in a mountain cabin with a man big enough to break her in two like a matchstick. A man who was fast regaining his strength, but not the gentle temperament that had held it in check. A man who had reason to hate her.

She drew a deep breath. "Do you need to use the chamber pot?"

As though the question was the last straw in the list of indignities that had been forced upon him, his hand shot up to grip her throat, tightly but not painfully. "You know," he said almost conversationally, "I could wring your neck for what you've done."

Delilah's gaze locked on his. "I am yours to do with what you will. If my death will ease the misery I've caused you, then by all means, kill me. I won't fight you."

A flicker of surprise crept through his eyes, and then was gone. He stared at her for a long moment and then, with a grimace of disgust, dropped his hand to his side. "Go," he said. "Just get away from me. I'm going out to the outhouse."

"I don't think—" Delilah started to argue that he wasn't ready, but she wasn't allowed to finish.

"Don't think," he snapped. "Leave me alone." He watched her as she walked to the stove and began turning the bacon in the pan. God, he hated her. He hated her for betraying him and throwing his love for her back in his face. He hated her for caring for him so tirelessly—as though that could possibly make a difference now. And he hated her for looking so fragile and beautiful despite the faint blue shadows beneath her eyes.

Ignore her, he admonished himself. Then slowly, cautiously, he pushed himself to a sitting position and swung his legs over the side of the bed. He was weaker than he'd imagined, he realized, as his arms shook with fatigue. Then, looking down at his legs, he realized he was damn near naked. "Where are my pants?"

"Hanging over the end of the bed. I was going to wash them and mend them, but I haven't gotten around to it yet."

"Don't bother," he muttered as he carefully worked his way a few inches toward the foot of the bed so that he could reach the trousers. One leg was torn and crusted with blood, but he donned them anyway and then, after a glance to ensure Delilah was turned away, he slowly stood to fasten them. His legs trembled alarmingly, and he looked around for something to use as a crutch or a cane. He'd be damned if he'd accept her help any more than was absolutely necessary. "Bring me that broom, will you?"

Delilah considered him for a second, as though contemplating arguing, and then, with a resigned shake of her head, did his bidding. Without a word, Samson accepted the broom and, using it as a cane, began to make his way toward the door.

"The outhouse is to your right and around the corner," Delilah said, and then added, "Just in case you're interested."

Samson scowled. He wished he knew who the devil Delilah Sterne was behind her ever-changing facade. Was she a lady who happened to gamble? Or a gambler who knew how to pretend she was a lady? Was she a lady sharpshooter who'd become a temptress and betrayer of men? Or a temptress who'd learned how to shoot? And who was this tireless nursemaid who'd suddenly appeared? Was Delilah none of them? Or all of them?

It took Samson quite some time to work his way to the outhouse, and when he finally arrived, he discovered he certainly didn't have the strength to stand any longer. Sitting there, alone for the first time in days, with his trousers bunched around his ankles, Samson sourly contemplated life as he tried to regain his breath and enough strength to make it back to the house. It was as he was pulling up his trousers that Samson heard the crackle of paper in his pocket. Frowning, he reached in and extracted a thick wad of paper.

Delilah's blasted letter! He was about to throw the missive into the outhouse hole when something suddenly stayed him. He remembered the questions he'd just had about her. Might her letter answer some of them? He wasn't about to forgive her, but it might not hurt to see what she had to say.

Sitting back down, he leaned against the plank wall,

pulled the letter from the envelope, and unfolded it. Angling the missive to catch the light coming through the door, he began to read:

Dearest Matt,

What I have to tell you is extremely difficult, and I know you shall never forgive my betrayal, which is why I haven't the courage to face you.

Anger clouded his vision for a moment, but he forced himself to read on. And then, gradually, he found himself caught up in her story despite himself.

I am not truly a widow, as I think you may have guessed, or at least suspected. I merely borrowed the persona in order to make my way in life on my own terms. I stole the name from a man who stole something very precious from me. But I've jumped ahead in my story again.

When my father began to awaken from his prolonged state of mourning, in order to support us, he returned to the occupation he knew best: bounty hunting. As you must know, bounty hunters make enemies, and my father was no exception. One day, when I was seventeen and Eve but fifteen, and Daddy was away tracking a killer, we received an unexpected caller, going by the name of Jacob Sterne. Sterne had learned that Daddy was responsible for taking his younger brother in to face a hangman's noose, and heedless of his brother's guilt or innocence, he wanted revenge. When Sterne discovered that Daddy wasn't home, and that neither Evie nor I could tell him where to find him, he decided to get his revenge in another way. A way that would bring Daddy to him.

Although Delilah did not say, in so many words, what had happened that day, Samson could well imagine the events, and he winced as the story continued to unfold. For although Delilah's penned words seemed to carry very little emotion, he sensed the depths of the tragedy she'd endured and perceived what it must have cost her to put it all down on paper. Temporarily setting aside his own anger with her, Samson wanted to soundly thrash the father who had left two young women, little more than girls, alone while he went off chasing a killer. He wanted to kill Jacob Sterne all over again—though, according to Delilah, Garrett Sinclair had accomplished the task quite adequately, albeit at the cost of his own life. And he wanted to hang Trent Lider, Delilah's supposed betrothed, for spurning her on the heels of such a painful incident, rather than lending her his strength.

After Daddy's death, we stayed on the farm. I was determined to try to make a home for Eve, but it didn't work out well. Very few of the townspeople offered sympathy, or help, or friendship. Rather, they seemed to avoid us, me in particular, as though the misfortune that had befallen us might in some way rub off on them. When I came to realize that Eve was as unhappy as I, we decided to sell the farm and move on to a place where no one would know us or the scandal that had transpired. I was still in mourning for Daddy at the time, and at one point in our journey, a fellow traveler mistook me for a young widow. That was when I decided to appropriate Jacob Sterne's name.

Samson paused a moment in admiration of her resourcefulness, her resilience. How many young women would have done as well? How many would have had the courage to manipulate the conventions of so-called polite society in a way that worked *for* her rather than against her?

I didn't begin to gamble until Eve married, for I wouldn't have submitted her to the stigma associated with my profession. But having no desire to enter into the wedded state myself, and certainly no desire to apply myself to making a living in the age-old manner which so many lone women are forced into, I turned my eyes to the saloons and the gaming tables. I found widowhood a boon for the freedom it afforded me, although as a man you undoubtedly will not understand that. And so, I embarked on a new life for myself. A life without responsibility for anyone but myself. Or so I thought until I received Eve's letter.

You see, dear Matt, I promised Daddy long ago that I would never let any harm come to my younger sister, and I take my promises very seriously. With Tom in such dire straits, when Eve informed me that she needed money to save her ranch, I could not refuse. Yet my luck seemed to desert me at the gaming tables, and I was not bringing in the income I needed—particularly on the nights when you were there. Your presence unnerved me, and yet you wouldn't leave me alone. I've been leery of men for years now, as you can imagine, and I was afraid of you. No, that's not quite true. I was afraid of the things you made me feel. I wanted you out of my life.

So, when I saw your face on the poster Pike brought to town, and recognized you, I saw the means to accomplish the two things I felt I needed to do most. And I'm more sorry than you could ever know. If I had known Telford's nature, I would not have done it. I told myself that you were probably innocent—for in my heart I never believed you guilty—and that a trial would only clear you and set you free. I convinced myself that my actions would benefit everyone all the way around, including you. I've never been more wrong in my life. Forgive me someday, if you can, as I hope to be able to forgive myself. My love, always, *Delilah Sinclair*. (How wonderful it feels to use my own name again!)

Damn! Samson crumpled the letter and thrust it back into his pocket, wishing that he'd never read it. She was right, he could never forgive her, but despite himself, he'd begun to understand her motivation, and that meant he couldn't hate her either. At least not quite as much as he had.

When he emerged from the outhouse, Delilah was standing on the porch, staring anxiously toward him. He scowled at her and she turned and went back inside. When he finally entered the house a few minutes later, leaning rather heavily on the broom, she said simply, "The food's getting cold."

He shrugged slightly and then winced as his healing ribs protested the action. "It'll do. I'll eat at the table this time." He stared at her, expecting her dissent. Expecting her to tell him that he'd already overdone it. But he was disappointed, for she merely nodded, and Samson realized he'd been looking for an argument. Looking for some fire, anything other than this meek facade she'd been presenting him with.

He was almost finished eating—beans and bacon had never tasted so good—when he noticed that Delilah was not eating. "Aren't you going to eat something?"

She shook her head. "I'm not very hungry. The mere smell of food makes me queasy lately."

Samson stopped chewing and stared at her. Thoughtfully, he assessed her appearance. She looked pale and tired. Naw, he decided he was probably worrying for nothing. It had only been a little more than two weeks since that night. And he hadn't noticed her being sick to her stomach.

A short time later, he spoke again. "I read your letter."

Her gaze flew up to lock with his, and she slowly swallowed a sip of coffee. "And?" she asked.

He frowned. He didn't even know why he'd told her. Just to see her reaction, he supposed. But now she was seeking something more, and he didn't know what to say. "You were right," he said. "I can't forgive you."

Her face went blank as she stared at him for a moment more. Then she nodded and rose to begin gathering the dishes. She turned to the stove, and he thought he saw a tear glisten on her cheek, but in the next instant it was gone, and he wasn't sure. It made him feel cruel and petty, and he didn't like it. Why the hell should he feel like that? She was the one who'd betrayed him. And what in blazes did she have to cry about? It wasn't as though she hadn't expected his reaction.

As the next few days passed and Samson finally began to spend more time awake than asleep, he began to sink further and further into a brooding, moody melancholy that he was powerless to throw off. Although, thanks to Delilah, he was alive, he had no life to return to, also thanks to Delilah. And if that wasn't bad enough, he'd now heard her vomiting on two occasions early in the morning, when she'd thought him still asleep. Damn! He watched her with hooded eyes as she moved about the cabin performing chores, caring for him. He was furious with her, but he couldn't deny that he still wanted her. Desperately. He wanted to hold her, kiss her senseless, and make her cry out her pleasure as he took her. And most certainly, if she was pregnant with his child, he wanted to hold it and see it grow.

Suddenly he thought to wonder about their sleeping arrangements. She was always sitting in a chair at the table when he fell asleep at night, and awake cooking breakfast before he woke in the morning. "Where have you been sleeping?" he asked bluntly, his words falling like stones into the heavy silence that pervaded the cabin.

Delilah jumped, and then turned to meet his eyes. "I have a bedroll," she murmured.

Samson's eyes narrowed as he noted the fatigue that now marked her face, her posture. Yes, she had a bedroll. But was she using it? That night, he feigned sleep, waiting, watching to see what Delilah would do—where she would sleep. About fifteen minutes after she believed him asleep, she lay her head down on her arms at the table. For an instant, he thought she was going to sleep like that, and then he realized that her shoulders were quaking with huge, silent sobs. The sight of her in such deep emotional pain hurt him more than he would have thought possible. And in that moment, he accepted her assertion that she was truly sorry for what she had done. But there was something else he had to accept too, and it was much harder to swallow: Samson had to accept the realization that, as much as he wanted to hate her, to put her out of his life, he didn't. He didn't trust her—might never trust her again—but he still loved her. And he was worried about her.

Slowly, carefully, he rose from the bed to go to her. So profound was her misery that she didn't even hear him approach, though he made no effort to be silent. She jumped when he placed his hand on her shoulder, jerking her head up to look at him with a blotchy, tear-stained face and red-rimmed eyes. Perhaps it was a measure of how irrevocably his heart was involved that he still found her beautiful. "What's the matter, Delilah?"

Her gaze slid away from his. "I'm just tired. I don't recall ever being quite so fatigued."

"Have you been sleeping?" He tried to see her expression, but she continued to avoid his eyes.

"Of course!" she said, but he thought her response might have been a trifle too fast.

"Come here," he said as he lifted her arm. He wanted nothing more than to sweep her up in his arms and carry her, but he knew that his ribs wouldn't allow it. "You're sleeping on the bed tonight, where you can get a good night's sleep."

Slowly she stood to face him, and then raised her brilliant blue eyes to his face. His breath caught in his throat. Damnation, she was beautiful. Too damn beautiful for his peace of mind. "Are you . . . still angry with me?" she asked in a small voice.

He nodded, for he couldn't deny it. "Yeah, but I'm working on it. All right?" Once again a small spark of something flared in her eyes, and she nodded. "Now," he said, "come lie down." Reaching for the lantern on the table, he extinguished the light.

Despite their mutual fatigue, they lay stiffly side by side while sleep remained as elusive as a wraith. Samson could not help thinking about Delilah's letter, about all she had said and so much she had not. He needed to understand. Finally, he spoke into the darkness. "Tell me about Jacob Sterne."

There was a moment of silence, and then she asked, "Why?"

Samson frowned, not fully understanding himself why he wanted . . . no, *needed* to know the details. Finally, he said, "I guess so that I can understand why you were so frightened of me."

After a long silence, during which Samson began to suspect she would not tell him, Delilah began to speak. And when she was finished, he understood better than ever before her fear of men. For the first time, he considered the possibility that perhaps he had been partially responsible for his own capture. If he had not pursued Delilah so relentlessly, watching her every move in the Lucky Strike, making his presence felt, would she have become desperate enough to follow the course she'd followed? He didn't think so.

Rolling onto his side, he stared down at her for a moment, saw her blue eyes gleaming in the darkness, and then leaned forward and kissed her. That gentle kiss said everything he could not put into words: *I forgive you; I miss you; I still love you; I want you;* and, most importantly of all, *I'm sorry. Sorry for not being able to trust you. Sorry for getting you pregnant. And sorry that I may not be here to help you raise our child.* If all went well, he would return to her. If not . . . she need never know what had happened to him.

In the morning, when Delilah awoke, he was gone.

Chapter Seventeen

At first Delilah thought he'd just gone to the outhouse. It wasn't until she and Poopsy went out to check on the horses and discovered that Goliath and one of Telford's big bays were missing that she learned otherwise. For an instant, she could only stare at the vacant stalls in stunned disbelief. And then realization began to sink in.

With a pounding heart, she raced back into the cabin to take an inventory of the things she knew should be there. The shirt she'd altered for him by sewing extra strips of material into the seams was gone. His trousers, and another pair of men's denims rescued from one of the bedrolls belonging to Telford's men, were gone. But most importantly of all, a number of their supplies were gone as well: The old coffeepot that had been sitting on the stove when they'd arrived at the cabin, along with one bag of the Arbuckle coffee she'd purchased, had disappeared. The last two cans of beans were gone, as was the last of the bacon. And, most telling of all, Samson's bedroll was no longer lying in the corner.

Finally, it sank in. He'd left her! He'd left her and her instincts told her he didn't intend to come back. Just when she had begun to think that perhaps they had a chance of working things out, he'd ridden out of her life. And it hurt far worse than she'd ever imagined.

Too paralyzed by shock even to cry, Delilah plopped onto a chair and stared sightlessly at the open door and the green meadow beyond. What was she going to do now? Her mind remained blank. Needing the solace of routine, she made a pot of coffee in the new pot she'd purchased and sat sipping the strong hot beverage as she tried to plan. But it was midmorning before her numbed mind slowly began to function and she thought to wonder about Samson's precipitous departure.

Where would he go, after all? Certainly not back to Red Rock, where the whole town now knew his true identity and, regardless of how well he'd been liked, somebody would take it upon themselves to try to collect the reward. Would he go off and try once more to begin a new life? No, she was certain he wouldn't. Not with the threat posed by Telford and his reward always looming in the background. So what would he do?

But even as she asked the question, she knew, because she knew what kind of man Samson was. Despite his brooding anger of the last while, his rudeness and resentment, Samson was a good and honest man. He would not keep running forever. That could mean only one thing: Samson had gone to face Telford. To free himself, one way or the other, from the reach of Telford's vengeance.

Worry froze her in place. His ribs weren't even completely healed yet. "What was he thinking?" she murmured aloud. Poopsy, sitting in the open doorway, barked in response, and Delilah turned to look at her. "He's not in any condition to be going after a man like Telford." The little dog barked again, and stood, wiggling her hind end as she backed toward the door. Poopsy was telling her it was time to go. "You're right, Poochie," Delilah said, with the hint of a smile touching her lips for the first time in days. "It *is* time to go." She couldn't let Samson face Telford and his men alone. She didn't know exactly what she was going to do to help him, but she knew that she had to try. If she didn't, she wouldn't be able to live with herself.

Poopsy bared her teeth in satisfaction as Delilah rose.

After hastily packing her remaining supplies, Delilah freed the other big bay horse and the mule to roam the lush mountain valleys. She planned to ride Jackpot and use the smaller horse that had belonged to Telford's man as her packhorse. Thankfully, the combination worked well, allowing her to travel more quickly than the balky pack-mule had. Even riding hard, though, she was unable to catch up with Samson by nightfall. He must have been riding like a man driven by demons.

And perhaps he was, she reflected.

Making a late camp, Delilah ate some jerky because she didn't feel like cooking, and sat staring into the firelight thinking what-ifs and if-onlys until her eyes grew heavy and she lay down and fell into a fitful sleep.

After a few days of traveling, the days began to drift into each other, one inseparable from the other by their sameness. Coming across a village, she replenished her supplies and rode on, always, it seemed, a step behind Samson.

After about eight days, when Delilah had finally concluded that she would never catch up with him, she finally spied his campsite as she was riding down a steep trail. Samson had made camp early on the banks of a creek brimming with clear mountain runoff. A short distance away, a mineral hot spring bubbled out of the earth into a natural pond. He was in the process of taking a bath in that pond, and no doubt soaking his aching ribs as well, so he didn't notice her presence. Delilah found herself watching him, mesmerized by the sheer male beauty of him. The bruises on his back had faded, and once again his big body was sleekly bronzed, the muscles rippling smoothly. Then suddenly, surprising her, he stepped out of the water to dry himself, and Delilah discovered that he was as naked as a jaybird.

Good heavens! Her face flamed as she quickly averted her gaze. In all the time she had cared for him, she'd never once *looked* at that part of him. She'd preferred to preserve her modesty, such as it was, by helping him perform the tasks that had needed to be done beneath the shield of the blankets. But now, the sight of him standing so gloriously naked on the edge of that steaming pool of water, like the god Poseidon risen from the deep, was branded in her mind for all time.

After taking a deep breath to calm her wayward emotions, Delilah began to wind her way down the trail toward his camp. It was a good thing she hadn't expected an enthusiastic greeting, for she would have been sorely disappointed.

Having heard her approach before he saw her, he had drawn his gun in readiness. When he recognized her as she came around a wall of rock, he holstered the weapon he held in his hand, but that didn't mean his greeting was any more welcoming. "What in blazes are you doing here?" he demanded.

Delilah set her chin and said, "I'm going with you."

"Like hell." The coldness of his steel-hued eyes and the scowl upon his forehead were enough to frighten the wits out of braver souls than she. Yet despite everything between them, Delilah remained certain that he would never hurt her. Without responding, she simply dismounted, set Poopsy down to explore, and then turned to tend the horses. "What are you doing?" Samson asked.

Delilah looked at him over her shoulder. "Making camp."

"I didn't invite you to share my camp."

His rudeness hurt, but she refused to show it. "Fine." She nodded. "I'll go over to the other side of the pond." Then, remembering that Samson had once said he hated his own cooking, she added, "You're free to join me for supper if you wish."

Samson made no response, so Delilah simply ignored him as she went about the task of setting up her camp and making a fire. Then, carefully rinsing the beans she'd purchased at the village, she set them to cook over the coals. She knew there was a reason why she'd stocked up on more supplies than she'd needed, and now she realized what it was. She intended to ensure that all sorts of savory smells wafted across the pond to Samson. Of course, she had to compete with the slightly sulfurous smell of the pond, but she thought she was up to it.

With the beans cooking, Delilah eyed the pond speculatively. After days in the saddle, she was aching for a nice warm and *thorough* bath. Glancing at Samson, who sat drinking coffee and brooding next to his own campfire, she contemplated the situation. Then, finally, she called, "Samson?"

"What?"

"Um . . . would you mind turning around?"

"Why?"

"I'm going to take a bath."

He scowled. "So take one. You're the one who insisted on camping here."

Delilah stared at him. Darn him anyway! He thought that by refusing her request, she'd either go without her much-desired bath, or get angry and go off and find another camp. Well, he had another think coming. Raising her chin in determination, Delilah removed her jacket and began undoing the buttons of her shirtwaist. From beneath her lashes, she peeked at Samson to see what his reaction to her unaccustomed boldness might be, but the blasted man wasn't even looking in her direction. He was writing something on a piece of paper. Which, when she thought about it, should have been exactly what she wanted, for she'd asked him to avert his eyes. So why did she feel so disappointed?

It was because his not looking when he *could* be looking signified a distinct lack on interest on his part, she decided. And that was hurtful.

Sighing at the havoc her own mercurial emotions were wreaking lately, Delilah placed clean, dry clothing where it would be within easy reach of the pool. Then, undressing down to her bloomers and camisole—she simply didn't have the courage to bathe stark naked in the open as Samson had—she walked to the water's edge.

Despite his determination, when Samson next looked up from the plans he was making, he couldn't help glancing in Delilah's direction. Unfortunately, he'd also just taken a sip of coffee, which went spraying everywhere. Good God! "What in blazes are you doing?" he yelled. But his shout only made matters worse, because it startled her, making her stand up in the water, and the white camisole and bloomers she wore, now wet, left little to the imagination.

"Taking a bath," she responded evenly. "You said to go ahead." Then, as though realizing her predicament, she hastily sank back down into the water, but it was too late. The image of her, with her beautifully seductive body accentuated by the sheer fabric, would keep him awake for many nights to come.

This was too much! She was deliberately taunting him. And he was through being a sucker for her machinations. From now on, he was going to do what *he* wanted, and to hell with how she might feel. And right now, he wanted her. Striding toward the edge of the pond, he began to strip off his clothing.

"Wh . . . what are you doing?" Delilah asked, as her big blue eyes widened to the size of saucers.

"Joining you," he said smoothly. "That's what you want, isn't it?"

"No, I . . . that is, I never thought . . . Oh, my!" She hastily turned and headed for the opposite bank as he slid his trousers off. But she wasn't fast enough. With three large strides, he caught her, grasped her arm, and turned her toward him. Her hands came up to press against his chest, a barrier between them. Yet, as her fingers came into contact with his chest, she curled them into fists, so that she touched him only with the less-sensitive heels of her hands. Samson smiled, for it was a very informative gesture.

She stared up at him with wide eyes and asked, "What . . . are you going to do?"

He smiled again. "I'm going to make love to you."

She flushed a very becoming shade of red. "But . . . but you're angry with me."

He nodded. "That's true, but in your case, my anger doesn't appear to have any adverse effect on the part of my anatomy that's required."

She seemed to ponder that in confusion for a second and then, with a sudden widening of her eyes and a very telling glance downward, she said, "Oh! Oh, no! I really don't think this is a very good idea. I had meant only to invite you to share my supper. And if you're still angry with me—"

He cut off her flow of words with a kiss. It was a deep, hungry kiss, and Delilah seemed to freeze in surprise for a moment before tentatively responding. Ah, yes! Slowly, he broke off the kiss to feather kisses over her cheek and temple, and then down to her ear. "I'm sorry," he murmured. "You were saying something?"

"Hmm? Oh . . . yes, well, I just think . . ." Focusing on the fact that she could still talk, Samson let her words blur as he concentrated on changing that. Pulling back a bit, he slid his hands up her arms and casually extended his thumbs to brush over the hard nubbins of her nipples. He was rewarded by a halt in the flow of words from Delilah's mouth, as she gasped.

"Is something wrong?" he asked with feigned innocence.

"No . . . of course not." But a pulse pounding in the base of her throat belied her words.

"That's good," he said. Then, he gently squeezed the taut nipple of her left breast between his right thumb and forefinger, rolling it slightly.

Delilah gasped and sagged toward him, breathing an "Oh, my!" as her equilibrium deserted her.

"Delilah—"

"Hmmm?"

"I'm afraid I've lost track of the conversation again. What were you saying?"

She looked up at him with passion-glazed eyes that did one heck of a lot for his ego. "I . . . I don't remember."

"Well, then, I guess it couldn't have been too important," he murmured as he lowered his head to capture her luscious full-lipped mouth in a ravenous kiss.

Delilah tried to remain unmoved, to discourage his passion. She really did. But within seconds, her own body betrayed her. She was completely unprepared for the onslaught of sensation that catapulted her from the realm of reason into the foreign territory of passion. It was as though her body, having once experienced the delights to be found in Samson's arms, was now starving for more. And suddenly she was kissing him back with a fervor and intensity that startled her as the hunger consumed her. She couldn't get enough, couldn't touch enough, couldn't feel enough. She threaded her fingers into his overlong hair, reveling in the coolness of the silky strands. Her hands swept downward, learning the texture of his body, delighting in the strength of him. Her mouth left his to taste his smooth skin, nibble his earlobe, and rain tiny exploring kisses over his chest. And then, abruptly, Samson lifted her in his arms and began carrying her toward the shore.

"Your ribs!" she remembered to protest.

"They're fine," he murmured. And then, for a good long while, the only words spoken were words of loveplay and passion.

Some time later, they sat companionably sharing the beans Delilah had cooked. "Mmmm," Samson said appreciatively. "You're a good cook."

Delilah colored beneath his praise. "Thank you. I did a lot of cooking when I was younger, but I haven't had much opportunity in recent years. I'm glad I haven't lost my touch."

And then, unfortunately, Samson's expression grew more grave, and he changed the subject. "You can't come with me, Delilah. It's too dangerous."

She frowned. "Which is precisely why I must come with you," she argued. "Two guns are better than one."

He scowled. "Dadburnit, woman! Can't you trust me to know what I'm doing? I have a plan."

"Don't you trust *me* enough to share your plan with me, so that I won't worry?"

He stared at her with steel-hued eyes that, for the first time in a long time, Delilah couldn't read. Then, finally, he shook his head. "After what you did, Delilah, I don't know that I'll ever be able to trust you again, no matter how much I might want to. And I certainly can't trust you now. Not yet."

She nodded, expecting and accepting his words. "Well, then I'm afraid I can't trust your judgment either," she said. "Too many things can go wrong, and then I'd never know what happened. I couldn't stand that. Especially since your going to face him is my fault. I need to be there, Samson. Can't you understand that?"

He scowled but said nothing, and Delilah thought that finally he had accepted the inevitability of her involvement. They slept together that night, or rather part of the night. A good portion of the night was spent making love. Gentle, compassionate love. Hot, hungry love. And intense, passionate love. Delilah learned more about the bond between men and women in that single night than she had ever thought to learn. Unfortunately, though, she'd not learned enough to be prepared for what faced her at dawn.

Samson was gone. Again. Blast the man!

After another bout of the sickness that seemed to plague her most mornings, Delilah set about preparing herself to move on. *Morning sickness!* Having just picked Poopsy up to settle her in the saddlebag, Delilah froze in midgesture. Poopsy licked her nose, releasing her momentarily from her sense of shock.

Oh, my! She'd heard women speak of morning sickness. They'd associated it with the early months of pregnancy. Swallowing, Delilah frantically tried to remember when her menses were due.

Last week! Her monthly flow should have begun while she was at the cabin. Her knees suddenly lost their strength, and she sat down hard on the ground. She was pregnant! She, who had never prepared herself for the idea of marriage, let alone children, was going to bring a child into the world. She was going to be a mother!

Too numb with shock to know how she felt about the idea, Delilah placed her hand over her abdomen with a sense of mingled wonder and unreality. And then she thought to ponder over how Samson would feel about it, and some of the wonder faded. The way he felt about her right now, he would probably think she was trying to trap him into marriage. She'd heard of that happening, although no one had ever explained to her how one got pregnant without the man's cooperation. Still, she decided she wouldn't tell Samson about her condition. Not yet. Not until he forgave her enough to ask her to marry him again. That would be the proper time to tell him.

An hour out of camp, Delilah lost his trail. It wasn't the first time, but on each of the other occasions she'd been able to pick it up again. This time, the trail seemed to have vanished. Obviously Samson had taken care to ensure that she *couldn't* follow him. Halting, she looked around thoughtfully.

The town of Cedar Crossing had to be fairly close. She was in Wyoming Territory, after all. Since Cedar Crossing was undoubtedly where Samson was heading, if she just kept going, she'd eventually encounter him in the town. She hoped.

She hated to think of him doing something rash like heading directly to Telford's ranch. But since she hadn't a clue where the ranch was anyway, she had no choice but to seek Samson in the town.

Dirty, tired, and disheveled, Delilah reached Cedar Crossing two afternoons later. From her point of view, the town didn't have much going for it. Many of the buildings were dilapidated, some looking like they'd never received a coat of paint, and the people seemed surly, watchful, and unfriendly.

Stopping off at the hotel, Delilah left Poopsy and her supplies in her room before taking Jackpot and the packhorse on to the livery. The Cedar Crossing Hotel proprietor wasn't nearly as friendly as Mrs. Schmidt had been. Neither were his rooms quite as spotless. But with much more important things on her mind, Delilah didn't pay the conditions much heed. The important thing was that she'd learned that Samson wasn't registered at the hotel under either his own name or the name of Matt Chambers, and the proprietor said that no one matching his description had been in. Of course, Delilah hadn't been certain if she could expect to find Samson there or not. Since he'd refused to share his plans with her, she didn't know if he'd planned to be overt in his pursuit of Telford, or inconspicuous.

After arranging for the stabling of the horses, Delilah was on her way back to the hotel when she suddenly halted in her tracks. There was a group of armed men coming toward her, two of whom were limping rather obviously, and one of whom leaned on a crutch. They looked familiar. Very familiar. And it was only as she recognized the fact that Paul Telford's distinctly cold-eyed gaze was centered on her that Delilah stopped to consider the fact that he and his men now had reason to dislike her almost as much as they apparently hated Samson. "Oh, boy," she murmured. She'd been so worried about Samson that she'd forgotten to consider that. But running from them wouldn't help. Violent men were a lot like vicious animals: If they sensed fear, it increased their ferocity. So, swallowing her trepidation, she resumed walking. When she reached them, however, she was forced to halt for, although the men stopped, they did not make way for her. She stared Telford in the eye, but nobody spoke. The silence stretched. Finally she said, "Good afternoon, Mr. Telford."

A shadow of surprise flickered through his eyes. He nodded. "Mrs. Sterne."

"I wonder if your men would be so kind as to let me pass?"

He stared at her for a moment, the enmity glowing from his eyes like madness. And then he smiled. It was the most chilling smile Delilah had ever seen. "Sure, why not," he said quietly.

Slowly his men opened ranks, but just barely enough for her to pass through them. In fact, she felt a bit claustrophobic in doing so, as, for one brief instant, she was surrounded by them. And then she was through, and continued on her way. Her face reddened as she heard a lewd comment made by one of the men. It was immediately followed by the rumble of crude male laughter, but she refused to allow them the satisfaction of acknowledging their rudeness in any way.

By nightfall, Samson still had not put in an appearance, and she was beginning to doubt the wisdom of coming here. Had her arrival just alerted Telford to the possibility of Samson being in the area? She had no way of knowing.

Finally, with worry preying on her mind, she lay down on the first real bed she'd seen in more days than she cared to count, and tried to sleep. Surprisingly, sleep came quite easily, although she supposed she should have expected that. She continued to be plagued by that strange bone-deep weariness that had begun to afflict her while she was caring for Samson.

It was still pitch-dark when a sharp sound woke her. She sat bolt upright in bed. For an instant, she stared into the dense blackness in confusion, trying to identify the noise, and then she realized it was Poopsy barking and snarling with a viciousness Delilah had never heard nor expected from her.

Somebody was in the room! That was the only explanation.

Slowly, carefully, as she tried to see in the dense blackness, Delilah reached one hand beneath her pillow for her derringer. She didn't usually sleep with it, but after meeting Telford and his men in town, she'd wanted a little extra reassurance, and had placed it there on impulse while she was getting ready for bed. The precaution proved useless, however, for a hard, callused hand closed over her mouth while strong fingers jerked her roughly out of bed before she could grasp the weapon.

"Scream, and I'll kill you," a disembodied voice warned out of the darkness. "You got that?"

With her heart pounding in her throat like an Indian tomtom, Delilah could only nod.

"Good," he said, drawing the word out. "Now light the lamp and shut that goddamn dog up before I shoot it." As though to suit action to words, she heard him draw his pistol.

Delilah did as she was told, although she had to pick Poopsy up and cuddle her to get her to quiet, and even then the little dog continued to growl. When Delilah turned to face her intruder, she understood why.

The man in her room was Telford's foreman, Casey, and he looked meaner than a rattlesnake. His eyes raked her nightgown-clad form with an insolence that was familiar to her, that panicked her. For she'd seen it before—in the eyes of Jacob Sterne. His calculated leer was designed to terrorize. And she refused to let him know how well it worked.

"Where's loverboy?" he asked in a snide voice.

Delilah didn't bother pretending she didn't know who he meant. "If you mean Samson," she said, "I have no idea."

"Sure you don't." His eyes raked over her once more.

"Too bad you're wastin' a body like that on a creep like Towers," he said. "Maybe I should show you how it can be with a real man."

Delilah met his gaze head-on, and clamped her lips shut, refusing to be drawn. Still smirking, he lifted a hand and traced a terrorizing finger down the curve of her cheek until he reached her chin. His action set Poopsy off again, and he lifted his hand as though to grab her, but Delilah turned so that his grasp grazed her shoulder instead. With narrowed eyes, she gave him a hard stare and said one word in a tone barely above a whisper: "Don't!"

He eyed her for a second. "Yeah? And what are you gonna do about it?"

Delilah looked pointedly at his left shoulder, which still moved a little stiffly, and then, with all the Southern sugar of which she was capable, said, "Why, sir, I am a lady. I am merely reminding you, being the big strong man that you are, that hurting defenseless little animals is the trait of a bully. Or a coward."

His hand shot out to grip her throat, and Delilah knew she'd gone too far. Damn her Irish ancestors. Her daddy had told her on more than one occasion that she had to learn to rein in her very Irish tendency toward irony. "Listen, bitch," Casey ground out from between clenched teeth, "there ain't nobody that's ever called me a coward and lived, so I sure hope that's not what you were tryin' to say."

Delilah shook her head and tried to look innocent. "Of course not, Mr. Casey," she gasped out past the constriction of his hand. "I would never dream of insulting—"

"Shut up!"

Delilah clamped her lips shut.

"Now look," he ground out as he released her throat, "Towers was seen in town just after noon today. He stopped at the saloon, had a drink, and rode out again. Two hours later you showed up. Now, do you really expect me to believe that you don't know where he is?"

Delilah's eyes widened at that piece of information. So, Samson was here. But where? "Yes, I do," she said. "Because it's the truth."

Casey narrowed his eyes. "Okay. If that's the way you want it. Get dressed. You're coming with me."

"What! Oh, no. I don't think that's a good idea."

"Did I give you the impression that you had a choice? Because if I did, I must be losin' my touch." He smiled, and then barked, "Move it!"

Discretion being the better part of valor, Delilah cautiously sidled toward the dressing screen in the corner of the room. She set Poopsy down at her feet and ordered her to stay while she dressed.

Two hours later, Telford escorted her, with Poopsy in her arms, up the steps of his home as though she'd been invited for dinner. She jerked her arm from his grasp. "Why am I here?" she asked coldly, not taken in by his solicitous attitude.

"Why, you're bait, my dear. I thought a smart lady like you would have figured that out by now."

"Bait!" Delilah echoed. "Do you honestly think Samson is going to come after me?"

"Yep. I do."

"You're crazy!"

Telford's eyes took on an extra layer of ice. "I'd watch it if I were you, my dear. I can always have you killed with your lover."

"But it's simply not going to work," Delilah protested. "After the way I betrayed him, the man doesn't trust me. He'll never believe that I'm not in on any trap you have devised."

"Well now, I sure hope that's not the case," Telford

said. " 'Cause if he doesn't show up, you're gonna wish he had. After all, you're the reason for him getting away the last time. Not to mention the pain you caused me in the process. Yessir, I just might enjoy taking a little payment for my suffering out of your hide." He ran a finger over her collarbone. "And such pretty hide it is, too."

Chapter Eighteen

Samson stared down at the Cross T ranch in an agony of indecision. He had known that Delilah would follow him—the damnable woman had refused to listen to reason—but, short of tying her up and leaving her, he hadn't known what to do about it. He had assumed that she'd be safer alone than with him. Having been betrayed once by her, Telford should have realized that Samson would not have confided his plans to her. And her solitary arrival in Cedar Crossing should have enforced that perception. So what was going on?

For a moment, he entertained the thought that Delilah was, once again, siding with Telford. But he really didn't think that was the case. From the way she'd yanked away from Telford's grasp, she didn't look any too happy to be there.

Frowning thoughtfully, Samson considered the situation. His own strategy in showing up in town and then disappearing had been to get Telford's men combing the hills for him. He'd planned to taunt them with his presence occasionally, facing them one by one until Telford, finally lacking his army, would be forced to confront him man to man. Perhaps Telford's abduction of Delilah was the reverse side of the same strategy. Perhaps her presence was designed as a taunt for Samson. Bait to draw him in.

What he didn't understand was *why* Telford thought such a strategy would work. Samson wasn't even certain himself how he felt about her. After all, he still wasn't one hundred percent sure where Delilah's loyalties lay, except perhaps with herself and her sister.

Then again, he was reasonably certain that she was carrying his child.

Could he allow a woman he had feelings for—although those feelings refused to be defined at the moment—to remain in possible danger? He grimaced. No, probably not. Could he allow the woman who apparently carried his child to remain in potential peril? No, definitely not. So, he guessed that left him with only one course of action: He had to rescue her.

"Damn!" he swore beneath his breath. He sure as hell wished he was the type of man who could walk away, because this time he had the feeling that Delilah Sinclair just might get him killed.

He watched the ranch closely for two days, learning the movements of Telford's men. From what he could discern, Delilah appeared to be well treated during that time. She certainly looked as beautiful as ever.

Finally, Samson felt confident enough to move in. It was near midnight on a night that was cursed with a clear sky and bright moonlight. He pulled Goliath up in a clump of bushes as near to the ranch buildings as he thought he dared go on horseback, and then continued on foot. At the near end of the house, he could see Delilah's silhouette pacing back and forth in the room she'd been given. At the opposite end, the silhouette of another woman made an occasional appearance in the window as well. He didn't know who she might be, for he'd never seen her outside the house. Possibly Telford's wife; the man was said to be married.

Although there were a number of men patrolling the perimeters of the ranch, there were only three guards near the house—two that made periodic circuits of the immediate grounds, and one that simply lounged on the porch leaning on his rifle and smoking cigarettes. Samson watched the men circling the house. His plan was to move in as soon as they'd passed Delilah's window, and break her out before they came around again.

It sounded simple. He just hoped it would be. That blamed dog of Delilah's was an unknown element. If it barked . . .

Once away from the house, they would have to avoid the other guards. He planned to spirit Delilah off the ranch by following a path that would primarily keep them in the shadows. That meant, however, that he'd have to take the guard near the barn, and the guard near the chicken coop, out of commission on his way in. And that blamed ramrod, Casey, was a wild card: He seemed to roam where and when he willed, following no particular pattern. Still, Samson doubted that the situation would ever improve from his point of view, so he might as well get it done.

Delilah thoughtfully chewed a fingernail as she paced the room that had become her prison, her steps soundless on the thick Turkish carpet that blanketed the floor. In the two days she'd been on the Cross T Ranch, she'd learned a lot about Paul Telford, about his passions, ruthlessness, and arrogance. His only real passion was gambling which, had he been an honest gambler, Delilah might have been able to turn to her advantage. The problem was that he was not honest, and he didn't care a fig how he won, as long as he did. He liked to brag that he was a more accomplished gambler than most professional gamblers, and that he had, in fact, won his ranch in a poker game.

As for Telford's ruthlessness, well . . . The man's poor wife, Melissa Telford, a pale blond wraith of a woman whom Delilah had caught a glimpse of, had descended into laudanum addiction to escape his tyranny in the only way she could. Or so the cook had said in a whisper when queried by Delilah. Mrs. Telford would certainly be of no help to her.

Telford's arrogance was his belief that everyone else, lacking his ruthlessness and immoral nature, was somehow inferior to himself. He showed respect for no one, treated his employees like dirt, though he paid them well, and assumed that money could buy anything or anyone. Including Delilah as his mistress.

In just two days, Delilah had come to despise him.

But that didn't help her escape. And escape she must, for Telford's advances were becoming more and more bold. The fact that he carried the only key to her room worried her.

At just that moment, Poopsy growled deep in her throat, and Delilah's gaze flew to the door. But she didn't hear or see anything. Looking back at the little dog, she noted that Poopsy's attention was, in fact, focused on the window. What the . . . ? Could it be Samson? she thought, in a moment of breathless hope. She'd almost given up on him. Then she remembered the way Casey had been looking at her earlier. Uh-oh!

She looked around for something with which to defend herself if need be, but came up empty. Then she remembered the lady's hat on the upper shelf in the armoire. Rushing across the room, she quietly opened the armoire door, removed the hat, and examined it.

Yes! The hat pin was still attached. Upon extracting the eight-inch-long makeshift weapon, she positioned herself next to the window and waited, watching Poopsy as the little dog continued to growl quietly. Delilah didn't know how whoever it was planned to get the window open, because she'd already tried that and had come to the conclusion that it had either been painted or nailed shut. But if they managed to get it open, she fully intended to take advantage of it.

A moment later, the window broke, as an arm wrapped in the protection of some black fabric plunged through it in a short, controlled jab. Delilah jumped, startled by the explosion of noise in the dense silence, although in reality the sound created by the breaking glass as it landed on the thick carpet was little louder than the tinkling of a wind chime.

Well, shoot! Why hadn't she thought of breaking it?

"Delilah?" came a hoarse male whisper as the protected arm continued to clear the glass from the window ledge.

Delilah blinked and froze in place for a second as she struggled to identify the caller. "Samson?" she whispered in return. As though to confirm her conclusion, Poopsy leaped down from the bed and ran happily toward the broken window. Without preamble, a hand reached in to scoop up the little dog.

"Come on," Samson said, tilting his head to see Delilah, as she stood to the side. "We have to get out of here. Hurry!"

Delilah hesitated no more. Dropping the hat pin, she grasped Samson's offered hand and sat carefully on the window ledge to swing her legs out. A second later, still clasping his hand, she followed him through the darkness. She was frightened to death of being caught—more for Samson's sake than for her own—yet through it all her heart soared, singing one joyous refrain: *He came for me*.

After reaching Goliath, they had just placed Poopsy into a saddlebag and Samson was giving her a hand up, when the sound of a hammer being pulled back on a gun echoed like a gunshot in the still night. "Hands up, Towers," a cold voice growled out of the darkness. "Less'n you want me to shoot the little lady there."

Samson raised his hands as Poopsy barked and growled uselessly. A single glance at Samson's face made Delilah's heart sink, for he looked exceedingly grim. "Evenin', Casey," he said.

A few minutes later they were standing on Telford's front porch with the muzzles of numerous pistols trained on them while one of the hands woke Paul Telford. When Telford emerged from the house, strapping on his gunbelt as he came, he took one look at Samson and Delilah and smiled. But it was not a nice smile. "Kill him," he said to his men. "And take all the time you want doin' it."

Delilah panicked. They were going to beat Samson—again. And once again it was because of her. Because he'd come to rescue her. "No!" she screamed, clutching uselessly at the arms of the men hauling Samson off. She couldn't allow this to happen. "Please!" she cried, pinning her eyes on Telford, trying to appeal to any shred of mercy the man might have in his soul. "You can't do this. Please! It's not right."

Telford looked at her only long enough to say, "I can do anything I want, Mrs. Sterne. I thought you understood that."

Her eyes flicked briefly to Casey, who remained standing at Telford's side, but he seemed as unmoved by her pleas as his employer. "You can't just appoint yourself judge and jury. Let Samson stand before a court of law for his crime. Let a judge decide his guilt or innocence."

Telford shook his head. "He's guilty of killin' my son. No sense in wastin' a judge's time."

"But it was self-defense!" she argued. "Your son was going to shoot him in the back."

Telford pinned her with a cold stare. "Says him."

"There were witnesses!"

Watching his men as they began to hammer their fists into Samson, Telford shrugged without looking at her. "None that count for anything."

Delilah stared at him. "Meaning what? Meaning there were none you couldn't buy off? Meaning that the truth only counts if it can stand up against your money?"

Telford glared at her. "Shut up before I let my men shut you up. For good."

Oh, God, help me. I don't know what to say to move him. Delilah wrung her hands in frustration as tears began to track down her cheeks. "Please," she said, resorting to begging once more. "Please don't do this." But Telford ignored her. She looked at Casey. "Please, Mr. Casey, don't let this happen. It isn't right."

Casey looked uncomfortable. "Is what she says true, boss? Did the kid try to shoot Towers in the back?"

Telford turned and glared at him. "On my land, the truth is whatever I say it is. You got that, Casey? 'Cause if you don't, you're welcome to ride out."

Casey nodded. "Yes, sir." He continued to look thoughtful and, Delilah thought, a bit uncomfortable, but he made no move to help her or Samson.

The sound of a particularly loud blow landing on Samson's hapless body made Delilah flinch. "Samson—" she cried.

The cry drew Telford's attention again. "Shut up before you wake the whole house up. I never thought I'd see the day that you lost your poker face," he sneered. "Buck up, Mrs. Sterne. This won't take that long. And then you can leave and go on with your life."

But Delilah wasn't listening any more. Reminded of her vocation, and Telford's penchant for gambling, she began to grasp at straws. Drawing her tattered pride around her like a cloak, Delilah looked up at him. "Very well then, Mr. Telford. Since you have so kindly reminded me of my profession, may I propose a wager?"

"Wager?" He looked down at her. "What kind of wager?"

"You stop . . . this,"—Delilah gestured to the violence taking place—"right now, and we play a game of poker. If I win, you let Samson leave with me. If you win . . ." She swallowed, hating to even contemplate the outcome. "If you win, I'll leave without him."

Telford turned speculative eyes on her. "I heard you were pretty good," he murmured almost conversationally. "Course there ain't many men that can beat me, let alone a woman. You probably couldn't offer me enough of a challenge to make it worth my while." Shrugging, he appeared to dismiss her suggestion.

"Try me," Delilah returned in a soft-voiced challenge.

"Five card stud?" he asked, intrigued despite himself.

Delilah dipped her chin in a brief nod. "If you wish."

Then suddenly Telford seemed to reconsider. "I already have Towers," he said to her. "Why should I gamble for something I already have?"

Before Delilah could reply, Casey nodded and interjected. "That's right, boss. Why should you? She's a professional gambler, after all. Got quite a reputation in some quarters." He shook his head. "I don't think it's a good idea."

Delilah shot a look at him. What was he doing? Surely he knew that any intimation that she provided a challenge to Telford would only increase the powerful rancher's desire to play. Was Casey taking her side? She didn't know. Men like Casey had a twisted code of ethics. It was impossible to know what his strategy was.

"I don't pay you to do my thinkin' for me, Casey," Telford growled. "So shut yer trap."

Casey's expression was indecipherable; he said nothing.

Telford looked over Delilah's head at his men. "Hold up a minute, boys," he yelled. Then he looked back at Delilah with soulless cold eyes. "All right," he said, "I'll take your wager. But if you lose, you're only gonna have two choices: Either you become my mistress, or I'll give you to my men, and you can join Towers." He grinned evilly. "We'll bury you together."

Delilah's heart contracted, and a pulse pounded in her throat. "And if I win?" she asked.

Telford's grin widened. "Hell, if you win, I'll let you both go free."

Delilah considered. For the first time in her life, she was going to play a hand she could not afford to lose.

"Well?" Telford demanded. "Those are the terms. If you don't like 'em, then we'll forget this gamblin' thing right now and get back to business. Do we have an agreement or not?"

Delilah lifted her chin and met his gaze. "Agreed," she said quietly.

Telford looked up at his men. "Bring Towers over here, boys. The lady here is gonna gamble for his life. We might as well let him watch, seein' as how it kind of affects him. Heck! He can use the time to contemplate where he wants to be buried."

A moment later, both Delilah and Samson were escorted into Telford's parlor. Samson, Delilah noted, already had a swollen eye and a bloody lip. From the way he moved, it looked as though his barely healed ribs were probably bothering him again too. But it also looked as though he'd given as good as he'd gotten: More than one of Telford's men sported cuts and bruises. In fact, one looked as though he'd run into a brick wall nose-first.

"Bring the cards," Telford demanded of one of his men. The house servants were all abed, and probably determined to stay there despite the noise, or rather because of it.

"What have you done, Delilah?" Samson asked.

Telford didn't allow Delilah to respond. "Why, it's like I said, Towers. The lady is gamblin' for your life."

"And what happens if she loses?" Samson demanded.

Telford shrugged. "I've given her a choice, actually. If she loses, she can either join you in your grave, or she can become my mistress."

"Delilah—" Samson's tone demanded that she look at him, that she meet his gaze. The pain reflected there stabbed straight to her heart. "Don't do this, darlin'. Please. From what I saw . . . well, to be honest, you just aren't that good."

To Delilah's dismay, Telford took in every word. Feigning a casualness she didn't feel, Delilah said, "You only saw me at my worst. I only lost when you were there."

Samson swallowed visibly and, infuriatingly, pointed out, "I'm here tonight. You might not win."

She wanted to explain to him that his presence didn't unnerve her anymore because she was no longer afraid of the things she felt for him, but she couldn't, so she merely shrugged. "It's worth a chance."

"No it isn't!" Samson exploded. "Telford, you can't do this. She has nothing to do with what's between you and me. How much revenge do you need for the loss of a back-shooting kid who didn't understand the meaning of honor?"

Telford's face was suddenly suffused with rage. "My

son may have tried to shoot you in the back, Towers, but it was no less than you deserved after throwin' him in the water trough and embarrassin' him in front of the whole town. That town was gonna be his one day. He needed respect."

Samson stared at him sadly. "You don't bully respect out of people, Telford. You earn it. Jesus! The poor kid never had a chance with you for a father, did he? You're as much to blame for his death as I am."

"Shut up before I change my mind and kill you right now." And then his eyes widened. "That's what you're tryin' to do, isn't it? You're tryin' to piss me off so bad I'll kill you and let the little lady here go free." He clucked his tongue as he accepted the cards his man handed him. Then he looked at his foreman. "Casey, if he opens his mouth again, I want you to close it for him. Is that clear?"

Casey nodded. "Yessir." At a gesture from Telford, he pulled out a chair at the table for Delilah.

A very tense game of poker ensued. Delilah watched Paul Telford like a hawk. She'd already decided that if Telford cheated, she'd cheat too. Samson had been right. She, too, had her price, and she was going to gamble on not getting caught. She had to, because she could not afford to lose this game. If you had to cheat a cheat to play a fair game, was it cheating? She didn't know. All she knew was that she'd do what she had to do to save the life of the man who meant everything to her.

Not knowing whether the deck of cards Telford produced had been previously stacked, Delilah had insisted on dealing the first hand. She won, but not by much. Now it was Telford's deal.

"I'll take two cards," she said softly, discarding two that did not work well. Then, sliding the two new cards into her hand, she glanced at it before returning her gaze to the rancher. She had a good hand. A *very* good hand. Her luck was back.

Telford, having completed the deal, now held his right hand on the table, rigidly flat, with his fingers tightly together. He'd palmed a card! Delilah was almost certain of it. She doubted that he'd use it this hand, because he wouldn't be able to make the switch. But she'd have to watch him on the next hand.

On the next deal, she dealt a couple of cards from the bottom of the deck. Nothing remarkable. Just enough help to keep the playing field level. And so, the game progressed. Hand for hand, it looked as though the ultimate win could go either way. And the tension grew.

Telford began to look suspicious, and more than a little angry. Finally, he barked, "The bitch is cheating."

"I been watchin' her, boss, an' I ain't seen nothin'," one of his men countered.

"You couldn't see a goddamn wart on the end of your nose," Telford growled.

Delilah leveled a stare at him. "I assure you, sir, that in all the time I have gambled, I have never once resorted to cheating." *Until tonight*, she added silently, praying the Lord would forgive her dishonesty. "I am simply a very lucky person."

Telford growled something beneath his breath. Moments later, when the game ended and he'd lost, he stared at Delilah with murder in his eyes. "There's no way you could have won tonight if you hadn't cheated," he said.

"How can you possibly say that?" she asked.

For a moment she thought he would come right out and admit that he'd been manipulating the cards to win, but instead his face suffused with rage, and he looked at his men. "Take them outside and kill them," he demanded.

The hands hesitated. Then one asked, "Both of them, sir?"

"That's what I said, isn't it?"

"But, boss, she won," Casey pointed out. "The deal was that you'd let them go."

"She cheated!" Telford shouted.

He shrugged. "Reckon we can't kill a woman for defendin' herself." The insinuation was clear: Casey was admitting that his boss had cheated.

The erosion of his authority, on top of his loss of the poker game, seemed to make Telford almost insane with the force of his rage. Pushing and shouting and swearing vilely at everyone in his path, he sent ornaments crashing to the floor as he ordered everyone out of his house.

Grabbing Delilah, Samson herded her ahead of him as he looked at Casey. "Are we free to go?" he asked, forced to raise his voice to be heard over Telford's tirade.

Outside on the front porch, Casey nodded. "I don't like you, Towers, but I don't kill men for fightin' fair. I thought it was you who done the back-shootin'." His gaze flicked to Delilah. "And I don't kill women." It was about as close to an apology as they'd ever get from a man like Casey.

"I'll have to come back," he said to Casey. "You know that I have to finish it with him one way or the other."

Casey nodded. "I know."

With a nod, Samson began to lead Delilah toward the spot where they'd left Goliath—and Poopsy, still imprisoned in the saddlebag. Suddenly Telford exploded from the house. Before anyone knew what he was about, he grabbed one of Casey's pistols. "You're not going to get away with this, Towers," he shouted. "I've had enough of your interference in my life. You took everything from me. My wife. My son. It isn't fair." He continued shouting insanely, and began to wave the pistol around as he trailed after Samson and Delilah with an almost drunken gait.

"What's he talking about?" Delilah asked. "Do you know his wife?"

Samson shook his head and then shoved Delilah to the ground as Telford fired wildly. Damn! He needed a gun. How could he defend Delilah and their unborn child against a madman with a gun when he was unarmed? Samson looked toward Casey. Although the man looked uncomfortable with the way things were going, he didn't appear ready to pull his gun on the man who'd hired him.

Another shot whined past Samson's ear. He thought he heard Delilah murmur something, but he wasn't certain.

Desperately, Samson sought some protection. The nearest hand was only about ten feet away. Not far, but it might as well have been a mile. "Hey!" he shouted, attracting the man's attention. "Throw me your gun." But in the next instant, one of Telford's wild shots caught his own man in the shoulder, and the man spun, hitting the ground even further from Samson.

But there was no more time to hesitate. Looking down at Delilah's beautiful face as though, in that split second, he could commit it forever to memory, Samson said, "I've got to get a gun. Stay here. Don't move." And then he was snaking his way along the ground, as quickly as possible, toward Telford's fallen man. He'd just reached him, had pulled the gun from his holster, when there was a deafening blast and then . . . silence. Dead silence.

Afraid to look up, afraid of what he might see, Samson slowly looked toward Delilah. She was alive! She was looking over her shoulder in Telford's direction. Samson's gaze followed hers and his eyes widened, for

Paul Telford lay on the ground, unmoving. Quickly, Samson's gaze roved over those present, seeking the shooter. But although some of the men present had drawn their guns, all were looking toward the house with varying expressions of surprise on their faces. Samson rose to his feet to see what, or whom, they were looking at. A slight blonde standing on the front porch slowly lowered a rifle.

"Mr. Casey—" she called in a soft, cultured tone at odds with the results of the violence around them.

"Yes, ma'am?"

"You and the men now work for me. If you or any of them have a problem with that, I expect them to be off my property within the hour. Is that understood?"

"Yes, ma'am."

She nodded and then stepped down off of the front porch to make her way across the yard, not to her husband's side, but to the spot where Samson now stood with his arm around Delilah. As she came closer, Samson felt a tightening in his gut, a sense of recognition that left him reeling.

"Melissa—?" he asked in disbelief.

She stopped before him. "Yes, Samson, it's me," she said quietly. She stared at him for the longest time and then said, "If I had it to do over again, I would have left with you when you wanted me to. I want you to know that."

Samson nodded. He didn't know what to say. Melissa was still beautiful in a pale, fragile way, but he found that his heart no longer felt the connection to her that it had only a few years ago.

"You know," she said, turning away from him briefly, "it's ironic that everything I've wanted to escape for so many years now belongs to me. I think I'll keep it simply for the sake of revenge." She shrugged. "I have nowhere to go anyway, really. And the knowledge that a woman is running his ranch will keep Paul turning over in his grave for all eternity." She smiled and looked back at Samson. "Fitting, don't you think?"

Samson stared at her. "I think you have to find a way to let yourself be happy, Melissa. It's your turn." He gently tugged Delilah forward. "May I introduce you to Delilah Sinclair?" he said.

The two women greeted each other, sizing each other up as women are wont to do, and then Melissa said simply, "Make him happy, Miss Sinclair."

An hour later, Samson and Delilah had almost reached Cedar Crossing. They'd been riding in thoughtful silence, each concerned with how to go about healing the problems that still ailed their fledgling relationship, when Samson suddenly spoke. "You cheated Telford, didn't you, Delilah?"

She considered him. Considered trying to deny it, but knew that she couldn't lie to him. "Yes," she said. "I did. You were right. Everyone has a price, a point at which they will bend their principles to achieve an end." Unspoken between them lay the knowledge that his life had been her price.

"Well, I reckon I'll have to allow that gamblin' might not be all bad. But once we're married, I don't want you goin' into saloons without me. Is that clear?"

Delilah reined her horse in and sat staring at Samson's back as he kept going. Finally he seemed to notice that she was no longer beside him, and he pulled Goliath to a halt. "Is something wrong?" he called to her.

"Did you just ask me to marry you?"

Samson tilted his head as though considering. Finally he said, "I guess I did at that. But like I said, you'll have to curb those gamblin' tendencies of yours."

"But I haven't accepted your proposal yet," Delilah pointed out, not at all certain that she liked a man dictating to her after so many years of freedom.

He smiled a slow, sexy smile that heated her blood. "You will."

"How will we live? Do you think you can get your old job back in Red Rock?"

Samson shook his head. "Actually, I inherited some land in the foothills of the Colorado mountains a few years back from one of my uncles. I thought maybe it'd be worth takin' a look at it. It might be good ranch land. What do you say?"

Slowly, Delilah smiled. "I say *yes*."

Samson pondered her. "I gotta be clear on somethin', darlin'. Is that yes to Colorado, or to marryin' me?"

"Both."

He smiled, and as some of the tension flowed out of his muscles, Delilah realized he hadn't been as sure of her answer as he'd pretended. "Good," he said. "That's what I thought." He kicked Goliath into motion again.

A moment later, Delilah thought of something. She didn't want to begin their new lives with secrets between them. "Samson—"

"Um-hmm?"

"There's something I have to tell you."

His steel-hued eyes locked on her face. "What's that?"

"Well, I . . . that is—" She stopped and drew a deep breath, and then plunged. "I'm pregnant."

His left eyebrow arched. "You don't say?"

Delilah frowned. That wasn't exactly the reaction she'd expected. He didn't seem surprised at all. "You knew!" she exclaimed.

He nodded. "I was pretty sure."

They rode in silence for a bit longer, and then Delilah had to ask the question that plagued her, for some men didn't take readily to fatherhood. "Are you . . . happy?"

Samson pulled Goliath up short, looking at her with eyes that suddenly glistened with intense emotion. "Oh, darlin'," he said, "don't you ever doubt it." And then he sidled Goliath close enough to her mount for him to kiss her.

Oh, yes!

And in those seconds, the last clinging shackles of the past fell away from both of them, leaving them free to face their future . . . *together*.

Dear Reader,

I hope you've enjoyed my first foray into the realm of historical romance. I must admit that I had a wonderful time penning the story of this strong but gentle man and his impulsive heroine. And nothing pleased me more than ensuring that, this time, the story of Samson and Delilah had a happy ending.

I enjoy hearing from my readers. You may write to me at:

P.O. Box 262
Kitscoty, AB
Canada T0B 2P0

A self-addressed envelope and international postal reply coupon or fifty cents for Canadian postage to the US would be appreciated.

Sincerely,
Christine Michels

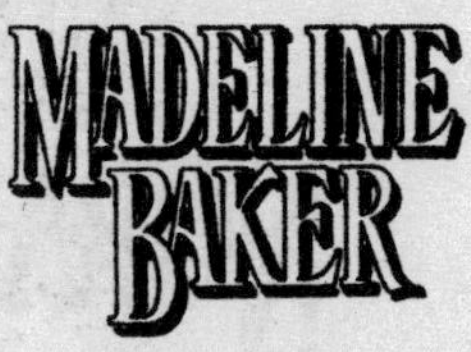

"Lovers of Indian romance have a special place on their bookshelves for Madeline Baker!"

—Romantic Times

Ruthless and cunning, Ryder Fallon can deal cards and death in the same breath. Yet when the Indians take him prisoner, he is in danger of being sent to the devil—until a green-eyed angel saves his life.

For two long years, Jenny Braedon has prayed for someone to rescue her from the heathen savages who enslaved her. And even if Ryder is a half-breed, she'll help him in exchange for her freedom. But unknown perils and desires await the determined beauty in his strong arms, sweeping them both from a world of tortured agony to love's sweet paradise.

_3742-4 $5.99 US/$6.99 CAN

Dorchester Publishing Co., Inc.
P.O. Box 6640
Wayne, PA 19087-8640

Please add $1.75 for shipping and handling for the first book and $.50 for each book thereafter. NY, NYC, and PA residents, please add appropriate sales tax. No cash, stamps, or C.O.D.s. All orders shipped within 6 weeks via postal service book rate. Canadian orders require $2.00 extra postage and must be paid in U.S. dollars through a U.S. banking facility.

Name____________________
Address____________________
City__________ State_____ Zip________
I have enclosed $________ in payment for the checked book(s).
Payment <u>must</u> accompany all orders. ❑ Please send a free catalog.

Winner of the *Romantic Times* Lifetime Achievement Award

Fleeing her abusive uncle, young D'lise Alexander trusts no man...until she is rescued by virile trapper Kane Devlin. His rugged strength and tender concern convince D'lise she will find a safe haven in his backwoods homestead. There, amid the simple pleasures of cornhuskings and barn raisings, she discovers that Kane has kindled a blaze of desire that burns even hotter than the flames in his rugged stone hearth. Beneath his soul-stirring kisses she is able to forget her fears, forget everything except her longing to become his sweet Kentucky bride.

_4046-8 **$5.99 US/$6.99 CAN**

Dorchester Publishing Co., Inc.
P.O. Box 6640
Wayne, PA 19087-8640

Please add $1.75 for shipping and handling for the first book and $.50 for each book thereafter. NY, NYC, and PA residents, please add appropriate sales tax. No cash, stamps, or C.O.D.s. All orders shipped within 6 weeks via postal service book rate.
Canadian orders require $2.00 extra postage and must be paid in U.S. dollars through a U.S. banking facility.

Name____
Address____
City_______________________State________Zip____________
I have enclosed $__________ in payment for the checked book(s).
Payment must accompany all orders. ☐ Please send a free catalog.